KISSED A SAD GOODBYE

ALSO BY DEBORAH CROMBIE

All Shall Be Well
A Share in Death
Leave the Grave Green
Mourn Not Your Dead
Dreaming of the Bones

DEBORAH CROMBIE

KISSED A SAD GOODBYE

MACMILLAN

First published in the United States of America 1999, by Bantam, New York

First published in the United Kingdom 1999 by Macmillan
an imprint of Macmillan Publishers Ltd
25 Eccleston Place, London SW1W 9NF
Basingstoke and Oxford
www.macmillan.co.uk
Associated companies throughout the world

ISBN 0 333 73503 X

Copyright © Deborah Darden Crombie 1999

The right of Deborah Darden Crombie to be identified as
the author of this work has been asserted by her in accordance
with the Copyright, Designs and Patents Act 1988.

All rights reserved. No part of this publication may be
reproduced, stored in or introduced into a retrieval system, or
transmitted, in any form, or by any means (electronic, mechanical,
photocopying, recording or otherwise) without the prior written
permission of the publisher. Any person who does any unauthorized
act in relation to this publication may be liable to criminal
prosecution and civil claims for damages.

1 3 5 7 9 8 6 4 2

A CIP catalogue record for this book is available from
the British Library.

Printed and bound in Great Britain by
Mackays of Chatham plc, Chatham, Kent

For Rick
who makes it possible

ACKNOWLEDGMENTS

Thanks to Kate Miciak, my editor, whose insight and encouragement made this a much better book; to Nancy Yost, my agent, for her support; to Gina Wachtel, for her heroic juggling of schedules; to Tom Cherwin, for his copyediting expertise; to Honi Werner, for capturing the mood of the story so well with her evocative jacket art; to Kathryn Skoyles, whose hospitality allowed me to experience the Island firsthand; to Karen Ross, M.D., of the Dallas County Medical Examiner's Office, for her medical advice; to those who read the manuscript and contributed suggestions: Carol Chase, Terry Mayeux, Barbara Shapiro, and the members of the EOTNWG; and special thanks, as always, to Rick and Katie for putting up with me in the midst of a book.

KISSED A SAD GOODBYE

CHAPTER 1

*The old dockland is still clear
in the minds of Londoners.
Generations of children grew up
in streets where the houses were
dwarfed by ships, whose sides
rose like cliffs over their back
gardens.*

George Nicholson, from Dockland:
An illustrated historical survey
of life and work in East London

HE SAW EACH NOTE AS IT FELL
from his clarinet. Smooth, stretched,
with a smokey luster that made
him think of black pearls against a
woman's translucent white skin. "If
I Had You," it was called, an old
tune with a slow, sweet melodic
line. Had he ever played this one
for her?

In the beginning she'd stood in the
street as he played, watching him,
swaying a little with the music. He'd
distrusted her power clothes and her
Pre-Raphaelite face. But she'd intrigued him as well. As the months
went by, he never knew when she

would appear. There seemed no pattern to it, yet whenever he moved, she found him.

It had been a day like this, the first time he'd seen her, a hot summer day with the smell of rain on the threshold of perception. As evening fell, the shadows cooled the hot, still air and the crowds poured out onto the pavements like prisoners released. Restless, jostling, they were flushed with drink and summer's licence, and he'd played a jazzy little riff on "Summertime" to suit their mood.

She stood apart, at the back of the crowd, watching him, and at last she turned away without tossing him even a cursory coin. She never paid him, in all the times after that; and she never spoke. It had been he, one night when she had come alone, who'd called her back as she turned away.

Later she sat naked in his rumpled bed, watching him play, and he had seen the notes disappear into the shimmering web of her hair. When he'd accused her of slumming, she'd laughed, a long glorious peal, and told him not to be absurd.

He had believed her, then. He hadn't known that the truth of it was beyond his imagining.

"I WON'T GO." LEWIS FINCH LEANED *back in his chair and obstinately planted his booted feet on the worn rail beneath the kitchen table.*

His mother stood at the cooker with her back to him, putting cabbage and potatoes on to boil for his dad's dinner.

"You'll need someone to look after you, if Da's called up," he ventured. "And if Tommy and Edward join—" He realized his mistake even as she whirled round to face him, spoon still in her hand.

"Shame on you, Lewis Finch, for trying me so. Do you not think I have grief enough with your brothers' silly talk of uniforms and fighting? You'll do as you're told—" She broke off, her thin face creased with concern. "Oh, Lewis. I don't want you to go to the country, but the government says you must—"

"But Cath—"

"Cath is fifteen next month, and has a job in the factory. You're still a child, Lewis, and I won't rest unless you're safe." She came to him and pushed his thick fair hair from his forehead as she looked into his eyes.

"Besides, it's all just talk now, and I don't for one minute believe we're really going to have a war. Now, go on with you, or you'll be late for school. And get your dirty boots off my table," she added with a telling glance at his feet.

"I am not a child," Lewis grumbled aloud when he'd banged his way out the front door, and for a moment he was tempted to give school a miss altogether. It didn't seem right to sit in a stuffy classroom on the first day of September.

He looked up Stebondale Street, thinking longingly of the newts and tadpoles waiting in the clay ditch behind the fence, but he hadn't anything to collect them in. And besides, if he was late Miss Jenkins would smack his hands with her ruler in front of the class, and his mum had threatened to send him to St. Edmund's if he got into trouble again. With a sigh, he stuck his hands in his pockets and trudged off to school.

The morning wore away, and through the open window of his class in Cubitt Town School Lewis could see the dark bulk of the warehouses lining the riverfront. Beyond the warehouses lay the great ships with their exotic cargoes—sugar from the West Indies, bananas from Cuba, Australian wool, tea from Ceylon. . . . Miss Jenkins's geography lecture faded. What did she know about the world? Lewis thought as she droned on about taxes and levies and acts. Now, the Penang, she could tell you about far-off places, she could tell you about things that really mattered. One of the few masted ships that still came up the Thames, she lay in Britannia Dry Dock for refitting, and just the smell of her made Lewis shiver. After school he'd—

The creak of the classroom door brought Lewis back with a blink. Mr. Bales, the headmaster, stood just inside the door, and the expression on his long, narrow face was so odd that Lewis felt his heart jerk. From the corridor rose a dull roar of sound, the chattering of children in other rooms.

"Miss Jenkins. Children." Mr. Bales cleared his throat. "You must all be very brave. We've just had an announcement on the wireless. War is imminent. The government has given orders to evacuate. You are all to go home and report back here with your bundles in one hour." He turned away, but with his hand on the door turned back to them and shook his finger. "You must have your name tags and gas masks, don't forget. And no more than an hour."

The door closed after him. For a moment the room held its breath, then a

from Ned Norris in the back row. "A holiday! We've got a

class took up the chanting as they surged out to meet the other children in the hall. Lewis joined in, pushing through the front doors and leaping from the steps with a Red Indian whoop, but his heart wasn't in it.

The children scattered, but as Lewis turned up Seyssel Street his feet slowed. He was suddenly aware of the sounds of the Island—the constant clangs, creaks, and whistles from the docks, and from the river the hoots of the tugs and the low thrumming of the ships' engines. How could there be a war, when nothing had changed?

He thought of the Penang *again, being fitted out for her return journey to Australia. He'd stow away, start a new life in the Outback, not be parceled off to some strange family in the country like a piece of stray baggage. Almost eleven was old enough for a job, he was big for his age, and strong—surely someone would have him.*

Turning into the top of Stebondale Street, he saw his father's old bicycle propped neatly against the front door of their house. His mother's lace curtains, fragile from so many washings, fluttered in the open front window.

He knew then that he couldn't run away, because he couldn't bear the thought of his mother's tears or his dad's gentle disappointment.

Lewis kicked hard at the bike and it toppled with a satisfying crash. He left it lying in a heap as he went through to the kitchen, and when he saw his parents' faces he knew that the news had come before him.

GEORGE BRENT SWUNG HIS ARMS AS much as the dog's lead allowed and picked up his pace a bit. He needed the exercise as much as Sheba these days, for even in this heat he ached when he got out of bed most mornings. He pushed away the fleeting thought of coping with the cold and damp of winter. No point whinging about something that couldn't be helped, and in the meantime it was a gloriously hot, summer day. Winter was months away, and his worst worry was the possibility of sunburn on his bald head.

Sheba trotted ahead of him, muzzle low in search of scent, her small black body quivering with energy. As they passed the Indian restaurant on Manchester Road, she raised her nose in a long sniff. The spicy smells emanating from its kitchen were as familiar to George now as the odor of cabbage and sausage had been in his childhood, but he'd never quite made up his mind to try the stuff—though he conceded that the urgings of Mrs. Singh might one day tip the scale.

He lifted his hand to Mrs. Jenkins in the dry cleaner next door to the restaurant, then quickened his pace yet again. He was late this morning, on account of helping Mrs. Singh with her telly, and most likely he'd missed his mates who gathered for coffee at the ASDA supermarket. But it was only fair, wasn't it, doing a good turn for a neighbor? Especially as good a neighbor as Mrs. Singh.

Smiling at the thought of what his daughters would say if they knew what he got up to with the widow next door, he turned the corner into Glenarnock. They thought he was past it, but he still had a bit of lead in his pencil. And it was hard to expect a man to go without after so many years of having it regular. He meant no disrespect to their mum's memory, after all.

As they came into Stebondale Street, Sheba tugged against the lead, sensing the nearness of the park, but George slowed as they reached the terraced houses across from the entrance to the Rope Walk. They made him think of the program on the Blitz he'd heard on the radio the evening before. As he'd sat snug in his kitchen with his evening cup of tea, it had brought the memories flooding unexpectedly back— the sound the planes made as they came in for a bombing run, the sirens, the devastation afterwards.

Coming to a halt, he told Sheba to sit. He took the houses for granted now, passed them every day without a thought, but this one short block of half a dozen homes was all that had survived of Stebondale as he'd known it before the war. The rest had been destroyed, like so much of the Island, like the house he had grown up in.

He'd been too old to be sent to the country, so he'd seen the worst of the bombing in the autumn and winter of 1940. The corners of his mouth turned up as he remembered the relief he'd felt when he'd presented himself at the recruiting office on his seventeenth birthday. The real war, he'd been certain, would be better than just waiting for the bombs to fall.

A few months later those nights in the Anderson's back garden shelter had seemed an impossibly safe haven. But he had come back, that was the important thing, and his time in Italy had taught him to let the future fend for itself.

Sheba's yip of impatience ended his reverie. He moved on obligingly and soon she had her anticipated freedom, running full tilt off the lead. George followed after her at his own pace, along the Rope Walk between the Mudchute and Millwall Park, then huffed a bit as they climbed to the Mudchute plateau. There Sheba disappeared from view as she followed the rabbit trails though the thick grass, but he stayed to the narrow path that followed the boundaries of the park. The dog always seemed to know where he was even when she couldn't see him, and she wouldn't stray far.

When he reached the gate that led down to the ASDA supermarket, he glanced at his watch. Half past nine—his mates would most likely be gone. The sun had moved higher in the sky and he was sweating freely—the thought of a cuppa, even on his own, was tempting. But the longer he tarried, the hotter it would be going home.

Mopping his head with his handkerchief, he walked on. Here the brambles encroached on the path, catching at his trouser legs, and he stopped for a moment to unhook a particularly tenacious thorn from his trainer laces. As he knelt he heard Sheba whimper.

He frowned as he finished retying his shoelace. It seemed an odd sound for Sheba to make here, where her normal repertoire consisted of excited barks and yips—could she be hurt? Unease gripped him as he stood quickly and looked ahead. The sound had come from further down the path, he was sure of that.

"Sheba!" he called, and he heard the quaver of alarm in his voice.

This time the whimper was more clear, ahead and to the right. George hurried on, his heart pounding, and rounded a gentle curve.

The woman lay on her back in the tall grass to the right of the path. Her eyes were closed, and the spread of her long red-gold hair mingled with the white-flowering bindweed. Sheba, crouching beside her, looked up at George expectantly.

She was beautiful. For an instant he thought she was sleeping, even hesitantly said, "Miss . . ."

Then a fly lit on the still white hand resting on the breast of her jacket, and he knew.

CHAPTER 2

*Down by the Docks is a region I
would choose as my point of
embarkation if I were an
emigrant. It would present my
intention to me in such a sensible
light; it would show me so many
things to turn away from.*

Charles Dickens (1861)

AT FIVE MINUTES TO TEN ON AN
already hot Saturday morning, Gemma found herself looking for an
address in Lonsdale Square. A few
minutes' walk from her Islington
flat, the square was lined solidly
with the cars of residents at home for
the weekend. A posh neighborhood,
this, the preserve of upwardly mobile Blairites, and Gemma wondered
how the woman could afford such
an exclusive address. The terraced
Georgian houses looked severe, their
gray-brick facades relieved only by
trim in black or white . . . except for
the one with the glossy red door.
Gemma checked its number

against the address on her notepad, then climbed the steps and rang the bell. She tucked a stray wisp of hair back into its plait and glanced down at her casual Saturday clothes—jeans and sandals and a linen shirt the color of limes. What did one wear for the occasion? Maybe she should have—

Before she could talk herself into retreating, the door swung open. "You must be Gemma," the woman in the cherry-red jumper said, and smiled. She wore little makeup other than the red lipstick outlining her full lips, her short dark hair was fashionably ragged, as if it had been trimmed with nail scissors, and against her pale skin her eyes were a clear and luminous hazel. "I'm Wendy."

"I like your door," said Gemma.

"I find it breaks the ice. Come in." The room into which she led Gemma faced the street. It stretched towards the back of the house, long and narrow with simple lines and a high ceiling. A formal Georgian mantel on the outside wall divided the room into two perfectly proportioned halves.

Beyond that all Gemma's expectations failed. The walls were crayon yellow, the furniture sixties contemporary in primary colors, and above the mantel hung a huge poster of the Beatles crossing Abbey Road.

An upright piano stood against the long wall, between the fireplace and the rear of the room. As Gemma looked round, the woman touched her arm and gestured towards the sofa.

"Sit down. I've made us some coffee. This morning we're just going to get acquainted."

"But I thought . . ." Gemma's nervousness flooded back. Whatever had possessed her to make this appointment, to give up a free Saturday morning that could have been spent with Toby? It had been a stupid idea, a chance thought followed up when it should have been dismissed, and now she was about to make an utter ass of herself. Thank goodness she'd told no one but her friend Hazel what she meant to do.

Wendy Sheinart sat down beside Gemma and lifted the coffeepot. "Now." Smiling, she filled Gemma's cup. "You can tell me why you want to play the piano."

•　•　•

KINCAID HAD PACKED THE SORT OF picnic he thought a boy would approve of—thick ham sandwiches, potato crisps, Cokes, and the pièce de résistance, an enormous slab of chocolate gâteau from the bakery on Heath Street. He stowed the hamper, specially bought for the occasion, in the Midget's boot, then put down the car's top with a grateful glance at the clear blue arch of sky visible over Carlingford Road.

After the heavy rains of the first few weeks in June, the prospects for Wimbledon Finals had looked dismal. But Kincaid had persevered in his quest for tickets, finally securing two center-court seats for the day, and it seemed that the weather gods had seen fit to reward his diligence.

Offering up a silent thanks, he hopped into the car with an unaccustomed sense of anticipation. The Midget's engine roared obediently to life, and as he eased it into gear he felt a spasm of guilt for having even considered getting rid of the old car. Abandonment seemed a poor compensation for its years of faithful service—a bit like putting down a good dog—not to mention the fact that Kit would probably never forgive him. The boy had fallen in love with the car at first sight, and the last thing he needed now was another loss, however small.

Since his ex-wife's murder in April, Kincaid had done what he could to fill the gap in her son's life. He had also come to feel sure that Kit was, in fact, not Vic's second husband's son but his own child, conceived just before he and Vic had separated twelve years ago—though he had yet to tell Kit what he suspected was their true relationship.

Turning into Rosslyn Hill, Kincaid headed south, into Haverstock Hill, then into Chalk Farm and Camden High Street. When he'd passed through Camden Town on his way home from Gemma's earlier that morning, the street vendors had been setting up their booths. Now the Saturday market was in full swing and the display of colorful cotton skirts and dresses made him think of Gemma. The clothes would suit her, and she'd enjoy the bustle of it all. Perhaps one day soon they could bring Kit for a Saturday outing.

He wondered how she meant to spend her Saturday. She'd assured him that she hadn't felt left out over the tennis, that he and Kit needed a bit of male bonding, but she hadn't offered any hint of her own plans. Or had he simply failed to ask?

The sudden braking of the car in front caused him to give up his ruminations on the minefields of relationships and to concentrate on survival. The traffic crept along the rest of the way to King's Cross, but still he found a space at the curb and made his way to the platform with time to spare.

When the Cambridge train eased to a stop a few moments later, Kincaid felt the same flash of excitement he'd known as a child on meeting a train. In his small Cheshire town the trains had brought a whiff of the outside world, of adventures yet to be had, people yet to be met.

He craned for a sight of Kit's fair hair through the mill of disembarking passengers, then waved as he spotted him. Smiling to disguise the painful jolt that Kit's resemblance to Vic still gave him, he gave the boy a friendly thump on the shoulder before holding out his hand for their customary high five. "Hullo, sport. Anyone for tennis?"

Grinning, Kit slapped his palm, then swung his holdall over his shoulder as they walked towards the exit. "Colin was *so* jealous. You should've heard him moaning and whinging about it. Laura was that fed up."

"And I'm sure you did your best not to rub Colin's nose in it," Kincaid said wryly as he opened the boot and took Kit's bag. "No, don't look in there." He snapped the boot shut before Kit could see. "I've got a surprise."

"A surprise? Really?" Kit's eyes widened, proof that eleven was not too old for treats. He swung himself over the passenger door into the Midget with the finesse of a hurdler. "What kind of surprise?"

"The edible sort," Kincaid teased as he started the car. "Wait and—" His phone shrilled just as he eased the nose of the car into the street. Swearing under his breath, he slipped it from his pocket with one hand while maneuvering the car back into its parking space with the other.

"Kincaid," he snapped, and heard in answer the familiar voice of the Yard's receptionist telling him to hold.

"What is it?" asked Kit.

Covering the mouthpiece, Kincaid said, "Work." Then he added, with more confidence than he felt, "Won't take a minute."

Chief Superintendent Denis Childs came on the line, sounding as unruffled as always. Kincaid had been guilty more than once of wishing for a natural disaster, just to see if Childs were capable of an elevated pulse.

"Look, Duncan, I'm sorry." The smooth rumble of the superintendent's voice hinted at his bulk. "I know you're not on the rota this weekend."

Kincaid's heart sank. An apology up front was not a good sign.

"But it's been one of those days," his boss continued. "The other teams have already been called out, and we've just had a homicide report that the local team feels needs our intervention. Their DCI is away for the weekend, and their guv'nor feels it might be a bit much for the newly promoted inspector on call this weekend."

"A proper baptism," Kincaid agreed. "Where's the body, then?"

"The Isle of Dogs. Mudchute Park."

"Oh, Christ." Kincaid hated outdoor crime scenes. At least indoors you had some hope of containing the evidence.

"A young woman," continued Childs. "From the preliminary reports it sounds like a strangulation."

"Are the SOCOs on the way?" Kincaid asked, grimacing. An outdoor *sex* crime. Even better. "Have the uniformed lads cordoned off the area?"

"In the process. How soon can you be there?"

"Give me—" Kincaid glanced at his watch, and the movement brought Kit's white, tense face into his focus.

He had forgotten him.

"Guv—" Then he stopped. How to explain his predicament to his chief? "Under an hour," he said at last, with another glance at Kit. "I've some things to take care of first. What about Gemma?"

"The duty sergeant's ringing her now. Keep me informed," Childs added, and rang off.

Kincaid switched off the phone slowly and turned to Kit. "I'm sorry. Something's come up, and I'm afraid I'll have to go to work."

"Can't you—" the boy began, but Kincaid was already shaking his head.

"I've no choice in the matter, Kit. I'm really sorry, but you'll have to go back to Cambridge—"

"I can't," said Kit, his voice rising. "The Millers have gone away for the weekend. Don't you remember?"

Kincaid stared at Kit. He'd forgotten that as well. He was finding it increasingly difficult to coordinate the demands of his job with his commitment to Kit, and now he seemed to have run up against an insoluble dilemma.

"I suppose you'll have to stay at the flat on your own, then," he said with a smile, trying to soften the blow.

"But the tennis—" Kit bit down on his lip to stop its trembling.

Kincaid looked away, giving the boy time to collect himself. Then an idea occurred to him and he said slowly, "Maybe we can work something out. Wait and see."

"CORNSILK," THE PAINT SAMPLE HAD READ, and Jo Lowell had liked the name as much as the color. As she painted, Jo imagined it spreading over her kitchen and dining room walls like warm butter, and when she'd finished, the rooms seemed to glow with perpetual summer sun.

There was nothing like a bit of fresh paint to cheer you up if you were in the doldrums, she often told her clients, but she seldom found the time to take her own advice. And of course her clients almost never did the actual painting themselves, but she thought the physical labor might be the most effective part of the therapy. Perhaps she should change her business cards to read *Interior Decorating and Mood Counseling* and raise her hourly rates.

The small smile raised by the thought quickly vanished as she thought of the previous evening. Her cheery yellow walls and soothing green trim had done little to prevent the very eruption of tempers she'd meant to avoid. She'd intended a little civilized dinner party—a means of making peace with Annabelle without actually having to offer forgiveness, because in spite of everything that had happened between them, she had missed her sister.

Jo had been good at entertaining, once, but this had been her first attempt without Martin, and it had been difficult to find the right mix of people. One of the worst things she'd found about divorce was the division of friends into *his* and *her* camps. Martin's friends, of course, were out of the question, but she hadn't dared bring her own partisan supporters into contact with Annabelle, whom they viewed as the vil-

lain of the piece. So she'd invited guests she'd felt sure would con-
tribute to a pleasant, neutral evening—a couple who were recent
clients; Rachel Pargeter, a neighbor who had been a close friend of
their mother's; Annabelle and Reg. And it had almost worked—until
her son Harry had told his aunt what he thought of her.

Carefully, Jo slipped the last of the bunch of early sunflowers into
the vase on the dining room table. The kitchen door slammed and
Sarah's high, piping voice carried clearly from the back of the house.
"Mummy, Mummy!"

"In here, sweetheart." Gathering up her shears and the florist's paper, Jo headed for the kitchen. Her daughter stood just inside the door,
her dark hair disheveled, her cheeks pink from the heat. She'd spilled
something that looked suspiciously like Coke down the front of her tee
shirt, and the waistband of her little flowered shorts had worked its
way below her navel. At four, Sarah was a highly articulate and skilled
tattletale.

"Harry's in the shed, Mummy. You said he wasn't to go in there.
And I know he broke something, 'cause I heard it smash."

Jo felt the swiftly rising bubble of anger; she clamped down on it.
Sarah didn't need any encouragement for her righteous indignation.
"I'll deal with Harry—you wash your hands at the sink. You've been
into the Coke again, haven't you, missy?"

Sarah glanced down at her shirt, and Jo saw the swift calculation
pass across her heart-shaped face before she said earnestly, "It wasn't
me, Mummy, really it wasn't. Harry got it out and he spilled it on my
shirt." She tugged the stained fabric away from her chest as if removing any association with it.

"Oh, dear God." Jo closed her eyes and breathed a prayer. Her precious baby daughter was going to be an actress or a criminal, and she
felt incapable of dealing with either possibility just now. She took a
deep breath. "Right. When you've finished with your hands I want
you to pick up your toys in the sitting room, and I don't want to hear
any more stories. Is that clear?"

Sarah put on her best injured face. "But, Mummy—"

Jo, however, was already pushing open the door to the garden. She
was learning that the only way to manage her daughter was to disen-
gage from the dialogue, because if she continued to participate the

child would eventually wear her down. With Harry, things had been different. The slightest reprimand had been enough to bring the boy to tears, as if his emotions ran uncontainably close to the surface. And now that sensitivity seemed to have been translated into a sullen anger she was unable to breach.

The garden was quiet except for the drone of the bumblebees in the lavender, and it seemed deserted. The only signs of suspended activity were a chipped cricket bat and an old rubber ball lying in the thick grass, but at the bottom of the garden the door to the shed stood open. The small mail-order building was her retreat and studio.

She'd painted the outside a color called Labrador Blue and picked out the trim in white. Inside, she'd washed the walls with diluted emulsion, then furnished the space with bits and pieces of old furniture, a few watering cans, and books. Here she experimented with the custom finishes that were her trademark, or read, or sometimes just tried to sort out her life. And the shed was strictly off-limits to both children.

Slowly, she crossed the lawn and stepped inside. Harry sat on the floor with his back to the bookcase, his knees drawn up to his chin. Beside him lay the cut-glass jug she'd filled with roses from the garden, its handle snapped off. Water pooled on the floor and ran into the rag rug; roses lay scattered like flotsam from a storm.

Jo knelt and touched him on the shoulder. "Did it cut you? Are you all right?" When he didn't answer she pried his hands from his knees and checked them. They were unblemished. She kept one hand in hers and tried again. "Harry, did you break the vase because you were angry with me? You know what you did last night was wrong, but maybe I was wrong to punish you instead of talking about it."

Harry turned his head further away from her and the sunlight slanting in from the window lit his hair like a flame. What an irony it was, thought Jo, that while Sarah had inherited her own dark auburn coloring, Harry might have been cloned from her sister's genes. And her father, who had always adored Annabelle at Jo's expense, had fastened his expectations on Harry as the heir to, if not the family name, at least the family tradition.

"Sometimes mums can be wrong, too," she continued. "But somehow I have to make you understand that you can't say things like that to people. I'm sure you hurt Annabelle very—"

"I don't bloody care." Harry snatched his hand away and for the first time looked at her. "She's a *whore*. I meant to hurt her." He blinked and tears spilled over into his pale lashes.

"Harry, you mustn't use words like that. You know better—"

"I don't care! I *hate* her."

"Harry, darling—"

"Don't call me that." He pushed himself up from the floor and stood over her. "I'm not your darling, and I hate *you*, too!" Then, with a slam of the door, he was gone.

THE COINS CLINKED INTO GORDON FINCH'S clarinet case in a staccato, irregular rhythm. The children tossed them, then stood as close as they dared, rapt with attention, moving their bodies unself-consciously to the music. Both the small girls and boys were bare-chested in the heat, the definition of their ribs showing like the delicate tracery of the branching veins in a leaf. Their faces were flushed from the sun, and some held half-forgotten ice creams in sticky fingers.

He envied them their uncomplicated innocence, intact until some-one came along to bugger it up for them. Thank God he hadn't the re-sponsibility for the shaping of a life. Caring for Sam was about as much as he could manage, and he'd been off his nut to think otherwise.

He finished "Cherry Blossom Pink" and wiped the clarinet's mouth-piece. The children watched him, large-eyed, jiggling up and down in expectation. Their parents stood behind them, some half sitting on the knee-high iron railing that separated the flower bed from the round, brick bulk of the Isle of Dogs entrance to the foot tunnel. Lifting the clarinet to his lips again, he played a bit of "London Bridge." The chil-dren giggled and he thought for a moment, searching his memory for tunes they might like, then improvised "Here We Go Round the Mul-berry Bush."

A pied piper with a clarinet, he slid into "Ob-La-Di, Ob-La-Da," then "When I'm Sixty-Four," from the Beatle's *Sgt. Pepper* album, and the children bounced and swayed happily. But after a bit their parents grew restive, and one by one the families began to drift away. They all had agendas, he thought as he watched them leave—places to go, things to do, people to see. Surely he didn't envy them that as well?

Finishing the piece, he drank from the bottle of water he'd bought at the refreshment kiosk a few yards away. He stood with his back to the spreading plane tree at the far end of Island Gardens. Behind him, just the other side of the tree, ran the river promenade. People strolled by at the undemanding pace dictated by the hot summer day, pausing occasionally to rest on the benches or gaze at the bright glint of the Thames. Directly across the river, the twin, white domes of the Royal Naval College irresistibly drew the eye, echoed by the round dome of the Greenwich end of the foot tunnel.

Between the Naval College and the tunnel rose the tall masts of the *Cutty Sark*, in dry dock at Greenwich Pier. The ship was the last survivor of the lovely clippers that had once unloaded their cargoes in the East End's docks, and he'd often wished he had been born in time to witness the end of that era. But near the *Cutty Sark*, the much smaller, flag-bedecked *Gipsy Moth* proved that adventure was still possible, for in 1967, Sir Francis Chichester had single-handedly sailed the tiny yatch around the world.

A voyage around the world would present an easy solution to his own present predicament, but Gordon knew even as the thought flitted through his mind that he was too well-rooted here, in the place where he'd spent his childhood, and that running away would solve nothing in the end.

Squatting, he sloshed a bit of water into the bowl he always carried for Sam. "Thirsty, mate?" The dog raised his head, then lumbered to his feet with an air that spoke more of duty than desire. After a few obliging laps of water, he circled twice on the patch of bare earth he'd chosen as his bed and settled himself again, nose on his front paws. Sam's movements were visibly slower these days, but it was hot, after all, and the heat made everyone lethargic. Still, Gordon had made up his mind not to take the dog down into the tunnel anymore—the seeping dampness couldn't be good for the animal's joints.

Not that he wanted to play in the tunnel anyway, after what had happened last night. Of course, he'd known he would see her—it was inevitable, living and working in such close proximity. Yet he had stayed on the Island, playing in the park, in the tunnel, beneath the shadow of the cranes on Glengall Bridge, tempting fate. Even today, as good as this pitch was, there were places he might have done better. Maybe he should pack up and try South Ken, or Hampstead High Street, or Islington again.

He knelt, hands on the clarinet as he prepared to break it apart, and before his eyes flashed an image of Annabelle's face, white and furious. Last night, anger had stripped her of the cool veneer of detachment she'd maintained even when he'd told her he wanted no more to do with her. He'd thought that, perhaps for the first time, he'd had a glimpse of who she really was, what she really felt, but still he'd not been willing to believe her. Now, doubt gripped him and he wondered if he had been blinded by pride.

What if he'd misjudged her? What if he had been wrong?

JANICE COPPIN'S HEART HAD JUMPED WITH a peculiar mixture of dread and excitement when the phone rang. Getting called out on the job was always difficult on the weekends—with Bill gone, she had to send the children to the center, and at ten pounds per child, per day, she sometimes wondered if she'd be better off on the dole. Not that Bill had been worth much as far as looking after the kids went—or good for much of anything at all, for that matter, the big lout, except dropping his trousers and getting her pregnant. She should have listened to her mum.

Her daughter, Christine, came in and sat on the edge of her bed, watching her with the intensity Janice always found a bit unsettling. The eldest of her three children, Christine was an awkward girl who took her responsibilities seriously, as if perpetually making up for having been conceived among the bushes in the Mudchute with Bill's leather jacket for a bed. Her chubby body stubbornly refused to acknowledge the onset of puberty and her straight brown hair looked as if it had been cut using a bowl as a guide, but she seemed as yet oblivious to these deficiencies.

"What is it this time, Mummy?" she asked, pushing her spectacles up on her short nose.

Working one foot into a new pair of tights, Janice glanced at her daughter. A suspicious death, the duty sergeant had said, and as her guv was away for the weekend, the case would be hers. But she answered, "Don't know yet, love": she tried not to discuss cases she thought would upset the children. "Shit!" she added as she stood and the tights laddered. Last pair; they'd have to do. It was her day for the hairdresser's, so it meant going at least another week without a cut or color. And it was too hot for her wool suit. She'd have to wear it anyway, no matter if she stank like a stevedore at the end of the day—it was the most professional-looking thing she had, and if this was going to be her big day she was bloody well going to look like it.

"Will you be home before the center closes?" Christine ignored her swearing, though the boys would have jumped on her because she was always on at them about it. "The boys won't want to go to Granny's."

"Tough on them, then," Janice replied impatiently, and sighed. She slid her feet into her new navy shoes and put on her jacket. Already she could feel the wool scratching through the thin fabric of her blouse. "Chris, you know I'll be home as soon as I can. I'll ring the center, okay? When I see how it's going."

Christine nodded, her eyes solemn behind the spectacle lenses.

"You collect the boys from next door and take them along to the center—tell them I said to mind or else." She grabbed keys and handbag from the chest of drawers on the way out of the room. Glancing back, she saw the unmade bed, the pile of dirty laundry she hadn't found the time to wash; thought of the dishes waiting in the kitchen sink and the littered sitting room. *You wanted this,* she reminded herself. *You wanted out of uniform; you pushed and stepped on toes to get here.*

Outside the door of the flat, she gave Christine a quick hug, then stood watching her as she ran next door. Across the street her neighbor washed his car, his bulging gut stretching his thin cotton vest. His trousers rode so low that when he bent over half his arse was exposed. Janice turned away, feeling slightly nauseated, knowing he'd smile and whistle if he saw her looking. *The bastards; they thought you wanted them no matter how they looked.*

She hesitated, debating whether to walk across Glengall Bridge. It was the most direct route—taking the car meant driving right round the dock, but on the other hand arriving at a crime scene on foot wouldn't do much to establish her authority.

A few moments later she pulled her Vauxhall up beside the assembled pandas in the car park of the ASDA Superstore. DC Miller came to meet her, his spotty face pale—on closer inspection, he looked decidedly green about the gills.

"Tell me this is a joke," she instructed him. "Manufactured by that old fart George Brent just to ruin my Saturday morning."

Miller blanched a bit further. "No, ma'am. There's a body." He pointed at the slope leading to the park. "Just up there."

A *derelict,* thought Janice, *just found himself a nice peaceful place to pass away. Inconvenient but not messy. Not on this weekend when her guv was off drinking himself into a stupor at his son's wedding.*

"It's a woman," said Miller. "Young. Crime scene team is on its way."

Janice felt the prickle of sweat in her armpits. It was her show, then, ready or not.

CHAPTER 3

The Mudchute is an area of land which originally belonged to the dock authorities. Covering about 30 acres, roughly square in shape, it has high clinker banks (on which grass and wildflowers now flourish). These banks were built to contain a lake of silt dredged up from Millwall Dock in the 1880s and 1890s.

Eve Hostettler, from Memories of
Childhood on the Isle of Dogs, 1870–1970

KINCAID HAD TO STOP AND CON-sult his *London A to Z* twice, much to his chagrin, but it had been some time since he'd worked a case in the East End, and he'd seldom had reason to venture further east than Wapping or Limehouse. It was all called "Docklands" east of the Tower now, but not even the massive re-building scheme of the last decade had managed to completely erase the character of the individual neighbor-hoods.

A glance at his map as he passed Canary Wharf told him that he was entering the Isle of Dogs peninsula.

He drove south on Westferry Road, following the line of new housing developments and unfinished building sites sprouting like mushrooms between the road and the shore. Many of the hoardings displayed the legend *Finch, Ltd.* in a bold graphic.

Occasionally he caught a glimpse of the river between the buildings, and once a flash of an enormous passenger liner, white and clumsy as an iceberg. As he neared the bottom of the horseshoe he turned left on East Ferry Road, heading north again, up the center of the Island.

To his left he saw a row of Victorian terraced houses that formed part of a prewar housing estate; to his right lay a wasteland of construction. This had to be the extension of the Docklands Light Railway he'd read about, which would take the train under the river to Greenwich, and then to Lewisham, but he hadn't visualized the extent of the chaos the controversial project would generate.

The engineers had managed, however, to keep East Ferry Road passable, and beyond a hoarding on his right the land rose steeply to the plateau of Mudchute Park. Kincaid bypassed the first entrance to the park, a steep, arched tunnel across from the Millwall Dock, and soon came to the entrance of the ASDA supermarket.

As he turned into the car park he saw the pandas, blue lights flashing, clustered in front of the ASDA service station. Gemma's battered Escort stood a little to one side; a pair of uniformed constables held back a gathering crowd of interested onlookers.

Pulling up between Gemma's car and a red Vauxhall, Kincaid got out and headed for the knot of people gathered at the rear of the car park. The bodies shifted and he had a glimpse of Gemma's copper hair and green shirt as she turned to meet him.

"Guv." Gemma greeted him with a brief nod. "This is DI Janice Coppin. She's the senior officer here."

Kincaid held out his hand to the woman in the navy suit, who gripped it as briefly as courtesy allowed. The expression on her blunt face imparted no more welcome than her handshake, and even her stiff blonde hair seemed to radiate displeasure.

"What have we got, Inspector?" Kincaid asked easily, but he remembered his chief's comment about the newly promoted DI not being considered up to the job, and thought it wouldn't surprise him if Coppin felt hostile towards Scotland Yard for invading her patch.

"Up there." DI Coppin stepped aside so that he had a clear view of the entrance to the Mudchute, tucked away in the heavy shrubbery that lined the perimeter of the car park. "A woman's body, exposed by the side of the path. We were waiting for you," she continued. "The pathologist's finished, but we couldn't move the body until you had viewed it in situ."

Kincaid had no intention of apologizing to her for his tardiness. He said merely, "Let's have a look, then," and started towards the park entrance.

The litter strewn over the car park tarmac spilled onto the ground, clustering thickly along the paved path that climbed towards the plateau and the entrance to the park. The rubbish made a mockery of the pastoral, wooden arbor built over the park's swinging gate, and would prove a headache, he knew, for the team collecting evidence.

The wooded slope was gentle, but by the time Kincaid had pushed carefully through the gate bars, he'd begun to sweat. The path forked before him, and even after the rains of the past few weeks, its surface was trampled hard enough to resist an impression from his rubber-soled shoes. Ahead and to the right it climbed towards a dividing hedge and beyond that the high open spaces of the park; to his left it wound along the edge of the steep bank, and a dozen yards along it he saw a cluster of white-overalled crime scene technicians.

Kincaid slipped on an overall and started towards them. Out of long habit, he put his hands behind his back as he followed the line of the blue and white crime scene tape. It removed the unconscious temptation to touch.

The technicians parted at the end to let him through, and he saw her then, half in the hedge's shadow.

"She was a looker, all right," said Willy Tucker, the photographer, at his elbow.

She lay on her back, between the edge of the path and the hedge that separated this alley of park from the higher ground. His first impression was that her clothes had been straightened.

The short skirt hugged her thighs too neatly. The long, black linen jacket was still held together by its pewter buttons, though one cream satin bra strap showed where the jacket had slipped a little from her shoulder. She wore no blouse.

Glancing at Tucker, Kincaid said, "Her tights—they weren't disturbed?"

"Not that we could see without moving her."

The tights were sheer, the merest whisper of black against her pale skin, and both legs had laddered. One foot was bare, the other encased in a black shoe with a high, chunky heel.

Kincaid squatted, still keeping his distance, and at last looked at her face. It was a smooth oval, the skin unlined even in the strong light. The nose was straight, the lips well-defined. As the patch of shade retreated, sunlight sparked from the cloud of her red-gold hair. So alive did it look that if not for the slight congestion of her face and the hovering flies, one might have thought she had simply lain down for a rest.

An earthy, spicy smell rose from the crushed vegetation beneath his feet and her body, making him think of lovers entwined in a hillside bower. "Have you found her other shoe?" he asked.

The photographer shook his head. "Not so far. The uniformed lads have started a radial search."

All dressed up and nowhere to go, Kincaid thought as he stared down at her still body. He stood, resisting the urge to smooth the fine wayward hair from her cheek. "Maybe she left it at the ball."

GEMMA WATCHED KINCAID MAKE HIS WAY back down the cordoned path, his face shuttered as always in such circumstances. "Have we got ourselves a nutter, then, guv?" she asked when he reached them. You didn't say "serial killer," not when there was the remotest possibility of being overheard by the long ears of the press, but it was always the first thing you thought with a young woman murdered like this.

Glancing back at the crime scene technicians crouched like strange white insects near the corpse, Kincaid shook his head. "I think her killer knew her. It looks as though someone arranged her clothing, and if she was sexually assaulted it's not obvious. We'll know more after the postmortem."

"I'll arrange for the mortuary van now," said DI Coppin. "If that's all right with you, sir," she added with unconcealed hostility.

Kincaid's eyebrow lifted a fraction, but, once again, he didn't rise to the challenge. "Go ahead, Inspector. The sooner the better, in this heat. It's a good thing the temperature dropped last night."

Coppin made an awkward descent, hampered by the narrow skirt of her wool suit. Gemma watched her until she'd cleared the swinging gate and vanished from sight, then turned to Kincaid. "Listen, guv—"

Before she could continue, Kincaid motioned her into a small patch of shade, away from the uniformed officers. "It's too bloody hot to stand about in the sun," he said, pulling a handkerchief from his trouser pocket and blotting his forehead with it.

A curving, split-rail fence separated the grassy area bordering the path from the sloping ground that marked the park's edge, and from where Gemma stood it drew her eye towards the entrance. The flat, trellised top of the wooden gate gave it the look of a Japanese shrine; beyond the thick screen of trees, the gleaming buildings of Canary Wharf rose incongruously against the pastoral view.

The comfortingly familiar smell of bacon and eggs cooking in the ASDA's cafe reached them on a faint puff of breeze and Gemma's stomach rumbled loudly in response. Too nervous to eat before her piano lesson, she'd meant to treat herself to a late breakfast afterwards. But she should have known better, as her mobile phone had rung before she and Wendy Sheinart had finished their half hour's conversation.

"About the DI, guv," she said, glancing at the uniformed officers to make sure they were out of hearing. "Her chief inspector's off at his son's wedding this weekend, and it seems he called us in without informing her. She feels it should have been her case, and I can't say I blame her. Maybe if you could go a bit easy on her—"

"Sets a bad precedent," Kincaid said, grinning, then sobered. "It's a tough break for her, but if she's going to be an effective officer, she'll have to learn to cope."

Gemma's own experience was proof enough of that, but she felt sympathetic nonetheless. "Still, I'd not like to be in her shoes."

"My guess is they pinch," he said under his breath, for Coppin had finished with the radio and begun the climb back up the hill from the gate.

Reaching them, the DI made a visible effort to regulate her breathing before she spoke. "They're on their way. What next, sir?"

"Tell me what the pathologist found." Kincaid pulled his small notebook from the pocket of his trousers.

Coppin consulted her own notebook. "The pathologist estimates that the victim died sometime in the night or the early hours of the morning—can't have been much longer than that in this heat or the deterioration of the body would be marked. There are no outward signs of sexual assault, but there is some obvious bruising on the throat."

"Any identification?"

"No, sir. We've not found her handbag, nor any obvious dry cleaner's markings in her clothing."

"Who found her?"

"A pensioner, sir. George Brent. Lives in the council flats down the bottom of the park. He was out walking his dog when he saw her at the edge of the shrubbery, but I'm surprised no one called it in sooner—she was visible as a bloody beacon."

"Has he been interviewed?"

Coppin frowned. "No—I didn't see much point. I know him—he's a harmless old man, not likely to have noticed anything important."

After a moment's pause, Kincaid said evenly, "Inspector, at this stage of an investigation, we don't know what's important, and *everything* has a point. I'll see Mr. Brent myself."

"But—"

"In the meantime, we'll need to get the house-to-house inquiries started as soon as possible and the incident room set up. Our first priority is identification, and we had better be prepared to make use of the media."

A SHREDDED PIECE OF PLASTIC BLEW fitfully across the section of the ASDA car park visible through the screen of trees. Watching from her balcony, Teresa Robbins thought of a film she'd seen once about tumbleweeds in the American desert. The giant weeds had blown in a similar way, in erratic bursts, as if they had a life of their own. The movement of the bit of rubbish made her feel vaguely uneasy, as did the hot breeze that animated it.

Yet she stayed, leaning against the chipped iron railing, craning to see beyond the trees. She'd seen the first police car arrive mid-morning, while she'd been hanging out washing on her half of the narrow concrete balcony. There was a cluster of cars now, pulled up in a rough circle beyond the petrol station. It worried her, not knowing what was happening, but she couldn't bring herself to join the crowd of onlookers gathering in the car park.

A loud thump from next door warned her that her neighbor was up, and that her time on the balcony was limited. Teresa prized her quiet mornings there, especially Saturdays, when she had the time to tend her geraniums and petunias. The evenings were his, given over to heavy metal music and six-packs of lager, and he fueled their ongoing skirmish by leaving fag ends in her flowerpots for her to clean out the next morning. She knew she should tell him to bugger off, but standing up to people was never as easy for her as it was for Annabelle.

She'd improved at it, though, in the five years she'd worked for Annabelle Hammond. It simply never occurred to Annabelle that she wouldn't get what she wanted, whether professionally or personally, and Teresa had often watched with quiet amusement as her boss sailed into a meeting with unsuspecting executives who had not been prepared to take her seriously because she was female. By the time they stopped gaping at her looks, Annabelle would have their signatures on the dotted line.

Although Teresa knew she could never aspire to Annabelle's flair, she'd worked at her job as the firm's bookkeeper with a zeal and efficiency no one from her Croydon comprehensive would ever have expected from her—a girl so ordinary that she'd once overheard a teacher describe her as "the girl most likely to disappear."

After a series of accounting jobs that hadn't quite fit, she'd started at Hammond's with little expectation. To her surprise, she'd soaked up the business like a sponge, discovering a talent for organizing as well as figures. She learned she could juggle things in her head, and had even begun to develop a passion for tea that rivaled Annabelle's. A year ago, Annabelle had promoted her to chief financial officer.

They made a good team. Between them, they had taken Hammond's Fine Teas from the past into the nineties, and it was only in the past few months, as Annabelle had begun to address the future of the firm, that Teresa had seen her display any doubt or hesitation.

She frowned as she thought of the breakfast Annabelle had organized with Sir Peter Mortimer at the Chili's in Canary Wharf this morning. Annabelle had not shown up, and it was unthinkable that she would not keep such an appointment. Reg and Teresa had entertained Sir Peter as best they could, but without Annabelle, they had not dared broach the reason for the invitation. And as the day wore on with no word of explanation from her, Teresa felt increasingly worried.

Next door, another thump was followed by the sudden blare of music—the heavy repetitive bass and growling lyrics that made her head ache. With a grimace, she turned and gathered her things from the wooden drying rack. She'd ring Annabelle at home again, and if there was no reply, she'd go to the office in case Annabelle showed up there.

As Teresa glanced down at the car park once more before retreating into the flat, an unmarked white van moved slowly across the tarmac.

WHILE THEY WAITED FOR THE MORTUARY van, Gemma nipped down to the supermarket cafe for a bacon-and-egg roll and a cup of tea, not knowing when she might have another chance to eat. The air-conditioned market provided a welcome refuge from the heat and she looked round with interest as she peeled the cling-film from her roll.

Cavernous and comprehensive, the store was the sort Gemma hadn't much opportunity to visit, but she assumed it was what the inhabitants of the posh developments expected. It was only when she'd watched the shoppers for a few minutes that she realized most of them were solidly working class. Curious, she quickly finished her sandwich and entered the main part of the store. To her surprise, although the shelves were well-stocked, there was a distinct shortage of gourmet items and a preponderance of white bread.

She bought a packet of ginger-nut biscuits for emergency rations, tucking it in her handbag as she emerged into the glare of the street. The mortuary van was parked unobtrusively at the rear of the car park, its rear doors standing open. She crossed the hot tarmac, and as she reached the path leading up to the Mudchute, she saw that the attendants were attempting to maneuver the stretcher and zipped black body bag through the cubicle of the swinging gate. They were red-faced and sweating, and one swore steadily and inventively. Kincaid stood a few yards up the hill, his hands in his pockets, his lips pressed together in impatience.

The attendants put the stretcher down and looked up at him. " 'Fraid we're going to have to upend her, guv," said the one with the rich vocabulary.

"Just be careful, will you?" Kincaid admonished them, and Gemma heard him mutter something about "buggering up the physical evidence" under his breath.

"We'll get some straps."

Gemma took advantage of their descent to the van to slip through the gate and join Kincaid.

"Feeling a bit better?" he asked.

"Much. Where's the inspector?"

"Limehouse Station, getting things organized. Just our luck they closed the old station here on the Island and the new one's not finished."

Looking up at him, Gemma noticed the small spot on his chin he'd missed with the razor that morning, shaving in her cupboard-sized bathroom. She was close enough to smell her soap on his skin and the thought of their shared shower brought a smile to her lips. "Sorry about your Saturday," she said. "What about Kit?"

"The Major stood in for me."

"Kit must have been disappointed, just the same."

"Yes." Kincaid didn't meet her eyes.

"How rotten for you." Gemma knew he hated to let Kit down, and she also suspected that any guilt he felt over failing in his commitment to Kit was strengthened by his guilt over Vic's death. Although he didn't talk about it, she'd sensed it gnawing at him the past few months, and she felt it driving a wedge between them.

"Worse for him, poor little beggar."

Gemma thought of Toby, who accepted her frequent unexpected absences with equanimity because it was all he'd ever known. "He will get used to it, and you've not much choice, have you?"

"We'll have her out of here in a tick, guv," called out the talkative attendant, returning from the van.

Glancing at Gemma, Kincaid seemed about to reply, then shrugged and turned his attention back to the corpse on the stretcher. Frowning, he said, "If she were dumped here, how did the killer get her into the park? That gate would have made things bloody difficult."

"I suppose you could get through it with a body over your shoulder, if you were strong enough. But you'd be visible, even at night. There must be other entrances." Watching the men strap down the body, then hoist the stretcher into an upright position and maneuver it through the gate, Gemma added, "Did you find anything under the body?"

"No. Nor any definite evidence of dragging. But the ground's hard. It might not have left traces."

Leveling their burden on the far side of the gate, the stretcher-bearers moved down the path to the car park. As Gemma and Kincaid followed, the attendants slid the stretcher roughly into the van and slammed the doors.

Gemma winced as she thought of how carefully the woman's body had been placed in its bower of grass. "That wasn't necessary. There's no bloody hurry now, is there?"

Kincaid gave her a surprised glance. "You know it doesn't mean anything to them. She's not a person anymore."

Gemma shook her head. "She is to someone, somewhere."

"She did look remarkably peaceful," he said, and she heard the understanding in his voice. It was odd, thought Gemma, that the more disfigured the corpse, the easier it seemed to distance oneself from the victim's humanity. With a light touch on her shoulder, Kincaid added, "I suppose we'd best get on with it. I think we should see the pensioner who discovered the body. And I'd like to have a look at the geography of the park on our way."

When he'd retrieved his jacket and his *A to Z* from his car, they climbed back up to the Mudchute plateau. Skirting the crime scene, they continued eastwards along the path. To their left lay a steep bank, and at its bottom the high-fenced back gardens of a new housing estate. The dense growth of brambles and bindweed that covered the slope and spilled over to crowd the edge of the path showed no signs of trampling. Pausing to look down, Gemma felt the palpable weight of the sun beating against her scalp as the air over the high ground of the park shimmered in the mid-day heat.

Beside her, Kincaid picked a ripe blackberry and popped it in his mouth. "From the map, it seemed possible that she'd been killed in the housing estate, then dragged up into the park." He shook his head. "But there's no access, unless you can fly."

Gemma tentatively considered a blackberry. She'd read about berry-picking in books, but it was something she'd never done—in her childhood berries had come in punnets at the greengrocer's, and her family hadn't had time for holidays in the countryside. As Kincaid moved away she reached out and plucked one. It left sticky purple stains on her fingers, and as she hurried after him, the wild, sweet-tart taste of it on her tongue gave her an unexpected sense of liberation.

Before them both path and bank made a sharp right turn. Gemma thought of the brief glimpse she'd had of the slightly irregular square of park on the map. "I thought it would be an ordinary city park, but it's more like the rolly bits of Hampstead Heath laid out on a tabletop, isn't it?"

"A living tablecloth?"

"I suppose so. But it is an odd place, and an odd name."

"The Mudchute was built from the silt dredged up from the Mill-wall Dock—I think the mud was quite literally pumped through a chute," Kincaid said. When Gemma gave him a surprised look, he smiled and added, "I asked Inspector Coppin about it and got the penny lecture from her for my pains. The land belonged to the Dock and, being off-limits, was a huge temptation to the local children for years. It was only made a park about twenty years ago."

They had reached a bench set back from the path, a sort of natural lookout point. Gemma stopped and gazed round at the rolling, scrubby grassland, dotted with the occasional tree. "But it's enormous. What was it all for?"

"Dockworkers' allotments, mostly, and timber storage. Look, there's someone's garden." He pointed down the now-gentle slope at a small vegetable patch fenced off with chicken wire. "Some of the park is still used for allotments, though I wonder if they'll be kept up when the pensioners are gone. There's a demonstration farm here now, used mostly for educating schoolchildren."

"It sounds like you managed to thaw Inspector Coppin."

He grinned. "Only because she enjoyed knowing more than I did."

Ahead of them, the path disappeared into a wide, level expanse of dirt, and the breeze brought them a distinct whiff of manure. "Is that a road?" asked Gemma.

Kincaid consulted the map. "We're coming to the farm now, and it looks as though a track comes up from the farm entrance. We'll have to see if it's accessible at the bottom."

"If you could drive a car this far, you could carry a body to where we found her."

Looking back along the path, Kincaid mused, "A good walk, carrying such a burden." He knelt and felt the dry earth with his fingers. "But as hard as the ground is, you might be able to drive partway along the path without leaving a trace."

They started down the gentle incline and soon reached the main farm buildings. Inside the central courtyard a group of small children ate ice creams bought from the concession kiosk. "A thriving business, that," said Gemma. The sight of the children made her think of Toby, left in her sister's care by default. A day spent with Cynthia's little hellions and her son would be wound up like a top for a week, but what choice had she had?

Where the dirt farm road met paved street, a large, metal-barred gate stood propped open. A rusty padlock hung from a chain looped through its leading edge.

"Doesn't look as though it's been closed recently." Kincaid rubbed the toe of his shoe against the dusty road surface. "No sign of scraping or dragging that I can see."

Gemma touched the pitted surface of the gate. "So the murderer *could* have driven her into the park." She looked round at the council flats lining the paved cul-de-sac. "But in this area you'd surely run a risk of being seen even in the middle of the night. Nosy neighbors."

"They might remember seeing an unfamiliar car, even if they thought it was just teenagers looking for an uninterrupted cuddle."

Smiling at his choice of words, Gemma touched his arm briefly as they turned towards the street. "How delicate of you, Superintendent. Where do we find Mr. Brent, then?"

He consulted the map. "This is Pier Street. It should take us right into Manchester Road if we continue along it."

The council houses they passed as they walked were built of the gray concrete blocks typical of the sixties, but most appeared well-kept. Front doors stood open in the mid-day heat, and although the bead curtains hanging in most doorways afforded inhabitants a bit of privacy, they allowed cooking odors an easy escape. Gemma sniffed appreciatively at the scent of garlic mingled with spices not quite as familiar.

Some of the tiny front gardens had been paved over entirely, others had a few pots and hanging baskets or revealed a small attempt at a plot of flowers, but the garden of the flat they approached would have made a garden center green with envy. Every inch of the eight-foot square was filled with something blooming, and as they came nearer Gemma saw that one would have to squeeze through a gate held ajar by a mass of purple clematis.

She checked the number over its door. "Mr. Brent, I believe."

"The inspector said something about his prize flowers."

"An understatement." No bead curtain covered this doorway, and as they brushed their way down the narrow path, the smell of roasting meat competed with the cloying scent of the flowers. From inside, a telly blared forth the theme from *Grandstand*.

Kincaid tapped on the doorjamb, waited a moment, then called "Hullo!" over the din.

"Just coming," answered a woman's voice. She appeared from the rear of the house, wiping her hands on a flowered pinny. "Can I help you?"

"We're here to see Mr. Brent."

Grimacing, the woman said, "Hang on a moment while I turn this racket down."

As she slipped through the sitting room door, they saw a flash of television screen, then the noise stopped.

Returning to them, she nodded. "That's better. Bloody thing drives me crazy. Now, what did you say you wanted?"

"Mr. Brent," answered Gemma. "We're from the police. We'd like to talk to him about this morning."

The woman's face instantly creased with concern. "A terrible thing. Dad's been that upset, it's taken me the whole morning to get him settled. I had to promise him roast chicken and potatoes, in this heat, and now you want to get him all riled up again." She was small and wiry, with cropped hair kept black with the help of the dye bottle. Beneath the flowered pinny she wore stretchy trousers and an open-necked tee shirt.

Kincaid smiled. "I'm sorry, Mrs.—"

She touched her hair, then held her hand out to Kincaid. "Hubbard. Brenda Hubbard, *née* Brent. I'll just—"

"Bren!" a man's voice called from the back of the house. "Who is it, Bren?"

Brenda hesitated a moment, then shrugged. "It's the police, Dad. They've come to see you." Stepping back, she led the way into the sitting room.

Gemma instinctively drew in her arms as they entered, for the small room was stuffed so full of things that movement was restricted to a narrow path through its center. The fringed lamp shades competed with the poppy-sprigged wallpaper, which shouted in turn at what was visible of the bold floral carpet. Souvenir-type knickknacks and family photographs jostled for space on every flat surface, but the photos held the advantage by spilling over onto the walls.

Brenda Hubbard looked back at Gemma, then gestured at the photos. "I tell Dad there'll be no room for him one of these days, but he can't bear to part with any of them."

Pausing, Gemma examined a group of particularly ornate frames atop a bookcase. "School class?" she asked, pointing at the photo in the largest.

Smiling, Brenda said, "Family. There were fourteen of us. Thirteen girls and a boy, the last. Mum was determined, I'll give her that." She briefly touched a photo of a faded, sweet-faced woman surrounded by children, then moved on.

The blue plush reclining chair in front of the television provided the room's sole island of solid color, but it was empty. The glass door to the small, concrete patio stood open, and in the shade of a garden umbrella sat an elderly man in a white plastic patio chair. Beside him, a Patterdale terrier raised its slender black head from its paws at their approach.

"Mr. Brent." Kincaid held out his warrant card as they followed Brenda onto the patio. Glancing at the dog, which was now sniffing his ankles, he added, "I'm Superintendent Kincaid and this is Ser—"

"Get down, Sheba." George Brent scolded the dog gently, then scrutinized them with alert blue eyes. "Janice Coppin sent you, did she? I'd not have credited her with that much sense."

Brenda Hubbard gave an exasperated shake of her head. "Dad, that's not a nice thing to say and you know it." With a look at Gemma and Kincaid, she added apologetically, "Janice was at school with our Georgie, and Dad took against her over some silly thing that no one else even remembers."

"Your mum remembered. And it wasn't a silly thing to our Georgie—she stood him up for the Settlement Dance." Having made his point to his daughter, George Brent held out his hand to Kincaid. His grip was strong, and the arms and shoulders revealed by his cotton vest still showed muscular definition.

Kincaid pulled over two more plastic patio chairs. "Do you mind if we sit down, Mr. Brent?"

"Oh, forgive my manners." Brenda Hubbard sounded a bit flustered as she helped them arrange the chairs. "Can I get you something to drink? Tea? Or some orange squash?"

"Squash would be lovely," said Gemma, as much to remove the distraction of bickering with his daughter from Mr. Brent as to quench a genuine thirst.

As Brenda disappeared into the kitchen, Kincaid began again. "Mr. Brent, we don't want to upset you, but we need you to tell us about what happened this morning."

"Whoever said I was upset?" Brent gave a dark glance towards the house. "Load of bollocks," he added under his breath, but as he spoke he reached down and buried his fingers in the dog's rough coat.

"It's not every day you find a dead body, Mr. Brent," Gemma said gently. "It would upset anyone."

Brent looked away. Gemma saw the movement of his Adam's apple as he swallowed, and the spasm clenching the hand still resting in the dog's fur. "Beautiful. She was so beautiful. I thought she was sleeping, like a fairy princess."

Returning with their drinks, Brenda served them without interrupting, then pulled another plastic chair into the shade and sat down.

"Why don't you start from the beginning, Mr. Brent," suggested Kincaid. "You took your dog to the park?"

"You'd had your breakfast, hadn't you, Dad?" prompted Brenda. "You always take Sheba for her run after breakfast."

"That's right. Right round the park we go, every morning and every evening. Keeps us fit, doesn't it, girl?" He stroked the dog's head; the animal's tail thumped.

"What time was this, Mr. Brent?"

"A bit later than usual, on account of helping Mrs. Singh next door with her telly. About half past eight, I'd say, and already hot as blazes."

Gemma sipped her drink, then asked, "Did you take your usual route?"

"We always go the same way, don't we, girl?" said Brent, and Sheba's tail moved again in assent. "Up from the bottom of Stebondale Street, into the park at the Rope Walk, across and up the other side." He shook his head. "Bloody construction mucking things about. Can't hear yourself think."

"That's along East Ferry Road?" asked Kincaid.

"Farm Road, we always called it. There were still farms round about when I was a boy, though you'd not think it now. I remember when we lived in Glengall Road, before the bombings—"

"Mr. Brent," Kincaid interrupted gently. "Tell us what happened next."

George Brent took a handkerchief from his trouser pocket and rubbed it slowly across the polished dome of his head as he watched Sheba, now happily digging in a patch of the small flower bed at the edge of the patio. "You're a right devil, aren't you, girl?" he said softly, then met Kincaid's eyes. "Most mornings I stop at the ASDA for a cuppa, meet my old mates, you know, though Harry Thurgar for one is getting a bit past it . . . but I was too late this morning, so we went on along the top."

His gaze strayed again, back to the dog. "I let her off the lead—she's always after rabbits, or what she thinks is rabbits. Then I heard her whining, and when I caught up to her . . ."

At the word "rabbits" Sheba sat back on her haunches and cocked her head expectantly, then moved to her master's side. Her long, elegant profile made Gemma think of the paintings of dogs on Egyptian friezes. Hadn't the Egyptians believed that dogs followed their masters to the underworld?

"Did you touch the body, Mr. Brent?" she asked.

"No, I . . . Well, maybe I did, just a bit, to see if . . ."

"But you didn't move her?"

Brent shook his head. "All I could think then was to get help, I don't know why. Ran to the ASDA, silly bugger; too old to run like I used to. Used the phone to ring 999."

"You waited for the police?" asked Kincaid.

"Didn't know they'd send Janice Coppin, did I?" Brent scowled and Sheba responded with a low humming in her throat. "Treated me like a child, or a dimwit. She's no better than she should be, that woman, and her husband's a no-account—"

"Dad, that's enough," said Brenda. "And Bill's her *ex*-husband now, you know that." She looked at Kincaid and Gemma. "If that's all . . ."

"Just a couple of questions more, Mrs. Hubbard." Kincaid turned back to her father. "Had you ever seen the woman before, Mr. Brent?"

"I . . . I'm not certain." Mopping his head again with the handkerchief, George Brent seemed suddenly to age, as if his uncertainty weighed heavily.

"You don't have to be sure." Gemma smiled to put him at ease. "Just tell us where you think you *might* have seen her."

Brent said hesitantly, "At the shops, just along the road. That hair, so lovely . . . but I never quite saw her face."

"Recently, Mr. Brent?"

Gemma heard the hint of excitement in Kincaid's deliberate drawl.

Brent shook his head. "No, I . . . My memory's not what it used to be. I think it was nearer the spring, maybe Easter. I'm sorry," he added, as if he'd seen the disappointment in their faces, but Gemma had the distinct feeling that the old man hadn't told them everything he knew.

Kincaid rose. "You've been a great help, Mr. Brent. And we're going to let you have your lunch now. There's just one more thing. You said you walked Sheba yesterday evening—did you go the same way?"

"Have to put her on the lead to stop her, wouldn't I? Like a clockwork dog round that path, she is." Brent chuckled at his own wit.

"What time was this?"

"Nine o'clock news was just coming on. Hate to miss the news, but it's too dark after."

"And you're sure the body wasn't there?"

Brent bristled. "I'd have seen her, wouldn't I, even in the dusk. I'm not bloody blind."

"Of course not, Mr. Brent," Kincaid reassured him as Gemma stood. "And we do appreciate your time."

As they turned to go George Brent called after them, "You tell that Janice she's a silly cow. Our Georgie would never have left her on her own with a pack of rotten kids."

REG MORTIMER SELDOM DRANK. A SOCIAL pint occasionally, or a glass or two of wine with dinner, but urgings to more than that he usually fended off with a smile and an offhand remark about keeping fit. Reg could never bring himself to admit the truth—that it made him ill, revoltingly, nauseatingly, childishly ill.

His hand trembled as he lifted the glass to his lips—Jack Daniel's because he found the sweetness of the Bourbon easier to stomach than the tangy bite of Scotch. Could one call this medicinal? The half glass he'd drunk had done nothing to still the panic fluttering beneath his breastbone. Nor had it helped him decide what he ought to do.

Turning, he glanced at the phone in the corner, then again at the thinning crowd in the bar. At lunchtime people came in the Henry Addington at Canary Wharf to see and be seen, though this being Saturday the men had traded their business suits for carefully pressed Levi's and khakis, and in this heat the women wore shorts and bright sundresses. Beyond the windows in the pub's curved marble front wall, the sun blazed, making a molten sheet of the water, muting even the reds and purples of the buildings at Heron Quays across the dock.

Lunchtime was easing into afternoon, and there was still no sign of Annabelle. It had been a thin chance, coming here, where they often met on a Saturday, but he had rung her flat until the phone seemed glued to his ear. Then he'd gone round and pounded on her door, and he'd done the same at the warehouse.

Not that Annabelle ever made a habit of instant availability—he sometimes thought she enjoyed putting him off, teasing him. But she always returned calls, and although he suspected she was still angry with him, he couldn't imagine Annabelle missing a meeting as important as this morning's for personal reasons.

Of course, he'd lost his temper last night—he'd be the first to admit it, if she would only give him a chance—but the fact that the party at Jo's had turned into a fiasco hadn't been his fault.

Despite the heat in the bar, Reg shivered. He thought of what he had revealed to Annabelle last night, spurred by jealousy, and of what he had kept from her. He had driven her away, and he couldn't bear the thought of losing her. Not now, with so much at stake. But how could he repair the damage he'd done?

And why hadn't Annabelle turned up this morning? As hard as he and Teresa had tried to smooth things over at breakfast, his father hadn't been fooled for a minute. Sir Peter's support was crucial—they all knew that—but what Annabelle and Teresa didn't know was how desperately Reg needed things to work out the way they'd planned.

He'd phone Annabelle again. Surely she would answer—it had been an hour since he'd last rung, plenty of time for her to have returned home. Perhaps she had even been trying to ring him. Yet even as he stood, a bit unsteadily, a wave of dread coursed through him, as certain as the nausea that followed.

"THERE'S NO POINT SENDING SOMEONE ROUND the shops in Manchester Road until we get a photo." Kincaid leaned against the corridor wall outside the incident room at Limehouse Police Station, sipping tepid tea from a polystyrene cup.

"I've sent one of the lads to pick up the prints," said Gemma, adding, "Hope there's one that will be palatable to the public." Kincaid couldn't tell if her grimace reflected the prospect of dealing with hysterical residents or the thought of the nasty liquid in her cup.

He nodded agreement. "The photos should be all right. Her face was remarkably well-preserved." The afternoon having so far yielded no clues to the woman's identity, the distribution of photographs to the inquiry team became the logical next step.

Gemma's empty cup squeaked as she crumpled it. "Will you release a drawing to the media?"

During the course of the afternoon, they had set the routine of investigation in motion; the first round of house-to-house inquiries, concentrated on the supermarket and the streets immediately adjacent to the park; the intensive search for physical evidence, always a race against contamination of the crime scene; the checking of the victim's description against the Police National Computer's missing persons reports. But he'd delayed speaking to the media until he'd prepared a formal statement describing the dead woman and asking the public's help in identifying her or reporting suspicious sightings in the area. "No, not yet. We'll try the description first, and if that doesn't produce results, we'll have the police artist make a sketch." Finishing his tea, he tossed his cup in the bin and pushed himself away from the wall. "I suppose I'd better face the lions." He pulled up the knot on the tie he'd rescued from the boot of the car, then ran his fingers through his hair.

Gemma smiled. "You're quite presentable. They're waiting in the ante—"

The incident room door swung open and Janice Coppin came out. Although the passing hours had taken their toll on both starched hair and suit, they'd done little to temper the inspector's prickliness, although Kincaid had found her to be competent and patient with her staff. "There you are," she said as she saw them. "The duty officer's just rung from downstairs. There's a bloke at the window raising holy hell because they won't let him register a missing person until the twenty-four-hour limit's up."

Kincaid heard the intake of Gemma's breath as she said, "A match?"

Coppin shrugged. "His girlfriend didn't come home last night. Her name's Annabelle Hammond, lives just at the end of Island Gardens. And he says she has long, red hair."

CHAPTER 4

*By 1797, over 10,000 coasters
and nearly 3,500 foreign-going
vessels were coming up to
London annually. The West India
vessels contributed particularly
to the river's traffic jam. . . . In
September 1793, [the West India
Merchants] held a meeting in an
attempt to resolve it, which was
to lead in due course to the
building of London's first
commercial docks.*

Theo Barker, *from* Dockland

"BLOODY POSER," JANICE COPPIN
muttered, jerking her head towards
the interview room, where she had
sequestered the man who wished
to make a missing persons report.
"Ought to have his mobile phone
surgically implanted in his ear."

Gemma knew the type all too
well. They indulged in the prolonged and very public use of their
mobile phones in the trendier cafes
and coffeehouses, and this disregard
for both cost and manners apparently served as a badge of social status. "Do you think we should take
this seriously, then?" she asked.

"Can't see him as a practical

joker," Janice answered reluctantly. "And his distress seems genuine enough. It's just that he fancies himself a bit." With a dark look at Kincaid as he came through the door at the end of the corridor, she added in Gemma's ear, "But I imagine you're used to that."

Before Gemma could come up with a retort, however, Kincaid joined them. "I postponed the media a bit longer, until we see what this chap has to say. Have you told him anything?"

Janice shook her head. "Just that someone will speak to him. And I sent one of the constables in with a cuppa."

"Right. Then let's not get the wind up with an abundance of police presence. Why don't you run a check on—what's his name, Inspector?"

"Reginald Mortimer." Janice articulated each syllable distinctly, crinkling her nose as if she found it distasteful.

"Run a check on Mr. Mortimer, then, Inspector, while Gemma and I have a word with him."

"Sir—"

Kincaid stopped, hand on the doorknob.

Janice hesitated, then shrugged. "Never mind." As she turned away, Gemma saw her glance at her watch.

It was the time of day when domestic arrangements needed adjusting if you weren't going to get home, and as Gemma followed Kincaid into the interview room, she wondered when she'd have a chance to check on Toby. She told herself, as she often did, that her frequent absences would only make her son stronger and more independent, but the argument never quite convinced her.

The interview room was larger than most, with a frosted-glass window on the corridor side, but it was still stuffy with the remainder of the day's heat. It contained the usual laminate table in an unsightly orange and a half-dozen mismatched chairs of dubious heritage.

The man sitting on the far side of the table looked up at them and started to rise, his expression anxious. As Kincaid stepped forward with an introduction, Gemma studied Reginald Mortimer. Janice had been right. Mortimer wore sharply creased khaki trousers and the knit shirt with designer logo required of a yuppie. Thrown over the back of the chair was a nubby linen jacket; the most expensive of mobile phones peeped from the inside breast pocket.

Of slightly above average height and slender build, he had wide gray-blue eyes and shiny brown hair that flopped over his brow with a slight wave. She wondered if Kincaid would notice the man's physical resemblance to him.

Reg Mortimer smiled as he shook Kincaid's hand, and the likeness lessened. His features, she decided, were all just a bit too delicate, and he looked nearer her age than Kincaid's. He smelled slightly of alcohol and nerves.

"I'm sure this is all a mistake. You must think me a dreadful ass," he said. His voice was pitched higher than she found pleasing, and no doubt it was his fruity, upper-class accent that had set Janice's teeth on edge.

"Sergeant James," Gemma said, pressing his damp palm with her own as she settled into a chair and took a pen and notebook from her bag. "Can we get you some more tea?"

"No, I'm fine, really." Reg Mortimer shook his head and she saw his eyes dart towards the tape-recording equipment. "Look, I never meant to make such a fuss. I got a bit carried away in the heat of things, then when your sergeant chap on the front desk didn't seem inclined to be cooperative . . ."

If he'd had a drink to steady his nerves, he didn't appear to be drunk. Gemma heard no slurring in his speech, and his eyes tracked steadily as he looked at them.

"Don't let the equipment put you off, Mr. Mortimer." Kincaid waved a hand at the tape recorder as he sat down. "This is all quite un-official—we just needed a quiet place to have a chat." He smiled and pulled his chair a bit closer to the table, as if to emphasize the infor-mality of the interview.

"Never been in a police station before." Mortimer's attempt at in-souciance didn't quite come off.

"They don't rank high on the list of pleasant work environments, complete with mod cons. Now, Mr. Mortimer," Kincaid continued, and Gemma felt tension rise at his change of tone. "Something must have worried you quite a bit to bring you here. Why don't you tell us about it."

Looking from Gemma to Kincaid, Reg Mortimer began hesitantly,

"It's my fiancée, Annabelle . . . Annabelle Hammond. She didn't come home last night."

"Do you and Miss Hammond live together, then?" Kincaid asked.

"No. No, we don't." Reg Mortimer's answer seemed reluctant. "Annabelle has a flat just opposite the Island Gardens DLR Station. On Ferry Street."

Kincaid crossed his ankle over his knee and adjusted his trouser cuff. "So you can't be sure she didn't return home?"

"Well, no, I can't be positive, but I've checked quite thoroughly."

"Could Miss Hammond have decided to go away for the weekend without telling you?"

Mortimer shook his head, stirring the lock of hair that fell forward on his brow. "It wasn't like that. We were together last night. We'd been to a party in Greenwich, at her sister Jo's. But Annabelle wanted to leave—"

"What time was this, Mr. Mortimer?"

"Half past nine–ish, I think, but—"

"A bit early for leaving a party, wasn't it?" Kincaid raised a doubtful eyebrow.

"Annabelle wasn't . . . wasn't feeling well," Mortimer said, reaching for his tea. It would be cold and scummy by now, Gemma thought, only appealing as a distraction.

"Mr. Mortimer." She chose her words carefully. "Has it occurred to you that perhaps Annabelle made an excuse, because she had other plans?"

"I'm sure she didn't." He met her eyes. "We were going for a drink, after. We started back through the foot tunnel—we'd walked to her sister's—when . . . Well, it was all very odd. . . ." He faltered.

With a glance at Kincaid, Gemma continued the questioning. "What was odd, Mr. Mortimer?"

Frowning, he rubbed his palms against his knees. "The lifts were closed, so we took the stairs down to the tunnel level. She was fine then; it was only when we started down the slope of the tunnel itself that she went very quiet—have you ever been in the tunnel?" He looked at Gemma as he spoke and she shook her head. "It *is* a bit creepy," he continued. "Cold, and the sound echoes everywhere—but

Annabelle never seemed to mind before. But her steps got slower and slower, until after a few yards she stopped and told me to go on, she'd meet me at the Ferry House for a drink in a few minutes."

"And you left her there?" Kincaid asked. "At the edge of the tunnel?"

Mortimer flushed. "There's never any point arguing with Annabelle when she makes her mind up about something. But I did try. She said she was all right, she just needed a few minutes on her own. So after a bit I went on. The funny thing is . . . when I was halfway up the other side I looked back, and I could have sworn I saw her talking to the street musician."

"There was a busker in the foot tunnel?" Gemma asked, surprised. It seemed an odd place, but then she'd seen them often enough in the tube station tunnels.

"There usually is, in the center of the flat stretch. But I don't remember seeing this chap before."

Kincaid uncrossed his ankles and leaned forward a bit, a signal to Gemma that his attention was fully engaged. "Did you go back, then?"

Mortimer wrapped his hands round his cold cup as if for comfort and shook his head. "I wish I had, now."

"Did you see her again?"

"I waited at the pub for an hour, then I waited outside her flat."

"You don't have a key?" Kincaid's tone indicated skepticism.

"No. Annabelle is adamant about her privacy," Mortimer answered without defensiveness. "I went back to the tunnel, but there was no sign of either of them. Then I tried the flat again, and rang her from my mobile."

"And then?"

"I went home. I started phoning again at first light, and I've been round to her flat and to the office—we work together—periodically all today. This afternoon I rang her sister, but she hadn't heard from her, either."

"Does Miss Hammond make a habit of going off like that?" Kincaid asked.

"Not that I'm aware of," Mortimer said dryly. "And she's certainly never done anything like this before. You think she's gone off with some bloke for a dirty weekend, and I'm having a fit of the vapors over it, don't you?" he added, his voice rising.

"Not at all," said Kincaid. "We're very interested in what you've told us."

Reg Mortimer's eyes widened and Gemma heard the quick intake of his breath before he said, "What is it? What's happened?"

"Just bear with us a bit longer, Mr. Mortimer," Gemma said gently, in an effort to put him at ease. "We don't know that anything has happened to your fiancée, but it would be helpful if you could give us a bit more information about Miss Hammond."

After a moment's hesitation, Mortimer answered. "Annabelle's thirty-one. She was thirty-one in January. She's the managing director of Hammond's Teas. It's her family's business—Annabelle took over from her father five years ago. I handle the marketing side of things. The warehouse is just down the far end of Saunders Ness Road."

Gemma hadn't a clue where that might be, but she wrote it down in her notebook. "And what does Annabelle look like?" She saw the tendons flex in Mortimer's hands as they tightened on the mug. "Height?" she prompted, not wanting to give him any longer to ponder the significance of the questions.

"About like you. And she's slender, with red hair." He studied Gemma. "But not like yours—it's lighter, almost golden, and longer, too."

"Eyes?"

"Blue."

"And can you tell us what she was wearing last night?" Gemma asked, eyes on the pen poised over the page of her notebook.

She felt his gaze on her face before he answered softly, "A black jacket. Long, with silvery buttons. And a little black skirt."

Making a conscious effort not to glance at Kincaid, Gemma wrote deliberately in her notebook. She felt none of the elation she'd expected over an almost certain identification. Until this moment, the anonymous woman had been merely a puzzle; now she had become real, someone with a name, a job, a family, a lover.

Kincaid rested his fingertips on the edge of the table. "Mr. Mortimer, you've been very helpful, and we appreciate that."

Gemma looked up and reluctantly met Reg Mortimer's eyes, knowing she needed to observe his reaction as Kincaid continued.

"But I'm afraid I have to tell you that the description you've given us of Annabelle Hammond matches that of a woman found this morning in Mudchute Park."

Mortimer's face was still, expressionless. He licked his lips. "Dead?"

"I'm afraid so."

For a moment longer Reg Mortimer stared at them, the only change the draining of color from his face. Then the handle of the tea mug he still held snapped cleanly off. He looked down at the shard of cheap pottery in his hand, as if he couldn't quite work out where it had come from.

"If you could make a formal state—"

"Since when?" Mortimer demanded.

"Sometime last night. I'm afraid we can't be more definite than—"

"How?"

"Mr. Mortimer, we're not sure of anything yet. If you could just give us her sister's name and—"

"I want to see her."

"I'm afraid it's customary for a family member to make the identification," Gemma said gently. "If you could just—"

"Surely you won't make Jo . . ." His voice broke.

"It's procedure, Mr. Mortimer. I'm—"

"I don't think I can bear not knowing."

Although she understood his plea, Gemma shook her head. "I'm sorry," she said again.

Mortimer rose unsteadily to his feet. "Then I think I'd like to go home."

Kincaid pushed back his chair. "We'll arrange it. But if this busker was the last person to see Annabelle, we'll need to talk to him. Had you seen him before? Can you describe him?"

For a moment, Gemma thought Mortimer hadn't heard, but he wiped a trembling hand across his mouth and seemed to make an effort to collect himself. "The street musician? I'd never seen him before. And I didn't really look when I passed him in the tunnel. . . . But when I looked back . . ." He closed his eyes, frowning, then gripped the back of his chair for support as he swayed a little. "He was tall. . . .

I remember Annabelle was looking up at him. Short hair . . . fairish. Military clothes."

"What instrument did he play?" Gemma asked.

Reg Mortimer opened his eyes. "I remember I thought it a bit unusual. The clarinet."

KIT STOOD IN THE CENTER OF Kincaid's sitting room, watching the millions of sparkling, dancing dust motes illuminated by the late afternoon sun that blazed in through the open balcony doors. Having placed his holdall at the end of the sofa, he'd unzipped it and taken out one of his natural history books, placing it carefully on the coffee table so that he'd feel like he belonged here. He'd only spent the night in the flat once before—usually Duncan came to Cambridge and took him out somewhere, or he stayed with the Cavendishes in the big house while Duncan stayed with Gemma—and he had so looked forward to this weekend, just the two of them on their own.

Sid, Kincaid's black cat, lay curled on a patch of sunlit carpet, eyes slitted in contentment. Kneeling, Kit ran his fingers through the cat's silky fur and scratched behind his ears. He felt the vibration of the cat's purr travel through his fingers and up his arm until it seemed as if it were reverberating inside his brain. The contact made him miss Tess with an almost physical pang.

Cats were all right, he supposed—he'd never had one, never had a dog for that matter until Tess had come into his life—but there was nothing like a dog for making you feel less lonely.

He stood and shoved his hands in his pockets. He wouldn't bloody cry, not even here on his own, though these days he fought a constant battle against the tears that seemed to hover behind his eyelids, waiting to pounce on him at the most humiliating moment.

This morning had been a near thing when Duncan told him he'd have to go to work—it made him flush just thinking about the way his eyes had filled and his voice had quavered. But things hadn't turned out as badly as he'd expected. He had liked the Major, rather to his surprise, because the old man hadn't fussed over him—hadn't patted him or said "poor boy" or looked at him in that pitying adult way. An adventure, the Major had called it as they set off on the tube to

Wimbledon, and Kit had done his best to master his disappointment. But even though the tennis had been glorious, it hadn't been the same without Duncan. It just wasn't bloody fair.

Since the Major had left him here and gone down to his own flat, Kit had poked about at his leisure, examining books and CDs and the photos on the walls. He'd tried the telly remote control, zapping through the channels, but there was no Sky TV and he flicked it off in disgust. For a while he'd stood on the balcony, looking down into the bright blooms of the Major's garden, but he'd come in again when the emptiness of it began to make him feel queer.

His face felt stretched and hot from sunburn and he realized suddenly that he was thirsty. Wandering into the kitchen, he opened the fridge and stared at the contents. A carton of orange juice, a pint of milk past its sell-by date, a cola, and two cans of lager. For a moment Kit was tempted—he was nearly twelve, after all, and he ought to take advantage of being on his own to do something grown-up—but there were only two beers and Duncan was sure to notice if one went missing. With a shrug he chose the cola, popping the top and tossing the ring into the rubbish bin. He rummaged idly through the kitchen drawers as he drank, thinking that if he found a fag he'd try that instead, but then he remembered he'd never seen Duncan smoke.

Why hadn't Duncan rung him like he'd promised? Where was he now? It must be a murder—that's what he did, after all, even though he didn't like to talk about it. Kit tried to imagine a body, riddled with bullets like the ones in the videos he liked, but he couldn't erase the one image he didn't want to see—his mum lying so still on the kitchen floor in their cottage.

Throwing the empty cola can into the bin, he glanced at the clock—almost seven. He'd refused the Major's invitation to come down to his basement flat for baked beans on toast and a game of cards, but he supposed he could change his mind. Anything was better than staying here on his own.

THE COACHES THAT WOULD TAKE THE *children to the railway station waited at the curb in front of Cubitt Town School. Parents clustered round them, straining for a last glimpse of sons and daughters as the children were marshaled into untidy queues by the teachers. Many of the mothers were weeping, and the sight of his mum's tear-streaked face caused Lewis almost as much embarrassment as the paper name tag pinned to the breast of his jumper. He felt like a bloody parcel, and a parcel without a destination at that, for they hadn't been told where they were going. Many of the children had been bundled into winter coats and stank of sweat and damp wool; some of the smaller ones had already been sick from the heat and excitement.*

The queue shifted suddenly as the children in the front began boarding the first bus, and a gasping moan rose from all the parents at once. Little Simon Goss's mum burst into sobs, arms outstretched as she begged them not to take her baby. As Lewis turned away in mortification, he glimpsed his father at the back of the crowd. Their eyes met: he saw that his father's were filled with tears.

Swallowing hard, Lewis lifted his hand in a wave; then the momentum of the queue overtook him, carrying him along until he was pushed and shoved up the steps of the bus. He clambered over bodies until he managed to secure a seat at the nearside window, and from there he watched as the remainder of the children were loaded. Finally they were ready, and he lifted his hand once more to his parents as the bus rumbled into life.

Then they were moving, and he felt excitement fizz in his chest—in spite of the uncertainty, in spite of the fact that his suitcase lacked many of the items on the required list, in spite of the humiliating name tag and the gas mask in its cardboard box banging against his chest. Yet as the bus began its lumbering turn into Manchester Road, he twisted round in his seat for one last look at the life he was leaving behind.

At first, as the coach rumbled and belched its way down the Commercial Road and then over the Tower Bridge, he thought they might be going to Waterloo. At home, he had a worn and treasured map of London, and if he closed his eyes he could see the placement of the great railway stations as easily as if he held it in front of him. Paddington, King's Cross, Euston, Marylebone, Victoria, St. Pancras, Waterloo. The trains left each station in a different direction, so that when he learned their point of departure, he'd have some idea of their final destination.

But as they continued south into Lambeth, he knew they'd left Waterloo behind, and soon they were crossing the Thames again over the Lambeth Bridge. Victoria. They were going to Victoria, then, and from there— south. . . .

Giddily, he stared up into the station's vaulted arches as he was herded across the concourse to join the queues of strangely silent children snaking down the platforms. Steam hissed and swirled round the trains; the only sounds were the shouts of the porters and conductors and the echoing of whistles in the cavernous space.

In spite of the teachers' efforts at order, the boarding of the train entailed much pushing and shoving as the children scrambled for seats next to windows and friends. Lewis's carriage was packed with several classes, but still he managed to secure a window seat, and taking pity on little Simon Goss, he squeezed the boy in beside him. There was a wait, then a great roar from the children as a guard waved a green flag and the train began to move.

As they chugged out into the sunlight, sandwiches were pulled from paper wrappers and chocolate bars were opened. The silent apprehension of the queues gave way to holiday chatter and absently Lewis ate the bread and drippings his mother had given him, his face pressed to the glass. The suburbs seemed to go on forever—Clapham . . . Wandsworth . . . Balham. . . . Splotches of green began to spring up between the clusters of buildings. Then the splotches spread together until it was the clumps of houses that stood out, dark patches against the green of the rising hills.

The children grew quiet again, absorbing the strangeness of the countryside, and the temperature continued to rise. When the train ground to a halt, a moan of tension ran through the car and Lewis felt a wave of nausea. They waited, whispering, but soon the train began to move again.

As the heat grew and the children became more anxious, the special treats eaten by many inevitably came back up. To make matters worse, it was soon discovered that the train had no toilets. Lewis tried pinching his nose to block the stench, but it only made his thirst worse. Simon Goss had gone to sleep, slumped against Lewis's numb shoulder. The younger children who weren't sleeping grizzled for their mothers, a continuous keening of misery.

The train slowed once more. Lewis opened eyes he had squeezed shut against the glare. His eyelids felt sticky. Licking his parched lips, he squinted at the station sign as the train squealed and shuddered to a stop.

Dorking. *Wherever* that *was. He closed his eyes again and leaned his head against the window, wondering if he'd dozed and dreamed that they were doomed to stay on this train forever.*

The sound of an engine roused him. He looked out, blinking. A green coach pulled up to the station, then another, and another. Men shouted commands and the buses were maneuvered into position beside the platform. Lewis felt his heart thud as the children woke and a stir ran through the car.

The loading of the buses went smoothly, as most of the children were too hungry and exhausted to cause any trouble. Lewis's class was put with another, and as their coach pulled away from the station, the children clutched their parcels and stared out at the red-bricked buildings of the high street. But they soon left the town behind, and the road ran west into wooded, rolling hills and the afternoon sun.

Lewis had found himself near the front of the coach, and to quell the panic rising in his chest at the sight of all that openness, he spoke to the driver. "Where are we, mister?"

The driver, a thin man with a leathery face and wispy hair, glanced back at him and smiled. "Surrey, lad."

That didn't mean anything to Lewis. He tried again. "How far is it? Where are we going, mister?"

Another flick of the man's eyes in the mirror and he replied, "Ten miles or so. Not far. You'll see."

Subsiding in his seat, Lewis thought the man had a funny sort of accent, all stretched-out and blurry-sounding. But at least they'd be off this bus soon. The twisting and rising and falling of the road was making him feel all-over queer, and he wrestled with the catch on his window until he managed to get a bit more air.

He tried closing his eyes, but that only made it worse, so he looked at the great, green hump of land rising away to the right.

Following Lewis's gaze in his mirror, the driver said, "That's the north Surrey Downs, lad. Old earth, that is. Feet have walked that way since the Dark Ages."

Lewis did not find the thought comforting.

After a bit they turned off to the left into a lane no wider than the coach. The lane dipped down between thick hedges, curving and turning, and at every bend Lewis gasped in terror and squeezed his eyes shut. Surely

*they would crash into the hedge, or meet something coming the other way,
but the driver seemed unconcerned and eventually Lewis relaxed a little.*

*Then the hedges disappeared, and a triangular bit of grass appeared. A
few houses were clustered round it, and a ways up the hill on the opposite
side rose the steeple of a church. The coach continued past the green and into
another narrow lane, but this one had houses either side, and it came to a
dead end at a long, low building that bore the legend:* Women's Institute.

They had arrived.

"KIT SHOULD BE BACK AT THE flat by now." Kincaid disconnected the
mobile phone as he negotiated the entrance to the Blackwall Tunnel.

He'd left the top down on the Midget, and Gemma held back the
strands of hair that had blown loose from her hair grip with one hand
while she turned the pages of the map book with the other. "I'm sure
he's fine," she reassured him without looking up. "The Major will keep
an eye on him." She traced a spot on the *A to Z* page with her finger. "I
think I've found the street, but it doesn't look like much on the map.
It's just above the old center of Greenwich."

"Right. I think I can get that far."

They were on their way to interview Annabelle Hammond's sister,
having been given her address by Reg Mortimer.

"Did you find anything on Mortimer?" Gemma asked as they
emerged from the tunnel into the evening sunlight. She'd been arranging for a car to run Mortimer home while Kincaid had a word with
Janice Coppin.

"Sod all, at least in the system. Not even a traffic ticket, as it seems
our Mr. Mortimer doesn't drive." He squinted as he turned west into
Trafalgar Road and the low sun blinded him. "What did you think of
his story?"

"Holes you could drive a lorry through," Gemma responded. "If
Annabelle Hammond left her sister's party because she felt ill, why
would Mortimer have left her on her own in the tunnel?"

"And why not go back when he saw her talking to the busker? Unless . . . he invented the busker so he wouldn't seem to be the last person to have seen her alive," Kincaid mused.

"In that case, why call attention to himself by reporting her missing?"

Kincaid shrugged. "We don't know for sure that it *is* her. We're way ahead of ourselves." Glancing to his left, he saw the beginning of Greenwich Park, its manicured lawns rising up the slope of the hill that housed the Old Royal Observatory. He remembered how crushed he'd been when he'd learned that Greenwich Mean Time was now measured from Deptford. A little bit of childhood romance had died at that moment. "We'll have to bring the boys here," he said, pointing. "Tour the *Cutty Sark*, visit the Observatory. Kit would be interested, don't you think? *And* there's a tea kiosk."

"For the bottomless stomach," Gemma said, smiling. "You'll turn left just ahead, pass the police station, and turn right on Circus Street, then turn left again on Prior."

He followed her directions, winding ever upwards until they came to the tiny unpaved lane with the rather grandiose name of Emerald Crescent. It turned out to be more of a Z than a crescent, a narrow, twisty alley flanked by hedges, back gardens, and a few large, old homes. Just past the final sharp zag to the left they found the address they'd been given for Jo Lowell, Annabelle's sister.

Square and symmetrical, with charcoal brickwork and white trim, the house was separated from the lane only by the iron railings that marked the basement entrance. Through the window to the left of the front door they could see a vase of sunflowers on a table.

Kincaid reversed past the last bend until he found a spot of verge large enough for the car. He killed the Midget's engine, then climbed out and stood for a moment, listening to the sounds of early evening in the lane. A child shouted, a dog barked, and somewhere dishes clattered. "A peaceful evening," he said softly as they started walking towards the house.

"Until now." Gemma moved a bit closer to him, her shoulder brushing against his. "Can't be helped."

He looked down at her, appreciative of the implied comfort. She knew how much he hated this part of the job. For a brief moment as they reached the door, he let his hand rest on the small of her back in acknowledgment. Then he pushed the bell.

The chimes echoed, and as a voice called out, "Coming!" the door swung open. The woman who stood before them stared at them with the blank expression reserved for the unexpected caller, then she smiled tentatively. "Can I help you?"

Kincaid smiled back. "Are you Josephine Lowell?"

Her brow creased. "Yes, I'm Jo, but look, if you're selling something—"

"We're with the police, Mrs. Lowell." As Kincaid introduced himself and Gemma, displaying his warrant card, her dark eyes dilated. "What . . ." She glanced towards the back of the house, where the sounds of children in dispute could be clearly heard.

"We need to ask you a few questions, Mrs. Lowell. If we could come in?"

"Oh . . . of course." She stepped back. "Do you mind if we talk in the kitchen? I was just putting dinner together and I think things have got a bit out of hand."

They followed her through a dining room that was painted a soft yellow and accented with the sunflowers they'd seen through the window, then into a comfortable kitchen that looked out on the back garden. A small girl stood on a step stool at the cooker, stirring something in a pan, and an older boy seemed to be trying to wrestle the spoon from her hand. The room smelled of onions, garlic, and spices, overlaid with the sharpness of cooking tomatoes. Spaghetti sauce, Kincaid guessed.

"Give over, Sarah. You've got sauce all over the cooker." The boy made another grab for the spoon but the girl snatched it back and turned with a howl.

"Mummy! I wanna *stir*!" Tomato sauce dripped from the spoon to the floor in patterns like blood spattering.

"All right, you two, that's enough." Jo Lowell removed the spoon from her daughter's fist as she scooped her off the stool, then swiped the floor with a kitchen towel from the roll on the worktop.

The boy flushed to the roots of his red hair. "I was just trying to help. It's not my fault she's made a mess. You always—"

"Harry, please." Jo Lowell's exasperation made it clear that this was an oft-played scenario. "Would you take Sarah out into the garden for a few minutes?"

As if alerted by something in his mother's voice, the boy turned and really looked at them for the first time. "But—"

"Harry." Jo's tone was firm.

With a last glance at them, he capitulated. "Okay, okay." Taking his sister by the hand, he said as he led her towards the door, "Come on, Sarah. I'll let you bat."

Gemma smiled as the garden door banged after them. "A great sacrifice, bowling to your little sister."

Jo shook her head. "Harry's life seems to be full of trials these days. But you don't want to hear about that. Please sit down." She gestured towards the breakfast alcove to the left of the back door, then turned to the cooker. Steam billowed from a large pot behind the saucepan. "Let me just turn these things off." As she adjusted the knobs, the gas flames dwindled to blue, then sputtered out. She turned and leaned against the cooker, arms folded across her chest. "Can I get you something?"

"No, we're fine, thanks," Kincaid said, studying Jo Lowell as he pulled out a chair for Gemma. A smudge of tomato sauce adorned her tee shirt, and her jeans were stained with splotches of paint; a cotton scarf held her dark auburn hair back in a careless ponytail. She wore no makeup and her skin was slightly freckled. He thought she looked a bit too thin, and there were dark shadows beneath her eyes, as if she hadn't slept well. Although attractive, she bore little obvious resemblance to the dead woman in Mudchute Park. But then there was the boy's hair. . . . He seated himself so that he could see out the large window into the garden. "We'd just like to ask you a few questions about your sister."

"My sister?" Her surprise seemed so genuine that he wondered what she had been expecting.

"Her fiancé, Reginald Mortimer, has made a missing persons report. He said he'd rung you?"

Jo gave a dismissive wave of her hand. "Yes, he did, but I just assumed Annabelle was still narked with him and had made herself temporarily unavailable."

"Then this has happened before?"

"Well, no, it's just that last night . . ."

Before Jo's hesitation could develop into real caution, Gemma interposed. "What happened last night?"

"They were here—Reg must have told you—and I think they had a bit of a row. That's Annabelle's way if she's cross with you—she cuts you off for a bit."

"Is that why they left? Because they'd had a row?"

"Why do you want to know?" asked Jo Lowell. "Look, I think you'd better tell me what's going—"

"Have you any idea what the row was about?" Kincaid said, not yet willing to be deflected.

"No, I'm sorry, I don't." Shifting her stance against the cooker, Jo clasped her hands together.

"This was a dinner party?" prompted Gemma. "Celebrating anything in particular?"

Through the open door, they could hear Harry's continuous grumbling and Sarah's high, strident voice making the occasional response. Jo glanced out the window over the sink, then said, "No, it's just that my husband and I are divorced, and this was my first attempt at entertaining on my own."

"Must have put quite a damper on your party, your sister and her fiancé having a row," Gemma said sympathetically.

"It was a bit uncomfortable," Jo admitted, frowning.

"I understand they work together. It must be awkward there, as well, if they don't get on."

Jo shrugged. "I'd say they get along better than most—they've had long enough to work out their differences."

"They've known each other a long time, then?" Kincaid asked.

"Since we were children. Our parents were friends. In fact, it was Father who encouraged Annabelle to take Reg on."

"In the professional sense, you mean, not the personal?"

"Father's always had dynastic ambitions for Annabelle, and Reg fits the bill quite nicely all round. A merger of the Hammonds with the Mortimers would almost make up for not having a son in the firm."

"What's so special about the Mortimers?" asked Gemma.

"Sir Peter—Reg's father—is rather a big cheese in restaurants and hotels, that sort of thing. I'm quite fond of him, actually. Annabelle could do worse in the way of a father-in-law." Frowning, Jo added, "What is this all about? Surely you're not taking this missing persons thing seriously?"

"Mrs. Lowell, have you seen or heard from your sister since she left your house last night?" He knew he was slipping into policespeak, but, like the ceremonial and familiar language of funerals, it had its uses.

Jo stared at him. "No, but there's nothing unusual about that. Sometimes we don't talk for weeks. What—"

"Mrs. Lowell, I think you should sit down."

She came slowly, unwillingly, to the table, slipping into a chair without taking her eyes from them. Her expression was anxious. "What's happened? Is Annabelle all right?"

He looked out the window at the tableau formed by the two children on the green square of lawn. Sarah Lowell stood with her back to them, bat raised, and as her brother threw the ball the sun glinted from his hair.

If they were wrong, Jo Lowell would endure the trip to the morgue for nothing. And if they were right, he wished he could preserve for her this moment untouched by loss, bound by the sound of the children's laughter on the evening air.

KINCAID HAD SENT GEMMA HOME AFTER their return from the morgue. They'd not make any further progress on the case tonight, and he'd only to tidy up the tag ends of the paperwork at Limehouse Station. Or so he'd insisted, but the truth of the matter was that he'd needed a bit of time on his own to sort out his impressions of the day.

Jo Lowell's quiet identification of her sister's body had been harder to take than tears. His condolences had sounded stiff and intrusive even to himself, and he'd had her driven home without attempting to question her further.

Now that they had put a name to the face, the investigation would move into the sifting of evidence and the tracing of every connection with Annabelle Hammond. The constable dispatched to the Greenwich Foot Tunnel had found no sign of the busker described by Reg Mortimer, but from the beginning Kincaid had had his doubts about the story's authenticity. It was just too bloody convenient, and he'd begun to suspect that Reg Mortimer had a great capacity for inventiveness.

Having organized his makeshift desk as best he could, he said good night to the officers still on duty in the incident room and left the station through the side entrance. As he retrieved the Midget from the car park, he heard music and laughter pouring out of the pub next door. The image of Kit waiting alone in the flat squelched the temptation of a pint before it was fully formed, and he climbed in the car and started the engine. Tomorrow he'd pick up an unmarked Rover from the Yard, but tonight he would enjoy the rare treat of driving through the warm darkness with the top down.

He loved London at night, when the streets had emptied and the lights ran together in a kaleidoscopic blur. As he pulled out into West India Dock Road, he could see to his left the flashing beacon atop Canary Wharf's Canada Tower. He wondered if Annabelle Hammond had seen it last night as she emerged from the Greenwich Tunnel, and who had been with her. . . .

Of course, they couldn't overlook the possibility that Annabelle had been killed by a stranger, perhaps an attempted rape gone wrong; she might simply have been in the wrong place at the wrong time. But his instincts told him that there was more to it than that. He guessed Annabelle Hammond had been the sort of woman who aroused strong emotions, and that it was this quality in her that had led to her death.

The drive from Limehouse to Hampstead took him half as long as during the day, and when he reached Carlingford Road he found a parking space near his flat, a miraculous feat at this time of night. The windows of the Major's basement rooms were dark, so he entered the building and climbed the stairs to his own flat.

Carefully, he slid his key into the lock and eased open the door. His sitting room was in semidarkness, lit only by the small lamp on the kitchen island and the soundless, flickering images on the telly. Kit lay on the sofa in jeans and tee shirt, sound asleep, one arm outstretched, Sid curled up on his chest. The cat opened green eyes and blinked at Kincaid; the boy didn't stir.

As Kincaid stood watching, he had the same odd sensation in his chest that he'd experienced the last time he'd seen Kit sleeping—the day he'd found the boy hiding in the Grantchester cottage after his mother's death.

Turning away, he discovered on the kitchen island a covered plate of sandwiches, a glass of milk, and a note in Kit's small, neat hand.

Dear Duncan,

We saved you some sandwiches from the picnic. But we (meaning me!!) polished off the cake. The Major wants to take me to Kew Gardens tomorrow, that is if you have to work.

PS I fed Sid. He really likes ham sandwiches.

PSS The tennis was brilliant! But I wished you were there.

This missive was signed with a large calligraphic K and embellished with birdlike squiggles.

Kincaid found a light blanket in the linen cupboard and covered Kit as far as the cat. Then he put the sandwiches and milk in the fridge, quietly poured himself a finger of twelve-year-old Macallan, and carried the note and his drink across the room to the armchair. There he sat for a long time, motionless except for the occasional lifting of his glass, watching the gentle rise and fall of Kit's breathing.

AFTER SHE HAD PUT THE CHILDREN to bed, Jo slipped next door and let herself into her father's house with her key. He had taken Sir Peter and Helena to dinner at the Savoy, but he would be home soon and she had steeled herself to break the news to him then.

She hadn't been able to bring herself to speak to the children, not yet, although she knew she'd have to face it in the morning. They'd gone to bed without a fuss, a signal that they sensed something was wrong, but they hadn't asked. Nor had they questioned her unexplained absence when the police had driven her to the morgue, though Harry had made a token complaint about being sent to the neighbors' for a while.

Standing in the hallway, she listened to the sounds of the empty house. The grandfather clock ticked; the floor creaked; from the kitchen came the low hum of the fridge and the intermittent drip of the tap. She had grown up in this house, and to her it seemed a living, breathing entity, as familiar as her own body. It had its own unique smell, and she closed her eyes as she tried to pick out the individual components. Was there the faintest hint of tea rose still, four years after her mother's death? It had been her mother's scent, and the house had been filled with the garden's roses from spring to frost. Did odors linger like ghosts, invisible, yet there for those able to perceive them?

She gazed up at the portrait of her mother on the landing. The beaded lace veil and headdress Isabel Hammond wore in the portrait hid most of her red-gold hair, but the eyes that looked down at her were Annabelle's.

The only blessing Jo could see in her sister's death was that her mother had not had to endure it. Although her mother had seen Annabelle more clearly than most, she had loved her fiercely nonetheless. As Jo loved her own children, despite their faults—and she found her mind could not fasten on the thought of their deaths, at any age.

Moving into the dining room, she encountered her father's essence; the muskiness of his shaving soap, overlaid with the sharpness of glue and the slight spiciness of balsa. He had always been good with his hands, and when her mother's ill health, and then his own, had compelled him to turn the day-to-day running of the business over to Annabelle, he'd begun building scale models of tea clippers. Since childhood he'd been fascinated by the intricacy and precision of the ships that had first brought tea to Britain.

The dining room table served as his workbench, and he'd not only given up any pretense of using the room for its original function, he'd built special illuminated shelves to hold his creations.

Jo picked up the half-completed model in her hands, running her fingers over the curve of the hull, searching for imperfections. Would his bits and pieces of wood be enough to compensate for the loss of a daughter he had valued above all else?

He still lived on income from his interest in the firm—as did she, to some extent. The money from her shares supplemented her own business, allowing her to work from home, and to be there for the children. Would Hammond's provide security for any of them, with Annabelle gone?

Jo shook her head and went to the drinks cabinet. No point thinking that far ahead, yet. There was this evening to get through first; tomorrow she would think about the next thing. She'd learned that when her mother died. And that there was no harm in the occasional numbing drink. Pouring some of her father's treasured Courvoisier into a snifter, she carried it to the sitting room and sank into the armchair by the empty fireplace. The windows stood open and the edges of the drapes moved fitfully in the night air.

Green velvet; her mother's choice. If Jo stood near them she thought she could smell the pipe tobacco her father had smoked when they were children. It had been Annabelle who had bullied him into giving it up. She'd claimed it made her feel sick, that she couldn't bear to be in the room with him when he smoked; then she'd administered the coup de grâce by refusing for weeks to kiss him good night. As a power play it had been brilliant, a harbinger of things to come.

Jo's hand jerked at the sound of a car coming up the lane and the brandy sloshed over the lip of the glass. She held her breath. How could she possibly do this? What preparation had she in her thirty-four years that would allow her to tell her father this terrible thing? For a brief moment she hoped that Reg Mortimer had phoned his parents, and that Peter and Helena had told him; then she cursed herself for a coward. Gravel crunched as the car turned into the drive. She heard the gears shift as it began to climb.

Carefully, she set the glass on the end table and rose. Her limbs felt awkward, uncoordinated as a toddler's, and once she had managed to unfold herself from the depths of the chair, she stood rooted to the spot. The car door slammed and a moment later she heard her father's key in the door she had left unlocked.

The door swung open. "Jo?"

She found her voice. "In here, Dad."

"Good. I could have sworn I'd locked the door, and I'd hate to think I was becoming an absentminded old dodderer." Coming into the sitting room, he offered his cheek for a kiss. He wore the light gray summer suit that set off his silver hair. In his late sixties, William

Hammond was still a handsome man, and since Isabel's death he'd had a time of it fighting off what Annabelle called "the widows' club."

Had called, Jo reminded herself. She swallowed. "Dad—"

"Peter and Helena send their regards. I see you've got a drink already. I think I'll join you in a nightcap. Didn't want to overdo and drive; you know how touchy they are these—"

"Dad." Jo touched his arm. Her hand was shaking. "I need you to sit down."

William peered at her face. "Are you feeling all right, Jo?"

"Dad, please." She saw his expression of mild concern turn to alarm. "What is it, Jo? Are the children all right?"

"They're fine. It's—"

"Is it Martin?"

"Dad, please." She pressed her hand against his chest so that he was forced to retreat a step. When the backs of his legs hit the edge of the sofa, he sat involuntarily. Jo dropped to her knees before him. "Dad, it's Annabelle. She's dead."

"What?" He stared at her, uncomprehending.

"Annabelle's dead." *Annabelle's dead.* The phrase echoed in Jo's head like a children's nursery rhyme.

William drew his brows together. "Don't be silly, Jo. Whatever is the matter with you?"

Jo reached out and grasped his hands in hers. The skin on his knuckles felt like silk under her fingers. "The police came to my house. Reg reported her missing because she didn't come home last night."

"But surely they've just had a tiff of some sort—"

"That's what I thought when he phoned me this afternoon. But the police found her body. I know. I saw it."

"No . . ." The muscles in William's face began to sag with shock, like modeling clay held too close to a flame. He shook his head rigidly. "There must be some mistake, Jo. Annabelle can't be dead. Not Annabelle . . ."

Not Annabelle. Never your precious Annabelle. "Daddy, I'm so sorry." As she squeezed her father's hands, she felt the enormity of it overwhelm her. Annabelle had always been there, to love and to hate. However would she manage without her?

CHAPTER 5

*Isle of Dogs, the intended site [of
the West India Docks], was then
a lonely, boggy waste used for the
pasturing of cattle. It was said to
have only two inhabitants: one
drove the cattle off the marshes
and the other operated the ferry
to Greenwich.*

Theo Barker, from Dockland

WHEN KINCAID'S ALARM BLARED,
he was sleeping with his pillow over
his head. It was already full daylight
at six o'clock, and when he emerged
from his cocoon, the air from the
open window smelled fresh and clean.
That made him a bit less reluctant
to roll out of bed, though it didn't
quite compensate for having to get
up at such an ungodly hour on a
summer Sunday morning. The postmortem on Annabelle Hammond
was scheduled for eight o'clock, and
he'd arranged last night to meet
Gemma at the Yard beforehand and
go together from there.

Although he showered and shaved

as quietly as he could, when he tiptoed into the sitting room on his way to the door, Kit stirred and opened his eyes.

"What time is it?" Kit asked sleepily, propping himself up on his elbow. "Did you just get home?"

"It's half past six in the morning, and I've been home but I have to go out again." Kincaid bent down to stroke Sid, who had abandoned Kit and was rubbing madly about his ankles, purring. "I was going to leave you a note."

Kit threw off the blanket and sat up. "Can I go with you?"

"Sorry, sport. It's work."

"But it's Sunday."

Kincaid sighed. "I know. But that doesn't matter when there's a case on."

"It's a murder, isn't it?" Kit stared at him, wide awake now.

Pushing Sid gently out of the way, Kincaid sat on the edge of the coffee table.

Before he could answer, Kit continued, "You could take me with you. I'd wait in the car. I wouldn't be any trouble."

Kincaid thought of the body that would be laid out on the stainless steel mortuary table, and of what would happen to it. "Kit, I can't. It's just not on, and I have no idea how long I'll be."

"But I have to get the train back to Cambridge tonight." Kit's blue eyes widened in alarm. "I've got school tomorrow; it's exam week. And there's Tess—"

"I'll get you to the train, don't worry. And in the meantime, why don't you take the Major up on his offer. I think you'd like Kew." Kincaid glanced at his watch. "I'm sorry, sport, but I've got to—"

"There's nothing for breakfast." Kit's mouth was set in the stubborn line Kincaid had begun to recognize as his way of coping with disappointment.

"I know," Kincaid said with a rueful smile. "I'd planned we'd do the shopping together." He thought for a moment. "I've an idea." Removing his wallet, he peeled off a few notes. "There's a good cafe round the corner on Rosslyn Hill. Why don't you treat the Major to a proper breakfast. There's enough for the tube and your admission to the gardens, as well." He tucked his wallet back into his pocket, then hesitated a moment, not knowing how to make Kit understand that he wasn't abandoning him by choice.

"I'll see you tonight," Kincaid said finally, and as he let himself out of the flat, it occurred to him that perhaps his justification wouldn't hold water, because he had, after all, chosen the job.

"MILE END AT EIGHT O'CLOCK ON a Sunday morning," muttered Gemma as they made their way down into the bowels of the hospital. "Just where I wanted to be." She hated the smell of disinfectant and the underlying, cloying smell of illness.

To distract herself, she thought of the music store she'd seen as she walked to the Angel tube station this morning. It had been closed, of course, but she'd crossed Pentonville Road and peered in the windows. Maybe tomorrow she'd have a chance to buy the music books Wendy had recommended, and at next Saturday's lesson—assuming this case allowed her to go—she would actually start playing the piano.

Last night, after putting Toby to bed, she'd dimmed the lights and poured a glass of white wine from the open bottle in the fridge. Then she'd stood, hesitating, looking out into the twilit garden. As much as she valued her all too infrequent opportunities for solitude, she'd felt itchy, unable to settle; she wondered if a few minutes' quiet chat with Hazel would help her erase Annabelle Hammond's image from her mind.

As she'd quietly let herself out of the flat and made her way across the garden, she blessed the chance that had led her to the Cavendishes. Hazel had not only offered to care for Toby, along with her own daughter, while Gemma worked, but she'd become a much-valued friend as well. In many ways, Gemma felt closer to Hazel than she did to her own sister, for she'd learned blood was no guarantee of sympathy or common interest.

She'd found Hazel and Tim sharing a quiet moment at the kitchen table, drinking mugs of hot cocoa. "I'm interrupting," she'd said, one hand still on the doorknob. "I'll just say good night."

"Don't be silly. Come and sit down," Hazel had said, patting the chair beside her. "I'd offer you cocoa, but I see you've brought your own tipple," she'd added with a glance at Gemma's wineglass. "Hard day?"

"A right bugger." Gemma had wandered over to the table but hadn't sat. "And you can imagine what Toby was like after a day at Cyn's. He fought going to sleep like it was the end of the world, then passed out from one second to the next." Touching the soft knitting wool in Hazel's basket, she'd added, "Would you mind if I went into the sitting room for a bit?"

Tim had looked up from his paper and smiled. "Help yourself."

She'd wandered into the sitting room, drawn by the piano. Sliding the cover back, she'd run her fingers lightly over the keys just for the smooth feel of them, then pressed a few randomly, listening to the notes vibrate and die away. She couldn't imagine that she would ever be able to string the notes together in a way that would make music—and after her talk with Wendy Sheinart, she found herself trying to work out why she had such a strong desire to do so.

There had been a case the previous autumn that had unexpectedly opened up the world of opera for her, and she'd found herself fascinated . . . and since moving into the garage flat, Hazel's wide-ranging collection of CDs had allowed her to sample everything from piano concertos to improvisational jazz . . . and then in the spring there had been the street musician with the clarinet, who had drawn her to listen whenever she passed the Sainsbury's on her way home from work. An odd coincidence, she thought fleetingly, that Reg Mortimer had described a busker with a clarinet, but surely it was no more than that.

Having asked her why she wanted to play the piano, Wendy Sheinart had accepted her fumbling attempt at an explanation with a smile. "You don't have to understand it," she'd said. "I think perhaps a need to make music is innate with some of us, and background and experience don't figure into it. And it really doesn't matter. I just wanted to be sure you were doing this for *you*."

"Here we are." Kincaid touched her arm, and with a start Gemma realized she'd been about to walk past the doors to the morgue. He gave her a quizzical glance. "Why do I get the feeling you're not all here this morning?"

Gemma smiled and pushed the bell for admittance. "Sorry. I was gathering wool."

"Then I envy the sheep."

The door swung back and they identified themselves to the pony-tailed young man in spectacles.

"Dr. Ling's expecting you," he informed them as he ushered them in.

Kincaid frowned. "Dr. Ling? Would that by any chance be Kate Ling?"

"In the flesh," said a white-smocked woman as she emerged from the postmortem room. Dark hair as straight as broom bristles framed her pale, oval face and swung just above her shoulders. The pathologist's dark eyes gleamed with the wicked humor Gemma remembered. They had worked with her in Surrey the previous autumn, on a case that had resulted in the death of one of Gemma's friends and the near-fatal injury of another. The unexpected rush of memory was sudden and painful enough to leave Gemma momentarily speechless, but Kincaid carried on in the breach.

"What are you doing in London?" he asked, shaking Kate Ling's hand warmly.

"A promotion of sorts," Kate answered. "The Home Office had a vacancy needed filling, and I drew the short straw. But I can't say I'm minding the bright lights all that much, and I get a nice variety of clientele." She nodded towards the room at her back. "Nice fresh one, this, and just out of the cooler. Shouldn't be too unpleasant for you, if you're ready."

They followed her into the room, masking and gowning as Kate retied her mask and pulled the instrument trolley up to the autopsy table. Was it possible to envy the dead? Gemma wondered as she looked at Annabelle Hammond's body. The breasts were perfectly formed, neither too large nor too small; the neck slender, the shoulders well-shaped; the waist small and belly flat; the thighs smooth and slim. Even her feet and ankles were beautiful, and Gemma had seldom seen a set of toes worth writing home about. Fat lot of good all that loveliness did her now, of course—and it might even have got her killed. But it had certainly been a body to inspire passion, even obsession.

"Did you do the on-scene yesterday?" Kincaid asked Kate Ling. "Sorry to have missed you. Bit of a balls-up there."

"The old headless-chickens routine," Kate agreed as she pulled a new pair of latex gloves from the dispenser. "But I imagine we'll cover everything now."

As she reached up to switch on the microphone over the table, Kincaid said, "What about time of death? Off the record?"

The corners of Kate's eyes crinkled as she smiled beneath her mask. "Half past twelve." She laughed aloud as she saw Kincaid's skeptical expression. "You asked me for off-the-record, and now you don't believe me? Seriously, though, I'd say it's not likely she was killed before midnight, although the calculation of body cooling is made a little more difficult by the fact that the ambient temperature began rising rapidly as soon as the sun came up. Lividity was fixed, but the corneas had just begun to cloud, and rigor was not fully established."

Gemma looked up from her notebook, pen poised over the page. "Eight hours or less, then?"

Shrugging, Kate said, "There are always unanticipated factors. Perhaps the tox report and stomach contents will help you."

"Spoken like a true pathologist," Kincaid said, grinning, and it abruptly occurred to Gemma that he found Kate Ling attractive. It wasn't that he was flirting, exactly, but there was somehow an extra degree of attentiveness in his responses. And his interest was a dangerous thing, as she well knew.

"Was she killed where she was found?" Gemma asked, diverting Kate's attention from Kincaid.

"It looks that way, unless she was moved very shortly after death. The lividity corresponds to the position of the body."

"Can you hazard a guess yet as to how she died?" Kincaid asked.

"Now that *would* be telling." Kate reached up and switched on her microphone, then stated that she was continuing the external examination of Annabelle Hammond. She tilted the head back so that they had a good view of the throat. "We won't know until we get into the tissue if there was any crushing of the larynx. But the bruising on the throat is minimal, as is the facial congestion."

"Anything else obvious?"

Kate lifted one of Annabelle's hands and then the other, examining the long, slender fingers. "No visible blood or tissue under the nails, but we'll send samples to the lab just in case."

When she'd finished her careful scraping of the nails, she buzzed for the attendant. "Gerald, let's have a look at her back."

Gerald turned the slender body with the ease of practice, and Kate began her examination of the back of Annabelle's head, carefully parting the mass of red-gold hair with her gloved fingertips. "Here's something," she said after a moment, glancing up at them. She used a magnifier for a closer look. "I think it's possible we have some blunt force trauma here. There's a bit of loose hair and tissue, maybe a bit of swelling. We won't know for sure until we peel back the scalp."

Gemma swallowed and focused fiercely on her notebook. This was the part she hated most, even more than the initial incision and the removal of the internal organs. She'd always assumed that this part of the job would get easier for her the more exposure she had, but that hadn't turned out to be the case, and somehow it was always worst when the corpse was as unblemished as this one.

"What about fluids on the body?" she heard Kincaid ask as she stared at the loops and dashes of her shorthand.

"Nothing came up on the swabs, and I've not found anything else obvious. No evidence of recent intercourse, either."

"There's no indication that this was a sex crime, then."

Gemma heard Kate's shrug in her voice as she said, "Not unless it's a nutter who just likes to fantasize about it afterwards. But they usually leave something behind."

When Kate had finished with Annabelle Hammond's back and had Gerald turn the body again, she said, "Unless you have something else in particular you want me to look for, I'm ready to start the internal now."

As Kincaid shook his head he met Gemma's eyes. He knew she'd be struggling, but he wouldn't embarrass her by saying anything. And from his expression, he wasn't too keen, either.

Kate chose a scalpel from her array of instruments and spoke into the mike. "Right, then. Let's begin with a Y incision."

Gemma concentrated on breathing through her nose and recording Kate's observations in her notebook. *Healthy female. Probably an occasional smoker. No sign of a pregnancy, or of previous pregnancies.*

When the internal organs had been removed and weighed, Kate said, "We'll get the stomach contents off to the lab—should have something for you shortly. Now let's have a look at the neck."

Gemma glanced up just long enough to see the scalpel poised over Annabelle's white throat; then she forced her gaze back to her shorthand.

"Look." Kate sounded as though she'd found a prize in her Christmas cracker. "There's some bruising on the tissue that didn't show up on the skin. Odd, but you sometimes see that. And the hyoid cartilage is intact."

"Are you saying she wasn't strangled?" Kincaid asked, frowning.

"No, just that it's not obvious. And there's always the possibility of vagal inhibition. But let's have a look at that head injury."

Gemma took a deep breath and focused on Annabelle Hammond's toes.

EVEN WITH THE AID OF A sedative, Reg Mortimer had slept poorly. He had dreamed of Annabelle, disjointed fragments in which she had either dismissed him or furiously accused him of something he could not remember. In the last dream, they had been children again, and he had watched helplessly as she stepped into an abyss—then it had been he who was falling, and he'd awakened with mouth dry and heart pounding.

He forced himself to bathe and dress, to eat a bowl of cornflakes and drink a cup of tea, but through it all he had the strangest feeling of unreality, as if any moment he might wake again and find that everything, even the dreaming, had been a dream.

By half past nine, the walls of his flat had begun to close in, and not even the much-prized view of the Thames from his sitting room window offered relief. He had loved the playful conceit of his building, with its architectural mimicry of a great steamliner, but now he had a sudden vision of the building tipping, plunging to the depths and taking him with it.

Reg blinked away the vertigo and grabbed his keys from the entry table. The central lift whooshed him to the ground floor and the lobby doors ejected him into a fine morning. His feet took him south, along the river path and the blinding, molten sheet of the Thames, then into Westferry Road and round the corner into Ferry Street.

The sight of the blue and white tape fluttering from the door of Annabelle's flat brought him up short. A uniformed constable stood near a van, talking to a man in a white overall. Reg stood for a moment, watching, then forced himself to go past. Whatever impulse had driven him there was spent, but he knew now where he should go.

By the time he'd crossed under the river and climbed halfway up the hill in Greenwich, he was sweating. He entered Emerald Crescent from the bottom end, slowing his steps as his sense of unreality deepened. The lane had the peculiar Sunday morning sort of quietness that spoke of families sleeping in or lazing over coffee and newspapers; birdsong swelled from the hedges, and death seemed an impossibility.

As he neared the top of the lane, the land rose sharply on the left and through the thick screen of trees on the hillside he could glimpse William Hammond's pale blue door. Ahead, just past the lane's right angle, Jo's house sat foursquare and level with the lane. The back gardens of the two properties were adjacent, but not connected.

Jo and Martin Lowell had bought the house during Isabel Hammond's last illness, and while he would find it difficult to live next door to his father, he could understand Jo's choosing to settle so near her parents. His own family had lived in a Georgian terrace in Knightsbridge, and when he'd come here as a child he'd been fascinated both by the secret quality of the lane and by the Hammonds' house. Perched at an angle on the side of the hill, canopied by trees, it had seemed magical.

But this morning he didn't want to see Jo—he wasn't ready to think about what had happened there on Friday evening. It suddenly occurred to him that she might be with William and he hesitated a moment, then shrugged and began climbing the steps cut into the thick ivy on the hillside. It would be all right; Jo wouldn't say anything in front of her father.

A sound made him spin round, almost losing his balance on the steep steps. He could have sworn he'd heard a high, faint laugh, but there was no one there. Then as he turned back something flickered in his peripheral vision—a girl running up the steps away from him, bare-legged and with a long red plait bouncing on her back.

Blinking, he took a breath. Nothing there. He shook himself like a dog coming out of water and continued to climb, slowly—a lack of sleep and proper meals, that's all it was, and too much thinking about the past.

By the time he reached William's front door he had recovered his equilibrium. He rang the bell and waited.

William Hammond answered the door himself. As Reg gazed at him he realized that until now he hadn't thought of William as old. He'd been too much in awe of him as a child, and he had somehow kept that image fixed in his mind. But this morning William seemed to have shrunk. The black suit he wore emphasized his frailness, and against his silver hair his skin looked pale as driftwood.

Swallowing, Reg said, "Mr. Hammond. I'm so sorry. Is there anything I can do?"

William smiled and extended a hand that trembled as if he had palsy. "Reginald, my dear boy. How good of you to call. Do come in and have some tea."

Reg followed him through the house and into the kitchen. William put the kettle on the hob, then motioned Reg into a chair. "Jo said she'd bring over some cakes, but I'm afraid she hasn't managed it quite yet."

"It's all right, Mr. Hammond. I'm sure Jo has enough to deal with this morning."

"Yes, yes, she's taking things in hand. Telephoning and such. She and Annabelle are always so good at organizing, just like their mother." William set delicate cobalt and russet teacups on a tray, then reached for a brightly colored foil packet of Ceylon tea adorned with the Hammond's emblem. Annabelle had developed the blend herself, and it had been her favorite.

Reg stifled the urge to rise and snatch the packet from William's hand. "Would you mind if we had the Assam? Somehow I don't think I . . ."

William seemed to see what he was holding for the first time. "Oh, of course. Quite right . . ." He stood for a moment, as though the interruption had caused him to lose his place in the ritual, then he ex-

changed the tea packet and went methodically on with his preparations. When the pot had been warmed with the hot water, he filled it
and brought the tray to the table. Reg saw that his hands had stopped
shaking.

Suspended between the ticking of the kitchen timer and the tocking
of the grandfather clock in the hall, they waited for the tea to steep.
Feeling no sense of discomfort in the silence, Reg looked round the familiar kitchen. Here since his childhood had hung William's collection of framed Hammond's advertisements, some of them going as far
back as the 1880s, when a young man named John Hammond had left
his Mincing Lane employer and made the unprecedented move of setting up as a tea merchant on the Isle of Dogs. He had been William's
great-grandfather.

"I always loved these." Reg gestured towards the black and white
drawings. "Especially the ones from the *London Illustrated News*."

"Yes. That was Anabelle's favorite, the one with the little China-
men." While a pretty woman in late Victorian dress dozed in an armchair, a swarm of Chinese the size of pixies struggled to pull a canister
of tea to the top of a table, where a teapot and cup sat waiting. "I'm
afraid now it would be considered racist, but I've always thought the
poster had great charm, and Annabelle made up stories about the little
men—even named them, I believe. Their faces are so individual."
William stared at the drawing for a long moment, then said softly,
"I'm afraid I've not taken it in yet, not really."

"Have you seen the police?"

"The police? No. But Jo says . . . Jo says they told her we can't
bury . . . we're not to arrange the funeral, because . . ." The kitchen
timer dinged, and William lifted the teapot with apparent relief. He
pushed his spectacles up on his nose and carefully poured a little milk
into his cup before adding the tea. *The milk first, always, after steeping
the loose tea at least five minutes in a warmed pot.* Annabelle had taught
Reg that when they were children, and she had learned it from her
father.

And like her father, she had always insisted on bone china, arguing
that the development of English china and the drinking of tea were so
intertwined as to be inseparable. It had been an esthetic preference as

well, because she felt the delicacy of the porcelain affected the taste of the tea, and because the perfection of the ritual mattered to her as much as the quality of the tea itself.

Forcing himself back to the present, Reg said, "I'm sure the police don't mean to be insensitive," although he didn't like to think of the reasons they might need to keep Annabelle's body. "You can understand that they have to be thorough about these things." He took his cup and added a spoonful of sugar. Annabelle had nagged him into cutting down from two spoons to one, insisting that too much sugar blunted the taste of the tea. He added a second teaspoon and stirred.

"I don't understand how something like this could happen," William said slowly. "They say she was in the park. . . . But why would she have gone alone to the Mudchute at night? Surely Annabelle would never have been so foolish. . . ."

Surely not, thought Reg, but had any of them known Annabelle as well as they thought? And how could her death have been random, a grotesque coincidence unconnected with the events of the past few days? But beyond that, his mind closed in upon itself, refusing to follow the chain of probabilities to a possible conclusion.

Looking up, William met Reg's gaze. He grimaced. "I'm so sorry, my dear boy. I didn't mean to imply that you had been remiss in any way. This must be difficult enough for you as it is. Your plans . . ."

How could he tell William that it had been months since Annabelle had been willing to discuss their wedding, and that when he'd asked her point-blank to set a date, she'd refused? Lifting his cup with both hands, he sipped at the tea. It was too hot, but he welcomed the mingled sensations of pain and pleasure on the delicate tissues of mouth and tongue. Anything was better than numbness. Carefully, he said, "You and I know how headstrong Annabelle could be. And I'm sure we both learned that most of the time it was easier to let her have her own way than to fight a losing battle. But this time I let her go too far. . . ." His eyes filled with tears.

Reaching out awkwardly to pat him on the shoulder, William said, "You mustn't blame yourself. It's just as you said: Annabelle liked her own way about things. But she was a dear girl, all the same, everything a father could have wanted." His face convulsed with emotion and he looked away, staring into the leafy rectangle of the kitchen window.

Reg gave him time. Without asking, he added a little milk to William's cup, filled the cup with fresh tea from the pot, then rose and retrieved the still-steaming kettle from the hob. When he'd topped up the pot with hot water, he turned back to the cooker and stood gazing, like William, out of the window. He felt the air move round his face, heavy as a hand, warmer than his skin; it seemed to have no power to dry the sweat sliding under his collar.

Jo's children were playing in her garden next door—he could hear their voices fading in and out intermittently, like a radio broadcast from a far-off country. It might have been himself he heard, his voice mingled with Jo's and Annabelle's as they played in this same garden. . . . Had it been this green when they were children? Perhaps it had, for he remembered suddenly that Annabelle had liked to pretend it was the jungle in Sri Lanka, and that her mother's hedge of rhododendrons was a plantation of tea bushes. He wondered if there was some genetic factor involved in the inheritance of passions, for in Annabelle William's fascination with tea had appeared full-fledged and undiluted, while in Jo it had never aroused more than a mild interest.

When she'd been too young to read the more complicated text in her father's books, Annabelle had demanded explanation of the pictures, and they'd fueled her imagination. One wet spring day in the garden, she'd decided they would pick tea. It would be the finest tea, a royal tea, she'd proclaimed as she armed Reg and Jo with baskets and instructed them to pluck only the bud and the first leaf from each stem.

They had not been discovered until the poor rhododendrons had been stripped of almost every tightly furled pink bud, and when confronted by her furious and baffled mother, Annabelle had shouted that she'd only been doing the job properly. She'd spent a week in her room after that.

"Do you remember when Annabelle plucked the rhododendrons?" he asked.

William smiled. "And when her mother allowed her out of her room, she nearly burned the shed to the ground, trying to dry the leaves."

Reg walked round the table and sat again, slowly. He wrapped his hands round his Wedgwood teacup and stared at the skin forming on the surface of the tea, clouding it, just as time would cloud their memories and Annabelle's sharpness would disappear beneath a film of kindly self-deception. She would become the "dear girl" William thought her, and her father's illusions would remain unmarred by the less-than-perfect person Annabelle had been.

Looking up, he met William's eyes. *"Nothing* meant more to Annabelle than the business. I know that." Reg heard the bleakness, unexpected, in his own voice, but he continued. "We have to carry on the way she would have wished. We owe her that."

JANICE COPPIN TOOK A LAST BITE of her donut, then brushed the flakes of sugar icing from her desk. Sipping her coffee to wash away the sweetness, she reshuffled her paperwork and scowled. She'd groused under her breath last night when Mr. Scotland Yard had sent her to Reg Mortimer's flat. While she thought Mortimer a bit of a poser, she hadn't relished seeing him white and ill with the news, suddenly bereft of all his charm.

But perhaps she hadn't been quite fair to the superintendent. There were worse tasks, including the one Kincaid had undertaken himself last night—informing the dead woman's sister and accompanying her to the morgue. And he *had* asked her if she wanted to attend the postmortem this morning—she just hadn't been able to admit that she wasn't sure she had the bottle for it, and she couldn't have borne embarrassing herself in front of him.

It was even remotely possible, she supposed, that when Kincaid had told her to go home last night and see to her family, he hadn't been condescending to her because she was female. His sergeant had mentioned having a young son, so he would be familiar with the difficulty of making arrangements.

Janice wondered if they were sleeping together. It happened often enough, and she sensed an unspoken familiarity between them that went beyond the requirements of the job. Not that she cared, of course—if the woman was daft enough to get involved with her superior officer, that was her problem.

But if she was going to give Kincaid credit for some sensitivity, perhaps she ought to give his advice a second thought as well. He'd said there was no such thing as an unimportant witness in a murder investigation, even old George Brent—though they'd got no further forward when they'd interviewed him.

This was her patch, her neighborhood; she had history and a knowledge of these people that outsiders couldn't begin to appreciate. It was time she put it to good use. She'd have another word with old George, even if it meant apologizing for some long-ago slight.

First things first, though. Standing up, she dropped the donut wrapper in the bin and flicked the crumbs from her jacket. Reg Mortimer's description of the busker in the tunnel had brought immediately to mind the controversial son of Lewis Finch, a local property developer who had made his name and fortune in the rebuilding of the Docklands. She couldn't imagine what connection Gordon Finch could have had with the late Annabelle Hammond, but she had a pretty good idea where she might find him.

THE THREE TERRACED HOUSES AT THE end of Ferry Street had been built in the late seventies, the first phase of a massive waterside housing scheme that had failed because of the oil recession. Only the jutting angles of the rooflines were visible now over the brick wall and well-established private gardens that separated the houses from the street, but they were spectacular enough to make Kincaid wish he could see them from the river.

Janice Coppin had been his informant—when she'd heard the address last night, she'd wrinkled her nose and pronounced that the houses looked like a house of cards in the process of collapsing. He smiled now at the aptness of the description, but he found he liked the playful quality incorporated into the strong geometric design, and he wished the economic climate had allowed completion of the project.

According to Janice, in the intervening years, the economy had recovered, plummeted, and recovered again. Recently, an old building that stood between the private gardens and Ferry Street had been converted into flats, and it was here that Annabelle Hammond had lived.

The door to Annabelle's flat faced on the side street, a bit of pavement running down to the water. A bronze plaque set into a concrete base informed Kincaid that this was Johnson's Drawdock, and was the site of the old ferry to Greenwich. He turned and looked across Ferry Street, his eye caught by the bright red and blue cars of the Docklands Light Railway thundering across the old Millwall viaduct into Island Gardens Station, almost directly across the street.

Crime scene tape fluttered across the flat's entrance alcove, where Gemma stood chatting with the uniformed constable left to keep an eye on things. "The lads were a wee bit impatient with the lock," the constable was saying as Kincaid joined them. "So I'm to hang about until we get it sorted."

"Go get yourself a cuppa," said Gemma. "Or even a bite of lunch?" she added with an interrogatory glance at Kincaid.

Kincaid nodded. "I expect we'll be here a few minutes. Time enough for a quick break if you'd like."

"Right, sir. Cheers." He gave them a wave as he started across the street towards the park.

Kincaid raised an eyebrow as he looked at what was left of the lock on Annabelle Hammond's door. "I think 'brutal' might be a bit more descriptive."

"Inconsiderate of her not to have left us with a key," Gemma said as she pushed the door wide and Kincaid followed her in.

He glanced at her, concerned. Gemma seldom indulged in sarcasm, but when she did it was her way of whistling in the dark. The door swung closed behind them and suddenly the silent vacuum of the airless hall seemed louder than a symphony. "Good soundproofing," he commented as he switched on the lights and scooped up the post scattered on the floor. After flipping quickly through the letters, he put them on a side table. "Nothing too interesting, but we'll go through it later."

"No revealing letters addressed to herself?"

"No such luck. Just bills, from the look of them." He glanced from Gemma to the closed doors lining the T-shaped corridor. "Eenie meenie?"

Gemma considered, then pointed to the door at the other end of the T's short arm. "That one."

"Right." The sand-colored Berber felt soft under his feet as he walked down the hall. "No expense spared on the carpet," he commented.

"No expense spared anywhere, I should think," said Gemma, close behind him. "A flat in this building must have cost a pretty penny."

Opening the door, he found that they had chosen the sitting room. They stood on the threshold, staring. It was a large room, done in simple, spare furniture, the color scheme one of neutral sands and oatmeals. On its far side, French windows looked out over an enclosed garden, and it was the greenery framed in the glass panes that provided the room's focal point.

"It's beautiful," murmured Gemma, moving into the room. "Restful. She must have loved the garden."

From a small, flagged patio, steps led down to a walled oasis. A white wooden table and chairs stood under the trees at one end, a few pots of impatiens provided splashes of color, and on the lush rectangle of lawn, a croquet set had been abandoned, as if someone had been called away mid-game.

The waiting garden gave Kincaid a stronger sense of life interrupted than he'd felt standing over Annabelle Hammond's body in the morgue.

Turning away, he examined the room curiously. The SOCOs had been a bit more delicate in here, it seemed, and had left little evidence of their presence other than the thin dusting of fingerprint powder. There was a fireplace on the left-hand wall, fitted with gas logs and framed on either side by custom-built shelves filled with books. What people chose to read never failed to fascinate him, and he crossed the room to take a closer look.

There were a number of hardcover best-sellers, and a handful of titles that he recognized as being novels about successful women overcoming obstacles. None showed a particularly adventurous or introspective turn of mind, and all were tucked neatly between brass or alabaster bookends, with the spines arranged according to height rather than by content or author. It seemed as though Annabelle Hammond had been as tidy in her reading habits as she was in her housekeeping, and had reserved her passions for things other than books.

"Anything interesting?" asked Gemma as she came to stand beside him.

"Interesting by its absence, maybe. And obsessively neat."

"So I noticed." Gemma gestured towards the coffee table, where a few upscale design magazines were precisely stacked. "There's no sign of anything in progress—no half-read books or magazines, no newspapers left open, no basket of knitting or needlework." Turning back to the shelves, she touched the CDs stacked beside the stereo system. "She liked music, though, and her taste was a bit more eclectic. There's jazz and classical here, as well as pop."

His hands in his pockets, Kincaid resumed his wandering about the room, stopping to peer in the small kitchen alcove at the back. It was as neat and neutral as the sitting room, with a few expensive appliances that looked unused. The refrigerator contained a pint of milk, some orange juice, butter, a bottle of wine, and some olives. It reminded Kincaid of his own.

"She must have eaten all her meals out, or had take-away," he said. Gemma didn't answer, and when he stepped back into the sitting room, he saw that she was still standing before the bookshelves, staring at the single photograph in its ornate brass frame.

It was of Annabelle, alone. She stood in a meadow, wearing a barley-colored dress. She was laughing into the camera, and her hair shimmered like molten gold in the sun.

"You know," Gemma said slowly, "I don't think this room is about being peaceful at all. I think it's about not competing with Annabelle." She turned to him. "It's a stage. Can you imagine how she would have stood out in here, against this neutral background? You wouldn't have been able to take your eyes from her—not that I imagine that was easy to do under any circumstances."

One could see bone structure in the dead, but not the shape of a smile, or the sparkle in a glance, and the photograph gave animation to the face they had experienced as beautifully formed but without personality. Kincaid lifted it for a closer look. "She was truly lovely. And you might be right."

"I wonder who took the photo," Gemma said as he returned it to the shelf. "I'd say that either she felt a connection with that person, or she was a marvelous actress."

"There's a sense of mischief, of daring, even, in this photo that's not evident here." Kincaid gestured round the room. "I don't think this was where she lived—emotionally, I mean."

"So where did Annabelle Hammond express herself?" Gemma mused. "Let's have a look at the rest of the flat."

In the bedroom, Annabelle had incorporated soft, sea blues into the sand-colored scheme, but it was as tidy as the sitting room. No clothing lay draped over chairs or dropped hurriedly on the floor, but a look in the wardrobe caused Gemma to whistle through her teeth. "We can certainly guess where she spent a good deal of her money," she said, fingering the fabrics.

Kincaid glanced into the adjoining bath. Towels were draped over the radiator, a silk dressing gown hung from a hook on the back of the door. "I've a feeling she made the bed as soon as she got out of it. She might have even dried the bath."

Next they tried the middle door in the hallway. The room was a small office with a built-in desk, filing cabinets, and work area. A printer stood on the desk, alongside a lead and connector. "She must have kept her computer at the office," Kincaid said as he opened drawers, poking about for anything that looked interesting.

"Look at this." Gemma stood before a corkboard that had been mounted on the wall. "Seems Annabelle had a personal life, after all." Gently, she lifted layers and shifted drawing pins.

There were photographs, many of which Kincaid recognized as Jo Lowell and her children. In one Annabelle sat in a garden, a red-haired baby in her lap, an older couple standing behind her. The man was tall and silver-haired, the woman had a faded beauty that might once have equaled Annabelle's. "Her parents?" Kincaid guessed, touching the photo. "And her nephew, Harry?"

"The children's christening invitations are here, too," Gemma said. "But there's something odd. Look. There are several pictures of little Sarah as a baby, then nothing. It looks as though Annabelle was a most devoted aunt, yet there are no recent photos of either of the children."

Kincaid sifted carefully through the items. There were birthday cards and restaurant menus, bits of ribbon, a dried rose, a postcard of a Rossetti angel that bore a remarkable resemblance to Annabelle, and a flyer for a musical program in Island Gardens. He caught a glimpse of a red-haired child, but on closer inspection the photo bore the subtle signs of age. The child was Annabelle herself, he felt sure, a sunburned sprite with a mop of red-gold curls and a butter-wouldn't-melt expression. On one side stood a thin boy with Reg Mortimer's recognizable, guileless smile; on the other, Jo Lowell frowned into the camera. "The Three Musketeers, it seems," he said softly. But Gemma was right—in the last few years, her niece and nephew seemed to have disappeared from Annabelle's life.

"Look at this one." Gemma handed him a page torn from the *Tatler*. The full-lengh photo showed a grown-up Reg and Annabelle in the full splendor of black tie and ball gown. Arms clasped, both smiled into the camera's eye. "A gilded couple."

He glanced at Gemma. "What is it, love? Not envious of their social accomplishments, are you?"

She shook her head. "It's just that she seemed more than ordinarily alive—charmed, even. How could someone snuff out such beauty?"

"Perhaps she was killed *because* she was beautiful, not in spite of it," Kincaid suggested. "I think such beauty could inspire a dangerous jealousy."

"Reg Mortimer doesn't strike me as the type to fly into a jealous rage, but I suppose anything is possible." Moving to the desk, Gemma reached for the answering machine beside the telephone. "Let's see if Mortimer rang as often as he says he did." She hit *play*, and after a moment they heard Mortimer's voice.

"Annabelle, it's Reg. I'm at the Ferry House." There was a pause, then he added, *"Look, do come."* A beep ended the message, followed by another beep beginning the next. *"All right, I deserve to be punished. But enough is enough, don't you think? I'll apologize on bended knee."*

After that there were two calls without messages. "Mortimer again?" Kincaid speculated, but before Gemma could respond, a new message began.

"Annabelle? Where are you? Ring me at home." A man's voice, deeper than Mortimer's, used to giving commands. Another beep, and the same voice said, *"Annabelle, where the bloody hell are you? It's Lewis. Ring me back."*

There were several more calls without messages, then a woman's voice saying, *"Annabelle, it's half past nine. I know you can't have forgotten—we're waiting for you,"* and again, *"Annabelle, where are you? We've finished breakfast. We can't stall Sir Peter any longer. Please ring me at home."*

The last caller he recognized as Jo Lowell, sounding relaxed and a little amused. *"Annabelle, Reg says you've abandoned him and he's worked himself into a real tizzy over it. Do put him out of his misery. Ring me when you get in."*

Kincaid looked at Gemma and raised an eyebrow. "I'd say Reg and Annabelle did have a row, from the sound of that."

"Yes, but it supports his statement that he waited at the pub."

"Maybe," Kincaid answered with some skepticism. "Would Sir Peter be Reg Mortimer's father, do you suppose? And who is Lewis?"

His phone rang. While he extricated it from his pocket with one hand, with the other he brushed the backs of his fingers against Gemma's cheek, feeling a sudden swelling of desire at the nearness of her. He touched her lips with his fingertips, heard the quick intake of her breath. The flat was empty, after all. . . .

"Kincaid," he said impatiently into the phone.

"It's Janice Coppin here, sir. I think I've found our busker."

JANICE MET THEM AS THEY CAME into Limehouse Station from the car park. Her nod to Gemma held the slightest suggestion of a wink as she said, "I've put him in the interview room to cool his heels. He's not too happy about helping us with our inquiries."

"Have you told him anything?" Kincaid asked.

"No. Just confirmed where he was night before last, though he didn't like to admit it. Told him we had a dozen witnesses willing to swear he was in that tunnel."

"Is that where you found him? In the tunnel?"

"In the park. Island Gardens. From the description I guessed who he was, and he has a few regular pitches on the Island. He's one of our local activists—you know, does his part to keep the yuppies at bay." Her sidelong glance at Kincaid as she spoke made it clear she was pleased enough with herself to risk sending him up. "The ironic thing is that he's Lewis Finch's son."

"Lewis Finch?" Kincaid repeated, and Gemma thought of the message on Annabelle Hammond's answering machine. "Who's he when he's at home?"

"Our legendary Lewis, the saint of the East End, according to some.

He's responsible for redeveloping and restoring many of the old warehouses and factories on the Island."

Gemma heard skepticism in Janice's voice. "Is that not a good thing?"

Shrugging, Janice said, "I can see the dissenters' point. Once most of these places are tarted up, none of us who grew up here on the Island can afford to live in them." She nodded towards the interview room. "You can see where the son gets his looks, if not his views. According to rumor, Lewis Finch is quite the ladies' man."

Was it possible that Annabelle Hammond had been one of his conquests? wondered Gemma as they entered the interview room.

Then, as Kincaid said, "Why don't you begin the questioning, Janice," Gemma stopped dead on the threshold.

The man stood in the center of the room, facing them, hands jammed in the pockets of his army-issue trousers. The sleeves had been cut out of his camouflage jacket, revealing the muscular definition of his suntanned arms. Since she had last seen him, his fair hair had grown out a bit and he'd added a gold earring in his left ear.

"You've no right to keep me here like this," he said, and she remembered how unexpected she had found his educated voice. "Either let me leave or I'm calling my solic—" He saw her, and faltered.

His surprise, thought Gemma, must have been greater than hers, because she realized now that at some level she'd made the connection between Reg Mortimer's description and this man.

For a few months, he had played his clarinet in front of the Sainsbury's on the Liverpool Road, until he had become a regular if enigmatic part of her life. Although he had seldom spoken or smiled, she'd been drawn to him in a way she could not explain. But when she'd at last ventured to speak to him, he'd answered so brusquely that she'd felt a fool, and shortly after that he'd vanished from the area. She had not seen him since.

Sitting down, Janice Coppin switched on the tape recorder and gave the date, then addressed the busker. "Your name, please, for the record."

Without taking his eyes from Gemma, he said, "It's Finch. Gordon Finch."

CHAPTER 6

*Bounded on three sides by the
river Thames, and communi-
cations hindered (in those days)
by the swing bridges at the
entrances to the working docks,
[the Island] had (and still has) a
special feeling of isolation, which
separates it from the rest of East
London.*

Eve Hostettler, from Dockland

"SIT DOWN, MR. FINCH." JANICE
Coppin positioned her chair squarely
in the center of the interview table;
after a moment, Gordon Finch sank
reluctantly into the chair on the
other side. Kincaid and Gemma sat
on either side of Janice and a bit
back, so that Janice became the natural focus of attention.

Gemma was glad Kincaid had
given Janice the lead, for it gave her
a chance to study the busker, who
hadn't met her eyes again. It had
been some time since she'd seen him,
and she thought perhaps he'd lost
weight. Surely the planes and angles
of his face seemed more pronounced.

His short cap of fair hair stood up in tufts where he had run his fingers through it, and darker stubble shadowed his chin.

"I want my solicitor," he said. "You've no right to hold me here without my solicitor present." How many street musicians, wondered Gemma, had a solicitor at their beck and call?

"You are free to ring your solicitor, Mr. Finch," Janice countered. "But you understand that we are not charging you with anything—we merely want your help in answering a few questions."

"What sort of questions?" Finch said warily, not sounding reassured.

Janice lined up her notebook at a right angle to the table's edge. "You're aware, of course, that busking is in direct violation of—"

"Oh, come off it, Inspector. It's Sunday afternoon, the best day of the week, and most likely you've made me lose my pitch. If you mean to slap me with a fine for busking, do it. Otherwise let me go back to work before all the punters pack up their pushchairs and their picnics and go home." He moved his chair back, as if to rise.

Kincaid clasped his hands over his knee and smiled, making it clear he had no intention of terminating the interview. "Are you an observant man, Mr. Finch? It seems to me that your particular line of work would provide you with a unique opportunity to witness the vagaries of human nature, as well as its more ordinary comings and goings."

"Vagaries?" Gordon Finch stared at him, and Gemma chalked one up to Kincaid. "What the bleedin' hell is that supposed to mean?"

Kincaid grinned. "I don't believe you suffer from the constraints of the verbally challenged, Mr. Finch, but I'll tell you exactly what I mean. You're the ideal witness. You observe everything, but people don't see you. How many people who pass you could say later what clothes you wore? Or what piece you played?"

Finch shrugged, but Gemma saw interest in his light gray eyes. "Ten percent, maybe. On a good day."

Beside her, Gemma felt Janice Coppin stir with the impatience of one not used to Kincaid's interview methods.

"Frustrating, I should think," Kincaid continued conversationally. "Not to be appreciated. Like playing the violin in an Italian restaurant."

"They're punters—what can you say?" Finch shrugged dismissively. "But there are some who listen, some who even come back," he added, glancing almost imperceptibly at Gemma.

She looked away, shifting her gaze to his hands. Although he seemed more relaxed, his hands rested awkwardly on the tabletop, as if he were used to having something in them.

"On Friday evening, you were busking in the Greenwich Foot Tunnel," said Kincaid. "I want you to tell us what you saw."

"Sorry, I don't follow you." Finch frowned slightly.

"Did anything at all unusual happen?" Kincaid leaned forward, as if he could will an answer from him.

Finch thought for a moment, then shook his head. "Not that I remember. What are you getting at, exactly?"

"About half past nine—is that right, Inspector?" Kincaid glanced at Janice.

Janice made a show of looking through her notebook, although Gemma felt sure she knew the time perfectly well. "Yes, sir. Between half past nine and ten o'clock."

"About half past nine, a man and a woman entered the tunnel together, from the Greenwich end. But according to her companion, the woman suddenly refused to go on, insisting that he leave her there and meet her later. We thought perhaps you could corroborate his statement."

"How could I possibly know something like that?" Finch sounded more baffled than irritated.

"Because the woman was a strikingly beautiful redhead, and her companion says she spoke to you."

Gemma saw the involuntary jerk of Gordon Finch's hands, but when she looked up at his face, his expression was guardedly neutral. "I don't remember anyone speaking to me. What's all this about, anyway? Why don't you just ask her, if you're so anxious to know what this woman did?"

Kincaid settled back in his chair, absently turning the pen he'd picked up from the interview table round and round in his fingers. "I'm afraid that's not possible, Mr. Finch. She's dead."

Gemma watched Gordon Finch's face now, looking for the telltale signs of guilt—the nervous blink, the uncontrolled twitch of the mouth—but she saw only the blankness of shock.

"What? What are you talking about?" He looked directly at Gemma this time, as if trusting her to tell the truth.

"Her name was Annabelle Hammond." Gemma's voice felt as if it needed oiling. "She was killed on Friday night, sometime after she left the Greenwich Tunnel."

"But—" Finch shook his head once, sharply, and Gemma saw the flicker of some intense emotion in his eyes before his face settled into an impassive mask and he said flatly, "I can't help you."

Holding his gaze, Gemma said, "Then you wouldn't know if your father knew Miss Hammond, or the nature of their relationship."

"I've no idea. My father's affairs are his business. Now, either charge me with something or let me get back to work before my day is a total sodding loss, all right?"

Gemma knew they'd no further cause to hold him. But she also had no doubt that Gordon Finch had known Annabelle Hammond, and known her well.

TERESA STOOD AT HER SINK, WIPING the same plate over and over with a tea towel. After Jo's call she'd sat for a long while on the edge of the sofa, the phone still in her hand. Then, stiffly, she had stood and searched out the dust cloth, and after that the vacuum.

It was Sunday. She always did her chores on a Sunday, to be ready for the week. Whenever she tried to fix her mind on the thing Jo had told her, the thought skittered away, elusive as a bat at dusk, and she returned to the familiar loop. *It was Sunday. She did her chores on Sunday.*

The strident buzz made her jump and the plate flew from her hands, clattering unharmed to the lino. It was a moment before she connected the sound to her doorbell, and then her heart leapt with hope. It had been a dreadful mistake, of course; she should have seen that.

Dropping the tea towel in a sodden heap on the floor, she wiped the damp palms of her hands on her jumper and hurried through the sitting room. She flung the door open and stared at Reg Mortimer, who stood with his finger poised over the buzzer.

In all the time they'd worked together, Reg had never come to her flat, though she'd had a few guilty and quickly squelched fantasies in which he had. She'd told herself often enough that Reg Mortimer floated through life like oil atop water—he was seldom ruffled, never shaken, and if anything stirred in the depths, he did a good job of keeping it to himself.

But today she hardly recognized him. The skin beneath his eyes looked bruised with exhaustion, his lips were bloodless and clamped in a thin line, and she saw that his raised hand shook slightly.

"Teresa, I . . . I thought Jo must have rung you. . . ."

So it must be true—his presence here told her that, as did the sight of his face. "Jo said . . ." She faltered, then swallowed, forcing herself to continue. "But I didn't really believe it."

He nodded, once, an undeniable confirmation. She stepped back and he came into the flat, closing the door behind him. For a moment they stood staring at one another, then Reg touched her shoulder awkwardly. "Teresa, I'm so sorry."

That he should express concern for her, when he and Annabelle had been everything to each other, pulled the last prop from her fragile composure. She covered her face with her hands and began to weep like a child.

Reg gathered her into his arms, and it was not until her sobs had at last subsided into hiccups that Teresa began to take stock of her position. Her wet face was crushed uncomfortably into Reg's knit shirt, just beneath his chin, while he rubbed the middle of her back with the palm of his hand. He smelled faintly of sweat and aftershave—and with that thought she realized with horror that her nose was running and she hadn't a tissue. She pulled herself free of his arms and turned away. "Oh, God, I'm sorry. I'm a mess." Sniffing, she groped blindly for the box of tissues on the coffee table, knocking it to the floor.

"It's all right. You're fine." He retrieved the tissues and pressed a wad of them into her hand. "You have a good blow, and I'll make you a cuppa."

"But I . . . but you won't know where—"

"I'm sure I can manage that much in your kitchen. Sit down, please."

Teresa sat, because her rubbery knees threatened to give out if she did not.

She heard the opening of cupboards and the burble of the kettle, and a few moments later Reg reappeared, cradling a mug. He lifted a brow as he sat down beside her and transferred the mug to her hands. "Tea bags? What heresy."

"Only for emergencies." Teresa attempted a smile, but the tremble in her lip threatened to betray her. She sipped gratefully at the tea, even though it was too hot and too sweet.

"Then I'd say this qualifies."

She glanced at him. "I should have known yesterday morning, when she didn't show up for breakfast with Sir Peter. Annabelle would never have missed that meeting without letting us know. I should have realized—"

"Don't torment yourself over it, Teresa. Nothing you could have imagined would have helped Annabelle. She was already dead."

"They're sure?"

"As sure as the police are likely to admit about anything."

"But you knew, didn't you? Jo said you went to the police, that was how they identified . . . her body. You knew because you were closer to her. . . ." She touched his arm in a gesture more familiar than she could have imagined an hour ago.

He stood abruptly. "I don't believe that. It was logic, that's all. I knew what you knew—that she'd never have missed that meeting, not unless . . . And I knew she hadn't come home."

"But you were together—"

"Not the whole evening." Moving restlessly to the balcony door, he looked out. "After Jo's party she asked me to meet her later at the Ferry House. But she never came."

"But . . ." Teresa stared at his back. What he was telling her didn't make sense, but she didn't feel she could push him. "The police . . . did they say how . . ."

Reg shook his head. "No. Didn't they tell Jo?"

Teresa hesitated. This must be horribly difficult for him, she knew, but surely he'd thought of nothing else, and perhaps she could set his mind at rest. "Only that they didn't believe she'd been . . . you know . . . assaulted."

"And that's supposed to make it more acceptable?" His tone was bitter. "Along the lines of 'she led a full life'?" Seeming to sense her shock, he turned towards her, shrugging in a gesture of apology. "I'm sorry. I know that sounds horrible, but just now . . . nothing seems any consolation. She's gone and—" He turned away for a moment, then spun round and came back to the sofa. Sitting on its edge so that he could see her face, he took her hand and gave it a squeeze. "Don't mind me. I'm just feeling bloody." He smiled and released her hand. "I went to see William this morning."

With horror Teresa realized she'd not even thought of William, had not thought of anyone's grief other than her own, until Reg had appeared at her door. "How was he?"

"Shocked. We talked a little."

"About Annabelle?"

Reg turned her empty mug carefully on its coaster. "And the business. He's asked me to look after things for a bit. But I can't manage without your help. Things are going to be difficult enough as it is."

A jolt of alarm shot through her and she sat upright. "You didn't tell him what we meant to propose to Sir Peter?"

"Of course not. But we'll not be able to keep Hammond's out of the red for much longer without taking some sort of action—"

The phone rang, startling them both. Teresa stared at it as if a serpent had appeared without warning on her coffee table.

"Hadn't you better answer?" said Reg.

She lifted the phone slowly and pushed the *talk* button. "Hullo?" She listened for a moment, then said, "Yes. Right. Half an hour." She clicked off and looked at Reg. "It was the police. They want me to meet them at Hammond's."

LEWIS AND THE THREE OTHER REMAINING *children sat on the cold lino in the hall of the village's Women's Institute. The two girls were thin and plain and wore spectacles, and fat Bob Thomkins had blubbed so much that his face had come out all splotches.*

The adults had come in one or two at a time, walking among the children as if choosing from damaged groceries. They'd taken the smallest and prettiest children first, often separating siblings who had pleaded to stay together. A kind-looking lady in a flowered dress had chosen Simon Goss, shaking her head regretfully when the little boy had clung to Lewis's hand

and cried. So sorry, she'd said, she could only take the one, and she'd a son the same age as Simon.

Lewis had known hunger often enough, and grief, when his baby sister, Annie, had died of the smallpox—but he had never in his ten years felt unwanted. The only thing that gave him a small bit of consolation was that no one wanted the teachers, either, and Miss Jenkins and Miss Purdy looked as forlorn as he felt.

A gas lamp flared as the billeting officer lit it, sending long shadows jumping across the walls and floor. A few scarred wooden chairs had been pushed into a circle near the door, and there the officer and the two teachers conferred in low voices. Lewis thought he heard the words "last resort" as they flicked worried glances at the remaining children.

At that moment he made up his mind to go home. As soon as their backs were turned he would slip away and find the road out of the village. A vision of the darkness sliding over the great, empty countryside he had seen from the coach gave him pause, but then anything was better than this waiting. He could thumb a lift back to London, and if he was lucky, maybe he'd find something to eat.

As he drew his legs under him, tensing his muscles for a chance to bolt, he heard a familiar sound. A horse's hooves clip-clopped on the pavement, just like old Snowflake's when he pulled the milk float at home. But milk came in the morning, not in the evening. A shiver of fear ran down Lewis's spine as the hoofbeats stopped and the horse blew loudly just outside the open door of the hall. He stood, heart hammering.

The man who came into the hall didn't look frightening. He wore a black uniform and a cap, like the chauffeurs Lewis had seen at the cinema, and might have been a bit older than Lewis's dad.

"John, how good to see you," Mrs. Slocum, the billeting officer, gushed with relief. "I knew we could count on Edwina to take the rest of the children."

Removing his cap with a nod to the teachers, the man said a bit brusquely, "I'm sorry, Mrs. Slocum, but Mrs. Burne-Jones only gave me instructions to bring the one." Glancing at the children, he pinched his lips together. "You say this lot is all you have?"

"I'm afraid so," said the billeting officer, and Lewis wondered if the note of apology in her voice was meant for the children or for the man in the uniform. "But surely—"

"And needs must it's a boy, as she means to put him in the room above the stable," John said firmly. The thin line of his lips almost disappeared as he regarded Lewis and Bob Thomkins. He lifted a finger. "I suppose that one will do."

Realizing that the finger was pointing in his direction, Lewis looked wildly behind him, just in case some other boy had materialized.

"All right . . . Lewis, isn't it? Get your bag. You'll be going up to the Big House with Mr. Pebbles here," said Mrs. Slocum, her disapproval of the unknown Mrs. Burne-Jones's stubbornness plainly evident. Then she forced a smile. "John, do tell your mistress that we've three more without a place to lay their heads. And there are the teachers, of course. Surely she could find room for them, even temporarily."

John motioned Lewis towards the door. "I'll put it to her, Mrs. Slocum, but you know what she's like when she's made up her mind." He touched his cap and followed Lewis outside.

The white horse gleamed palely in the dusk. It stamped and shifted in its harness as they approached, rocking the dogcart. John jumped up to the seat and gathered the reins, then frowned down at Lewis. "Well, what are you waiting for, boy?" Then he added, a bit more kindly, "Have you never seen a pony cart before?" He patted the seat beside him with the flat of his hand. "Hop up here, quick now. We've a ways to go and supper's waiting."

The word "supper" fell enticingly on Lewis's ears. Deciding he could always run away afterwards if he didn't like the place, he tried to climb up on the cart as if he'd done it often.

John clucked to the horse and they set out at a gentle pace. The village was dark as pitch with the enforcing of the blackout, except for a splash of light as someone pulled aside the curtain over the door of the pub on the village green.

Lewis's heart lurched with homesickness at the brief sight of the men gathered near the door, pints in hand, enjoying the warmth of the evening. But they soon left such comfort behind, and as the lane began to climb, the darkness grew ever more dense. The horse's footfalls were muffled by a carpet of leaves, and Lewis sensed as much as saw the interlacing of the boughs above their heads. He felt lost in the blackness, as insubstantial as the mist he'd seen forming in the hollows.

Fixing his eyes on the faint glimmer of the horse's rump in front of them, Lewis asked, "How does he know where to go in the dark?"

A snort that might have been a laugh came from the man sitting beside him. "Have you never driven a horse before, lad? He knows my signals from the reins, but he doesn't need me up here. He can find his way home just as well as you or I."

"What's his name?" asked Lewis, encouraged by the patient answer.

This time the chuckle was unmistakable. "Zeus. Daft name for a horse if you ask me, but then nobody did."

Lewis glanced at his companion, relieved that the sharp nose he could see faintly silhouetted under the peaked cap did not seem to indicate a bad temper. "Are you the groom, then?"

"You are a cheeky sort."

"It's just that I thought you might be a chauffeur," Lewis hastened to add, afraid he'd overstepped the bounds with his new friend. "But you've not got a car."

"It seems I'll be driving whatever Miss Edwina requires," said John, and Lewis was relieved to hear the undertone of amusement again. "Young Harry Watts, the groom, ran off yesterday to join up. It's Harry's room you'll be getting, lad. Not that he did much anyway, with only two horses to look after, old Zeus here and Miss Edwina's hunter. She prefers the automobile, but she wasn't inclined to waste petrol on fetching a London ragamuffin up from the village."

Lewis considered taking offense at being called a ragamuffin, but decided his pride didn't warrant drying up his font of information. "What sort of an auto is it?"

"There are two, lad. The MG Roadster Miss Edwina drives herself, and the Bentley I drive for her."

"Blimey," Lewis whispered under his breath. The autos were the stuff of legend, beasts not glimpsed among the lorries and tradesman's vans of the Island. Just what had he got himself into? "Who is Miss Edwina?" he ventured. "Is she very rich?"

John chuckled. "That's Mrs. Burne-Jones to you, lad, and I suppose she does well enough for herself. You'll see for yourself in half a tick. We're almost there."

Lewis couldn't see any change in the dappled, leafy darkness surrounding them, but talking to John had made him feel a bit less frightened of it. After a moment's silence, he risked one more question. "Is there a Mr. Burne-Jones?"

"Broke his neck in a hunting fall the first year they were married. But if you ask me, she was just as glad to come back here. The house belongs to her family, the Haliburtons, drafty old pile that it is. Now hush, lad, and grab on to the cart." Twitching the reins, John made a clucking sound to the horse. Zeus turned sharply to the left and the cart lurched into a rut, rocking Lewis half out of his seat.

When he'd righted himself he realized they had emerged from the trees. He could see stars now, flinty specks against a sky as black as deep water. A spicy, green scent filled his nostrils as the cart brushed against a hedge; when he reached out to touch the leaves they felt soft against his fingers.

Then the road curved round a bend and he saw a darker shape rising against the sky, and to him it seemed as massive as one of the great ships. He gave a silent gasp of amazement—nothing he'd heard could possibly have prepared him for the sheer size and grandeur of this house.

As he gaped, he heard John chuckle beside him. "Miss Edwina's grandfather built it. Knew how to do things proper in those days, not like these modern things they throw up now. It must have been a sight, with a full staff and more gardeners than you could shake a stick at."

Lewis only half heard, his eyes fixed on the bulk of the house as the drive curved round it and the great peaks of the roof shut out the stars. John coaxed the horse to a stop and jumped down, then lifted Lewis's battered case from the back. "I'll turn you over to Cook now. You might just sweet-talk her into giving you a bite of supper."

"But Miss Edwina . . . won't I see her?"

"Don't hold your breath, lad." John put a hand on Lewis's shoulder and marched him up to a door. "She has folks visiting from London, but I daresay she'll get round to you eventually."

His mouth suddenly dry with terror, Lewis turned and clutched John by the sleeve. "You'll come in with me, won't you?"

For a moment he thought the man would refuse, but then his new friend sighed and said, "I'll have to answer to my Mary for keeping her supper waiting. But I suppose I can get you settled in the kitchen, then I'll come back and take you to your room after you've had a bite to eat. It must be hard, away from home on your own. Where's your family, lad?"

"The East End," answered Lewis, thinking of the comfortable muddle of his neighborhood. "The Isle of Dogs." Looking up at the dark walls looming in front of him, his question popped out before he'd thought *whether or not he should ask it. "It's so big—the house—why wouldn't Miss Edwina take the others?"*

John Pebbles shook his head. "Because she's a stubborn woman, and she's made up her mind there's not going to be a war. She always wants to think the best, does Miss Edwina, but I've no doubt she'll be sensible enough when the time comes." He sighed in the darkness. "And come it will, sooner rather than later, I fear." With that, he opened the door and nudged Lewis into the warmth and light of the kitchen.

HOW LIKE HER EX-HUSBAND, TO WEAR a button-down shirt and trousers on a day when everyone else had exposed their skin to the legal limit, thought Jo as she watched Martin Lowell cross the street and enter the park. She'd phoned and asked him to meet her here, near the outdoor tea garden.

When Harry had been small they'd come here every fine Sunday afternoon. They'd had tea and read the Sunday papers with Harry in his pushchair; then as he grew they'd helped him toddle up the hill towards the Observatory; and later still they'd crossed the road and explored the Maritime Museum.

Her choice of rendezvous had been instinctive, comforting, but obviously it hadn't inspired any fond memories in Martin. As he reached her, he pushed his tortoiseshell spectacles up on his nose and glowered at her.

"I don't know what you're trying on, Jo, but I'm not having it. This is my afternoon with the children and I don't want to hear some silly excuse—"

All the civil and reasonable words she's rehearsed as she walked down the hill were washed away on a flood of anger so intense it left her trembling. "Martin, shut up, will you?"

He stared at her, too surprised for a moment to respond, then said, "Don't take that tone with me, Jo. There's no—"

"Martin, listen to me. Annabelle's dead. She's been murdered."

"What?"

"You heard me. They found her body in Mudchute Park yesterday morning." Jo watched him, wondering how long it had been since she'd seen his face wiped clean of his perpetual disapproval.

Then his lips twisted and he said, "Serves the bitch right."

"Martin, don't—"

"What was she doing, shopping her wares in the park? That's what happens to whores like her. You should have known—"

"You bastard!" Jo's hand seemed to lift of its own accord. Through a haze of fury she felt the impact of her palm connecting with his cheek; her eyes filled with tears as her skin began to smart. Cradling her injured hand with the other, she stepped back, afraid of retaliation, then realized that Martin was far too aware of the stares of passersby to risk incurring any more attention. She'd made a public spectacle of him, and there was nothing he hated more.

"That was bloody uncalled-for," he hissed at her. Her handprint stood out white against his flushed cheek. "Have you completely lost your mind?"

"I don't care what sort of villain you've chosen to make of her, she was my sister. My sister! How could you—" Swallowing, she looked away, not trusting herself to go on. She gazed at the tea garden, where the interested spectators had gone back to their drinks and conversations, with only an occasional glance towards Martin and her.

"Don't you ever get tired of playing the martyr, Jo? I should think that even you would have to put some limits on forgiveness—"

"It doesn't matter what I feel now. I've got to tell the children. And I thought you might . . ."

"Might what? Tell them a little morality tale? Explain to them that this is what happens to tarts and home-wreckers?"

Jo felt her anger drain away as quickly as it had come, and she swayed with exhaustion. It had been a hopeless quest, and now she wanted only to go home, but she couldn't, not yet. "Promise me you won't talk to the children about Annabelle. Promise me you won't say these things to Harry."

Martin stared at her, the chin she had once thought strong thrust out in obstinate refusal. "Why shouldn't I tell them the truth? You'll make a saint of her—"

"At least promise me you won't see them until they've had a chance to absorb it. They're children, for God's sake. Can you for once think of someone besides yourself?"

"That's rich, coming from you," he said venomously, and she suddenly saw the same endless argument, spiraling down through all the days of her life. And she'd been foolish enough to think that divorce would mean an end to it. She closed her eyes and his voice faded until it was a faint, tinny squawking.

"Jo, what's wrong with you? Don't you dare bloody faint on me, do you hear me?" Martin's fingers bit into her shoulder, pulling her back. "Did you hear me? I said I'd not take them this afternoon. Now go home."

He released her and, shoving his hands in the pockets of his trousers, walked away.

KINCAID DID HIS BEST TO JUGGLE a ham salad sandwich as he drove. One hand for steering and one for shifting left none for eating, and as he transferred the sandwich to his right hand while shifting with his left, he had a fleeting fantasy that one day the Yard would put comfort before budget and equip fleet cars with automatic transmissions. Next he'd be dreaming of air-conditioning, he chided himself.

"Want to switch?" Gemma asked as she polished off the crumbs remaining in her clear, triangular sandwich box.

"Almost there," he said through a mouthful. Swallowing, he added, "And we'll be a bit early, I think."

"In that case, we might've had these in luxury." Gemma tucked her empty box into a rubbish bag and sipped at a bottle of fruit juice.

"In the canteen? Right." The smell of hot grease in the stifling mid-afternoon heat had encouraged them to grab their prepackaged sandwiches from the canteen at Limehouse Station and make a hasty exit.

He turned right into Ferry Street and pointed. "There, on the right. That's the pub where Reg Mortimer says Annabelle meant to meet him. The Ferry House."

"*Says?*" Gemma glanced at him.

"Well, we haven't any proof, have we?" The street jogged abruptly to the left just after the pub, so that it ran parallel to the river on one side and Manchester Road on the other. Kincaid drove slowly, taking advantage of the Sunday afternoon calm to study the flats between the pub and Annabelle Hammond's. "We'll have to send someone to have a word at the pub, and extend the house-to-house along this stretch here. Someone might have seen something." He tucked the last bit of sandwich in his mouth. "Mortimer might have invented the story about the busker as well."

"I don't think so." Gemma frowned. "Did you believe him? Gordon Finch, I mean?"

Kincaid thought while he chewed, then said, "If he knew why we'd brought him in, he's a bloody good actor. But I'd also swear he knew Annabelle Hammond, and that the idea of her having a connection with his father didn't surprise him."

"I don't believe he knew she was dead."

"Meaning he can't have killed her? Then why not admit he knew her?"

"I don't know. Maybe he's not in the habit of dealing cooperatively with the police," Gemma said with a hint of sarcasm.

"I thought we were quite civilized." They'd reached Annabelle's building and he swung in towards the curb, idling for a moment. "For now, I suppose we'll wait and see what DI Coppin turns up before we get out our hobnailed boots." Janice Coppin had informed them that the tunnel employed security cameras, and she'd set out in search of the videotapes. "And we'd better have a word with the owners here, too," he added. The gates that led to the three attached riverside houses were open, allowing a glimpse of a green and inviting enclosed garden.

As he moved on, one of the cheerful-looking red and blue DLR trains pulled into the elevated Island Gardens Station across the street. Gemma watched it, her brow furrowed. "She could have gone anywhere."

"What?"

"There are three hours unaccounted for between the time Reg Mortimer says he left Annabelle in the tunnel and the time Dr. Ling estimates she died. The train was so close, she could have gone anywhere in London."

At Island Gardens Station, Ferry Street became Saunders Ness Road, and Janice had instructed him to continue along almost to its end. He glanced at the round-domed entrance to the tunnel as they passed, and at the crowds still making the most of their Sunday afternoon in Island Gardens. Through the park's spreading plane trees he could see the glint of the Thames, and across the river the white, classical symmetry of the Royal Naval College. "Then someone brought her body back, to make it look as though she were killed on her doorstep?"

"We can't rule it out."

"No, but let's not complicate things any more than necessary for the moment. It's just as likely she never left the Island, or even this neighborhood." Once they were past the park, new developments of flats lined the river, each one of slightly different character and architectural style.

"This looks an odd place for a business." Gemma touched his shoulder as she leaned across to look out his window.

"This was one of the first areas to be heavily redeveloped. Most of the old riverside warehouses have been razed in the last few years to make way for upmarket flats."

"You've been grilling Janice again."

"Might be more accurate to say she's been instructing me, whether I like it or not. Hammond's is one of the last of the old warehouses on this stretch of the river. Look, this must be it."

He parked the car at the curb and got out, studying the building. It was four-storied, brown-bricked, a square bastion of Victorian industrial prowess, but its grimness was relieved by an arch of orange brick set in above each of its many windows, and another over the main door. A pediment rose above the flat roof, giving the facade an incongruously playful air, and beneath that had been set in plaster *Hammond's Fine Teas, 1879.*

Joining him, Gemma tried the glossy, dark blue front door. "Locked. But at least it's a bit cooler this side if we have to wait."

Kincaid examined the school across the street. Although the main complex ran to uninspired postmodern, a separate structure at the front proclaimed its Victorian origins with the same triangular embellishments and orange trim as the warehouse. "Not much hope of finding a good witness for Friday evening here. Let's have a look round the back of the warehouse," Kincaid said as he turned towards the river. There were no windows along the side at ground level.

The building was flush with the waterline in the back, so that the bricked pedestrian walkway that ran along the river was forced to detour round the front. "Dead end," he reported, exasperated. "The place is a bloody fortress."

"People stole things from warehouses in the old days, too." The tide was out; Gemma wrinkled her nose at the dank smell rising from the exposed mud.

"True, but there must be ground access round the far side. They needed loading bays for wagons even in the days when they brought goods in from the water."

"The river probably smelled worse then, too," Kincaid added, leaning over the walkway railing for a look at the rubbish revealed by the receding water. "And people probably just left a different sort of litter. Not very encouraging, is it?" He gazed at the three dark smokestacks of the power station across the river, then at the gleam of the Naval College further round the curve. "Sometimes I wonder if we've made any progress at all." Pointing across the river towards the college, he added, "Look at what Christopher Wren accomplished."

"I'll vote for plumbing, thank you," said Gemma, and he realized it was the first time he'd seen her smile all afternoon. The bridge of her nose had turned pink from the sun and the faint dusting of freckles across her cheeks had darkened.

"You all right?" he asked, brushing her cheek with his fingertip.

"Just hot." She pushed a tendril of damp hair from her brow and looked away.

"I thought—"

A car door slammed nearby. "That came from round the front," said Gemma, listening. "Someone's here." She retraced their steps towards the front of the warehouse and he followed, wondering just what he had meant to say.

A SLENDER, FAIR WOMAN IN JEANS and a yellow tee shirt stood before the door of the warehouse, keys dangling from her hand.

Kincaid called out and she whirled round, looking startled.

"Sorry," Kincaid said as they reached her. "Didn't mean to frighten you. We're with Scotland Yard." He showed her his warrant card and introduced Gemma, then asked, "Are you Teresa Robbins?"

"An Inspector Coppin rang me. . . ."

"She's the local officer on the case. We'd like to ask you a few questions, if you don't mind." Kincaid smiled, hoping to put her at ease.

"But I don't see how I can possibly help you." Teresa's thin face was pleasant, if unremarkable, and bore signs of makeup hastily applied to cover the ravages of weeping.

"You can start by looking round very carefully as we go in. I want you to tell us if you see anything at all out of the ordinary."

"But why—"

"Could Miss Hammond have come here on Friday night to finish up some work?" Gemma suggested.

Teresa put her keys in the lock. "I suppose it's possible." She pulled open the large door and stepped back, but Kincaid motioned her to go first.

It took a moment for Kincaid's eyes to adjust to the dim interior, which was streaked by sunlight slanting in from the high south and west windows. Then Teresa flipped a switch by the door and electric light chased the shadows from the corners.

The room was large, comprising the first two floors of the building. To the right was an industrial lift serving the upper floors; to the left were offices reached by a catwalk that looked down on the main floor. Halfway along the left-hand wall Kincaid saw the loading bays which he guessed must give access to lorries.

But these features he took in gradually, for first to draw his eyes were the chests. Ceiling-high stacks of square, steel-bound, silver-edged wooden chests filled the room. All bore exotic-looking stamps, in red or black ink, and those nearest him read, *Produce of India, Dar-jeeling*, followed by a series of numbers. The air in the warehouse was earthy and sharp with the unmistakable smell of tea.

Teresa had stepped a few feet into the room, looking carefully round her. "Everything looks just the way I left it on Friday."

"When did you last see Miss Hammond?" Kincaid asked.

"Annabelle left about half past five, I think. I was finishing up the accounts and just said 'Cheerio.' You know how it is. I didn't think I wouldn't see her—" Teresa swallowed hard.

"You worked late?" Gemma gave her a sympathetic smile.

"I usually do. Especially on Friday, so as to be caught up for the week."

"You said you did the accounts—you do the bookkeeping for the business?" Kincaid asked, wondering if Annabelle Hammond would have confided in her employee. But then she had been engaged to an employee, after all, and he supposed you couldn't get more democratic than that.

"I'm the chief financial officer." Teresa smiled shyly. "That sounds a bit glorified for what I actually do. I handle the accounts and the financial planning, but it's a small business, and we all tend to have a hand in everything."

"I understand that Annabelle and Reginald Mortimer were engaged. Did that make working together awkward for them? Or for you?"

"Awkward?" Teresa stared at Kincaid.

"Surely they had some conflict over things at work?"

"Sometimes men can be a bit sensitive about their authority," Gemma added with a glance at Kincaid. "You know the sort of thing."

Teresa shook her head vehemently. "Not Reg and Annabelle. They agreed about things, they wanted the same things for the company. And Reg . . . Reg worshiped Annabelle."

Kincaid thought he detected a hint of wistfulness in Teresa's voice. Had it been difficult for her, always on the outside, looking in? "When was the wedding to be?" he asked.

"The wedding?" Again Teresa gave them a surprised look, as if the question hadn't occurred to her. "They'd not set a date. Not an official one, anyway."

"And how long had they been engaged?"

Teresa frowned. "Coming up on two years, I think."

"Not much reason to delay a wedding these days—both of them independent, with their families' approval—"

"But they couldn't have just an ordinary wedding. They had social obligations, and I doubt Annabelle wanted to spare the time from work just now to plan the sort of affair expected of them." Teresa put forth this theory with great seriousness, as if determined to convince herself.

"Were you and Annabelle close?" asked Gemma. "Would she have confided in you if she'd got cold feet?"

"I . . . I don't know." Teresa lifted her chin defiantly. "Look, I don't understand why you're asking all these questions. Jo said that Annabelle was killed in the park, attacked by some pervert. What can that possibly have to do with us, or Hammond's?"

"Annabelle was *found* in the park. We don't know that she was killed there," said Kincaid. "Can you tell us why she might have been wandering round the Mudchute alone, after dark? In her party clothes and high heels?"

"No, that's daft. But . . ." Shadows from the slowly revolving ceiling fans flickered across Teresa's face, and Kincaid saw the irises of her pale blue eyes dilate like speading ink. "You can't think here. . . ." She folded her arms beneath her breasts and looked round as if seeing the warehouse for the first time.

"Did Annabelle tell you what she meant to do on Friday evening?" Kincaid asked.

"They were going to her sister's. She and Reg. The party had been planned for weeks."

"And she didn't contact you later in the evening?"

"Why should she have rung me?" Teresa sounded baffled.

"What if she were worried about something?"

"Annabelle wasn't the sort to worry," Teresa replied sharply. "And she wasn't in the habit of ringing me in the evenings, or of coming back here."

"Would there have been anyone here on Friday night? Do you run a night shift?"

"We don't *make* the tea, Superintendent. We blend and package it, and our production and shipping staff works five-day weeks. The equipment's upstairs, if you'd like to see, but *this* is the heart of the business." She gestured at the large table in the room's center, and Kincaid sensed her relief at treading familiar ground.

One side of the table's length held ranks of worn, tin tea caddies and plain foil bags; the other a neat row of rectangular, white porcelain dishes filled with mounds of loose tea, and another row of identical, white porcelain bowls. Gemma touched a finger to the tea in the last dish. "It smells good. What is all this?"

"The tasting table." Teresa glanced at them and Kincaid thought they must have looked blank, for she frowned and continued, "We don't sell just any tea. First it must be blended, and Hammond's has been famous for its blends for a hundred and twenty-five years. We buy the tea at auction—mainly from India and Sri Lanka, but since the late seventies China has opened up to us again, and some tea is exported from Africa and even South America."

"Sri Lanka—that used to be Ceylon?" Gemma moved round the table studying the tin caddies. "Some of these say Ceylon."

"Teas from Sri Lanka are known as Ceylon teas in the trade. But in Sri Lanka alone there are over two thousand different tea gardens—those are the estates on which tea is grown—and each estate has a number of different pluckings, or harvests, a year, depending on its altitude. And the tea from each of those pluckings can vary in taste and quality." Teresa lifted her hands, palms up, in a gesture that indicated the complications of the task.

Kincaid had never thought beyond a vague vision of India or China when he plopped a tea bag in his morning cup. "It's exponential, then?" he asked.

"Theoretically, yes—in reality, no." Teresa tucked a strand of straight blonde hair behind her ear and rubbed at the sweat beading her forehead. Although it was cooler in the warehouse than outside, it still felt like a tropical hothouse. "We've a history of dealing with certain gardens, and we tend to look for their produce. Annabelle . . . Annabelle visited some of the gardens in Ceylon and in India after university, but she wanted to go to China for their honeymoon. . . ." Teresa's eyes filled with tears. Sniffing, she tugged a tissue from the pocket of her jeans and blew her nose. "Sorry. I just can't . . . Some of our buyers didn't take Annabelle seriously at first. It's traditionally a male-dominated business, and I suppose they thought she was dabbling until she found something better to do.

"But the truth of it was that she *loved* tea. She'd been fascinated by every step in the process of manufacturing tea since she was a child, and she wanted to experience it firsthand."

"And for that she had to go to China or India?" asked Kincaid.

"Yes. All tea is processed right after picking, on the estate where it's grown. It has to be withered and rolled and dried within hours, or it loses its freshness. And the degree of fermentation must be perfect—if it's overfermented the tea will taste flat; if it's underfermented it can go moldy once it's packed for shipping. The tasting and blending we do here is only the very last stage." Her gesture took in the chests and the tasting table and the smooth boards of the old warehouse floor, polished from long use to a satiny sheen.

"Was Annabelle in charge of the tasting?"

"No, that's Mac—Mr. MacDougal. Tea merchants have professional tasters, and Mac's one of the best in the business. But Annabelle's . . . Annabelle *was* very good, and some of the blends she and Mac created have increased our market share considerably. I simply don't know how we'll manage without her." Teresa's voice threatened to break and she pressed her lips together in an effort at control. She turned away and led them to racks of shelving against the far wall. "This new design is only part of Annabelle's vision."

Kincaid saw that the shelves held round tins bearing the familiar Hammond's logo. The tins were an unusual shape, tall and thin, and of a striking cobalt blue and russet design, with the logo embossed in gold. He remembered seeing them in some of the more expensive gourmet shops, and at Harrods.

"They're lovely," said Gemma, turning a tin so that she could see the design all the way round.

"She chose the colors to please William—her father—after his favorite tea service. She—" Teresa closed her eyes. Shaking her head, she whispered, "I'm sorry."

"Come sit down." Gently, Gemma took her by the elbow and led her to the brightly cushioned grouping of rattan chairs positioned near the tasting table. "Let me get you some water."

"No, I'm fine, really," Teresa protested, but she sank gratefully into a chair, shivering as if she were cold. "It's just . . . I'm still not sure I've taken it in."

Gemma sat beside her. "I think Mr. Mortimer said that Annabelle had assumed the running of the business from her father?"

"His wife was very ill, you know. Cancer. Then after she died, he wasn't well himself for some time. From the shock, I suppose. Otherwise he'd never have given up control to anyone."

"Could Mr. Hammond not step in again?"

Teresa's brow creased in a worried frown. "It's been five years since William was directly involved with the day-to-day running of the business, although he drops in at odd times of the day and night. I think he can't bear to let it go altogether."

"Then with his experience—"

"It's more complicated than that. Annabelle was taking the company in directions William didn't approve—"

"But if you've been successful, surely he'd want to continue as Annabelle intended."

"No, you don't understand. To William, it's tradition that's important. Even though his great-grandfather began the business as a gamble on the new tea estates in Ceylon, he can't see that it was risk-taking that put Hammond's on its feet in the first place. He wants things done the way they've always been—"

"Such as?" Kincaid asked, intrigued.

Sighing, Teresa sat back in her chair. "I don't know where to start. Tea bags, for one. Until recently, Hammond's has never sold tea in bags—there's simply no comparison between our teas and the low-quality blends that are used in most mass-produced tea bags. But Annabelle was convinced that you *could* put fine tea in a bag, and that if you suffered some loss of quality in the processing, you made up for it by introducing consumers to better teas. A taste for tea needs developing, like a taste for wine, and Annabelle was sure we could switch the customer from bags to loose tea eventually.

"It was the same with flavorings. There's a huge market for flavored teas, especially in the States, but William wouldn't hear of it. Annabelle convinced the board that most tea drinkers start out with flavored teas and move on to appreciating the tea itself, but I'm not sure William ever really accepted the decision. He—"

There was a click of a latch and the front door swung open. Kincaid could make out nothing but the tall silhouette of a man, but Teresa pushed herself up from her chair. "Mr. Hammond. What are you doing here?"

"Teresa, my dear." Coming forward, he took her outstretched hand and gave it a pat. "Jo shouldn't have asked you to do this. It's the family's responsibility to look after things here." He turned to Kincaid and Gemma. "I'm William Hammond. How can I help you?"

Gemma would have recognized Hammond from Annabelle's photos without the introduction, although his expensive dark suit added an austerity to his courtly good looks. She wondered fleetingly how he could bear the suit in this heat, but his palm felt cool against hers as he shook her hand.

Teresa touched his arm, and when he turned back to her, she said, "Mr. Hammond. I'm so sorry—"

"I know you and Annabelle were very close," William Hammond answered with what seemed an effort. "She depended on you a great deal. As does Reginald. He came to see me this morning—" He broke off. "This is a terrible thing for us all. My daughter said you had some questions, Superintendent. And unless Teresa can be of further help, I think she'd like to go home."

"That's fine." Kincaid directed his reply to Teresa. "We know how to reach you."

Teresa hesitated for a moment and then, with a nod at Kincaid and Gemma, left.

"Sit down, please." Hammond took the chair Teresa had vacated and motioned for them to follow suit.

"I know how difficult this must be for you, Mr. Hammond," Kincaid said, tugging at the knot on his tie. He'd abandoned his jacket in the car mid-morning, and Gemma wagered the tie wouldn't last much longer. He glanced at her, a signal for her to take over.

"Have you any idea why someone would want to harm your daughter, Mr. Hammond?" She clasped her hands over the notebook she cradled unobtrusively in her lap.

He stared at her, his eyes tearing. "Annabelle was so beautiful. You couldn't begin to understand unless you knew her. No man could have asked for a more perfect daughter."

"I'm sure that's true, Mr. Hammond," Gemma said gently. "But we think it's possible Annabelle may have known her killer. Are you aware of any enemies she might have made through the business? Or of any rifts in her personal life?"

"Of course not. That's an absurd idea. Everyone loved Annabelle."
Gemma changed tack. "How did you feel about her engagement to
Reginald Mortimer?"

"Her engagement? What has that to do with this?" Hammond
drew his brows together impatiently.

"You approved of the engagement?" Gemma pressed.

"Of course. I've known the boy since he was an infant. You couldn't
have found a couple more suited to one another, and his family is of the
highest quality. His father, Sir Peter, serves on our board as well as being a personal friend. Peter and Helena have taken this very hard. . . .
They looked on Annabelle as a daughter."

"Reginald and Annabelle got along well, did they?" Kincaid interposed. "No tiffs or rows?"

"As far as I know, they got on extremely well, and if they had any
disagreements, they didn't share them with me." With a frown, he
added, "I hope you haven't been upsetting Reginald with these sorts of
questions. The poor fellow's had enough to deal with as it is."

Kincaid allowed a pause to lengthen before he asked, "Mr. Hammond, in your experience, would you say Reg Mortimer is a truthful
person?"

"What do you mean by that?" Blue veins stood out on William
Hammond's hands as he clasped them over his knees. "He's a fine
young man. Peter Mortimer and I have known one another since Oxford, and I have the greatest confidence in father *and* son."

Confidence enough, wondered Gemma, to marry your daughter off
to him, and bring him into your company with no more incentive than
friendship? She framed an idea into a question. "You said Sir Peter
served on the board. Does that mean he has a financial interest in
Hammond's?"

"Naturally he owns a number of shares. I'm sorry, but I really don't
see the point to this, under the circumstances. And I've things to attend to—people will be coming by the house to pay their respects."
Although polite, it was a dismissal as firm as the one he'd given Teresa
Robbins.

"Thank you for your time, Mr. Hammond. You've been very kind.
We won't trouble you any further at the moment." Kincaid rose and
Gemma followed his cue, uncomfortably aware of her skirt plastered to

the backs of her thighs with perspiration. "Our technicians will need to have a look round, however," Kincaid added, as if it had just occurred to him. "Perhaps Teresa could arrange that for us?"

"Here? In my building?" William Hammond's voice faltered. He looked suddenly exhausted, and Gemma thought that for all his appearance of control, he'd reached the limit of his endurance.

"They'll do their best not to disrupt things," Kincaid replied soothingly.

Gazing at the dust motes swirling in the bars of sunlight that dissected the air, Gemma realized she had become aware of complex layers of scent—the mustiness of old wood and the nearness of water, mixed with the ripe aroma of tea. The sense-tickling smells, the golden light, and the slow movement of the air under the spinning fans made the warehouse suddenly seem a timeless place, and she wondered what other dramas it had witnessed. She turned to Hammond. "I think Teresa said your great-grandfather started the business? So Hammonds have always been here?"

"I've always seen that as rather a special obligation, carrying on the family tradition. And it meant so much to Annabelle. . . ."

"What will happen now?" asked Gemma. "Will Jo carry on in Annabelle's place?"

"Jo has her own career, and she's never had much interest in the business." Hammond met Gemma's eyes, and the desolation she saw in his made her flinch. "But I doubt it would matter if she had. No one can possibly replace Annabelle."

CHAPTER 7

That 'The Island is not what it
was', is a sentiment with which
every Islander over forty would
agree . . . whilst recalling with
affectionate regret the days when
'every door was open', and
'everyone knew everyone else'.
Such phrases recall a
neighbourliness, and a sense of
local identity, both of which have
been threatened with destruction
by almost everything that has
happened on the Isle of Dogs
since 1939.

Eve Hostettler, from Dockland

KINCAID SLID INTO THE CAR AND
gingerly touched the steering wheel,
then snatched his fingers back.
"Bloody hell. I'll bet you could fry
eggs on the dash."

They had left William Hammond
on his own, with his assurances that
he just needed a chance to get his
bearings, but to Gemma the weight
of grief in the warehouse had felt so
tangible that even the scorching
heat outside was a relief. "It's a terrible thing to lose a child, even if
they're grown," she said as she grappled with a seat-belt buckle that

seemed molten. "Do you suppose it's even harder if that child is as perfect as Annabelle Hammond seems to have been?"

"She can't have been all that perfect, or someone wouldn't have killed her."

"Are you saying it was her fault she was murdered?" Gemma retorted, then felt a little embarrassed by her defensiveness.

"Of course not." Kincaid glanced at her in surprise. "But let's look at what we've got so far." Starting the car, he pulled it forward into a patch of shade and let it idle, fan running. "Annabelle Hammond was extremely beautiful, which, you have to admit, usually implies some degree of self-absorption. She was headstrong, even going against her father's wishes in the running of the family business, which leads to the next point—she apparently had a real passion for her job. Passion makes people dangerous."

Gemma thought of Gordon Finch, wondering if Annabelle's passion had extended to him. She said, "I suspect she'd got cold feet about marrying Reg Mortimer. Otherwise, why put it off?"

"We keep coming back to Mortimer, don't we? Why don't we stop at the Ferry House, see if we can confirm his movements on Friday night."

Realizing with a start that the afternoon had stretched into early evening, she pulled her phone from her handbag. "It's getting late. I'd better give Hazel a ring first and check on Toby."

"Oh, shit."

"What?" She looked up in alarm, her finger poised over the keypad.

"I completely bloody forgot. I promised to take Kit to the station." He glanced at his watch as he jammed the car into gear. "And there's no one else."

"The Major?" Gemma suggested, but even as she spoke she remembered he didn't drive.

"No car. And I've imposed upon him enough this weekend as it is. I'll have to drop you at Limehouse, and get back to Hampstead as quickly as I can."

Welcome to the world of the single parent, Gemma thought, but she had the sense to keep it to herself.

• • •

KINCAID BERATED HIMSELF AS HE TURNED into the bottom of Carlingford Road. He'd meant to ring during the day and check on Kit, and he'd certainly meant to keep the promise he'd made to him about tonight, but once he'd got involved in the case, his good intentions had come to nought.

Kit sat on the steps leading to the flat, his arms wrapped round his knees, his bag beside him. He watched, unsmiling, as Kincaid pulled up to the curb, and did not rise to greet him.

Kincaid got out and crossed the street. "I'm sorry, Kit. I got hung up."

Kit didn't look at him. "I've rung Laura and told her not to meet the train."

"We'll get you on the next one, then I'll let her know when to pick you up." When Kit didn't respond, Kincaid jingled his keys impatiently in his pocket and added, "Have you said goodbye to the Major?"

This elicited a scathing glance. "Of course I have. And thanked him. Do you think I was brought up in a barn?"

Kincaid closed his eyes for an instant and took a deep breath, the equivalent of counting to ten. "Well, shall we go, then? The sooner we get you to the station, the sooner you'll be . . . back in Cambridge." He had almost said "home." But since his mother's death in April, Kit had been without a real home.

Kit stood, his face averted, and trudged to the car as if his feet were mired in treacle. When Kincaid had stowed the boy's holdall in the Rover's boot, he got in beside him, pausing when he put the key in the ignition. "We'll go on to King's Cross, then if there's time before the next train, I'll take you for something to eat. And you still won't be very late back."

"It doesn't matter now. I'll have missed Tess's obedience class," Kit said stonily, his eyes fixed on some invisible point in the windscreen.

"You didn't tell me Tess had an obedience class."

"I never had a chance, did I? I've hardly seen you all weekend."

"Kit. I said I was sorry. But sometimes things come up—"

Swinging round to face him, Kit spat out, "You're always late." Red spots flared across his cheekbones and he rubbed the back of a fist across his trembling lower lip. "You say you'll do something, then you don't keep your word. You're just like my dad."

Kincaid clenched his hands round the steering wheel. "Give me a chance, will you, Kit? I've never done this before. It's hard enough for me to juggle my job—"

"Then don't bother." Kit turned away, his lips clamped tight and his chin thrust up in defiant bravado. "It's just the same old crap, isn't it? My dad—"

"Just because I have a commitment to my job doesn't mean that I don't care about you. I'm not going to lose interest, and I'm not going anywhere."

"Dad did. He—"

"Goddamn it, Kit, we're not talking about Ian, we're talking about me. And *I'm* your dad." Kincaid heard his words with horror, but it was too late to recall them.

Kit stared at him. "That's bollocks. What are you talking about?"

Bloody hell, Kincaid thought. What had he done? Shaking his head, he said, "I never meant to tell you this way. But I'm certain I'm your father. I thought—"

"That's daft. My dad's in France."

"Look at me, Kit." Kincaid reached for Kit's shoulder, but the boy flinched away. "Look at my face, then look at yourself in the mirror." He flipped down the passenger side visor. "You are the spitting image of me at the same age. My mother saw it instantly. I see it every time I look at you."

"I don't believe you," Kit said, but he darted a look at the glass.

Pulling his wallet from his pocket, Kincaid extracted two dog-eared photos. "My mother sent me this one. I was eleven." He handed it to Kit, who accepted it reluctantly; then he held up the second photo. "This one I took from your mum's office." Vic and Kit stood arm in arm in the back garden of the cottage in Grantchester, laughing into the camera. "You can see the resemblance, too, can't you?"

"No." Kit shook his head and dropped the photo of Kincaid in the console. "I don't believe it. My mum wouldn't have . . ." His eyes strayed to the photo again.

"This doesn't mean your mum did anything wrong, Kit. You know we were married before she married Ian. She must have been pregnant with you when we separated."

"She'd have told me. Mum told me everything."

"You must see that she couldn't. She was with Ian by then, and she wanted you to think of him as your father." And then Ian had abandoned them. After Ian's defection, Vic had brought Kincaid back into her life, and Kit's, but they would never be sure what she'd intended for them.

Kit kneaded the knees of his jeans with his fingers, refusing to meet Kincaid's eyes.

"I didn't know about you until that day I came to Grantchester. Your mum never let me know she'd had a child."

A tiny rip in the denim grew larger as Kit picked at it. "You're not my dad. You can't prove it." His barley-fair hair fell over his forehead, hiding his eyes, but the stubborn set of his jaw was clear.

Kincaid looked out at his quiet street in the early evening light. Next door a man and a boy washed a car, laughing as they got soaked in the spray. He could smell the smoke from someone's barbecue, hear the high voices of children in the back gardens. It was the language of families, and he didn't know it. "I *can* prove it, Kit, with a DNA test, but I won't try until you want me to. Give me a chance at being a dad. I know we can work things—"

"Like this weekend?" There was a ripping sound as Kit pulled at the bit of fabric he'd worked loose. "Like you let my mum die?"

"Kit, I—"

"I want to go back to Cambridge. Tess needs her dinner and she won't have been eating well with me away." Kit reached for his seat belt, snapped the buckle into place. He hugged his arms across his chest and stared straight ahead.

They drove to the station in silence.

LEWIS FOUND THE KITCHEN NOT ALL *that different from his mum's. Although the room was enormous, the oak table in its center was scarred and bleached from much scrubbing, with a bottom rail worn by generations of feet. Tea towels hung drying on a rack suspended above the old cooker, the room smelled of baking, a muted wireless played dance tunes in the corner. And Cook, a plump and floury woman as different from Lewis's willowy mother as chalk from cheese, scolded him in the same affectionate way.*

Cook had fed him part of a steak-and-mushroom pie and some cold ham—what she called bits-and-pieces—but it was more meat than Lewis had ever seen at one sitting. With the addition of a pot of cider, he could hardly keep his eyes open by the time John Pebbles returned to fetch him.

John carried a shaded lantern, and he led Lewis across the cobbled yard by its dim light. When Lewis caught his toe on a stone, John steadied him and clucked with disapproval. "Shame on Cook, plying a mere lad with cider."

"She said I needed nourishing," Lewis explained.

John gave a disgusted snort. "Hot, sweet tea, or a jug of milk from the dairy, would have done better. You remember that next time and don't let Cook teach you bad habits. Here we are, then," he added as they reached the stable.

As they entered through the central doors, John uncovered the lantern, and Lewis caught a glimpse of stalls to the right. One held Zeus, who looked curiously at them over the door, and the other a dark brown horse with a white blaze down the center of its face.

To the left the old stalls had been torn out, and two humped, canvas-covered shapes filled the open bays. But before Lewis could exclaim, John said, "Tomorrow, lad," and nudged him up the steep flight of stairs. "You can have a look at the autos then. In the meantime, you'll be snug enough up here."

Lewis saw a small, bare-planked room with a single, blanket-covered bed. A straight-backed chair and an old chest with a china basin and ewer atop it completed the furnishings. His battered case sat neatly beneath the heavily curtained window.

"There's an oil stove, but you won't be needing that tonight. The pump's in the yard, and there's a privy on the far side." John seemed to hesitate, then said, "I'll leave you the lantern, but you must promise to take care with it, and don't forget the blackout." He set it gently atop the chest, then went to the door. "You just go across to the kitchen in the morning. Good night, lad." His heavy footsteps clumped down the stairs, and the door at the bottom banged shut.

At home, Lewis had always slept in the same room as his brothers, and his mum or his sister had always been there when he came home from school in the afternoon. Now, he found himself completely alone for the first time in his life.

He sat down on the rough blanket and stared at the lantern light wavering on the walls. Although the room still held the day's heat, he began to shiver. He got up and extinguished the lantern, then curled himself into a fetal position on the narrow bed, his fist pressed to his mouth to keep the grief welling up inside him from escaping.

And so he slept, deeply and dreamlessly, until the morning sun brought a faint brightening round the edges of his window.

Awakening brought a moment of comfort, until he realized he couldn't smell his mother's cooking, or hear faint snatches of the songs she sang as she moved about the kitchen. Reality flooded back into his awareness, and with it the sense of being watched.

He opened his eyes, blinking stickily at a shadow in his doorway. As his vision cleared, the fuzzy form resolved itself into a boy about his own age, who crossed the room and pulled aside the curtains. Light flooded in, and Lewis saw that his visitor was tall and slender, and wore a navy blazer with a school tie. His dark hair was slicked neatly back above a pale face.

"Cook sent me to fetch you," the boy said in an accent Lewis had heard only on the wireless. "And I wanted to see you for myself. I couldn't get away last night—Mummy kept me fetching and carrying for Aunt Edwina while they talked about the war."

Lewis sat up and rubbed his face. "The war? Has it started, then?"

The boy leaned against the window frame. "Not officially, but they expect the announcement sometime today. Aunt Edwina has the wireless on in the sitting room, and Cook's listening in the kitchen. Aunt Edwina has a wager on with my dad that it will all come to nothing. 'A bloody old windbag' is what she calls Hitler. I think she's wrong, though. There is going to be a war."

"Is that why you're here, too?" Lewis asked, feeling confused. He couldn't imagine this elegant boy being sent away from home like a mislaid parcel.

"Edwina's my godmother," the boy explained. "Edwina Burne-Jones, she's called. This is her house. Mummy is certain the Huns will bomb London, and my school with it, so she wants me to stay down here for a bit. Edwina says you come from the Island. My family's business is there—Hammond's Teas."

"That's just across the street from my school," Lewis exclaimed with pleasure at encountering something familiar. "Are you a Hammond, then?"

"Oh, sorry." The boy pushed himself away from the window and came towards Lewis with his hand outstretched. "I should have said. My name's William. William Hammond."

KINCAID KNOCKED AGAIN AT GEMMA'S DOOR. There was no response, even though her car was pulled up on the double yellows in front of her garage flat. He'd driven straight from King's Cross without ringing first, something he seldom did, and now he realized he'd not considered whether he would be welcome.

But the thought of his empty flat was too sharp a reminder of his failed weekend, so he let himself through the wrought-iron gate that led into the Cavendishes' garden. Perhaps Gemma had gone next door, as she often did.

The walled garden lay in the cool, rose-scented shadow of early evening, and as he made his way along the flagged path that led to the big house, he saw Hazel on her knees in the perennial bed next to the patio. She wore shorts that had seen better days, and a pink tank top that bared her lightly freckled shoulders.

"Gemma's taken Toby to the park," Hazel called out. "You'll have to make do with me for a bit, unless you want to go after them."

"I think you'll do admirably. Although you look like you're working entirely too hard."

"Dandelions among the daisies," Hazel said by way of explanation as he sank into a chair on the patio. "That's the problem with this gorgeous weather. The weeds love it as much as we do." She wiped her hand across her brow and left a dirty streak. "There's some lemonade in the jug." Frowning, she gave him a closer look. "Unless you'd like something stronger. You look a bit done in."

He took a glass from the tray on the small table, then reached for the silver jug, its frosted surface traced with runnels of condensation. "No, this is fine, really. You're a marvel, Hazel."

"Tell that to my child. We've had a spectacularly bad day. Tim finally had to separate us and send me outside for a bit of earth therapy." Sitting back, Hazel drank from the glass she'd placed on the flagstones.

"Oh, come on, Hazel. I've never seen you even out of sorts with the children."

She laughed. "You should have heard me today, screeching like a fishwife at Holly because she refused to pick up the toys she'd deliberately thrown on the floor. Toby came in for his share of it, too, but he can't push my buttons in the same way. There's something about your own child. . . ." Hazel picked up her spade again and thrust it beneath the spiky leaves of a dandelion.

"Doesn't your training as a psychologist help?"

"Much to my dismay, I'm discovering that understanding children's behavior intellectually doesn't always make dealing with it easier." The dandelion came up with a spray of dirt and she shook what remained from the roots before tossing it into a pail.

"I don't even have that small advantage." He couldn't keep the bitterness from his voice.

Hazel glanced up at him. "What's going on? Did you and Kit not have a good weekend?"

"That's an understatement," he said with a derisive snort.

Hazel pushed herself up from the flagstones, dusted off her bare knees, and came to sit beside him. "What happened?"

Kincaid looked away. The white lilies in Hazel's border had begun to glow in the dusk. "I blew it. He was being stubborn and unreasonable, and I just lost it—blurted out that I was his dad, without thinking of the consequences."

"And?" Hazel prompted.

"He—" Kincaid shook his head. "He was furious. Accused me of lying to him, and told me to bugger off, more or less."

Hazel nodded. "That's not surprising. Remember how shocked you were at first? And you've turned Kit's world on end without warning. Not even his mother's death will have made him doubt his perception of things in the same way."

Frowning, Kincaid said, "I don't understand."

"You've made a lie of his life, his image of who he is and how he came to be. Especially now, with Vic gone, that image is all he's had to sustain him."

"You're saying I shouldn't have told him at all?"

"No." She touched his arm for emphasis. "Only that you need to understand the depth of the charge you've planted. What started the argument?"

"Work. A case came up this weekend—Gemma will have told you—and I couldn't do what I'd promised. Kit felt I'd let him down. And I had." He moved restlessly in his chair. "I'd thought that having him live with me was the obvious solution, once he'd had a bit of time to adjust. Now I'm beginning to wonder if my seeing him at all is doing more harm than good."

"I'm sure that's not true. But I don't think you realized the extent of the commitment you made," Hazel added, sighing. She reached for a box of matches and lit the citronella candle in the center of the table. "You haven't any experience with that sort of responsibility, and your job makes it doubly difficult."

"I know. But I still can't see any alternative to having Kit with me. He can't stay with the Millers indefinitely, as kind as they've been to have him through the school term."

"No word from Ian McClellan?"

Vic's ex-husband had returned to Cambridge just long enough to agree to Kincaid's arrangements for Kit, then he had hightailed it back to his lover. "Not a peep. I assume he's still enjoying the south of France with his nubile graduate student. But Kit hasn't given up hoping Ian will send for him." Kincaid shook his head. "I thought that if Kit learned *I* was his father, not Ian, it might make Ian's desertion a bit more bearable."

"It may, in time. But you're asking Kit for belief based on nothing but your word. You have no proof."

He thought of the day of Vic's funeral, when his mother had taken him aside and told him he was blind not to have seen the resemblance the boy bore to him, or to have calculated the number of months between the time Vic left him and Kit's birth. His first reaction had been denial; his second, panic; it was only the fear of losing Kit altogether that had made him realize how much he wanted it to be true.

Inside the house the kitchen light flicked on, and he heard the rattle of crockery clearly through the open window. "Kit has more to accept than the fact that he's *my* son," he said slowly. "He blames me for Vic's death."

"Duncan, Kit's a child. He has no other way of resolving what's happened to him, unless the trial—"

"That's no help. It may be two years before Vic's murder comes before the courts. And what if Kit's right—and I did fail her?"

Leaning forward so that the light shining from the kitchen window illuminated her face, Hazel said forcefully, "You know that's not reasonable. You did all anyone could have done for Vic."

Had he? Since Vic's death he had tried to convince himself of it, but now his nagging doubts leapt out like reaching shadows. "What matters now is Kit," he said, pushing the thoughts aside. "How can I salvage the mess I've made of things?"

Hazel gave him a searching look. "The important thing is not to give up on him. Make him see that you aren't going to reject him, no matter how he behaves." Frowning, she thought for a moment, then added, "I'd say he's testing you—and protecting himself. If he drives you away now, he doesn't have to worry that you'll run off and leave him the first time he's not perfect."

"Like Ian did."

"Yes. If you have to break a promise, make it up to him in some way, as soon as you can. It's the only way he'll learn to trust you. And Duncan—be patient with him."

"That doesn't seem to be my strong suit these days." Suddenly, a wave of exhaustion swept through him, as if the adrenaline that had carried him through his row with Kit had drained away. With an effort, he finished his lemonade and stood, looking out across the garden. Gemma's windows were still dark.

"You're not going to wait?" Hazel asked. "I've a quiche in the fridge, and some white wine chilled."

He hesitated, then shook his head. "I think I need some time on my own tonight. But thanks, Hazel. Will you tell Gemma I came by?"

"Of course." Hazel got up and gave him a brief hug. "I'd better see if I can make up to Holly with a half hour of *Winnie the Pooh*."

If only it were that easy, he thought as he let himself out the garden gate and unlocked the Rover. But he and Kit had no comforting rituals to mend the rifts between them.

As the car's interior lights came on, he noticed that the center console contained only some peppermints and pocket change. Surely Kit had dropped his old photo there, the one his mum had sent of an eleven-year-old Duncan in scouting uniform, sporting a toothy grin.

When a quick search between the seats and on the floor yielded nothing, he remembered leaving Kit alone in the car for a moment at the station, while he fetched his bag from the boot.

If Kit had changed his mind and taken the photo with him, perhaps there was hope he might come to terms with the idea of their relationship. Kincaid felt his throat tighten with unexpected hope.

A BIT OF SALAD WITH THE first tomato and cucumber from his vegetable plot, peas, two potatoes roasted in their jackets, and two lovely chops from the butcher along Manchester Road. George Brent surveyed this bounty with pleasure and a certain anticipation, for it was the first time he'd prepared supper for Mrs. Singh.

He was quite proud of his developing culinary skills, as the wife had done most of the cooking in the more than forty years they'd had together. Never too late to learn, his old dad had been fond of saying.

It was never too late for some other things, either, he thought with a sly smile. A clean shirt after his bath, a liberal splash of aftershave on his newly shaven neck and jaw—he was undoubtedly as irresistible as one of those young studs on the telly, although when he'd been that age he'd have thought it daft to bathe more than once a week.

When he was a lad, before the war, the Saturday bath had been an occasion. They'd heated water for the big, old, tin tub in the scullery, and they'd each had their bit of Sunlight soap. And on fine days, they'd taken their bit of soap down to the river. The water had been clean, then, and the great ships had been as familiar to them as the furniture in their parlors.

The thought of the war reminded him that he'd meant to listen to that program on the wireless again, the one about the Blitz he'd heard on Radio Four the other evening. The events of the previous day had driven it from his mind—that and his daughter Brenda's fussing, which had only served to remind him of the dead girl every time he turned round. He'd even seen her face in his dreams.

In an effort to put it out of his mind, George imagined Mrs. Singh on the other side of the small table, her knees touching his under the cloth. And the little table did look inviting with two places set on the oilcloth and the jug of bright flowers he'd picked from the garden—a perfect setting for a bit of romance.

As he peeked at the potatoes in the oven and turned the chops over in the pan, the doorbell rang. He glanced at the clock. Mrs. Singh was early, but he liked promptness in a woman. Wiping his hand on the tea towel, he went into the hall.

Janice Coppin stood in his open doorway. "Hullo, George. Surprised to see me?"

"What do you want?" He scowled at her, but she smiled back at him, unfazed.

"Just a word. Can I come in?"

"I'm expecting someone."

"It won't take long."

"All right, then," he said grudgingly, and led the way back to the kitchen, where he turned off the fire under the pan.

"A lady friend?" inquired Janice, taking in the jug of flowers and the carefully laid plates as she sat in one of the kitchen chairs. "George Brent, you old goat."

"None of your business, miss," he growled, but he could've sworn he heard admiration in her tone. She wore shorts and a tee shirt rather than her stiff police-lady suit, and looked, George decided, altogether more human.

"It's about the dead woman, George," she said. "The one you found in—"

"I know which one. How many dead women do you think I've run across lately?"

"Then you remember the sergeant who came to see you?"

He glared at Janice, not bothering to answer. He'd liked the kind-voiced policewoman, a nice-looking lass with her pretty red hair—but that brought to mind the other one, lying so still in the grass. . . .

"Sergeant James said you didn't seem quite sure about where you'd seen the dead woman, George. I thought you might have remembered something else."

George didn't like to admit how much it had been bothering him, especially to Janice Coppin. "I'm not senile, you know," he said, but he heard the hesitation in his voice.

"No, of course you're not," Janice agreed. "And I've not given you credit, have I? For noticing things, and remembering things."

"Would you like a cuppa, lass?" he asked, thinking that maybe Janice Coppin wasn't so bad after all.

"That'd be lovely."

He put the kettle on, and opened the package of Hobnobs he'd bought specially for Mrs. Singh.

When he'd given Janice her tea and biscuit, she said, "I've been thinking, George, that if you didn't want to say where you'd seen the woman, maybe it was because she was with someone you knew, and you didn't want to get anyone in trouble. But if we're to catch her killer, we have to know everything we can about her."

George met her eyes, then looked away, fidgeting with the tea towel he'd used to wipe the sloshed tea from her saucer. "You're an Islander, lass. You know what it's like, though you won't remember the best days, before the war."

"My mum says she knew everyone when she was a girl, all the neighbors—"

"Hard to get into trouble in those days," George agreed with a smile. "Someone would rat on you for certain. We played in the street on fine days, hoops and marbles, not like the things kids do today."

Closing his eyes, he could see it all as clearly as if it were yesterday. "The girls had tops with colored paper stuck on them and they looked so lovely when they spun. . . . And we all played cricket together, girls and boys, while the grown-ups stood round chatting. . . ." He opened his eyes and found Janice watching him intently. "I knew him then. Just a little lad, and I was already in my teens. Who'd have thought things would turn out the way they did?"

"What things?"

"The war, his family . . ." George sighed and shook his head. "But he came back, and I've always admired him for that. He never forgot where he came from or what he owed. And he always had a kind word for me and a pint at the pub."

Janice held her teacup motionless, balanced in both hands. "Who, George?"

"Lewis Finch," he admitted reluctantly.

"You saw Annabelle Hammond with Lewis Finch?"

"Was that her name? Like Hammond's Teas?"

"Exactly. It's her family's business, and she was in charge of it. Where did you see them?"

George pleated the tea towel. "Once coming out of the Indian restaurant just down the road. He was holding her arm, friendly-like, and she was laughing. You couldn't help but notice her. Once in the Waterman's Arms. And another time, in his Mercedes. The windows were tinted but you could still tell it was her."

"Recently?" asked Janice.

"In the pub, a month or so ago. That time outside the restaurant, I'm not certain, except that it was nippy that day. In the autumn, maybe."

"And the time in the car?"

"It was just a glimpse, one day when I was taking Sheba for her run. It doesn't mean anything, that he knew her."

"No. But we'll have to have a word with him, just the same," said Janice, and George thought she didn't sound any happier at the prospect than he'd felt in telling her what he'd seen.

She finished her tea and stood up. "Thanks, George. I'd better let you tend to your supper."

With a regretful thought for his potatoes—likely cooked to a crisp—and cold chops, George saw her to the door.

From the walk she turned back and gave him a cheeky grin. "By the way, George—I'm sorry about the Settlement Dance. Tell your Georgie that for me one of these days, would you?"

GORDON FINCH STOOD AT THE WINDOW of his first-floor flat, looking out across East Ferry Road. A breath of cool air stirred the lace curtains. The street lamps had come on, and across the road in Millwall Park the bowlers had given up their game and retired to the pub.

All so normal, all so ordinary. For a moment he held on to the thought that he would turn and life would go on uninterrupted. Annabelle would be standing naked at his kitchen sink, brushing her teeth, holding the mass of her hair back with the other hand to keep it dry. She would lean forward, the angle of the light creating a hollow in the small of her back, highlighting the curve of her hip, then as she straightened the shadows would shift, playing over her skin like a lover's hands.

From the beginning she'd shed her clothes whenever she walked into his flat, throwing her expensive suits casually over a chair. Sometimes on colder days she slipped on a silk kimono he'd found at a street market. Captivated by the rich colors of the old silk, he'd bought it on impulse. It was the only gift he had given her, hanging ready from a peg on the back of the bathroom door.

He saw the gold and russet folds of the robe fall open, revealing a slice of creamy skin as Annabelle sat at his small table, eating Indian take-away with a plastic fork. The candles he'd stuck in saucers guttered and smoked between them. Laughing, she'd called him a barbarian, but when he challenged her to invite him to her flat for a proper dinner, she refused.

She'd come to him for months before he learned her name, and even then she'd never talked about herself in the ordinary sense. It was only by chance that he'd seen her come out of the Ferry Street flat one day and learned that she lived just down the road—a few blocks and another world away.

Not that he'd needed confirmation that Annabelle Hammond was everything he despised, one of the privileged who take without considering those they trample in the process. Why had he thought he might be the undamaged exception?

Once, straddling him on his narrow bed, she'd held his clarinet between her breasts and asked him if he'd give it up for her. "Don't be daft," he'd said, but for a moment the abyss of obsession had opened before him. What might he have done for her, he wondered now, if he hadn't discovered her betrayal?

CHAPTER 8

*The Island population had
reached its peak of around
21,000 in 1900. . . . The green
fields had been replaced by
docks, warehouses, factories and
streets of terraced houses. In
this predominantly working-class
community, young people found a
job, married and set up home not
far from their parents.*

Eve Hostettler, from
Memories of Childhood
on the Isle of Dogs

IN THE MID-EIGHTIES, LEWIS FINCH
had chosen to live with a view of
Millwall Dock rather than a view
of the river; in fact, his housing estate had been one of the pioneering
Docklands developments, low-rise
and less than exorbitantly expensive.
Although he'd had many opportunities since to sell at a profit and move
into one of his own newer, more
glamourous riverside developments,
he liked the small scale of the place,
liked knowing his neighbors, and
he'd found himself loath to make a
change.

Nor did he care much for travel,
and having arrived home from a

weekend conference late the previous evening, he'd begun his Monday morning routine with a particular sense of relief.

Shower, shave, dress, then repair with a pot of coffee, a rack of toast, and a stack of newspapers to his tiny dockside balcony.

As he buttered his toast, he gazed out at the sun-pearled, early morning mist on the water. To the north, across the Outer Dock, he could see Glengall Bridge; to the northwest, the towers of Canary Wharf rose in the distance, barely visible in the haze; to the east were the DLR and the high ground of the Mudchute.

It was his small kingdom—the Island—and if he hadn't quite managed to re-create the past, at least he'd come to terms with his failures over the years, and with himself.

Or so he'd thought, until Friday night.

The things that had happened with Annabelle had exposed long-buried wounds, and his reaction had shocked him so deeply that he'd spent the weekend trying to regain his balance.

Today, he'd attempt to repair the damage, or at least control it. But it was too early yet to ring Annabelle at the office, so he would read the papers and drink his coffee, and try not to consider the prospect of his life without Annabelle in it.

He began with the *Financial Times*, as always, then the *Telegraph*, and last, the *Daily Post*—his daily prescription for taking the world's pulse.

The headline jumped out at him from the front page of the tabloid. WOMAN FOUND MURDERED IN MUDCHUTE PARK IDENTIFIED. He read on, at first with the sort of uneasy curiosity engendered by the mention of violence on one's own doorstop—then with unbelieving horror.

It couldn't be. He read it again, tracing the words with his finger as if he were a child, willing it not to be true.

At last, he lowered the newspaper with shaking hands, his vision blurred. What had he done?

Years of hatred had spilled in a moment of fury—then he had let her walk away, white-hot with her own anger. And he feared she'd gone straight to his son.

. . .

LOOKING IN THE OPEN DOOR OF Janice Coppin's dimly lit office, Gemma saw a television on a portable stand flickering bluely in one corner. "You wanted to see me?"

Janice sat on the edge of her desk, sorting through a pile of video-tapes. "Did the guv'nor reach you?" she asked, looking up. The room smelled of stale cigarette ends and Gemma saw that the tin ashtray on the desk was near to overflowing, although she didn't remember ever seeing Janice smoke.

"On my mobile," Gemma replied. She'd awakened to find Toby fractious and feverish, not a good omen for a Monday morning. By the time she'd got him settled in front of the telly at Hazel's, she was running late, and Kincaid had rung her to say he'd keep the appointment he'd made with Annabelle Hammond's solicitor on his own. She'd not had a chance to ask why he hadn't stayed last night, and he hadn't offered an explanation.

Coming further into the room, Gemma peered at the juddering black and white image on the telly screen, her interest quickening. "What have you got?"

"The security-camera video from the foot tunnel. I spent the morning in their office, watching the footage from all the cameras on the time-lapse VCR. Once we'd isolated this camera, they made me a copy."

Gemma noticed her creased blouse and flattened hair. "What time did you come in?"

"Crack of dawn, it feels like. But worth it." Janice put down the videos she was holding and picked up the remote. "Watch."

It was an odd perspective, with pedestrians moving in both directions in the foreground while the tunnel receded in the distance. Then Gemma saw what someone had momentarily blocked—Gordon Finch, standing against the curving tunnel wall, his clarinet case and his dog at his feet. Then the tape jumped jerkily to the next recorded segment, reminding Gemma a bit of an old silent film.

Now a woman stood in front of Gordon, her back to the camera, but Gemma recognized her sleek, black jacket and short skirt, and even in monochrome the wavy fall of her hair was unmistakable. It was Annabelle Hammond.

From her body movements, she seemed to be speaking, but Gordon didn't respond. Annabelle reached out, touching his arm in a gesture of entreaty. Only then did he look at her and shake his head. For a moment, Annabelle stood there, hand still on his arm. Then she shoved past him and walked away down the tunnel, anger visible in every stride.

The tape jumped again. Gordon Finch slowly broke apart his clarinet and knelt to put it in its case. Still squatting, he leaned back against the white-tiled wall of the tunnel, his eyes closed, one hand resting on the dog's head.

Then again, the now-familiar jerk and pause, and the frame showed nothing but moving pedestrians and an unoccupied segment of white-tiled wall. Janice stopped the tape.

Gemma realized she'd been holding her breath. "That's all?"

"There's no sign of either of them after that, on any of the cameras," Janice replied as she rewound the video. "But there's no doubt, is there, that it's Annabelle Hammond?"

"So he lied to us."

"It's certainly obvious he knew her." Janice slid off her desk and switched on the overhead light, then went round to her chair, brushing a speck from her trousers as she sat down.

That Gordon had known Annabelle came as no surprise to Gemma, but she had not been prepared for the emotional intensity of the eerily silent scene, or for the oddness of seeing Annabelle Hammond come to life. "But did he follow her?" she asked.

"It didn't look as though they were making an assignation," said Janice. "She wanted him to do something, and he seemed to be refusing."

Gemma sat slowly down in the visitor's chair, smoothing her skirt beneath her thighs. She'd pulled the coolest item she could find from her wardrobe this morning—a short, loose, Indian cotton dress. "Maybe she wanted him to meet her, and after she left he changed his mind."

"But she was the one who was angry. Why would *he* kill *her*?"

"We don't know what they were arguing about. Or what he might have been building up to," Gemma countered.

"Even if he met her later, it doesn't mean he killed her. And what about Mortimer? He says he saw them together—what proof do we have that Mortimer didn't wait for her?" Janice's blunt face was set in a stubborn scowl.

Gemma studied her. "You're defending him, aren't you? Gordon Finch, I mean. Why?"

"I'm not," Janice said hotly. Then she shrugged and looked embarrassed. "It's just that I'd admired what he stood for—you know, the Robin Hood sort of thing. Rich man's son comes back to his roots and supports the working classes. Probably all a load of bollocks, and it's not as if his father hasn't done his part for the Island. And speaking of the father," Janice added, "I've come up with something."

Gemma thought she detected reluctance. "He cheated on his income tax," she joked, but Janice didn't smile. "All right," said Gemma. "Out with it, then."

"You were right about George Brent. I went back to see him last night, and it wasn't too difficult to get him to 'remember' where he'd seen Annabelle Hammond."

"With Lewis Finch?"

"More than once. Coming out of a restaurant sometime in the autumn, then again fairly recently. And he described their behavior as 'friendly-like.' "

"So it *was* Lewis Finch on Annabelle's answering machine," Gemma mused aloud. "And we have evidence that she had some sort of relationship with his son as well." She nodded at the videotape.

"I think we can take for granted that Annabelle Hammond could lift a finger and have any man she wanted—but doesn't it seem a bit odd that she chose both the Finches?"

"Coincidence?" Gemma ventured, but she didn't believe it. "And at this point, we don't know that she had sex with either of them. Maybe her relationship with Lewis Finch was strictly business, and with Gordon . . ."

"Music lessons?" Janice gave her a skeptical look. "All right, let's just say she slept with them both. Why keep up her engagement to Reg Mortimer, if she was so inclined to sample other merchandise?"

"Men do it often enough. But if Mortimer knew, it gives him a hell of a motive for killing her." Gemma thought for a moment, then said decisively, "We'd better get all our ducks in a row before we pursue this any further. The guv will want to see Lewis Finch when he gets back from the solicitor's."

"And in the meantime, I suppose we'd better have Gordon brought in again." With a grimace, Janice reached for the phone.

"Wait." The request had been unpremeditated, and Janice's startled expression prompted Gemma to back it up. "I know it's not exactly protocol, but it's obvious he doesn't respond well to authority. He'll just be shouting for his solicitor. Let me go and have a word with him." She glanced at her watch. "It's only half-nine. I doubt buskers leave for work very early."

Janice stared at her, her hand still poised over the phone; then, with a sigh, she leaned back in her chair. "On your head be it, then."

LEWIS DID NOT MEET EDWINA BURNE-JONES *that day. After he had finished a breakfast in which the rashers of bacon seemed endless, John had taken him back to the stables and allowed him to help polish the autos. This Lewis had done with reverence, rubbing at the merest smudge on the Bentley until its black paint shone like glass. For the rest of his life he would associate the scent of automobile wax with comfort; for those industrious hours spent with John, listening to his stories and receiving the occasional word of praise, held homesickness at bay as nothing else could.*

In the afternoon, John officially introduced him to the horses, showing him how to fill their water troughs and mangers and how to sweep the soiled straw from their stalls, and promising that when Lewis felt a bit more comfortable, he would teach him how to use the curry comb and brush.

There was no further sign of the elegant William Hammond, and by the time Lewis fell into bed after supper, he had almost forgotten about him.

Sunday, September 3rd, dawned clear and mild. Lewis woke to a chorus of birdsong floating in through his open window. Not liking to think what his mother would have said about his consorting with Methodists, he'd refused John's invitation to attend chapel, and so found himself at a loose end after breakfast.

Cook, seeing a pair of idle hands, set him to work at the kitchen table peeling carrots and potatoes for Sunday dinner.

It was there, in the warm steaminess of the kitchen at eleven o'clock in the morning, that he heard Prime Minister Chamberlain announce over the wireless that Britain had declared war on Germany.

Cook sat down, fanning herself and clucking with dismay. "Oh, Lord, who'd have thought it, after the last one? All the young men will go— such a terrible waste." She shook her head. "I lost both my brothers in the Great War. Just boys they were, too young to die in the trenches."

At the sight of Lewis's face, she reached out and pressed her damp, red hand against his. "Oh, dearie, I am sorry. You told me you had brothers, didn't you?"

Lewis nodded, but the constriction in his throat kept him from speaking. What he hadn't told her was that his brothers meant to sign up the very second that war was declared, and had sworn him to secrecy. His mum would be inconsolable when she found out what they'd done.

"Well, mayhap it's a tempest in a teapot, and nothing will come of it," Cook said comfortingly. "And speaking of tea, I think a nice cuppa would brighten us up a bit," she added, heaving herself to her feet. Watching her ample backside as she bustled about the cooker with kettle and teapot, Lewis tried to come to terms with the fact of war. In spite of the weeks of preparing for the blackout, the talk of shelters, the antiaircraft balloons that floated above London like escapees from a child giant's birthday party, he hadn't really believed in it. He hadn't thought his evacuation would mean more than a week or two away in the country, and now it looked as though he was here to stay.

The door to the hall swung open and William Hammond came in. He was dressed as he had been yesterday, in school blazer and tie, but his hair had sprung up from its neat combing as if unable to contain itself. "I say, have you heard? Isn't it tremendously exciting?"

Cook turned from the kettle with an admonishing shake of her head. "You don't know what you're saying, Master William. If your mother heard you—"

"Mummy's had hysterics all over the parlor. Father's administered the smelling salts and sent her upstairs for a lie-down," William volunteered. "And Aunt Edwina wants to see everyone in half an hour, in the drawing room. I think she's going to make a speech. I'm to tell all the staff." With that, William charged out as energetically as he had entered, and Lewis was left to wait with Cook.

They gathered in the kitchen—John Pebbles and his wife, Mary, a delicate woman with soft brown hair; Kitty, the parlormaid, a girl not much older than Lewis; Owens, the Welsh butler with the singsong voice; Lewis; and Cook. As they waited, they muttered and exclaimed among themselves, yet when the bell summoned them they trooped to the front of the house in silence.

Lewis found himself last as they entered the drawing room, but that gave him a moment to take in his surroundings. After the smokey dimness of the kitchen and the polished, dark woodwork of the hall and staircase, the white-plastered room seemed garden-bright. A chintz-covered sofa faced the fireplace, flanked by needlepoint chairs displaying a profusion of roses. A side table held a large vase of late summer flowers, and a painting over the mantel carried on the soft reds and blues. Lewis drew his eyes from the oddly dressed children in the painting to the slender man who stood turned away from them, one elbow on the mantel as he gazed out the window.

Then the figure turned, and Lewis saw that it was not a man at all, but a tall woman in riding breeches and coat, with the shortest bobbed hair he had ever seen. Her face was sharp and browned to the color of oak, and she had blue eyes that stood out bright as cornflowers against her dark skin.

"You will all have heard the news," she said, lifting a packet of cigarettes from the mantel and lighting one with a silver lighter. "It seems I was wrong in believing it wouldn't come to war, but I hope that will not be the case when I say I don't think this can last long." Edwina Burne-Jones spoke with such conviction that for a moment Lewis felt his fear lift. "But in the meantime, we must take the necessary precautions. We will rigorously enforce the blackout. Owens, Kitty, from now on that will be your responsibility."

"Ma'am," Owens acknowledged calmly, but Kitty looked terrified.

Edwina drew on her cigarette, then continued as she exhaled. "Everyone should make sure that their gas masks are in working order. And if we have warning of a raid, the cellar should do as a shelter." She fixed Lewis with her startling blue eyes. "You're the boy from London?"

Lewis could only nod. Then John's elbow jabbed him sharply in the ribs and he managed to croak out, "Yes, ma'am. Lewis Finch."

"It looks as though you may be with us for a while, Lewis. Is there anything you need?"

Blushing crimson to the roots of his hair, Lewis stammered, "Ma'am. I lost my postcard—the one they gave us to send home."

The skin round the corners of Edwina's eyes crinkled up as she smiled. "I think we can arrange something for you," she said, going to the secretary near the window and removing a sheet of paper, an envelope, and a stamp, which she handed to Lewis. Under his fingers, the paper felt smooth as rose petals.

She studied Lewis, narrowing her remarkable eyes against a veil of smoke. "I understand from the billeting officer that your school class will meet at the Institute until room can be made for you in the village school. Lessons will start as usual tomorrow morning." Pausing, she raked the others with a swift glance, then added, "I want your position here to be clear, Lewis. You are a guest, not a servant. You may help John with his tasks if you wish—he is certainly shorthanded since that infernal boy ran off to join up—but you are not obligated to do so. Do you understand me?"

"Yes, ma'am," Lewis said, although he was not at all sure that he did. How could he be a guest in a place so grand he'd never set foot in its like before?

What he did know was that from that moment on he would attempt to walk on water if Edwina Burne-Jones asked it of him.

GEMMA TOOK THE FIRST PARKING SPACE she came to on East Ferry Road. To her right lay the green playing fields of Millwall Park, spanned by the old, brick aqueduct that now carried the red and blue trains of the DLR. To her left, across the street, was a terrace of simple, prewar houses, some painted and stuccoed, some still sporting their original brown brick. According to Janice's instructions, Gordon Finch lived just a few doors further along.

She started to roll her window up, then shook her head and reversed the crank. There was hardly anything worth stealing, after all, among the odds and ends of papers and food wrappers that littered the car's interior, and ten minutes with the windows closed would turn the Escort into an oven.

As she walked slowly up the street, checking the numbers on the houses opposite, she wondered what had prompted her to take this interview on her own, knowing it was against procedure, knowing that Kincaid would likely have her head for it.

She'd already stretched the limits of truthfulness by not telling Kincaid that she'd met Gordon Finch before—if you could call their brief encounter "meeting"—and the longer she put it off, the more awkward an admission would become.

But then she knew nothing more about Finch than that he had busked in Islington for a time, so what did it matter, really?

Somehow that argument didn't make her feel any better. Shrugging, she promised herself a compromise. She *would* tell Kincaid, the first chance she had to drop it casually into the conversation. And if she thought it necessary after she'd spoken to Finch, she'd send someone round to bring him in to the station.

Reaching the entrance to Millwall Park, she detoured long enough to peek through the wrought-iron fence at the deserted bowling green and the substantial-looking Dockland Settlement House behind it. She guessed this would be the center of working-class social life on the Island, and that Gordon Finch might be a regular here, but she had difficulty imagining him socializing even in the service of political aims.

Retracing her steps and continuing up the street, she'd only gone a few yards when she heard the light notes of the clarinet. She followed the sound across the street to the brown-brick house at the end of the terrace. The music came from the open upstairs window, and as she stood listening, she thought she recognized the Mozart piece she'd heard Gordon play once on the Liverpool Road.

There were two glossy, deep blue doors on the side of the house, and the one nearest the rear bore the number Janice had given her. He must have the upstairs flat, Gemma thought. She knocked sharply and heard the dog bark once in response. It was only when the music stopped that she realized she had no idea what she meant to say.

The door swung open without warning and Gordon Finch stared at her, looking none too pleased. His feet were bare, and he wore nothing but a thin cotton vest above his jeans. Sunlight glinted from the gold earring in his left ear and the reddish stubble on his chin.

"If it isn't the lady copper," he said with a look that took in her dress and bare legs.

Gemma was suddenly very aware of the fact that she was wearing only bra and knickers under the thin cotton dress. She felt both unprepared and unprofessional, and wondered why it was that tights gave one a sense of invincibility.

"I'd never have picked you for a snoop. Is this a social call, or are you just doing your job?" His tone made it clear what he thought of her choice of profession.

She collected herself enough to pull her identification from her handbag and flip it open. "I'd like to ask you a few questions, if you don't mind, Mr. Finch," she said, determined to regain her authority.

Gordon Finch ducked his head in a mock bow and gestured towards the stairs. "Be my guest." He stepped back to let her by, and when Gemma brushed past she was close enough to feel the warmth of his breath. The sound of her sandals thumping on the threadbare steps seemed unnaturally loud as he padded silently up behind her.

When she reached the top of the stairs, she went straight through the open door without waiting. Her momentum carried her into the center of the room and gave her an instant to take stock.

Gordon Finch's dog, Sam, lay on a round cushion near the open window. "Hullo, boy," she said. "Remember me?"

Lifting his head, the dog regarded Gemma, then returned his head to his paws with a sigh. She obviously had not made a lasting impression.

The single, large room was obviously used as a bedsit. To the back was a kitchen alcove with a small pine table and two chairs, to the front a single bed with a cotton spread in bars of bright reds and purples.

"Does it get your seal of approval?" Gordon Finch said behind her, and when Gemma turned round, he added, "What did you expect? Beer cans and rubbish?"

A bookcase held a CD player but no television, and a music stand was positioned in front of the window. His clarinet rested half out of the open case on the floor, and on the stand pages of sheet music fluttered gently, as if sighing. The flat was tidy and, even though sparsely furnished, looked comfortable.

Look, Mr. Finch, I'm not here to—"

"Mr. Finch?" he parroted, mocking her again. "Why didn't you say anything yesterday at the station?" He stood with his back against the door, arms crossed.

"Pardon?"

"You know what I mean. You'd have thought you didn't know me from Adam."

Gemma glared back at him. "Are you saying I do? We spoke once, as far as I remember, and I might as well have been a leper. Now I'm supposed to have claimed you as a long-lost cousin?" She'd come here to give him a break, and he'd immediately put her on the defensive. Angrily, she added, "And you lied to us."

"About what?" He stepped towards her. As Gemma instinctively stepped back, it flashed through her mind that maybe this visit hadn't been such a wise idea after all. But he merely picked up the packet of cigarettes on the table beside the bed and tapped one free.

"You told us you didn't know Annabelle Hammond, and that you didn't speak to her that night," she said as Gordon lit the cigarette with a match. The smell of smoke filled the room, sharp and pungent.

"So?" His offhand delivery might have been more effective if he'd met her eyes. He extinguished the match with a sharp flick of his hand.

She shook her head in exasperation. "We have the video surveillance tapes. I've seen them. Annabelle did stop and speak to you."

With the cigarette dangling from his lips, he stooped and lifted the clarinet from its case. "That doesn't prove anything."

But she'd seen the instant's freeze before he'd masked his reaction with movement. "It proves that you saw her shortly before she died, and that you had a disagreement."

Still holding his instrument, he sat down on the edge of the bed. "It wouldn't be the first time a complete stranger found my playing offensive. Or my looks. Does that make me a suspect?"

"What I saw on that video was not a disagreement between strangers," she replied. "It was an argument between two people who cared enough about each other to be angry. You knew her. Why are you so determined to deny the obvious?"

Taking a last drag on the cigarette, he crushed it out in a small black and white Wedgwood ashtray. With his gaze on the clarinet, he pressed the keys without lifting it to his lips. She waited in silence, and at last his fingers stilled. He looked up at her. "Because whatever there was between Annabelle and me is no one else's business."

"It is now. This is a murder investigation."

"I had nothing to do with her death. And what was between us had nothing to do with her death."

"Then doesn't it matter to you how she died?" Gemma demanded. "Someone killed Annabelle Hammond, and it's my guess it was someone she knew and trusted."

"Why? What makes you say that? Surely it was some . . . You said she was found in the park. . . . How was she . . ."

Although in her brief experience Gordon Finch had been sparing with words, it was the first time Gemma had seen him at a loss for them. "We're not releasing the cause of death just yet, but I will tell you that there was little sign of a struggle, and that she does not appear to have been sexually assaulted." She hesitated, then added, "And her body seemed to have been rather carefully . . . arranged."

"Arranged?" He stared at her. "Arranged how?"

She didn't know if the details would haunt him more than the images conjured up by his imagination, but she knew she'd said too much already and would have to answer to Kincaid for going over the mark. Temporizing, she said, "As if her dignity mattered. She looked very . . . serene."

"Annabelle, serene? That's an oxymoron." He stood again, lighting another cigarette.

"Why? What was she like, then?"

Frowning, he inhaled until the tip of the cigarette glowed orange-red. "She was . . . intense. Alive. More so than anyone I'd ever met." He shook his head. "That sounds absolute rubbish."

"No. Go on."

He shifted restlessly. "That's it. That's all I can tell you."

"But—"

"You don't understand. I knew how she *was* with me, but nothing else. Nothing." Going to the window, he pulled aside the lace panel and looked out. The sounds of the heavy equipment from the construction at the Mudchute DLR Station came clearly on the breeze.

When he didn't continue, she said, "Were you . . ."

"Lovers?" The word carried an undertone of amusement. "Past tense. I broke things off with her months ago."

"*You* broke it off with *her*?"

He spun round and took a step towards her. "Is that so hard to believe? Do you think I hadn't any pride? I'd had enough of games."

"What sort of games?"

"She came to listen to me play, just like you. And one night she came home with me."

Gemma felt the flush creeping up her chest and throat. Is that what he'd thought the evening she'd stopped and spoken to him about his dog? She wondered if he'd been more encouraging with Annabelle—not that she'd had Annabelle's motives, of course. . . . Or if perhaps Annabelle had liked the challenge.

"I should think you'd have been flattered," she said, aiming at nonchalance as she perched herself gingerly on the arm of the old chair near the bed.

Its fabric was worn, but he'd covered it neatly with a woven purple rug, and for an instant she imagined Annabelle sitting there, framed by the contours of the chair, her hair glowing against the purple backdrop. Gemma smoothed the rug with her fingers, feeling as though she were infringing upon a ghost.

"Flattered?" With a derisive snort, he added, "By the attention of a woman who didn't tell me her name for weeks? Who made it a point not to tell me where she lived or what she did?" He flicked ash from his cigarette end with a sharp tap of his fingertip.

"But you found out?"

"Only by accident. I'd just got off the train at Island Gardens one day. I looked down from the platform and saw her coming out of the Ferry Street flat. And once I knew her name, it didn't take too long to make the connection with Hammond's Teas."

"You must have wondered why she was so secretive—what she was hiding."

"The arrangement suited me well enough."

"Did it?" Gemma shook her head. "I wouldn't think the hole-and-corner bit suited you at all. Or that you'd like being treated as if she was ashamed of you."

"All right," he said sharply, and she knew her remark had stung. "I didn't like it. But she said she was engaged to someone in the company, and there were reasons she couldn't break it off."

"What sort of reasons?"

"She wouldn't say. I told you, she didn't talk to me about herself. She only said that much because—" He stopped, scowling, and ground out his cigarette in the ashtray next to the first.

"Because you threatened to call it off," Gemma finished for him. "Is that it?" When he didn't answer, she said, "Is that what ended things between you?"

"No. I just . . . got tired of her, that's all." He jammed his hands in his pockets and stared out the window.

"When did you learn about your father's connection with Annabelle?" asked Gemma, trying a different tack.

"I didn't know there was a connection—and I doubt you do, either. You're fishing, Sergeant."

"We have a witness who saw them together as far back as last autumn. And your father left a message on her answering machine the night she died."

"So?" Gordon challenged, but she thought his face had paled.

"When did you first see Annabelle?"

He lit another cigarette. "I don't remember."

"You said she came to listen to you play. You must remember what time of year it was," Gemma insisted.

"Summer, then. It was hot."

"And when did you break things off with her?"

"A few months ago. I suppose it was early in the spring."

Was that why he'd been so taciturn when she'd seen him in Islington? wondered Gemma. The timing fit. "And you'd not seen her again until Friday night?"

"Seeing and speaking are two different things. I'd seen her around— the Island's a small place—but I hadn't spoken to her."

A current of air lifted a sheet of music from the stand and sent it drifting lazily towards Gemma. Bending to catch it, she turned it right side up. "It *is* Mozart you were playing. I thought it must be."

Gordon looked surprised. "You were listening?"

"I couldn't help hearing. And I remember you playing it before."

"In Islington." He squinted against the smoke rising from his cigarette as he studied her. "You like music, then? Do you play?"

She heard the quickening of interest in his voice, free for the first time of mockery or caution. "No, I . . ." She hesitated, unwilling to part with her secret. But this was the first chance she'd seen of breaking through his defenses. Shaking her head, she left the chair and wandered over to the kitchen table. She turned to face him again, her handbag clutched against her midriff like a shield. Perhaps he wouldn't think her daft. "No. I don't play. But I . . . I want to learn the piano. I've started lessons."

He ground out his cigarette and came across to her, pulling one of the kitchen chairs away from the table until he could flip it round and straddle it. "Why?"

Gemma laughed. "You sound like my teacher. Why does everyone want to know *why*? I'm not silly enough to think I'm going to become a great pianist, if that's what you think. It's just that music makes me feel . . ."

"Go on."

"I don't know. Connected with myself, somehow." She smiled, as if making light of it would protect her from ridicule, but he merely nodded as if it made perfect sense. "What about you?" she asked. "You're good—I know that much. Why do you do this?" Her gesture took in the small flat, the clarinet, the signs of a meager existence.

"I like my life."

"But you could play in an orchestra, a band—"

"Oh, right. Sit in a monkey suit in a concert hall, or play in some poncey restaurant where no one listens to you?"

"But surely the money would be—"

"I make enough as it is. And nobody tells me when to go to work, or when to go home. Nobody owns me. I could pack up tomorrow and go anywhere, free as a bird."

Gemma stared at him. She was close enough to notice that his eyes were a clear, pure gray. "Then why don't you?"

The question hung in the silence between them. After a moment, she said, "That freedom is an illusion, isn't it? We all have ties, obligations. Even you, as much as you try to deny it. Is that why you broke things off with Annabelle? You were afraid she'd get too close?"

"No, I—"

"She wanted something from you, in the tunnel. What was it?"

He gave a mirthless laugh. "Good question. I asked her that often enough."

As if unsettled by the tension in their voices, Sam raised his head and whined. Gordon knelt beside him, putting a comforting hand on the dog's head.

Gemma moved a step closer. "What did she ask you that night?"

"To reconsider. She wanted me to . . . to go back to the way things were."

"And you refused her?"

He continued stroking the dog.

"Did you change your mind, go after her?"

"Do you think I killed her?"

Gemma hesitated, thinking of the shock she'd sensed when they told him of Annabelle's death. "No," she said slowly. "No, I don't. But that's my personal opinion, not a professional clean bill of health. And if I'm wrong about you, my head's on the block."

Standing up, Gordon faced her. "Why did you come here on your own? On the strength of that video, you could've had me hauled in to the station."

Gemma touched the pages on the music stand with the tip of her finger. "I don't know," she answered. "I felt she meant something to you, in spite of what you said."

Gordon hesitated, then said, "For what it's worth, I regretted turning her away so . . . abruptly. She'd never asked for anything before . . . or given me reason to think I was more to her than a bit of rebellion on the side." He shook his head. "But it was so unexpected . . . and it wasn't until afterwards I realized she'd been crying."

"Do you know why?"

"I came straight back to the flat—I suppose I thought she might come here." He looked away, and the muscle in his jaw flexed. "But she didn't. I never had a chance to ask her."

KINCAID SAT AT A TABLE NEAR the door in the pub just down the street from Hammond's; Gemma had agreed to meet him for lunch.

Smoke filled the air in spite of the open doors, VH1 blared from two televisions mounted near the ceiling, and the menu offered prepackaged pub food.

Frowning, he sipped at his pint, wondering if he and Gemma had miscommunicated about the time or place. Her tardiness had not improved his temper, already frayed by an interview with his guv'nor. Chief Superintendent Childs had expressed himself as not at all happy with their progress on the case, notwithstanding Kincaid's reminder that it had only been two days and they'd had very little to go on.

He'd just about made up his mind to place his order, hoping a meal would improve his perspective, when he spotted Gemma standing in the doorway. She saw him and smiled, then threaded her way through the tables to him.

"Guv." She looked flushed from the sun, and a damp tendril of hair clung to her cheek.

"What'll you have?" he asked as she sat down.

"Mmmm . . . a lemonade would be nice. Something with a bit of ice."

"Shall I order the food as well? Fish and chips?"

"Make it two, then," she said, fanning herself with the menu.

When he returned with her drink, he said, "Did you get Toby settled? How is he?"

"I just rang Hazel from the car. She says he's fine now, just a bit of the sniffles." Gemma drained half her glass, then sat back, looking much restored. Touching his arm, she said, "Duncan, about Kit . . . Hazel said you told him—"

He shook his head. After a night spent tossing and turning, just the thought of talking about it made him feel drained. "It's a proper cock-up. I wasn't naive enough to expect to be welcomed with open arms. But I hadn't thought he'd take it so hard." He shrugged, making light of it. He couldn't tell her the worst part.

"He's been through such a lot, poor little beggar. I don't imagine he knows what he feels. What are you going to do now?"

The barmaid arrived at the table and plopped loaded plates down in front of them, followed by serviette-wrapped cutlery and plastic packets of tartar sauce. Without a word, she went back to her tête-à-tête over the bar with a shirtless young man sporting a large and very well-endowed, naked lady tattooed on his arm.

Kincaid poked at his fish with the tip of his fork. "Give him more time, I suppose. Try to behave as ordinarily as possible. And have a talk with Laura Miller—see how she feels about having him through some of the summer hols."

"Why didn't you wait last night?" Gemma speared a chip. "We missed you by minutes."

"I'm sorry. I suddenly realized that I was too knackered to think."

Gemma gave him a swift glance but didn't pursue it. "Tell me about Annabelle's solicitor."

"A very high-powered lady with an office in Canary Wharf. But she was persuaded to give me the time of day," he answered, feeling relieved. "It seems Annabelle hadn't much to leave in the way of material things." Downing the last of his pint of Tetley's, he thought for a moment of ordering another, but decided it would only make him groggy in the heat. "Her flat was mortgaged, and bought recently, so there's very little equity. Her car was leased. Some debts, but nothing out of the ordinary."

"No assets at all, then?"

"I didn't quite say that. She had her shares in the company, and she left those to Harry and Sarah Lowell. She designated their father, Martin Lowell, as trustee."

Gemma looked up in surprise. "Not her sister?"

"The solicitor says that since Jo's divorce, Annabelle had discussed making a change, but hadn't actually done anything about it."

"Could Lowell benefit directly from the share income?"

"I imagine that would depend on how tightly the trust is structured. The question is, did Lowell know about the bequest?"

"Annabelle's death could have been convenient for him, in that case," said Gemma. Finishing her lemonade, she added, "But we've not had the impression so far that Hammond's Teas was a financial gold mine."

"Annabelle seemed to live comfortably on her income, but I'd assume she was also paid a salary."

Gemma pushed her plate aside. "I'd like to know if Jo Lowell was aware of the bequest."

"Then I suggest we ask her before we interview Martin Lowell. Shall we walk?" he asked, rising.

"I suppose it's quicker," said Gemma, but he thought she sounded less than enthusiastic.

As they left the pub and started down Saunders Ness towards the tunnel, she told him about Janice's interview with George Brent, and the appointment Janice had made for them with Lewis Finch that afternoon.

"I'm impressed with the inspector's initiative. So there *is* a connection between Annabelle and Lewis Finch."

"*And* between Annabelle and Gordon Finch. Janice found the video footage."

"You've seen it?"

"And I've spoken to him. It's clear from the video that she wanted something from him, and that he refused her. He says he had broken off their relationship, and that she wanted to mend things between them."

"Then why did he lie?" They'd reached the tunnel entrance, and as they waited for the lift, Kincaid glanced at her. "You had him brought in?"

"I went round to his flat. I thought he might be more cooperative." Kincaid frowned. "On your own?"

"That was the idea—a bit less police presence," she said defensively. "He's not the sort who responds well to authority."

"Gemma, for Christ's sake—the man could very well have murdered Annabelle Hammond. What were you playing at?"

"What was he going to do—bump me off in his flat in broad daylight, after I'd left word at the station where I'd be?" Gemma's sarcasm echoed the mulish set of her jaw. "That would be daft, and I don't think we're dealing with a lunatic. And besides"—she shot him a defiant glance—"I'm still here, aren't I?"

"That's beside the point. Just don't do it again—you might not be so lucky next time. Not to mention the fact that you've played hell with protocol."

"As if you never do," she muttered.

"Dammit, Gemma, I'm—" He stopped himself. Arguing would only make her more stubborn, he knew, and there was no point turning this into a full-blown row. He'd done enough damage losing his temper the last few days.

The lift doors opened, and as they waited for the disembarking passengers to exit, Kincaid saw that the lift was unusually large and had a uniformed operator. Once inside, he discovered the high-tech counterpart to this rather old-fashioned courtesy: a security camera and monitor, mounted near the ceiling.

They took up positions against the bench in the back as the other passengers crowded in. "If he admitted a relationship with her, I suppose your strategy worked," he said quietly.

She gave him a wary glance as they continued their descent, as if assessing his change of tone. The camera view shifted from the tunnel to the interior of the lift, and for a moment he saw himself with Gemma beside him. Then the lift sighed to a stop and the doors slid open, disgorging them into the white-tailed dampness of the tunnel.

As they started down the gentle incline, he saw that the condensation from the curving walls had collected into rivulets on the sloping concrete floor. The sounds of voices and footsteps ricocheted eerily round them; from somewhere he heard music. "What exactly did the video show?" he asked. "Did Finch leave with her?"

"It seems Reg Mortimer *was* telling the truth, at least to a point, about what happened here." Gemma moved closer to Kincaid, allowing a cyclist walking his bike to pass. *Bicycles Strictly Prohibited* signs had been plainly posted at the tunnel entrance. "Annabelle stopped and spoke to Gordon Finch, and Mortimer was nowhere to be seen. She seemed to be arguing with Finch, but he didn't respond. Then she walked away, and a few minutes later he packed up and left."

"Did he meet her afterwards?"

"He says he went straight home. I've asked Janice to send someone round this evening to check with his landlady."

Glancing at Gemma, he thought she looked pale, but he didn't know if it was due to the cold light reflecting from the white tiles or the thought of the weight of the river above them.

They walked in silence as they neared the flat stretch of the tunnel, and the echoing music resolved itself into a very bad vocal rendition of "Bad Moon Rising," accompanied by abysmally played guitar. Wincing, Kincaid commented, "I should think people would pay this bloke *not* to play. If Gordon Finch is anywhere near this untalented, Annabelle might have been trying to persuade him to give it up."

"He's—" Gemma stopped, giving him a look he couldn't read. Ducking her head, she fished in her handbag and tossed a fifty-pee piece into the busker's case as they passed. "I'm sure that wasn't the case."

"Did Finch admit to knowing about Annabelle and his father?"

"He says he'd no idea. And we can't be sure she was having an affair with Lewis Finch, just because she was seen with him."

"Right," Kincaid said sarcastically, a little amused at Gemma's determination to think the best of Annabelle Hammond.

They were climbing now, nearing the Greenwich end of the tunnel, and Gemma's pace had increased enough that Kincaid had to lengthen his stride to keep up with her. The music had faded until it came to them in intermittent, if still discordant, waves.

The tunnel's end came into view, with clearly visible daylight filtering down the stairwell beside the lift. Gemma bypassed the lift doors. "Let's take the stairs. I don't think I can bear being closed up another minute."

"Reg Mortimer and Annabelle would have come this way that evening. The lifts close at seven," Kincaid said. Then he added, with a glance at the spiraling steps above them, "But I daresay going down is easier than going up."

"Reg says they left the dinner party because Annabelle wasn't feeling well; Jo says they had a row; Teresa Robbins and Annabelle's father say they never fought about anything. So who's telling the truth?" Gemma mused as they climbed.

"I'd say Jo, as far as it goes—but I don't think she's told the whole truth. We'll need to talk to Mortimer again, but perhaps Jo can give us a bit more ammunition."

Emerging a few minutes later, a bit breathless, into sunlight and warmth that felt welcome for a change, they saw before them the tall masts of the *Cutty Sark*. They detoured round its bow to reach King William's Walk, then made their way through the center of Greenwich. Small and somewhat tatty shops nestled beside flower-bedecked pubs, and many businesses bore *Save Greenwich* placards on their windows.

"Save Greenwich from what?" asked Gemma as they passed a particularly inviting pub called The Cricketers.

"Developers, I imagine. With the underground extension going in, this will be a prime area for commuter flats." It would be a shame, he thought as they left the town center behind and began climbing up through the terraced streets, for Greenwich to fall to bulldozers now when it had escaped much of the devastation suffered by the Isle of Dogs during the war.

By the time they reached Emerald Crescent, he could feel a film of sweat beneath his shirt. The lane seemed even sleepier on a Monday afternoon than it had on a Saturday evening, but a knock at Jo Lowell's door brought a quick response.

Harry Lowell stared at them, eyes wide in his thin face. It was clear he knew them now as the bearers of bad news.

"It's all right, Harry," Kincaid told the boy gently. "We just want a word with your mum."

"She's in the shed. I'll take you." Harry turned and they followed him through the silent house. "Sarah's having a nap after lunch," Harry explained as they crossed the back garden, "and Mummy tries to work when Sarah's sleeping because she's such a little pest." When they reached the small blue shed, he put his head round the door and said, "Mummy, it's the police."

Jo Lowell came to the door, wiping her hands on a cloth that smelled of spirits. "What—"

"We'd just like to ask you a few questions, Mrs. Lowell," Kincaid said. She looked exhausted and untidy, as though she'd hardly slept or looked in a mirror since Saturday. A tank top exposed freckled shoulders pink with sunburn, and her dark hair was pulled carelessly back into a ponytail.

"I'm sorry." Jo glanced apologetically at her hands. "I was just trying out a new glaze. We can go in the house—"

"This is fine, really," he reassured her. "It won't take a minute."

"All right, then, but there's not much room." She stepped back and they followed her into the shed. The single room was clearly a retreat, and he understood her reluctance to allow their intrusion.

The worktable held a tin pail of garden roses and daisies as well as cans of decorating emulsion and brushes. Squares of board showed translucent yellow paint in various stages of crackling as it dried. On the back wall, shelves held an assortment of gardening and design books as well as bits of old pottery and dried herbs. A friendly-looking gargoyle regarded them from atop the iron frame of a mirror.

Jo gestured towards the single rush-seated chair and a small stepladder, then turned over an empty pail as a seat for herself. "Have you found something?" she asked.

Kincaid took the ladder for himself, offering Gemma the chair. "Mrs. Lowell, were you aware that your sister left her interest in Hammond's to your children?"

She stared at them blankly. "Her shares? To Harry and Sarah? But . . . She never said." Her dark eyes filled with tears and she wiped at them with the back of her hand.

"She designated their father as trustee," Kincaid continued, watching her.

"Martin?" Jo's face lost what little color it had, and for a moment she seemed too shocked to speak. Then, swallowing, she said, "Surely not . . . There must have been some sort of mistake. . . ."

A bumblebee blundered in through the open window and buried itself in the petals of a rose. The scent from the flowers was almost strong enough to mask the paint. Kincaid stifled an urge to sneeze and said, "Annabelle's solicitor said the arrangement was made several years ago, and that Annabelle had recently discussed changing it when your divorce was finalized, designating you as trustee. But she never got round to it."

"But this is dreadful. You don't know . . . Martin can be so . . . unreasonable. And this will give him a substantial voting block. How could Annabelle have done such a silly thing?"

"She didn't know there was any hurry to change it," Gemma said. "And perhaps Martin wasn't so difficult when she made the original bequest?"

"No. No, he wasn't. But that seems a very long time ago."

Gemma opened the notebook she'd taken from her handbag. "How exactly are the shares dispersed, Mrs. Lowell?"

"My father, Sir Peter Mortimer, and I own the majority—along with Martin, now. My mother bequeathed her shares equally to Annabelle and me upon her death. It's my income from the firm that's allowed me to start my own business, and to work from home. If Martin buggers it up . . ."

"We'll need to have a word with him, Mrs. Lowell. The solicitor gave us his home address but not his work. If you could tell us where we might find him?"

"Is that really necessary?" A look at their faces seemed to answer her question, and she went on reluctantly. "He manages the bank just as you come into the town center. You can't miss it." She stood. "Look, if that's all—"

"Just a few more questions, if you don't mind, Mrs. Lowell." As Jo subsided onto her makeshift seat again, Kincaid added, "You said your sister and Reg Mortimer had a row at your dinner party? Can you tell us exactly what happened?"

"I . . . I was washing up a bit before the pudding. Annabelle had been helping clear the table. Then she came in and said she wasn't feeling well, that she'd made her excuses to the other guests and Reg was waiting for her in the lane. She left through the garden."

"But you didn't believe she was ill?"

"It was so awkward, and so sudden. And Reg didn't even tell me good night." Jo managed a smile. "I've seldom seen his manners fail him."

"You didn't think it odd that your sister didn't tell you what was wrong?" asked Gemma.

Jo hesitated a moment. "Annabelle didn't always confide in me. Even when we were children. Still, I thought she'd ring the next day. . . ."

"But you were close, weren't you?" Gemma pressed. "I could tell from the photographs she kept that she was a very devoted aunt— much better than I am with *my* sister's kids—or at least she was when Harry was small."

"Annabelle loved the children. She'd have liked babies of her own, I think, but the company always came first."

"Was Annabelle partial to Harry?" Gemma remembered the discrepancy in the number of photos of the children.

"Oh, no, I wouldn't say 'partial.' " Jo pleated the hem of her khaki shorts between her fingers. "It's just that once she became managing director, she hadn't as much time for them. Harry took it rather hard.

He's very—" She paused, head cocked as she listened. "I think I hear Sarah. I'd better—"

"Just one more—" Marveling at the acuity of maternal ears, Kincaid stopped as Sarah's plaintive voice came through the open window. He hadn't heard a thing until now. "Just one more question, Mrs. Lowell. Do you know a man called Gordon Finch?"

"Finch?" Jo repeated, clearly distracted by her daughter's calls for her. "Not Lewis Finch?"

"What do you know about Lewis Finch?"

"Only that he and Father don't get on. It's not at all like Father, really."

"Do you know the cause of the friction?" Kincaid asked.

"I remember Mummy saying she thought it had something to do with the time Father spent in Surrey during the war."

"Your father was evacuated?"

"His mother was sure Greenwich would be bombed—they lived just next door. Father still does." She gestured towards the uphill side of the lane. "So his parents sent him to his godmother's. She was extremely eccentric—you know, the sort of woman who wore trousers when women didn't wear trousers." Jo smiled. "Father adored her. He often talked about her when we were children. Annabelle always loved hearing stories about the family."

"Did Annabelle know that your father disapproved of Lewis Finch?"

"Oh, yes. He never made a secret of it. Is Gordon Finch some relation to Lewis?"

"His son. And it seems as though your sister was well-acquainted with them both. Gordon Finch was the busker she spoke to in the tunnel that night."

"Lewis Finch's son—a busker?" Jo frowned. "How odd."

"You don't think it odd that Annabelle defied your father's wishes about the Finches?" asked Gemma.

Jo shook her head. "Not if you knew my sister. Annabelle was almost as obsessive about the family and the business as Father, but she had a perverse streak. She loved to meddle in things."

CHAPTER 9

*For the lonely cowherd of
medieval times, when the Isle of
Dogs was a desolate, windswept
marsh, as much as for the
youngsters who lived in the
crowded streets of the
industrialized Island, the river
has provided over the centuries a
moving, colourful pageant of
ships and boats, and a link with
the life of the great oceans and
the wide world beyond the
estuary.*

Eve Hostettler, from
Memories of Childhood

"ANNABELLE CAN'T HAVE LEFT VOT-
ing shares to Martin Lowell." Reg
Mortimer stared at Teresa as if she
had suddenly lost her mind.

She stood in the doorway of his
office, a sheet of scribbled notes in
her hand. The phone call from the
solicitor had come just after lunch,
but Teresa had sat for a while after
hanging up, trying to absorb the
news. "The solicitor wouldn't mistake something like that, Reg. And
she didn't exactly leave the shares to
him—he's just the trustee for the
children."

"Harry Lowell is ten years old, for

[153]

God's sake." Reg pushed his chair back until it banged against the file cabinet. "Lowell can do anything he wants until Harry reaches his majority, and by that time Hammond's may have gone to the wolves."

Teresa closed the door. "You're overreacting, Reg, surely. Why wouldn't Lowell want the company to do well, for his children's sake?"

Reg pulled at the knot of his tie as if it were choking him. "You don't know what he's like. Or how he felt about—" He shook his head.

"About what, Reg?"

"Nothing. He's a bastard, that's all." Patches of damp had begun to appear on his starched blue shirt. He'd come in that morning shaved and dressed with his usual smartness, but as the day wore on the atmosphere in the warehouse had seemed to exact a physical toll on him, as it had on everyone.

Teresa had arrived early, taking it on herself to inform the sales and production staffs of Annabelle's death. She had somehow got through it without breaking down, and they had all made a stunned attempt at business-as-usual. It was when she'd shut herself in the large office she'd shared with Annabelle that her composure had dissolved completely. She had wept again, but now that she'd got it over with she felt a bit more able to cope.

"Martin may not even vote the shares," she said now, attempting to calm Reg. "He knows nothing about the business, after all."

"He's a banker, for God's sake—he understands finance. And he'll realize he has the power to affect any decision the board makes." Reg grasped the front of his desk as if for support.

"He'd have to influence one of the other major shareholders to swing a vote. Annabelle said he and Jo weren't on good terms, and I can't see your father or William—"

"You know what we have to do. And we might be able to pull it off, unless bloody Martin Lowell interferes."

"You can't mean to approach your father now, with Annabelle—" Teresa swallowed hard.

"I don't see that we have much choice." Reg stood, still grasping the desk, looking up at her through the fringe of hair that had fallen over his brow.

Watching him, Teresa tried to recall the comfort she'd felt yesterday in his arms. But now he seemed to be disintegrating before her eyes, and for the first time she felt a little frightened. "Just wait a bit. Everything will be fine," she added, trying to reassure herself as much as him.

"Will it?" He pushed his hair back with a visibly shaking hand and came round the desk. "I wish I had your confidence, Teresa." Lifting his jacket from the hook on the back of the door, he stood, his face inches from hers. A fine tracery of red veins showed in the whites of his eyes. "Annabelle didn't deserve you," he said softly. "And neither do I." Then a draft of cooler air touched Teresa's cheek as the door swung shut behind him.

She went out to the catwalk and stood, staring down into the warehouse long after he had disappeared through the front door. When Superintendent Kincaid rang a few minutes later, she had to tell him she had no idea where Reg Mortimer might be.

STANDING IN THE LANE OUTSIDE JO Lowell's house, Gemma gave Kincaid a questioning look as he retracted the antenna on his mobile phone.

"No joy," he reported. "Mortimer is temporarily away from the office. We'll keep trying."

Gemma glanced at her watch. "We have some time before our appointment with Lewis Finch. I think we should have a word with William Hammond while we're here." She nodded towards the house nestled into the side of the hill above them, its pale aqua door just visible through the trees. "I'd like to see what he has to say about the Finches, and about Martin Lowell's unexpected inheritance."

"Aren't we going at this roundabout? We haven't talked to Lowell yet."

"We'll pass right by the bank on our way back through Greenwich."

"All right. Let's pay Mr. Hammond a call, then." Kincaid led the way as they crossed the lane and climbed the steps set into the hillside.

It was cooler under the trees, and the filtered light illuminated patches of multicolored impatiens among the vines. "Someone likes to garden," said Gemma. "Or liked to," she amended as they neared the top. "It's a bit wild now."

On closer inspection, the aqua door also showed faint signs of neglect, its paint chipped and peeling near the bottom. Gemma rang the bell, and as they waited she listened to the birdsong coming from the surrounding trees.

William Hammond answered the door. He wore red braces over a white shirt and suit trousers, and on his feet only stockings. For a moment he stared at them without recognition, and then said, "I'm sorry," adding, with a gesture at his attire, "you've caught me resting. I'm afraid I've not been sleeping particularly well." He ran his long fingers through his hair in an attempt to arrange it. "Have you any new information?"

"I'm sorry, no," Kincaid answered. "But there are a few questions we'd like to ask you. It won't take long."

"Please, come in," said Hammond so hospitably that Gemma had the feeling he didn't find their presence all that objectionable. Perhaps any company was better than time spent with his own thoughts, she reflected.

In the sitting room, dark green velvet drapes had been pulled wide to admit the smallest breeze. Gemma caught the faint scent of dust, and of something it took her a moment to recognize as glue. A pair of men's dress shoes sat neatly beside the sofa, and the cushion at one end bore the imprint of a head.

As she sat on the chintz-covered chair Hammond indicated, a glimpse into the adjoining room made Gemma catch her breath. "Oh, how lovely," she said, rising and going to the doorway for a better look. A model ship stood on a dining table, its slender masts a delicate sculpture, its hull gleaming like satin. "Is it the *Cutty Sark*?"

Hammond smiled. "No, this is the *Sir Lancelot*. She made the China-to-London crossing in a record eighty-eight days."

"She's exquisite," Kincaid said, joining them. "I remember attempting something from a kit when I was a boy, but this—" He touched the curving hull. "This is a work of art." Looking round the room at the other ships gracing the shelves, he asked, "How do you model them? I understood that the *Cutty Sark* was the only clipper of its class left in existence."

"It takes a good deal of research," Hammond admitted. "I use written accounts as well as paintings, sometimes with a dash of artistic license thrown in."

"It must take amazing patience." Gemma imagined the hours needed to complete the painstaking detail. She thought of her own aborted attempts at simple hobbies like knitting and needlework, and wondered again at her foolish determination to play the piano.

"What began as a childhood interest has become a bit of an obsession the past few years, I'm afraid. But since my wife died it's helped fill the hours, and now . . ." William Hammond gazed at the model, lost for a moment in a private contemplation, then he seemed to shake himself and return to them. "I'm sorry. And I've forgotten my manners. Let me get you something to drink—some tea, perhaps?"

Merely the thought of a hot drink made beads of perspiration appear on Gemma's upper lip. "No thank you," she said quickly. "This won't take a moment." At a small nod from Kincaid, she continued, "It's about your childhood, oddly enough, Mr. Hammond. We understand from your daughter that you were evacuated during the war."

They had returned to the sitting room, and Hammond sat down slowly on the sofa, his expression puzzled. "Yes, that's true, but why on earth should you be interested in that?"

"You were sent to your godmother's, in Surrey?"

"Just northeast of Guildford. A place called Friday Green. My godmother had a large estate there. But what—"

"I know the village," Kincaid said, smiling. "There's a nice pub—probably goes back that far. It's a lovely area. Paradise for a boy, I should think. Did you spend the whole of the war?"

"I . . . yes, I did, as a matter of fact. My mother was convinced we would be bombed here. As it turned out, we were very fortunate, and Hammond's suffered only minor damage."

"And it was during your evacuation that you came to know Lewis Finch?"

"Lewis Finch?" Hammond stared at Gemma blankly.

"I understand he's quite a prominent developer in the East End these days, known for his commitment to restoration."

"I—it's been a great many years but, yes, he was a fellow evacuee." He shook his head. "But what has this to do with my daughter's death?"

"Bear with me a moment, Mr. Hammond. According to Jo, you warned her and Annabelle not to have anything to do with Lewis Finch or his family."

"That's nonsense," he replied impatiently. "We simply don't move in the same social circles."

"Jo seemed to feel there was some sort of feud between you, and that it had to do with the war," pressed Gemma.

"A feud?" Hammond sounded surprised. "I can't imagine where Jo could have got such a melodramatic idea." With a slight frown, he added, "I might have said that I felt Lewis took advantage of his stay in my godmother's house to better himself, without giving credit where it was due, but I would certainly not consider that a feud."

"And you don't know Lewis Finch's son, Gordon?"

"His son? Why should I?" He seemed even more perplexed, and Gemma could see that he was tiring.

Wondering how much she should reveal, she glanced at Kincaid, but he merely gave her a minute shrug. Turning back to Hammond, she said carefully, "Sir, Annabelle seems to have been well-acquainted with both Lewis and Gordon Finch. In fact, she had been having an affair with Gordon for some months—and he may have been the last person to see her alive."

William Hammond stared at her, then drew himself up in his chair until his spine was ramrod straight. "There must be some mistake," he said crisply. "Annabelle would never have associated with Lewis Finch or his son. Nor would she have betrayed Reginald's trust." He turned to Kincaid. "I find it distressing, Superintendent, that you are wasting valuable time pursuing such lines of inquiry while my daughter's killer goes free."

As THE AUTUMN WORE ON, THE *threat of bombings receded, and very little disturbed the golden, waning days in the countryside.*

The war seemed very far away in Europe, and Lewis soon grew comfortably familiar with the household, for although he kept his room above the stable, Edwina gave him free run of the house. He and William both bathed in the large second-floor bathroom, and when Edwina did not have guests from London, the boys ate with her in the dining room.

Lewis still suffered the occasional pang of homesickness, but a Green coach was organized to bring the evacuees' parents down to visit every few weeks. In the meantime, there were apples to be picked, jams and pies to be

made, woods and quarries and the old Roman forts on the Downs to be ex-
plored, and most exciting of all, preparations for Guy Fawkes, for their
village had the biggest bonfire in the county.

Lewis did not see William Hammond at school, however, because while
the children from the Island had been integrated as well as possible into the
village school, William's parents had arranged a tutor to live at the Hall.
This privilege Lewis did not envy in the least.

On a bright Saturday morning in late October, William appeared in the
barn as Lewis was finishing up with the horses. He wore a heavy, cable-
knit cardigan and shorts with multiple pockets and carried a rucksack,
plus a large, carved staff.

Peering round Zeus's head, Lewis (who had long since lost his shyness
with William) snickered. "What is that getup?"

"It's proper walking gear," answered William. "My mum and dad sent
it for my birthday. I'm going to climb Leith Hill. They say from the Tower
you can see thirteen counties."

"You look like you mean to climb bloody Everest," said Lewis, but he
was intrigued nonetheless.

"You can come if you want," William offered in an offhand manner,
then sweetened the invitation with a bribe. "I've got sandwiches from
Cook. Ham and cheese."

Lewis finished spreading fresh straw into Zeus's stall and hung the fork
from its bracket on the stable wall. "I haven't any gear like that."

"Doesn't matter. You can use this stick if you want. I'll get another from
the gun room."

Brushing his palm against his trousers, Lewis accepted the stick, and
hefting it in his hand, he suddenly saw himself striding over tall peaks.
"All right, then, I'll come."

They were soon ambling down the road towards the village, sandwiches
and thermos of tea secured in William's rucksack. From one of the large
pockets in his shorts, William extricated a folded paper. "It's Aunt
Edwina's Ordnance Survey map," he said as he smoothed out the creases.
"Look. We can go by way of Coldharbour and come back through Holm-
bury, or vice versa. The climb is steeper the Holmbury way."

Lewis studied the map, not liking to admit he'd never seen one before
and didn't understand the markings. "Coldharbour, I'd say. I want to see
the Danes' Fort." He'd heard about the old earthworks from some of the

boys at school. "There were smugglers round these parts, too," *he added, glancing at William to judge the effect of this tidbit.*

"I never heard that," *William said with some skepticism.*

"Even John says so." *Lewis knew that would settle the matter, for they'd discovered that John Pebbles had an intimate and apparently infallible knowledge of the area. They walked on, pointing out spots they thought would have made good smugglers' hides.*

They followed the course of the Tillingbourne for some way, then began a steady ascent that took them into a dark and dense woodland. Lewis, who had not quite got over his claustrophobia under trees, began to fear they were lost, but would've died rather than said so.

As if reassuring himself, William said, "I'm sure this is the right way. I can read the map, and Aunt Edwina said it would seem a long way through the woods." *He moved a bit closer to Lewis on the soft, leaf-covered path.*

Suddenly, with a rustle and a crackling of brush, a deer erupted across the trail a foot in front of them. Lewis saw a flash of dark, startled eyes and white rump as he felt himself falling backwards, then he hit the ground, buttocks first, with a thump that knocked the wind from him.

William had staggered into the nearest tree and now hung on for dear life. They gaped at each other, wide-eyed, and started to laugh.

"Crikey, that nearly scared the piss out of me," *said Lewis between gasps as William helped him up. That only made them laugh harder, and they stumbled along, the woods ringing with their whoops, until they had to wipe tears from their eyes.*

As they neared Coldharbour the trees thinned, and they walked in companionable silence broken by the occasional episode of giggles. They spent an hour exploring the banks and ditches of the Iron Age fort, imagining battles that seemed more real to them than the rumors from Europe, and by the time they'd finished the climb to the summit of Leith Hill, they had worked up quite an appetite.

Having voted to eat their picnic before climbing the tower, they settled on a stone bench in the sun, facing the distant haze they surmised must be the Channel. His mouth full of ham and cheese, Lewis pointed into the distance. "If the Germans came, you could see them from here."

"If they come. My dad says they're calling it the Phoney War now." *William glanced at Lewis.* "Do you want to go home?"

Lewis washed down his bite of sandwich with some tea wh..
about his answer. Did he want to go home? A month ago h...
swered "yes" in an instant. Now, he said with a shrug, "I...
really. I miss my mum and dad. Sometimes I even miss my sister. But I like
it here, too." He dug in the paper sack for one of the apples Cook had
packed for them. "What about you? Do you want to go home?"

"Home I wouldn't mind, but I'd have to go back to school," William
answered with a grimace. "You don't know what it's like there," he added,
and glimpsing the expression on William's usually open face, Lewis didn't
pursue it.

"What about Mr. Cuddy?" he asked instead. "What's he like?" The
tutor, a thin, bespectacled man about the age of Lewis's father, had seemed
kind enough when Lewis encountered him.

"He's all right. Only it gets a bit boring being on my own all day, and
the maths are hard. That's old Cuddy's field, and I'm not very good at it."

"Maybe I could help you sometime," Lewis offered tentatively. "I like
maths. That's always my best marks at school. Composition's harder."

"I'm better at that. Maybe I'll write one for Mr. Cuddy about the deer,"
William said, grinning, and that set them to laughing again.

This conversation bore unexpected fruit a few weeks later, when Edwina
called Lewis into her sitting room and informed him that she had
arranged, with the permission of William's parents, for him to be tu-
tored along with William. "I've written to your parents, and they agree
that this is a wonderful opportunity for you. You're obviously a bright
boy, Lewis, and you deserve a better education than the village school can
provide."

"But I like school . . . and what about my mates?" Lewis said hesitantly, not wanting to seem rude.

Edwina lit a cigarette with the silver lighter on the mantelpiece and
the air filled with the sharp smell of tobacco smoke. "Warren Cuddy is
Oxford-educated and a fine teacher. He can open new worlds for you.
Friends come and go, Lewis, but the things you learn will always be yours,
to use as you will. You may not realize it now," she added with a smile,
"but from this day on your life will change in ways you cannot begin to
imagine."

•   •   •

"I'M BEGINNING TO SUSPECT THAT WILLIAM Hammond may have had a convenient blind spot where his daughter was concerned," Kincaid said as they walked down the hill towards Greenwich center in the intensifying heat of early afternoon.

"Surely that's not unusual," countered Gemma. "Most parents want to think the best of their children—especially if it has to do with sex. On the other hand, Jo Lowell certainly didn't seem surprised at the suggestion that her sister had cheated on her fiancé."

"I wonder where Mortimer fell in that spectrum. Did he think Annabelle beyond reproach? If that was the case and he found out about her affair with Gordon Finch, the shock might have driven him to kill her."

"Or if he was suspicious already and suddenly had his fears proved. But that doesn't explain the row at the dinner party—and we only have Jo's word about that—or the fact that he left her in the tunnel with Gordon Finch," argued Gemma. "And the answering machine messages seem to support his story."

They had reached Royal Hill and Gemma paused, looking in the window of a cheese shop. In the glass, Kincaid could see the reflection of the police station across the street. "He could easily have killed her, then left messages to give himself an alibi," he said.

Gemma walked on, swinging her handbag against the skirt of her cotton dress, leaving behind the temptations of white Stilton with ginger and Shropshire blue. "But you could hear the noise of the pub in the background, so it must have been before closing, and the pathologist says Annabelle died after midnight."

"We're not going to get anywhere with this until we see Mortimer again," said Kincaid. "And in the meantime, I'd like to know why Jo Lowell was so reluctant for us to interview her husband."

"Your curiosity is about to be satisfied."

They found the bank as easily as Jo had promised, and the clerk at the window directed them back to Martin Lowell's office.

"Mr. Lowell?" Kincaid tapped on the open door of the small cubicle. "We're from Scotland Yard—Superintendent Kincaid, Sergeant James." He showed his identification. "We'd like to ask you a few questions."

The man at the desk glanced up, a look of irritation marring his handsome face. Dark and clean-cut, he wore the banker's uniform of white shirt and dark tie, but he'd rolled up his sleeves against the heat. "Scotland Yard? How can I help you? I'm afraid I have a meeting in"—he glanced at his watch—"ten minutes, so I hope this won't take long."

"It's about your former sister-in-law, Annabelle Hammond," Kincaid said, adjusting one of the visitors' chairs for Gemma and taking the other himself. Lowell had neither risen nor offered his hand, and now he made no response to Kincaid's remark. "Has the Hammonds' solicitor been in touch with you?"

"Yes, this morning. But I don't see why this should be any concern of yours."

"Really?" Kincaid raised an eyebrow. "A murder and an unexpected disposition of property usually merit some interest, Mr. Lowell."

Martin Lowell smiled for the first time. "Are you suggesting I killed Annabelle for my children's interest in the firm, Superintendent . . . what did you say your name was? You must be quite desperate."

Kincaid had no doubt that Lowell remembered his name. "Your suggestion, Mr. Lowell, not mine." He smiled back. "I was merely wondering if you were aware of Annabelle Hammond's intentions."

"I'd no idea until the solicitor rang me this morning. I was certainly surprised, but I'm curious as to why you seem to think Annabelle's leaving her shares to her only niece and nephew an unusual bequest."

"It was the fact that she designated you as trustee I found odd, since you're no longer married to her sister."

Lowell shrugged. "According to the solicitor, she made the will shortly after her mother's death, and never got round to changing it. And she may have thought me better suited than Jo to look after the children's financial interests."

"Will you take an active role in the firm, Mr. Lowell?" asked Gemma.

Martin Lowell's glance at her was frankly assessing, and Kincaid saw Gemma flush.

"Any other course would be irresponsible, don't you think, Sergeant?" Lowell smiled, holding her gaze until she looked away. Then he stood, with another obvious look at his watch. "Now, if you don't mind . . ."

"Thanks for your time, Mr. Lowell," Kincaid said with mild sarcasm as he rose.

When they reached the street, Kincaid touched Gemma's shoulder. "What was that all about?"

Gemma scowled. "Who gave Martin Lowell license to think he's God's gift to women?"

To GEMMA, HERON QUAYS LOOKED CHEERFULLY informal compared with the classic lines of Canary Wharf just to the north, across the middle section of West India Dock. The complex was low-rise, and its slanting roofs, red and purple siding, and white iron balconies made her think of Swiss chalets gone riot. Janice had told her it was one of the early Docklands projects, and that Lewis Finch had kept an office there since the completion of the first phase in the mid-eighties.

As they walked along the waterside, Kincaid said, "I'm curious about William Hammond and the Finches, since Hammond denies having anything against them. Do you suppose Jo misunderstood what her mother said?"

Gemma shrugged. "Maybe he's just too polite to admit his class prejudices to us."

"Snobbery hardly constitutes a feud, and Jo Lowell doesn't seem the type to take it as such," Kincaid murmured as he opened the door emblazoned with the "Finch, Ltd." logo Gemma had seen on hoardings round the Island.

She breathed a sigh of relief as they entered the air-conditioned outer office. Outside, the sun glaring off the surface of the Dock had seemed to raise the temperature a good ten degrees.

When Kincaid had given their names, the rather harried-looking receptionist had smiled and led them into the left-hand office.

Gemma saw the view first—of the monumental Canada Tower across the Dock framed foursquare by the plate-glass window—then her attention was captured by the man who came towards them, hand outstretched.

She saw the resemblance at once—not so much in physical similarities, although those were evident, as in presence. Lewis Finch had about him the same sort of intensity that had first drawn her to Gordon, but in Lewis it had been translated into power.

"You've just caught me," said Finch, firmly shaking Kincaid's hand, then Gemma's. "Sit down, please. Normally, I'm out on site this time of day, but the officer who phoned said this was urgent?" He was in shirtsleeves, his tie loosened slightly at the collar, but that did nothing to detract from the instant impression of the sort of effortless elegance that came with wealth and success. Whatever advantages this man had been given, thought Gemma, he had put them to superb use.

"What can I do for you, Superintendent?" Finch asked, settling into the chair on the other side of his desk.

"You're aware of the death of Miss Annabelle Hammond?"

"I . . . Yes, I just learned of it this morning—I was away over the weekend. It's a terrible loss," he said, his voice heavy with regret, and Gemma suddenly realized that not once had Martin Lowell expressed any sorrow over his sister-in-law's death.

"You knew Miss Hammond well?" Kincaid asked.

"I'm not sure anyone knew Annabelle *well*, Superintendent. She was a very self-contained person. But we'd been friends for the past year or more. We met at a neighborhood meeting." The recollection made Finch smile.

"And you were . . . involved during the whole of that time?"

Finch studied Kincaid, and for the first time Gemma detected wariness in his manner. "If by that you mean did we have a sexual relationship, the answer is yes—when we both found it convenient. You have to understand that Annabelle was extremely independent."

"Tell us about her," said Gemma. "What was she like?"

When Lewis Finch looked at her, Gemma saw that his eyes were the same clear gray as his son's. "Annabelle had a talent for getting what she wanted—sometimes ruthlessly so—and she had the rare gift of knowing exactly what that was, at least in the professional sense. She was also intelligent, courageous . . . impossibly self-absorbed, and in some ways surprisingly loyal."

"A contradiction?" prompted Gemma.

Finch nodded. "Compellingly so."

"Were you aware that she was engaged to be married?" asked

Kincaid. "I don't know that her relationship with you constitutes a display of loyalty."

Finch frowned. "An odd sort of loyalty, perhaps. But in my experience, most people who stray outside a committed relationship justify their behavior by complaining about the injured partner. Annabelle never did that."

"Mr. Finch," said Gemma carefully, "were you aware that Annabelle also had a relationship with your son?"

Finch stared at her. "With Gordon? No, I was not."

"Annabelle Hammond seems to have been fascinated by your family. Have you any idea why?"

"No. She never said anything to give me that impression."

"And she didn't tell you that she was aware of your connection with her father?"

"What are you talking about, Superintendent?" Finch's voice was level, but Gemma felt the tension even in the room rise.

"Annabelle knew that you and William Hammond had been evacuated together during the war."

Finch blinked. "Yes, that's true. But we've had very little contact since."

"We believe that William Hammond may have warned Annabelle against you, and that she thought it was because of some sort of feud between you. Was there any basis to this?"

"Of course not. And I'm sure that if Annabelle had thought anything of the sort, she'd have spoken to me about it." He thought for a moment. "I did get the impression from Annabelle that William might have been getting a bit . . . odd, since his wife's death. Perhaps he's started to imagine things?"

"He seemed quite competent when we spoke to him. He said you had used those wartime connections to better yourself, and hadn't given credit where it was due."

"Did he?"

"Is that not true?"

For a moment, Gemma thought Lewis wouldn't answer; then he said very quietly, "Edwina Burne-Jones was a kind and generous woman who took a poor boy from the East End and treated him as if he were capable of accomplishing whatever he wished—but any gratitude

I feel towards her is no one else's business. Not William Hammond's, and not yours, Superintendent. Now, is that all?"

"One more question, Mr. Finch. When did you last see Annabelle Hammond?"

"We had dinner together several weeks ago. I can't give you an exact date," he answered, watching Kincaid, and Gemma felt sure he knew what was coming. He was far too intelligent not to guess they'd heard Annabelle's answering machine tape.

Kincaid appeared to deliberate for a moment before he said, "What you've told us seems to imply that your relationship with Annabelle was rather casual. And yet in the messages you left on her answering machine Friday night, you were quite clearly angry. Can you tell me why?"

"You've made an assumption, Superintendent. I never said our relationship was casual, only that it was irregular. Annabelle was sometimes difficult, but she was . . . unique. I've only known one other woman who approached life with such zest, and I—" He shook his head, and Gemma thought she saw a glint of moisture in his gray eyes. "I wasn't angry on Friday night—I was concerned. Annabelle had left a message at my flat that sounded quite unlike her—something about breaking off her engagement. I wanted to know what had happened."

"And did she ring you back?"

"No. I waited until after midnight, but I had a very early start the next morning for a meeting in Gloucestershire."

"Have you anyone who can verify your movements on Friday night, Mr. Finch?"

"I live alone, Superintendent. There's no one." Lewis Finch met Gemma's eyes. "No one at all."

WHEN THEY ARRIVED BACK AT LIMEHOUSE Station, they found Janice Coppin sorting through reports in the incident room, looking as though she'd have liked never to see another piece of paper.

"Any luck with the house-to-house?" Kincaid asked, perching himself on the edge of the desk Janice had commandeered.

"Only in the negative sense," Janice said with a gesture at the paperwork. "No one saw Annabelle Hammond anywhere that night. If she came home again her neighbors didn't notice, and none of them had much to say about her in any respect. Her neighbors across the little garden, a young German couple, admitted they'd seen her playing croquet with a nice young man, but their English didn't seem up to a description."

"Have someone show them a photo of Reg Mortimer, although I think we can assume it was he." With a glance at Gemma, Kincaid added, "If Gordon Finch is telling the truth, Annabelle never had him to her flat. And I don't know that anyone would describe Finch as a 'nice young man,' even taking language deficiencies into consideration."

"What about the pub, the Ferry House, where Mortimer says he waited for Annabelle?" asked Gemma.

"That's the one positive," said Janice. "From the description we gave him, the barkeep says he knows both Mortimer and Annabelle by sight, and that Mortimer came in alone around ten that evening. He ordered an orange juice, but it was a busy night and the barkeep can't swear to anything after that."

"But his impression was—" Kincaid prompted.

"His impression was that he stayed until last call."

"Could he have killed Annabelle when she came out of the tunnel, dumped her body somewhere, then moved her after the pub closed?"

"Not likely, unless he killed her in her flat. I can't see leaving a body anywhere outside in that vicinity. Too risky. But it seems Mortimer had good reason to be jealous." Kincaid went on to fill Janice in on the afternoon's interviews.

"A bit of a tomcat, wasn't she?" mused Janice when he'd finished. "The question is, did Mortimer know what she was up to?"

"I've been trying to reach him all afternoon." Kincaid had rung Hammond's again from his mobile when they'd left Lewis Finch, but the receptionist said Mr. Mortimer hadn't returned to the office; nor had there been any answer at Mortimer's home number. "We know he came into the office this morning, so I doubt he's scarpered. But he's first on the list for tomorrow, and I've left messages for him to ring us."

"Oh, that reminds me." Janice dug among the papers on the desktop until she found a scribbled memo. "You had a message passed on from the Yard. Someone called Ian McClellan is trying to reach you. Says he's in London and would like to meet with you tonight."

"Ian McClellan?"

"Here's the number he left. Is it a lead?"

"A lead?" Kincaid realized he must have sounded idiotic, and shook his head to clear it. He didn't meet Gemma's eyes. "No, it's . . . personal," he managed to say, tucking the memo in his pocket.

What the bloody hell was Ian McClellan doing back here now, and what the bloody hell did he want?

AT THE FLAT, KINCAID CHANGED INTO jeans and tee shirt, then tried ringing Kit in Cambridge. After putting him on hold for a moment, Laura Miller came back on the line and said rather apologetically that Kit didn't want to come to the phone just then. Kincaid heard the concern in her voice, but merely thanked her and said he'd try again later.

Looking through the open balcony door as he rang off, he saw Sid perched on the railing, watching the birds in the Major's garden with quivering interest. He went out and stroked the cat, finding a brief comfort in the fact that, unlike Kit, Sid always forgave him, no matter how badly he'd neglected him.

In the end, Kincaid chose familiar territory for his meeting with Ian McClellan: the Freemason's Arms, just across Willow Road from the Heath. The summer sun had begun its long evening slant through the treetops, and Hampstead Heath was filled with Londoners escaping flats stuffy with the day's heat. People strolled babies in pushchairs, played games of Frisbee and impromptu football, sailed boats on the Pond—and every glimpse of a boy with a dog reminded Kincaid of Kit.

When he reached the pub, he chose a table in the garden. He'd allowed time to get something to eat, but when the waitress brought his basket of chicken, he found he wasn't hungry. Nursing his pint, he picked desultorily at the chips and thought about Ian McClellan.

Vic's second husband, a political science fellow at Trinity College, had run off to the south of France the previous year with one of his graduate students. When Vic was murdered, McClellan had come back to England only briefly, and had refused to take Kit back to France with him. Although he admitted he'd long suspected Kit was really Kincaid's child, McClellan was still the boy's legal guardian, and he'd grudgingly acquiesced to Kincaid's temporary arrangements for Kit. Nothing had been heard from him since. Until now.

Glancing up, Kincaid saw McClellan walking across the grass towards him, pint in hand. He looked tan, but thinner than Kincaid remembered; on closer inspection his neatly trimmed brown hair and beard had acquired a liberal peppering of gray. This was the first time Kincaid had seen him divested of his corduroy, leather-elbowed jacket, but even in a short-sleeved cotton shirt he had about him an unmistakable professorial air.

Kincaid stood up to greet him, determined to get this meeting off to a better start than their previous encounters.

There was a moment of awkwardness, then McClellan shook Kincaid's hand firmly and sat down in the white garden chair. Having settled back and lifted his pint in mute salute, Ian broke the guarded silence. "I expect you're wondering why I asked to see you."

Kincaid nodded and sipped at his pint. "It was a surprise."

"Yes, well . . . Among other things, I believe I owe you an apology," Ian said slowly. "I've had time to think things through these last few months, and I can see now that my behavior was a bit . . . irrational. And irresponsible. The whole thing with Jennifer . . . and then Vic, and meeting you that way . . ." Sun glinted from Ian's gold-framed glasses as he looked away for a moment. "Things didn't work out with Jennifer when I went back to France. To be quite honest, I went right off the rails." Shrugging, he added, "Not quite what she bargained for, a middle-aged man in the midst of a breakdown. She came back to England to finish her degree."

"Is that why you came back? To be near her?" Kincaid asked.

Ian shook his head. "No. I'm not that foolish, although you might be surprised to hear it. But my sabbatical was up at the end of the summer, and the book had come to a dead halt, so there didn't seem much point in staying. . . ."

Kincaid waited in silence.

"How is he? Kit. Is he . . . coping? What about school?"

Kincaid thought of those first weeks, when Laura had found Kit clutching Tess every morning, crying, terrified to leave the dog long enough to go to school—certain something would happen to her while he was away.

"He's managed to finish out the term, at least. The school has tried to make things as normal as possible for him, under the circumstances.

"But that's what's on the surface—underneath, I don't know. He has nightmares. He's had difficulty eating, but that's a bit better lately." Kincaid paused, then added, "And he won't talk about his mother. Not even to Hazel Cavendish, who could probably squeeze confidences out of a rock."

"Is there any word on the trial?"

"The Crown Prosecution Service is still gathering evidence. There's no date as yet."

"And no resolution for Kit," Ian murmured. "Is her killer—"

"On remand, enjoying Her Majesty's hospitality. That's something, at least." Kincaid swatted at a late flying wasp that had landed on his glass. Dusk had settled on the garden with a cloak of cool air. The waitress came by, lighting the citronella candle on their table and bestowing a match-bright smile on them in the process. She wore a halter top and shorts no longer than her bar apron, and Kincaid noticed that Ian gave her an automatic smile. McClellan might have come to his senses over the latest affair, but old habits obviously died hard.

"There's something else," Kincaid said. "We're *neither* of us Kit's favorite people just now."

"Neither of us? I know he has reason enough to be angry with me, but why you?"

Having plunged in, Kincaid had no option but to continue. "I told him I was sure I was his father. Last night, as a matter of fact."

"*You* told him?" McClellan repeated, drawing his brows together. "You cautioned me not to speak to him about it. You said to give him time—"

"I thought I had. And we were facing making a change in his living arrangements—he can't stay with the Millers indefinitely."

Ian pushed his glasses up on his nose, a signal of agitation Kincaid remembered from their previous meetings. "How did he take it?"

Kincaid shoved his cold food to one side. "He doesn't want to believe it. He feels betrayed. And now you've come back. Why are you here?"

"Eugenia's been sending me threatening letters. I thought you should know."

"Threatening what? To spread more misery about in the world?" After Vic's death, Kincaid's dealings with his former mother-in-law had been acrimonious in the extreme, and promised no improvement. Kit had run away rather than stay in her care, and Eugenia was not likely to forgive Kincaid his part in making other arrangements for the grandson she considered as property.

"She's been a bit vague." Ian's smile held little humor. "First it was suing for grandparents' right to visitation. Lately, she's been leaning towards accusing me of legal abandonment and suing for custody herself."

"Dear God," Kincaid breathed, horrified at the thought.

"I don't think she has a leg to stand on as far as custody goes, but she might have a case for visitation. I've had a word with my solicitor."

The few chips Kincaid had eaten might have been lead in his stomach. "Kit ran away the last time he was forced to stay with her—that can't be allowed to happen again." Swallowing, he continued, "But there's no point talking about Eugenia without knowing what exactly you mean to do about Kit."

Ian studied his glass as he spoke. "The Grantchester house hasn't sold. I thought I'd take it off the market for the time being, until I get myself sorted out."

"You mean to live there?"

"For the time being. And I want Kit with me. I've a good deal of making up to do."

Kincaid pondered this in silence, then said, "You know I've no legal say in any arrangements you make for Kit. But if you abandon him again, I swear I'll do whatever it takes to ensure you never have another chance."

Ian met his eyes without flinching. "I want what's best for Kit, and I think it's this."

"What will you tell him about me?" Kincaid asked, his resentment rising.

"That it doesn't matter who his biological father is—he's still my son."

"And where does that leave me, now that you've suddenly become the ideal parent?" Kincaid couldn't keep the bitterness from his voice. He'd spent months trying to repair some of the damage McClellan had done, and now the bastard thought he could come back like the prodigal son.

"Look, Duncan." Ian leaned forward, his elbows on the table, and Kincaid realized it was the first time he had used his Christian name. "I'm not trying to shut you out of Kit's life. He needs both of us—"

"How would you know what he needs?" Kincaid's control was dangerously close to breaking.

"I can't make amends without starting somewhere, can I? And it doesn't sound to me as if you've any call for making threats or accusations—you've made a proper cock-up of things yourself," Ian added hotly.

They stared at each other, then Kincaid sat back. He took a deep breath. Getting at cross-purposes with McClellan would benefit no one. "All right. I'll admit that. But I was here, and I want it understood that I'm not bowing out of Kit's life now."

Ian gave him a crooked smile. "I'd say the question just now is whether he wants much to do with either of us. I'm going up to Cambridge tomorrow. I'll open the house, then fetch Kit from the Millers."

"Give him some time to get used to the idea," Kincaid countered. "A few days at least. He's found some security where he is . . . and he may find going back to the cottage difficult. . . . You know he won't leave the dog?"

"I'll give him a few days, then," Ian agreed, then grimaced. "And I suppose I can get used to the dog. Anything is possible."

Watching him, Kincaid felt a tingle of suspicion. It wouldn't do to take this latest declaration of intent entirely at face value. In his experience with Ian, anything was indeed possible.

WILLIAM HAMMOND WOKE SUDDENLY, HIS HEART hammering painfully in his chest. For a moment he wondered where he was, then the shapes in the dim room reasserted their familiarity. He lay in the high, old tester bed where he had slept with Isabel, his outstretched hand brushing against the hangings. She had loved the maize-colored satin, but the fabric was faded now, and stained.

The dressing table, there . . . the nightstand, there . . . and the pale oblongs on the right were the windows, admitting a faint light from Hyde Vale at the top of the lane. The curtains moved in the breeze and William pulled the duvet up to his chin, shivering.

In his dream it had been ripe summer, green and golden. He and Lewis stood knee-deep in the stream that ran through the bottom of the old pasture, picking watercress for Cook. They were laughing, their nut-brown faces turned up to the sun, but his feet and calves were cold as ice in the clear, running water. . . .

He had spent so many years forgetting, and yet it might have been yesterday, so real had the experience seemed for those few moments. Now the images began to dissolve, slipping away with the elusiveness of dreams, and William squeezed his eyes tight shut against the slow, leaking tears.

CHAPTER 10

*Another favorite haunt of Island
children for their outdoor games
was Island Gardens, a small park
on the riverbank opposite
Greenwich, created by the
London County Council in 1895.*

Eve Hostettler, from
Memories of Childhood
on the Isle of Dogs

GEMMA WAS AWAKENED FROM A
disjointed, early morning dream by
Toby's voice. Opening her eyes, she
made out his small form standing
beside her bed, silhouetted by the
dim light from the garden windows.

"Mummy, I had a bad dream."

"Did you, darling?" She sat up,
pushing her hair from her face. The
pale blue plush carousel horse her
son clutched to his chest had lost
most of its felt saddle, and its white
mane and tail were worn away to
stubble, but its black glass eyes were
still bright and Toby loved it with
fierce loyalty. "Did Horsey have a
bad dream, too?" she asked, feeling

the soft skin of her son's neck for signs of fever. "Was it monsters again?"

Toby nodded vigorously, and she made a vow to stop reading him *Where the Wild Things Are* at bedtime. "Climb in with Mummy, then, lovey, and go back to sleep." As she tucked him in between her body and the wall, she held her cheek to his for a moment and savored the sweet scent of him. He might look more like a little boy every day, but when he was warm and damp with sleep, he still smelled like a baby.

She lay quietly, listening as his breathing slowed with sleep. But she felt increasingly restless, aware of a nagging sense of disquiet, and after half an hour she slipped out of bed and went to the window. Opening the blinds, she stood for a while, watching the pale light creep across the garden and listening to the birds greet the day with revolting cheerfulness. Her head ached dully, a symptom she assessed as a mild hangover.

Last night, while waiting for Kincaid to ring after his meeting with Ian McClellan, she'd had a glass more than the two glasses of wine she normally considered her limit. But Duncan had not called, and at last she'd given up and crawled into bed, already regretting her overindulgence.

Surely Kincaid wasn't still cross with her over the business with Gordon Finch, she thought as she moved from the window to her tiny cupboard of a kitchen, where she filled the kettle. It was unlike him to hold a grudge, either personal or professional, but since Vic's death his moods and his temper had been unpredictable.

The kettle whistled as she finished grinding the handful of coffee beans she'd taken from the fridge, and as she poured the hot water into the cafetière, she thought about Annabelle Hammond. What secret had she possessed that had compelled others to accept life on her terms? It had been more than beauty, that much was becoming clear, and for an instant Gemma wished she could have known her—could have judged for herself whether she was saint or sinner.

AN HOUR LATER, AS SHE LISTENED to Toby singing happily over his cornflakes, she dressed carefully—camel trousers, a white cotton tee shirt under an olive linen blazer—determined today to present a professional front to the world, hot or not.

Although the morning had brought a small respite from yesterday's temperatures, the humidity had risen with the thin covering of cloud that spilled across the sky like curdled milk. As she drove towards the East End, she felt the moisture clinging to her skin and wondered if sheer willpower could keep her from wilting before the day had even begun.

Kincaid was there before her, leaning against the Rover he'd parked across the street from Hammond's. He smiled when he saw her and straightened, running a hand through his already wind-ruffled hair. "We might get some rain," he said by way of a greeting when she'd parked the Escort and joined him. "A break in the heat."

"Are you all right?" she asked, studying him. His good cheer seemed a bit manufactured, and he was not usually given to talking about the weather.

He looked back at her guilelessly, his eyes as blue today as the denim shirt he wore. "Why shouldn't I be?"

"You didn't ring. What did Ian—"

"I thought you'd be asleep." He looked away, leaning down to brush dust from the car's bonnet off his trousers. "And to be quite honest, I suppose I needed some time to sort things through." Glancing up at her, he added, "McClellan says he's here to stay. He's moving back to the Cambridge house. And he wants Kit with him."

"But . . ." Gemma tried to make sense of this. "After months of wanting nothing to do with him? Just like that? What did you say?"

"What could I say?" He gave her a lopsided smile. "You know the situation as well as I do."

Gemma searched for a reply, but everything that came to mind seemed both trite and facile. Finally, she touched his arm. "I'm sorry things are difficult just now. If there's anything I can do . . ."

"We could talk tonight, if the gods are willing." He took her elbow, guiding her towards Hammond's front door. "In the meantime, the guv'nor wants to see me mid-morning, and I'd like to be able to tell him we've made some progress on this case. Let's hope we find Reg Mortimer cooperative."

The first thing Gemma noticed as they entered the warehouse was the distinct aroma of tea; the second was the low hum of activity that had been absent on Sunday. As Kincaid spoke to the receptionist at her desk near the door, Gemma cocked her head, trying to sort out the sounds. From upstairs came the grumble of machinery and the occasional thump, and from the open doors of the loading bays drifted the sound of a radio. The ringing of a telephone punctuated the faint murmur of voices, but the atmosphere seemed subdued.

A balding man in a crisp green apron moved about the tasting table. He must be Mac, the tea taster Teresa had mentioned, thought Gemma, but before she could speak to him, the receptionist directed them up the stairs and along the catwalk.

As they passed the open door of the first large office, they saw Teresa Robbins seated at one of the two desks, telephone held to her ear. She glanced up, startled, and lifted one hand in an awkward gesture that stopped short of a wave.

Reg Mortimer awaited them in the office next door, rising from a neat desk to greet them. He wore a pale pink shirt and coordinated tie, but the flattering shade did little for skin made sallow by exhaustion. Gemma was shocked by how much his appearance had changed since she'd seen him three days ago. Guilt? Or grief?

"You've been rather elusive, Mr. Mortimer," Kincaid began as they sat down.

"Have I?" Mortimer smiled cordially enough. "There's been a good deal to see to—and to clean up." He ran the side of his hand across the polished surface of his desk. "Your lads don't exactly tidy up after themselves."

"Not part of their job description," Kincaid said, giving the office an interested glance.

Gemma saw no evidence that the forensic team had left traces behind, but she found the room's mixture of furnishings rather odd. The large, contemporary desk was of mirror-gloss ebony, the accompanying executive's chair black leather, while the straight-backed wooden visitors' chairs she and Kincaid occupied were likely older than Mortimer and had never been more than utilitarian. The chairs' ambiance was echoed in the scarred, wooden filing cabinets flanking the open, uncurtained window behind the desk, and atop one of the cabinets, a black-enameled fan oscillated with a gentle whirring.

After the fan, Gemma almost expected a Bakelite, rotary-dial phone on the desk, but a glimpse of the state-of-the-art unit tucked away behind Reg's Rolodex booted her swiftly back into the current decade.

As if he'd read her thoughts, Kincaid told Mortimer, "I see you've managed to update things a bit in the old building. Was this Annabelle's office?"

"No. Annabelle shared the one next door. It's been hard on Teresa, the last few days. The constant reminder . . . I don't think I could bear . . ." Mortimer shook his head. "We've always been short of office space here—that's one of the problems with this drafty old pile of brick. That and the damp," he added absently, and Gemma had the impression he was talking on autopilot while his mind was somewhere else entirely.

"There are just a few things we'd like to go over with you, Mr. Mortimer," Kincaid said. "Were you aware that Annabelle had left her shares in the company to Harry and Sarah Lowell, naming their father as trustee?"

Gemma pulled her notebook unobtrusively from her bag as she watched Mortimer's response. Although he didn't quite mask a grimace, he answered readily enough, and she thought he must have been prepared.

"I'd no idea until yesterday. Teresa and I are meeting with the solicitor this afternoon, to see if there is anything that can be done."

"So you share Jo Lowell's opinion that her ex-husband is likely to be difficult?"

"I've nothing against Martin Lowell personally. But we would be concerned at the idea of anyone without direct experience of the business controlling a large block of voting shares. I'm sure you can understand that," Mortimer said smoothly.

Gemma looked up from her notes. "Don't you find it odd that your fiancée didn't share something as important as the disposition of her assets with you?"

Mortimer tilted his chair back a bit and reangled the pen on his blotter. "Annabelle was rather obsessive about her privacy. And in any case, I'm sure it's not something she thought would be necessary to discuss," he added, his expression bleak.

"Perhaps she meant to wait until you were married, then sign them over to you," Gemma suggested.

"Trying to predict what Annabelle *might* have done seems a particularly fruitless exercise."

Spotting her opening, Gemma said, "Had Annabelle changed her mind about your engagement? Is that what your argument was about on Friday evening?"

Mortimer paled visibly. "What—what are you talking about? Of course she hadn't changed her mind. I've told you—she wasn't feeling well."

"That's funny," Kincaid said, picking it up. "Jo Lowell says the two of you had a row, and that you waited for Annabelle in the lane, not even saying good night to your hostess. I don't believe you'd have behaved so rudely unless you'd had a disagreement."

Mortimer glanced from Kincaid to Gemma. "It sounds so utterly stupid now." His eyes filled with tears and he brushed at them with the back of his hand. "And there's no taking any of it back, the things we said. . . ."

"Everyone has stupid rows," said Gemma, very deliberately not looking at Kincaid. "And if we're lucky we get to make them up. Don't let this grow out of proportion because you didn't."

A faint color rose in Reg's cheeks. "All right," he said after a moment. "Annabelle was furious because she thought Jo was flirting with me. . . . I told you it was idiotic."

"*Was* Jo flirting with you?" Kincaid asked. "Was there something going on between you?"

"No, of course not. Annabelle was just very out of sorts." Reg looked away, moving his shoulders in an embarrassed shrug. "Maybe I took a bit more notice of Jo than usual, just because Annabelle was being so bloody. And Jo seemed to be enjoying the attention, but that was all. It was silly, I know, but sometimes when you've known one another a long time, you seem to fall back into the way you behaved as children."

"Have you any idea why Annabelle was out of sorts?"

"Not a glimmer. Except that things had been more stressful than usual here lately." His gesture indicated the warehouse. "She'd been making changes that would have enormous impact on the future of the company—new products, new packaging, new marketing strategies. Now . . ." Reg slumped back in his chair with a shake of his head. "I don't know how we'll carry on without her."

Gemma thought of the distinctive tins Annabelle had designed, of Teresa Robbins's animation when she spoke of Annabelle's plans for pushing Hammond's into a new niche in the market, of the obvious grief and shock of the company's employees. Could Hammond's go on successfully, without Annabelle's drive and vision? "Was there anyone within the company who stood to gain from her death?" she asked.

"Not that I can see," Reg answered wearily. "Even Martin Lowell may find those shares more of a liability than an asset, without Annabelle behind them," he added, and Gemma thought she heard a trace of satisfaction in his voice.

Kincaid studied him for a moment. "Are you sure it was Annabelle who was jealous that night, and not you?"

"What?" Mortimer's hands, which had been idly rolling the pen back and forth, were suddenly still.

"It seems you'd have had good reason, Reg." Kincaid sounded sympathetic. "Were you aware that she knew the busker she spoke to in the tunnel? And that she'd been having an affair with him?"

"What?" Mortimer said again. His throat moved as he swallowed convulsively. "That's not possible. I . . . How could Annabelle possibly have known this chap, much less . . . A busker? You must be mistaken."

Gemma thought of the photos from the *Tatler* she'd seen on Annabelle's corkboard—Annabelle and Reg moving graciously from one society party to another, inhabiting a world that had no place for anyone outside its class or social set, unless the contact was made as an official act of charity.

She manufactured a smile. "He's really quite good. I'd say the entertainment's a bargain for a few coins tossed in a case." Too late, she felt Kincaid's swift, curious glance.

"But he's not just your ordinary street musician, if that makes you feel any better," offered Kincaid. "His name is Gordon Finch, and he's Lewis Finch's son."

This time Mortimer simply stared.

"Do you know Lewis Finch?"

Mortimer seemed to make an effort to pull himself together. "Of course I know Lewis Finch. Everyone on the Island knows who Lewis Finch is."

"Including Annabelle?"

"I . . . I suppose she did—she must have met him at some point."

"Would it surprise you to learn that she knew the father as well as the son, in the biblical sense? We're not sure which came first, the chicken or the egg, but it seems quite certain that she had an ongoing relationship with both of them while engaged to you."

"No!" Reg Mortimer stood, sending his leather chair flying into one of the filing cabinets. "I don't bloody believe it. I won't believe it. Can't you leave me *something*, for God's sake?"

When they didn't answer, he groped for the chair behind him, and sinking back into it, he covered his face with his hands.

"ALL RIGHT, IT'S JO LOWELL AGAIN," Kincaid said as they climbed into the Rover. "I'm beginning to feel like a bloody yo-yo." He'd just enough time for the run to Greenwich before his meeting with Chief Superintendent Childs. "Do you mind walking back through the tunnel?"

"Love to," Gemma answered as they turned north into Manchester Road.

"Do I detect a smidgen of sarcasm?" As Kincaid looked to the left, he caught a glimpse of George Brent's front garden, and George himself in a white string vest, deadheading the roses. He waved, but the old man was intent on his work and didn't look up. "It's a bit hard to believe that George Brent and Lewis Finch are of the same generation."

"I suppose George must be a half a dozen years older." Gemma rolled her window down, grimacing as a hot, gritty wind blasted into the car. "But you're right. I can't imagine Annabelle having a go at George."

"Do you think Reg Mortimer knew?"

"About Annabelle and Lewis, or about Annabelle and Gordon?"

"Either. Both."

"I don't know. He seemed pretty cut-up."

"In any case, I'll guarantee you that his story about the row at the party is a load of bollocks."

"You can't underestimate the power of sibling rivalry. Think about Jo, feeling awkward giving a party for the first time on her own. She might easily have been tempted into a little flirtation with her sister's boyfriend, and if that were the case, she wouldn't be dying to admit it under any circumstances."

"Very embarrassing. Not to mention it being a good reason for having had an all-out row with her sister," Kincaid added, considering the scenario.

"Which she wouldn't want to admit, either. But that doesn't solve the problem of what happened after Annabelle and Reg left the party."

They had reached the top of the Isle of Dogs peninsula, and he took Aspen Way to the right as it curved back towards the south and the approach to the Blackwall Tunnel.

As they entered the tunnel a draft of cooler air swirled into the car. Gemma leaned back against the headrest and closed her eyes.

Glancing at her, Kincaid said, "Were you just trying to get a rise out of Mortimer when you told him that Gordon Finch was good?"

For a moment, Gemma didn't respond, then she opened her eyes and gave him a swift look he couldn't read. "Not exactly. He was practicing when I arrived at his flat yesterday. But I'd heard him before, in Islington."

"In Islington?" he said, surprised. "When?"

She shrugged. "It's been a few months. But I wasn't sure until yesterday that it was the same person."

"I shouldn't think Gordon Finch would be easy to mistake," Kincaid said as the traffic slowed to a dead stop mid-tunnel. Although he'd learned he couldn't always tell what made other men attractive to women, he sensed that Finch had a certain magnetism, and if the man had appealed to Annabelle . . . "The strong, silent type, is he?"

"Who? Finch?"

"Or maybe it was the dog that impressed you?"

"As a matter of fact, I remembered the dog," Gemma answered

equably. "It was seeing him again yesterday that clinched it." She smiled, examining her fingertips, and he wondered who was taking the mickey from whom.

They rode the rest of the way to Greenwich in silence, but he couldn't quite shake the feeling that Gemma was holding something out on him.

Jo Lowell answered her door before Kincaid had lifted his finger from the bell, and at the sight of them her face fell. "I was just on my way out. I'm late for a meeting with a client. The children were dreadful this morning—" She stopped. "Never mind. What can I do for you?"

She was dressed to go out, in crisp trousers and a white silk blouse. A dusting of makeup minimized her freckles, her dark auburn hair was pulled back with a gold slide, and she wore a pair of simple topaz earrings. For the first time Kincaid realized how attractive she could be.

"It won't take a minute," he apologized, and she stepped back, ushering them in with good grace.

"Is this all right?" she asked, indicating the dining room.

The vase of yellow sunflowers still stood on the table in the pleasant room, and as they sat, Kincaid thought of Annabelle here, perhaps laughing at something someone said.

"We'll get right to the point, Mrs. Lowell. We've just had a chat with Reg Mortimer, and he admits that he and Annabelle had a row."

Had he imagined the swiftly controlled spasm of tension in Jo Lowell's mouth? "Are you sure your sister didn't tell you what the row was about?"

"No . . . I . . . What did Reg say?"

"That Annabelle was angry because she thought you were flirting with him."

For a moment, Jo stared, her mouth open; then she let out a peal of laughter. "Reg said *I* was flirting with *him*?"

"I take it you don't agree?" Kincaid asked.

"In his dreams." Jo subsided into slightly hysterical snickers. "I bloodied his nose once too often when we were kids, the little sod.

I could kill him!" She clapped her hand over her mouth. "I didn't mean—"

"I know you didn't. But could Annabelle have thought there was something going on between you and Reg? He says she was really narked about something."

"The bastard. It wasn't Annabelle who was angry—not in the beginning. He was the one furious with her."

"Why didn't you tell us this before?" Kincaid edged the vase of sunflowers over a bit so that he could see her across the table.

Jo sat back, sliding her hands into her lap, but not before he'd seen how tightly they were clenched. He was suddenly aware of her perfume, a fresh, grassy scent, and of the rising and falling of her chest in the warm, still room. "You knew all the time what the row was about, didn't you, Jo? Why didn't you tell us? And why did Reg lie about it twice?"

He waited, sensing Gemma beside him, but knowing she wouldn't break the tension, wouldn't give Jo an out.

"I didn't know, when you first asked me, that Annabelle was dead," Jo whispered at last, without taking her eyes from her clenched hands. "And then I was ashamed."

"You were ashamed?" Gemma prompted her gently. "Was it something you said?"

Jo shook her head, and the tears that had gathered on her lower lashes spilled over, streaking her cheeks. She didn't lift a hand to wipe them away. "It was Harry. You have to understand: It was Martin who poisoned him against Annabelle. I daresay she deserved it, but she adored Harry from the moment he was born, and I think it broke her heart."

Leaning forward, Gemma reached out as if to touch her. "Jo, start from the beginning. Tell us what happened."

"I don't want you to think badly of Annabelle." Jo lifted a curled fist to her breast in a pleading gesture.

"We won't," Gemma promised, without taking her eyes from Jo's, and Kincaid marveled, as he always did, at her ability to make an emotional link with a stranger.

Jo took a shaky breath and exhaled on a sigh, blinking back her tears. "It started when Sarah was a baby—before that, really. Martin and I had been having problems—I'd even thought about leaving him—and then Mummy got sick. And I got pregnant." Looking away, she shook her head and continued softly, "It was a stupid thing to do, crazy even, but it was like I couldn't help myself, I couldn't fight this urge. . . . I even cheated on my birth control." She looked back at them, her lips curving in a small smile. "It didn't help things with Martin, and it didn't keep Mummy from dying. But it gave me something to love, to fill the void. . . . Why am I telling you this? I've never said—"

Gemma touched her fingertips to Jo's outstretched hand. Kincaid thought he might have disappeared as far as the two women were concerned. "I have a son the same age as your Sarah. I know what it's like."

After a moment, Jo nodded. "Martin had been jealous of Harry, but with Sarah he felt completely shut out, and he was more angry with me than ever. And Annabelle . . . When Mummy died, Annabelle hadn't anything. . . ." The breath she took sounded almost like a sob. "They had an affair. Martin and Annabelle. Annabelle told me, after a few months. She said she couldn't stand it anymore, knowing that she'd betrayed me and the children, and that Martin wanted to keep on. I filed for divorce."

"Were you terribly angry with her?" Gemma asked it quietly.

"Of course I was angry. Furious. But she was my sister, and after a bit . . . I missed her.

"But Martin never forgave her; he swore she'd ruined his life, taken his children from him—as if he'd had nothing to do with it at all." Her voice rose on an incredulous note.

"And Harry?"

"Martin told him it was Annabelle's fault we weren't a family anymore, that everything would have been wonderful if she hadn't interfered. That was bad enough, but I thought that was all he'd told him. Until the night of the dinner party." Jo looked round the room as if realizing where she was sitting. "Annabelle hadn't been here often. . . . Things had been awkward between us, though we put up the best front we could for Father. But I thought it was time we mended things, so I invited them—Annabelle and Reg—and Mummy's friend

Rachel Pargeter who lives round the corner, and some clients who weren't biased one way or the other. . . ."

When Jo lapsed into silence, Gemma said softly, "What happened?"

"It was a disaster. Oh, not at first. Harry was rude to her, but I sent him to play outside with Sarah, and we got through dinner with flying colors. Then Harry came into the kitchen as Annabelle and Reg were helping me clear up. Annabelle had never stopped trying to make things up with Harry, you see. They'd been so close, and I don't think she really understood how deep the damage went. She touched him, called him a pet name, and he—lashed out at her. He said things . . . called her horrible names. . . ." Jo stopped. She'd gone pale under her tan.

"What sort of names?"

"Whore," Jo said, so quietly that Kincaid had to lean forward to hear her. "Filthy tart. He said if she hadn't . . . I'd no idea he even knew the words. Annabelle slapped him, and then Reg . . . started in on her."

"Reg was angry at Annabelle?" Kincaid frowned. "Not at Harry?"

"Reg hadn't known about Annabelle and Martin. He kept shouting at her, 'Is it true? Is it true?' and poor Harry was crying. . . . Then Annabelle stormed out and Reg followed her. I thought, the next day when he said she wouldn't answer his calls, that she had bloody good reason not to."

"And you didn't think, when you found out she was dead, that Reg might have killed her?"

"No. I thought . . . not Reg. For all his faults, the three of us have been together since we were children. Reg would never have hurt her."

"What about Martin? What if she went to see Martin after she left Reg in the tunnel?"

Jo's eyes widened with shock, and for a moment the room was so hushed Kincaid could hear his pulse pounding in his ears. Then Jo breathed, "Oh, God. Not Martin."

GEMMA STOOD BESIDE KINCAID IN THE lane as they watched Jo Lowell pull away in her small Fiat.

"Funny, Martin Lowell didn't happen to mention the fact that he'd had an affair with his sister-in-law when we spoke to him," Kincaid said, lifting his hand as Jo glanced back once before turning the corner into Hyde Vale.

"Or that he hated her. Although we might have guessed it." Not relishing the prospect, Gemma added, "I'll stop at the bank in Greenwich and speak to him again."

"Let's put it off until this afternoon. I think I'd like to be in on this one." Kincaid looked at his watch. "But I'd better not keep the guv'nor waiting. I'll ring you from the Yard." Unlocking the Rover, he added, "Hop in. I'll give you a lift to the town center on my way."

Gemma hesitated. "I'd like to hear someone else's account of that dinner party. Jo said her mum's friend lived just round the corner. I think I'll give her a try."

"You don't know which house."

"I'm perfectly capable of knocking on doors," Gemma retorted, waving him off.

She found Mrs. Rachel Pargeter on her second try, one house down from the corner on Hyde Vale. A tall woman in her sixties, with silver hair swept back in a neat twist, Rachel Pargeter wore a green canvas apron over her cotton blouse and trousers.

"Gardening gear," she explained in a husky voice when Gemma had introduced herself. "Come through to the back, and I'll just wash my hands."

Gemma smiled with involuntary pleasure as the woman led her into a glassed-in room whose doors stood open to a flagstone terrace and a shady garden. "It's lovely."

"Coolest room in the house. I'll just make us some tea—won't take a moment."

An enormous tabby cat lay on its back on the rattan sofa, all four paws in the air. It opened its eyes and blinked at Gemma, stretching sumptuously, and they had proceeded to the belly-scratching stage of acquaintance when Rachel Pargeter reappeared with a tray.

"Give over, Francis, you great beast," she said in a tone of affectionate exasperation. Then to Gemma she added, "Just shove him off. It will only hurt his feelings for about thirty seconds—short-term memory loss can be a blessing."

When Gemma had gently removed the feline and accepted a mug, Rachel Pargeter seated herself in the adjacent wicker rocker and studied her. "This is about Annabelle Hammond, I take it?"

"I understand you've been a friend of the family for some time."

"Oh, donkeys' years," Rachel admitted. "Isabel befriended me when we first moved here, thirty years ago. That was a great loss—Isabel's death. And now this." She sipped at tea Gemma still found too hot to drink. "I always felt a bit sorry for Annabelle, but I never thought things would come to this."

"You felt *sorry* for Annabelle?"

"I've always thought that exceptional beauty was as great an affliction as any physical handicap—perhaps more so. It is so difficult for the beautiful person, male or female, to develop a good character, isn't it? The odds are stacked against them from the start."

Gemma frowned. "How do you mean?"

"They are never required to *earn* the regard or affection of others through their behavior; rather, they come to expect it as their due. And they are forgiven almost anything, simply because of the way they look. Annabelle was more fortunate than others, because her mother kept her from being utterly spoiled."

Francis chose that moment to leap into Rachel's lap. The woman adroitly avoided spilling her tea, then stroked him as she continued, "The other tragic thing, in my experience, is that beautiful people so seldom have the security of knowing they are loved for themselves— who they are on the inside. But Isabel loved her daughter in spite of her beauty, not because of it, and she was scrupulously fair with the children." She sighed. "William, of course, was a great trial to her, but she didn't like to complain."

"A trial? How?"

"Annabelle was the child of his dreams—this beautiful girl who grew up with a passion for tea that surpassed his own."

"So he spoiled her terribly?"

"Oh, yes. And he placed on her the burden of perfection, which is a very difficult thing to live up to. It's no wonder Annabelle went off the rails a bit when her mother died."

"You knew about Annabelle and Martin Lowell?"

"I'm afraid so," Rachel said, nodding sadly. "Jo confessed it to me.

Poor thing, she had no one else to turn to—she certainly couldn't tell her father what his precious Annabelle had done." She gave Gemma a swift, intelligent glance. "And I suppose I'm betraying Jo's confidence now. But all this has been rather weighing on me. . . ."

"Jo told us herself, so you're hardly betraying a confidence," Gemma reassured her. "What I don't understand is how either of them could have fallen for Martin Lowell."

Rachel Pargeter smiled. "I take it you haven't seen Martin at his best. He can be quite charming—even I was smitten when they were first married and he asked my advice about the garden. He made me feel my opinion was the only one in the world that mattered. That intensity of his must have been awfully tempting to a girl used to playing second fiddle. Jo saw herself as Cathy to his Heathcliff."

"And Annabelle?"

"I suspect that after Isabel died she just desperately wanted to feel loved, and she mistook Martin's desire for that. I imagine she found out soon enough that Martin and love had no place in the same equation."

"But to betray her own sister!" Gemma hadn't realized until now how much the knowledge had upset her. She'd been able to justify to some extent Annabelle's betrayal of Reg Mortimer with Gordon Finch, but not her affair with her own brother-in-law.

"Sibling rivalry has existed since Cain and Abel. I expect Annabelle wanted what she thought her sister had—contentment in her marriage, children—and she was used to taking what she wanted."

"And Jo forgave her?"

"Eventually. But Harry didn't."

"It's about the dinner party I came to see you," said Gemma.

Rachel closed her eyes for a moment. "Oh, that was a terrible evening."

"You heard the argument."

"It's a small house, and they were shouting. Not that I was surprised, mind you. I'd had an idea what was brewing. Harry stays with me sometimes, and I'd seen what his father was doing to him." Rachel pushed the cat from her lap and set her empty cup on the table. "Martin's infidelity I could forgive, but not using his son to satisfy his own need for revenge. I'm surprised someone hasn't killed the bastard."

"Tell me what they said in the kitchen that night."

"I heard Harry first, shouting filthy words. Jo's poor clients were mortified—I think they thought it was the telly at first. Then Jo, shouting at Harry . . . and Harry sobbing."

"And Annabelle?"

Rachel looked away. "She was . . . pleading with Harry. Then Reg started in on her—I couldn't make out all the words, but he was outraged. Annabelle shouted at him. Then the back door banged, twice. Neither of them came back into the dining room. Jo returned a few minutes later, trying to put a good face on it, but we excused ourselves as quickly as we could."

"Did Reg and Annabelle seem all right at dinner?"

"Yes. A bit snappish, perhaps, but nothing out of the ordinary for a couple who knew one another well."

"And there was no mention of anyone, or anything else, that might have set off an argument?"

"Not that I remember." Frowning, Rachel added, "You're not thinking that Reg could have had something to do with Annabelle's death, I hope. He's not a bad lad—used to play with my Jimmy when he came to visit Jo and Annabelle."

"He was very angry with her."

"I think he may have been more upset on Jo's behalf than his own. That's what he shouted at Annabelle. 'How could you do that to your sister?'

"It is a shame that Annabelle hadn't the chance to see what she could make of herself—to see if she could mend her flaws," Rachel went on after a moment. "People always mourn the passing of exemplary souls, but I'm inclined to think they've done their bit and are ready to move on."

"But Annabelle wasn't."

"She had the potential to love. I believe she loved her sister—in spite of what she did to her—and I know she loved Harry. The child's rejection must have been a terrible blow, something she'd never experienced—and that pain might have been the flame necessary to forge her character," finished Rachel. She smiled at Gemma and began to assemble their tea things on the tray. "But it's facts you want, Sergeant, and I've given you nothing but idle speculation."

"It's been a great help to talk to someone who saw Annabelle clearly, Mrs. Pargeter."

"Do you think that?" Rachel Pargeter paused, her hand on the sugar bowl. "I'm not sure I saw her clearly at all. A good part of what I've said may be complete rubbish, wishful thinking on my part. Because I loved her, too, you know—not least because she reminded me of her mother. And love is a dangerous thing."

GEMMA HEARD THE MUSIC AS SOON as she stepped out of the lift in Island Gardens. It was Dixieland jazz, loud and rollicking and unmistakably live. She followed the sound round the side of the domed tunnel entrance, and when she turned the corner into the park proper, she saw the band beneath the plane tree that stood sentinel where the path met the river promenade.

The tree's trunk perfectly bisected the view of the Royal Naval College across the river, and the five musicians stood in the shade of its branches. All were middle-aged, graying, and bearded, and with their soft hats and shirttails hanging over their mismatched shorts they looked like businessmen out for an afternoon's lark. An occasional passerby tossed a coin in the open banjo case.

Gemma listened for a bit, unable to resist the toe-tapping rhythms, then wandered over to the refreshment kiosk and bought an Orangina. The park lay spread before her, so inviting that she decided to walk through it rather than go round by the road.

She took the path that cut straight through the center of the park, enjoying the clean fizziness of her drink, her steps still bouncing a bit with the music. Now they were playing a Benny Goodman tune she remembered her dad liking when she was a child, but she couldn't quite put her finger on the name of it. She hummed along, following the tune, gazing absently at the mothers with babies in pushchairs and the couples stretched out on blankets on the grass.

In front of her, an old woman in a zimmer frame navigated the path with tortoiselike deliberation, and beyond her a man lay beside a dog—it took Gemma's startled mind an instant to process the fact that the man was Gordon Finch, and the dog Sam. She stopped dead, staring, feeling as if she'd conjured him from her thoughts.

Gordon lay on his back, his eyes closed. He wore a tee shirt and jeans, his feet were bare, and a pair of boots rested neatly beside his clarinet case. Beneath his head, a folded jacket did duty as a pillow. The sun came out from behind the clouds, and the dappled light filtering through the leaves of the nearest plane tree played along his face and body.

Slowly, Gemma crossed the grass and stood over him. Sam lifted his head, and at the dog's movement, Gordon opened his eyes and looked up at her. "What fair vision is this?" he asked, straight-faced.

"What are you doing here?" Gemma said.

"Not up to sparkling repartee today, are we?" He sat, lifting his arms above his head and cracking his intertwined knuckles in a stretch. "It's a free park, i'nt it, lady? I could ask you the same. Join me?"

Gemma looked round as if a chair might materialize, then sank to her knees. "I need to talk to you."

Gordon nodded in the direction of the musicians. "I'm waiting a turn at this pitch, so I'm all yours as long as the band plays."

Although still mocking, he seemed more relaxed today than Gemma had seen him before.

"What is it?" he asked, looking at her more closely. "Are you all right?"

Surprised by his tone of concern, she stammered, "I . . . Yes, of course I'm all right, but—"

"Then sit down properly," he ordered. "You look like a sprinter at the blocks." She obeyed gingerly, but before she could cross her legs, Gordon laid a hand on her outstretched ankle. "And take your shoes off. You can't sit in the grass with your shoes on." He grasped her sandal by the heel and slid it free as Gemma jerked her foot back, protesting.

"I can't sit here in the park barefoot with you. It's not— What would—"

"What are you so afraid of, Sergeant?" He glanced up at her as he lifted her other foot and slipped the shoe off. "You can charge me with assaulting an officer, if it makes you feel better."

"Don't be absurd," she retorted, but she didn't retrieve her sandals.

Gordon wrapped his arms round his knees, regarding her impassively, while Sam got up and repositioned himself against Gordon's hip with a sigh. "You said you wanted to grill me?"

"I didn't mean—" Gemma bit off the rest of her protest. "All right," she said, tucking her bare feet under her in a cross-legged position. "Did you know that Annabelle had an affair with her sister's husband?"

The expression on his face told her he was taken aback. "No. I told you—she didn't talk about herself. And I expect that's the last thing she'd have told me." He seemed to hesitate, then said, "Was it . . . Do you know when?"

"Some time ago. It broke up her sister's marriage, and apparently he—Martin Lowell—blamed Annabelle."

"That's his name?" he asked, frowning. The upward slant of his brows echoed the sharp angle of his cheekbones. "She never mentioned him. But what has this to do with anything?"

"Her fiancé found out about her affair with Lowell on Friday night, at her sister's party."

"But if her sister's already divorced, it must have been before Annabelle was engaged to him—what's his name?"

"Reg Mortimer."

"So why get his knickers in a twist?"

"Maybe he knew, or guessed, that there was someone else. And he thought that if she could betray her own sister, why not him? Then he saw her with you, in the tunnel. . . ."

"Are you saying you think he waited for her? That he killed her?"

"It's a possibility, but so far the evidence doesn't seem to support it. Did she tell you that she'd broken off her engagement?"

"No. Had she?"

"We don't know. Your father says he rang her because she left him a message saying she'd called off her engagement, and that she sounded quite upset."

"My father?" Gordon's face was once again expressionless.

Gemma felt as if she were walking on eggshells, and fought against her inexplicable urge to protect him. "We've seen your father. He also told us that he and Annabelle Hammond had a long-standing relationship, and I'm having a hard time believing you weren't aware of it."

"I told you—my father and I aren't close. Why should I have known?" He kept his voice even, but Gemma could see the tension in the muscles of his jaw.

"Apparently she was seen about with him often enough. This neighborhood is as insular as any village, and considering the way information travels in that sort of environment . . . I should think you'd have heard sooner rather than later."

Gordon grimaced and looked away. After a moment, he said, "We lived here when I was a child. I started school here, just up the road. My father was already a presence in the neighborhood, gaining a reputation for trying to save the old buildings—that was pretty eccentric for those days, when most people didn't believe that the Docks could really die. But they respected his success. Everywhere I went I was Lewis Finch's son.

"Then, when I was eight, my mum decided we should move to the suburbs; that was her idea of success—bridge and cocktails—but my dad despised it. When they divorced, he came back to the Island for good."

"You stayed with your mum?"

"Lewis sent me to boarding school. Education meant everything to him, and he was determined I should have the best. What he couldn't accept was my not making use of what he provided for me—at least not in the way he'd had in mind."

Gemma thought of her own father, a self-made man in a small way compared with Lewis Finch, but still proud of the success he'd made of his bakery. Had he dreamed that his daughters would follow in his footsteps? If so, they had both disappointed him.

"He wanted you to join the firm?" she guessed.

Gordon buried his fingertips in the thick ruff of fur at the back of Sam's neck. "I lasted a year. Have you any idea what it's like to live in the shadow of someone like my father?"

Gemma studied him. His gray eyes were deep-set under the winged brows, his hair stuck up on the crown of his head in unruly spikes, there were hollows under his cheekbones and creases at the corners of his mouth that bespoke hard years. "So you remade yourself as far from his image as you could get: a street musician, an unconventional activist—"

"I found out what happened to the people who could no longer afford to live in their old neighborhoods," he protested.

"You could have gone anywhere. No one would have known who

you were. But you came back to the Island." She jabbed a finger at him. "Because you care about what happens here. You're your father's son, whether you like it or not. And I think that's why Annabelle sought you out."

"That's rubbish," Gordon said hotly. "She didn't even know my name in the beginning."

"I think she did. I think she was already seeing your father, and she became curious about you. So she came to listen to you play. Maybe that's all she meant to do at first, and it turned into more than she bargained for."

"But why? What could she possibly have wanted?"

"I don't know." Gemma plucked a blade of the soft grass under her hand. "But there is a connection between your families—your fathers were evacuated together during the war."

He stared at her. "I'd no idea."

"And you never heard that there was some sort of feud between your father and William Hammond?"

"No. And the idea's absurd."

"Annabelle's sister Jo says their father warned them away from your father and his family."

Gordon seemed about to reply, then stopped, his expression puzzled. "It is strange, now that you mention it. Annabelle was always asking questions about my family. I thought it was just ordinary curiosity until—"

"Until what?"

"Oh, it was nothing, really." He scratched Sam's ear for a moment. "One day I realized she wasn't curious about other things—you know, who my mates were, what I did when I wasn't with her, the usual female stuff."

Gemma gathered from the swift glance he gave her that he meant to get her dander up, so she let the remark ride.

"I . . ." Frowning, Gordon looked out at the river. "How very odd. You're sure my father knew Annabelle's when they were young?"

"They've both confirmed it."

"My father never talked about his childhood, and I certainly don't remember him mentioning knowing William Hammond. My mother, though . . . she always told stories about life here before the war. They

used to come here, to Island Gardens, on summer evenings, and watch
the pleasure boats on the Thames. The boats were strung with colored
lights, and music would drift from them over the water. Sometimes
people would dance, and my mother always wished she were old
enough to dance, too. But it never happened. Everything had changed,
after the war."

"Maybe that's where you got your love of music, from your mum."

He shrugged, his gaze still far away. "Maybe."

The band had stopped playing, but now the music started again.
First, a swingy beat, then the clarinet picked up the melody line with a
hint of melancholy. Gordon reached out and, grasping her hand,
pulled her to her feet.

"What—" she started to say, but he had placed his right hand in the
small of her back, guiding her firmly.

"You mean they didn't teach you to dance in police school?" he said
in her ear.

"Of course not. This is . . ." She had been going to say "absurd," but
the grass felt cool and springy beneath her bare feet, and the weight of
his hand on her back and the rhythm of the song seemed suddenly irresistible. "What is this?" she asked, fighting the temptation to close
her eyes. "It seems so familiar, but I can't quite . . ."

"Rodgers and Hart." Pulling her a little closer, he hummed along
with the melody. " 'Where or When,' it's called," he added, with a
trace of amusement in his voice.

The breeze lifted the hair on Gemma's neck, and for a moment she
felt herself floating, suspended between the music and his touch. "I'd
not have picked you for a dancer," she whispered.

"My secret ambition was to be Gene Kelly. . . ."

She felt his breath against her cheek, then she was aware only of the
music and the harmony of their steps.

The last flourish of the clarinet caught them in mid-step. They came
to an awkward halt, hands still clasped. Gemma felt the pulse beating
in her throat, then the rising flush of embarrassment.

She stepped back, freeing her hand. A low rumble of thunder vi-
brated in the air as she fumbled into her shoes and scooped up her
handbag. "I have to go," she said, and turning from him, she walked
away through the park without looking back.

IT WAS CHRISTMAS BEFORE LEWIS RETURNED to the Island for a visit. Evacuees had been streaming back into London for months, but the schools had closed at the beginning of the evacuation, and the returning children had no place to go. The government had not been responsive to appeals to re-open—the teachers had gone to the country with their charges, and many of the buildings had been taken over for civil defense.

"I'll not have you running the streets like a wild thing, not when you have a chance at a proper education," his mother had said firmly, but even though the government had launched a Christmas publicity campaign aimed at keeping children out of London—Keep them happy, keep them safe—she'd eventually given in to Lewis's pleas for a holiday at home.

His months in the country had been touched only lightly by the war. With the advent of petrol rationing in late September, Edwina's autos had been polished more often than driven, but to Lewis's delight, John had begun teaching him how to maintain them. Gardening was less to his liking, but he and William helped plant a winter garden behind the Hall kitchen. Edwina acquired two Jersey cows from a neighboring farmer as a hedge against the rationing of milk and butter, and on the Downs were ever-increasing signs of preparation as the army practiced training maneuvers and set up searchlight battery units.

None of this had prepared Lewis for the sight of London. He sat with his face pressed to a gap in the shatter-proof sticky-tape covering the window as his coach wound its slow way through streets empty of automobiles. People saved their petrol allotments for the weekends, managing as best they could on the overcrowded public transport. Sandbagged trenches, some painted in garish colors, scarred the public parks. The hurrying pedestrians were dressed all in somber grays and browns, as if they had adopted voluntary camouflage.

He walked from the bus stop to Stebondale Street, his footsteps growing slower as he climbed the last gentle rise. The street seemed meaner, dingier, than he remembered, and he felt a sudden uneasiness as his house came in sight. Would he find that things at home had changed, too? Going round the back, he entered the cluttered yard, then pushed open the kitchen door and peeked in. Familiar aromas assaulted him—cabbage and bacon and baking bread—and at the cooker, his mother stood with her back turned to

*him, her pink apron tied neatly at her waist. Pausing for a moment in her
stirring, she tilted her head in that listening way he knew so well.
"Lewis?" She turned, her thin face alight, and in a moment he was enveloped in a floury hug. "Let me look at you," she exclaimed, holding him
at arm's length. "Oh, my, your brothers will hardly recognize you, you've
grown so."*

*At the sight of his startled face, she laughed. "I wanted it to be a sur-
prise. Tommy and Edward have both managed a day's leave for Christmas. They'll be here tonight."*

*Cath came in then, high heels clattering on the floorboards, and gave
him a lipsticked smack on the cheek. Lewis stared at her in consternation.
"What's the film-star getup for?"*

*Cath tossed her head, but the motion didn't disturb her hair's smooth
waves. "I'm a grown woman now, Lewis Finch, and you should treat me
with some respect. I'm meeting someone, if you must know."*

*"Not if your da sees you like that," his mum said. "Lewis is right,
Cathleen. Wipe that muck from your face before your father gets home—"*

"But, Mummy, you know how long I had to queue to get this lipstick—"

*"You should have known better, then, shouldn't you, missy? And you'll
stay at home tonight with your brothers. I'll not hear another word."*

*"You should talk, anyway," Cath said, abandoning the argument and
pulling a face at Lewis. "Acting the toff like that."*

"What do you mean, toff?" he retorted, incensed.

*"Just look at you." She nodded at his pullover and trousers, castoffs of
William's, the trousers still a bit long. "And listen to you. You sound like
that reader on the BBC, what's his name, the one who talks like he has a
pencil stuck up his nose."*

"I do not—"

"You do so, Lewis Finch, and don't think I'm impressed one bit."

"And what makes you think I care?" He stuck his tongue out.

*Reaching out, Cath grabbed his earlobe between her thumb and fore-
finger and twisted.*

*He yelped and pinched back, his mum intervened, scolding them both,
and it was as if he'd never been away. As the day faded they gossiped over
cups of tea at the kitchen table until his dad arrived home from the ship-
yard, and shortly after that his brothers came in together, large and noisy,
looking like men—and strangers—in their new uniforms.*

That evening after tea, his dad took him for a stroll down to the river, their way lit only by moonlight on the melting snow. Although accustomed now to blackout in the country, Lewis had never seen the Island without light streaming from street lamps and headlamps and lace-curtained windows. It seemed a different city, an enchanted city, and he breathed deeply of the fresh air untainted by petrol fumes. In the still silence the occasional voice echoed oddly through the streets, and somewhere in the distance a bell chimed faintly for Christmas Eve services.

Lewis's dad walked without speaking, his hands clasped behind his back, puffing on the pipe he held clenched in his teeth. He had never been a man much for words, but Lewis didn't need them. He could sense his father's contentment in his company and he felt a stirring of pride.

When they reached Island Gardens, they had to feel their way carefully through the darkness under the trees, but as they emerged onto the moonlit promenade the river stretched silver and gleaming before them. The smoke from his father's pipe drifted out over the water like a fragrant cloud.

A barge passed by, lit only stern and prow by small, shaded lanterns. In the darkness and silence it seemed ghostly, primitive, a Viking longboat returned from the dead. Lewis shivered. Suddenly he felt a stab of homesickness as intense as those of his first few days at the Hall—and yet it was more than that. He wanted to freeze time, to hold everyone and everything unchanged, and the weight of his desire made it difficult to breathe.

"Da," he said, forcing the words out. "Let me stay here. The war's all bollocks anyway, everyone knows that. Nothing's going to happen—there's no reason I can't come home."

His father removed his pipe and sighed. "I wish it were so, Lewis. But the war's waiting. Like a beast, it is, before it pounces on you. I can feel its breath. Your mother can, as well."

Lewis had been away long enough to feel embarrassed by any reference to his Irish family's clairvoyance—something he knew William and Edwina would think of as superstitious nonsense, so he countered with his ultimate authority. "But they're saying in the newspaper and on the wireless—"

"It matters nought. They don't want a panic on their hands, so it's business as usual. But any fool can see the Germans won't stop where they are. It's only a matter of time, lad, and you're better off out of it." His dad tapped his pipe on the railing to empty it, then tucked it in the pocket of his coat. "Don't you see, knowing you're safe is the only thing gives your mum

any peace. We can't send your sister away, and your brothers have chosen their road—though before long I think it won't be a matter of choice for anyone young and fit enough to fight."

"I'll go, too, if it lasts long enough," said Lewis, smarting at always being thought a child.

"You know I'm not a religious man, lad—it's your mum who thinks so highly of the Church—but I'll say a prayer to all your mother's saints that this war ends long before that." He smiled down at Lewis. "And we'd best be getting back, or your mother will have Father Joseph out looking for us."

It was as close to a joke as his father ever came, and an effective means of ending an argument. Lewis matched his dad's steps, staying close beside him until they left the darkness of the park behind. They walked as briskly as the blackout allowed back to Stebondale Street, and the disappointment Lewis nursed became tinged ever so slightly with relief.

Even that disappointment was short-lived once they reached the house, for he was soon involved with the preparations for Christmas dinner. His family could have afforded few luxuries even had they been available, but his mother was adept at making do with little, and they sat down next day to a jolly table. Tommy and Edward had helped him make newspaper hats, and Cath had somehow procured a bit of colored tissue for homemade crackers. They'd filled them with bits of tinsel and mottoes concocted with much hilarity the previous evening. Lewis was even allowed a sip of Christmas gin, which inspired in him an affectionate glow and an unprecedented tolerance of his sister's teasing.

On this occasion, his family's gift seemed to have bypassed him altogether, for he had no premonition that this was the last time they would all be gathered together.

CHAPTER 11

*The great ships were brought
into the Island to loom over back
yards and gardens and the
foreign sailors were set down in
the dusty streets where the
children played.*

Eve Hostettler, from
Memories of Childhood
on the Isle of Dogs

KIT HAD BEEN WORKING DILI-
gently on his obstacle course since
lunchtime. The Millers' back garden
provided a level and shady area for
his endeavors, and he had managed
to persuade Laura and Colin to let
him stay behind while they went
into Cambridge for some shopping.

It was the dog show on the telly
last night that had given him the
idea. There had been the usual
best-of-breed judgings, which he'd
watched anxiously for dogs re-
sembling Tess. When he saw the
Norfolk terriers, with their shaggy
brown coats and bright black eyes,

he'd felt certain that Tess carried those genes somewhere in her ancestry.

But there had also been trials of agility and obedience open to all dogs, registered or not. He'd been particularly enchanted by the obstacle-course relay races, and the idea that Tess's lack of pedigree could be overcome in such a contest had given him a fierce sense of mission. Tess was as smart as any dog—smarter, even—and now he'd seen a way to prove just how special she was.

He'd constructed the jumps from last winter's leftover firewood—two logs for the supports, one for the crosspiece: just the right size for a small dog. Then he'd made a ramp from a piece of plywood and some milk crates he'd found in the garage, and a ring from an old tire rim. The only thing he hadn't managed to figure out was the dispenser for the tennis ball at the far end of the course; the idea being that Tess would run the course, retrieve the ball from the dispenser, then bring it back to him at the starting point.

At first Tess had bounded after him excitedly, jumping at the end of the lead dangling from his pocket, but when she'd realized no walk or games were immediately forthcoming, she'd retired to a shady spot under the oak tree. There she lay with her head on her front paws, her tail thumping occasionally as she followed him with her eyes.

Kit kept up a singsong running commentary on his tasks as he worked. Although this monologue was addressed to Tess, he found it helped keep him from thinking, and thinking was something he'd done his best to avoid the last few days.

Since he'd refused yesterday to take Duncan's phone call, Laura had been watching him with evident concern, but she hadn't questioned him about it. He'd even caught Colin giving him the odd worried look, and being nicer than usual, which was worse. He didn't want to talk to Colin, either—didn't want to talk to anyone about what had happened, and especially not to Duncan.

But every so often he'd found himself pulling the dog-eared photo of Duncan in his scout's uniform from his pocket. It was as if he couldn't help himself, and even as he finished a last adjustment to the log jump, his fingers slid into his pocket just far enough to feel the photo's edge, assuring him he hadn't lost it. The image had become so clear in his mind that he really didn't need to look at it anymore. It gave him the oddest feeling, like looking in a mirror that was ever so slightly warped—the hair a shade darker than his, the eyes a bit grayer, the nose a little less sharp.

But that wasn't the image he wanted to see. He'd locked himself in the bathroom last night after Colin fell asleep, searching his face in the mirror, trying to find the resemblance to his mother that people were always going on about.

He gave a sharp shake of his head, pushing the thought aside as he knelt beside Tess. "Come on, girl," he said as he took the dog's lead from his pocket and snapped it onto her collar. "Let's give this a try." He checked his supply of treats, giving her one for good measure, then started her trotting towards the beginning of the course as he clucked encouragement. As they neared the first jump, he picked up speed, urging, "Come on, girl, you can do it! Jump!"

Tess sat down hard in front of the log, tilting her head to one side and staring at him as if he'd gone completely daft. The expression on her face was so comical that he couldn't help laughing, but he was determined to go on nonetheless. Positioning himself on the far side of the log, he tightened the tension on the lead so that she couldn't go round, then held up a dog biscuit. "All right, girl, you want the biscuit, you come and get it. Come on! Jump!" He whistled coaxingly, and after a few aborted attempts to go round the sides, Tess jumped effortlessly over the log.

Kit whooped with delight as he fed her the biscuit, then flopped flat on his back in the grass while Tess tried to lick his face, one of their favorite games.

Suddenly, he had the odd sensation that he was being watched. He sat up, holding his squirming dog by the collar, and looked round the garden. It took a moment to make out the man standing by the gate, in the deep shadow of the yew hedge. His heart gave a thump of fear, then he realized there was something familiar about the figure.

The man lifted a hand to the latch and stepped through the gate, and as he moved into the sunlight, Kit saw his face clearly. Swallowing against the constriction in his throat, he said tentatively, "Dad?"

· · ·

"IT'S NOT IN THE BEST OF taste, is it?" Kincaid said to Gemma as he stared up at Reg Mortimer's building.

His meeting with Chief Superintendent Childs had left him distinctly out of sorts. Childs had just fielded a call from Sir Peter Mortimer, demanding to know why the police were badgering his son rather than making progress in finding Annabelle Hammond's murderer, and he had transferred his irritation to Kincaid with instructions to get somewhere bloody quick—and to go easy on Mortimer.

When Kincaid had suggested that the two things might not be synonymous, considering the fact that Mortimer had apparently lied to them from the beginning, Childs had warned him against making any allegations he couldn't back up.

Gemma shaded her eyes against the glare as she examined the building's little rounded balconies and portholes. Funnel-like structures rose from its top, while one side of the building cascaded downwards in a stepping-stone series of penthouse terraces. "I think it's jolly. A child's fantasy of living in an ocean liner, rather than a tree house. Looks a bit posh, though."

As he watched her, he thought she seemed remarkably unwilted for having slogged about in the heat most of the day. She'd been waiting for him at Limehouse Station and had soon caught him up on what had happened in his absence.

After her visit with Jo Lowell's neighbor, she'd rung Martin Lowell's bank, only to be informed that he was away at a meeting for the afternoon. But she'd at least finagled his home address.

While waiting for Lowell to get home, they had decided to try Reg Mortimer's flat, even though Mortimer hadn't answered his phone.

Only in passing had she mentioned to Kincaid that she'd seen Gordon Finch again, and that Finch had claimed he hadn't known of a connection between his family and Annabelle's or of his father's relationship with her.

It had been on the tip of his tongue to ask her why she hadn't pressed Finch harder, but he'd bitten back his comment, realizing he didn't trust his own motivations.

Following her now as she made her way round the building to the entrance, he wondered if the difficulty lay with him or with her. He was ordinarily comfortable with Gemma's interviewing skills, so why was he letting the matter of Gordon Finch get his nose out of joint?

As she reached the main doors, Gemma looked back and smiled at him, and he was glad he'd resisted his earlier impulse to snap at her. "Care for a cruise, mate?"

"Just as long as the ship stays firmly on dry land," he replied, holding the door for her.

Inside the building, a speedy lift whisked them up to the level of Reg Mortimer's flat. Kincaid knocked on his door, then they waited in the hush of the corridor. Gemma stood inches from him, and he could smell the sweet and distinctive scent of her skin. After a moment, he knocked again, looking at her with a shrug. "Where do you suppose—"

He stopped as the click of the dead bolt came clearly through the door. "It seems we're in luck, after all."

The door swung open. Reg Mortimer had discarded his tie; his pink shirt was rumpled and the tail had come partially untucked. He shoved back the brown hair that had fallen over his forehead in an unruly wave and groaned. "What is it this time?" he demanded.

Kincaid smiled. "People are always so happy to see us—I think we must be more popular than the dentist."

"At least the dentist doesn't bother you at home," Reg retorted. Then he stepped back reluctantly, adding, "I suppose you'd better come in."

The door opened directly into a large sitting room and Kincaid looked round with interest. The place struck him as faintly tropical. Two white, cotton-covered sofas faced each other across a round sisal rug. Table and bookcases were of pale, clean-lined oak, and the windows were dressed only in white linen shades pulled to half-mast. Light from riverside windows flooded the space. The room's color came from the lime and tangerine cushions tossed on the sofas and the contemporary paintings adorning the walls. The only immediate signs of human occupation were provided by a vase of wilted day lilies on the coffee table and a jumble of papers spread out on the gateleg table that stood half open against one wall.

"Nice flat," Kincaid said admiringly, taking a seat on one of the white sofas. "Hiding out from work, are you?"

Reg sank down onto the edge of the opposite sofa. "I kept thinking that Annabelle was just away for a bit, on a buying trip, maybe . . . expecting her to walk through the door. . . . It still doesn't seem real, somehow." He glanced at Gemma, who had moved behind him and was surveying the paintings with her hands clasped behind her back, as if visiting a gallery. "Is that usual?" he went on. "What I means is, you deal with this sort of thing all the time. . . . I've never experienced . . ."

"People find various ways of dealing with violent death. Perhaps that's why you've been less than truthful with us, Mr. Mortimer."

"What—what are you talking about?" Mortimer's eyes widened and in the bright light, Kincaid saw the sudden dilation of his pupils. There was no doubt the man was frightened of something.

"Did you think that Jo Lowell wouldn't tell us what really happened at that dinner party?" Kincaid asked, giving him a last chance.

"But I told you—"

"You can't have imagined we wouldn't check your story."

"You thought Jo would protect her sister, didn't you?" said Gemma, pulling up the chair that had sat in front of the gateleg table. "Was that the way it always was, Jo protecting Annabelle?"

"Yes— No— I mean . . . I can't think anymore."

"Then I'll help you, shall I?" said Kincaid. "You didn't know that Annabelle had had an affair with Martin Lowell until Harry blurted it out that night. But their affair happened before you and Annabelle became involved, so why were you so furious? Were you afraid she'd kept seeing him after she took up with you? Or was it because she hadn't told you the truth?"

"She said it wasn't anyone else's business—" Abruptly realizing his admission, Mortimer stopped and looked from Kincaid to Gemma.

"You argued about it after you left Jo's, didn't you?" asked Gemma. "You must have wondered what else she hadn't told you."

For a moment, Mortimer tensed as if he might deny it. Then his shoulders sagged. "How could Annabelle have betrayed Jo and the children that way? And if she could do such a thing to Jo . . ."

"Then she could betray anyone," Gemma finished for him. "Even you."

"It was too humiliating—I couldn't bear it. How could I tell you? And I didn't see how it could possibly matter—"

"You can't know what matters," Kincaid interjected sharply. "An investigation fits together like a puzzle—you can't know how your piece falls in with someone else's." He scowled at Mortimer and added, "Unless, of course, your piece is the only one that counts. Let's say that Annabelle added insult to injury. You were enraged with her already, angrier than you had ever been. You accused her of sleeping with someone else—" A look at Mortimer's stricken face told him he'd hit home, and he felt a pulse of excitement. "You demanded to know who it was. And she told you—didn't she, Reg?"

Through the flat's open windows came the hoot of a tug's horn, then the amplified voice of the tour guide on the Thames Ferry, extolling the architectural features of the riverside buildings in an exaggerated Cockney accent.

Reg Mortimer gaped at Kincaid like a rabbit mesmerized by a car's headlamps, his eyes wide and dilated, his breathing shallow. Then he clamped a hand over his mouth and bolted from the room.

A moment later they heard the sound of retching coming from the bathroom. Kincaid made a grimace of distaste.

"You certainly got a reaction," Gemma said softly. "The guv'nor is going to love you." She nodded towards the walls. "Have a look at those while we've got a moment."

The toilet flushed, then water ran. Kincaid stood and went to examine the paintings he'd only glanced at from a distance. Two of them echoed the limes and tangerines of the sofa cushions in more muted tones. The images were surreal, a bit jarring, but fascinating. Silvers and golds were predominant in the third canvas, an abstract study of amoeba-like shapes. When Kincaid saw the signature, his eyes narrowed. He went back and looked more carefully at the first two paintings. Again, the artist's name was one he recognized. If these canvases were original, he thought, they must have cost a pretty penny indeed.

Just as he moved to the gateleg table, he heard the water shut off in the bathroom. He only managed a swift look at the papers spread out on the tabletop before Mortimer came back into the room.

"I'm sorry," Mortimer said. His face glistened with perspiration. "I think I must be ill. Since Annabelle . . . I can't seem to keep anything down."

"It's very stressful, keeping things to yourself, Reg," Gemma said softly. "Why don't you tell us what Annabelle said that night?"

Reg sat down, clutching his middle protectively, then with a grimace he sat up straight and clasped his hands between his knees. "All right. She said she'd been trying to make up her mind to tell me for months. She'd fallen in love with someone else. She hadn't known, until she met him, what it was like to feel that way about someone—and she'd realized that even if he wouldn't have her, she could never be satisfied with less.

"And then she stopped, in the tunnel, with an astonished look on her face—you'd have thought she'd seen the Second Coming. She told me to go, but I said no, we had to talk, so she said she'd meet me at the Ferry House in half an hour, if I would just leave her for a bit. So I walked away, and it was just like I told you—when I looked back I saw her talking to the busker. But I'd no idea she even knew him, much less . . . Was it him she meant? Gordon Finch?"

"We can't be certain, but Finch says he broke off their relationship several months ago, and in the tunnel that night she pleaded with him to resume things. He says he refused her."

"Refused her? But why?"

Gemma didn't answer his question. "Did Annabelle tell you she wanted to end your engagement?"

"Not in so many words, no. But I suppose that's what she meant—I thought if I just gave her time to calm down, she'd change her mind."

"Did you wait for her?"

"No. I just walked for a bit, and the more I thought, the more it seemed that she couldn't really have meant those things she said. When I got to the pub I thought she'd be waiting to tell me it was all a mistake."

"And when she didn't come?"

"I've told you." Mortimer drew a breath. "I rang her, then went to her flat, but she wasn't there."

Kincaid regarded him with irritation. They knew Mortimer had gone to the pub, had rung Annabelle from there, just as he said. Forensics had not yet found any evidence that Annabelle's body had been moved in her car, Reg didn't own an automobile, and Kincaid couldn't come up with any believable scenario in which Reg had persuaded Annabelle to go with him to the park, then strangled her.

"Reg," said Gemma thoughtfully, "you knew Annabelle better than anyone, except perhaps her family—you'd been friends since you were children. She was very upset—shattered, even. What do you think she might have done when she left the tunnel?"

"Do you think I haven't asked myself that a thousand times?" Mortimer demanded. Then he frowned. "But . . . when she needed a refuge, she went to the warehouse."

"HOLD UP A BIT." GEMMA CLASPED Kincaid's elbow to steady herself as she slipped off her sandal and rubbed at her heel.

"Blister?"

She grimaced. "From the bloody tunnel, I think. I'd give anything for a plaster." After leaving Reg Mortimer's, they had walked from Island Gardens through the foot tunnel to Greenwich once again, avoiding rush-hour automobile traffic in the Blackwall Tunnel, but Gemma heartily regretted having worn new shoes.

"Not much further now," Kincaid said sympathetically. They'd reached the entrance to Martin Lowell's block of flats, not far from Greenwich center and the riverfront. The buildings here were red-brick, dark as dried blood, and showing signs of shabbiness. Rubbish had accumulated in corners of the courtyard, and the few shrubs looked stunted and neglected. "That looks like the flat number, straight across the court. A far cry from Emerald Crescent, I'd say."

Gemma slid her shoe back on and straightened up. "Right, then. Let's pay a call on Prince Charming."

Martin Lowell yanked the door open before Gemma had even rung the bell. "What the—"

"We'd like another word, Mr. Lowell," said Kincaid.

"I thought we'd done all that already. Look, I'm meeting someone—"

"It seems you left out a few things when we talked yesterday. Why don't we go inside, unless you prefer we tell your neighbors about your affair with your sister-in-law."

A door had opened two flats along and a woman with curlers in her hair was watching them with unabashed inquisitiveness.

His eyes still locked with Kincaid's, Lowell muttered, "Nosy bitch." But he stepped back, calling out as he allowed them into the flat, "It's all right, Mrs. Mulrooney, nothing to worry about."

Gemma looked round, thinking of the one time she'd visited her ex-husband's flat after they'd divorced. Apparently there were some men incapable of making a dwelling into a home on their own—Rob had been one, and it looked as though Martin Lowell was another. This flat looked clean, at least, which was more than she could have said for Rob's, but that was its only saving grace. The walls were the color of old putty, unadorned in any manner, and the sofa and matching armchair of a worn and undistinguished brown corduroy.

The obvious focal point of the room was a large new telly on a laminated stand. There was little else to speak of, other than a stack of financial magazines on the cheap coffee table, lined up neatly beside the remote control. The heavy mustard-colored drapes were pulled three-quarters of the way against the late afternoon sun.

"Why didn't you tell us it was your affair with Annabelle that broke up your marriage?" Kincaid asked, moving about the room as he spoke, touching the magazines, examining the television. He stopped by the sofa as if assessing its welcome, then continued with his wandering.

Martin watched him uneasily, but didn't invite them to sit. "I didn't see why I should. I hadn't seen Annabelle in a couple of years."

"Not since she broke things off with you, in fact?" Kincaid stopped his pacing to peer into the small kitchen.

"That's right. Was it Jo who told you?"

"Does it matter?" asked Gemma. "Were you expecting her to shield you?"

He gave her a bitter smile. "I see you've bought the Hammond sisters' story lock, stock, and barrel, and I'm the villain of the piece."

"Is it not true, then?"

"That I slept with Annabelle? Oh, that's true enough. But it would have been all right, if Annabelle hadn't told Jo."

Gemma stared at him in repelled fascination, wondering just how covering up an affair with your sister-in-law made it okay.

"I suppose Jo told you Annabelle was just trying to make amends? Set wrongs right, or some such righteous crap?" Martin continued. "The truth is, Annabelle liked to stir things. She discarded men like a snake sheds skin, and once she'd no use for you, she liked to amuse herself by shredding your life to bits."

"Are you saying Annabelle broke things off with you before she told Jo?"

"She'd set her sights on Peter Mortimer's son—more socially advantageous for a girl going places. I suppose she thought the match would benefit her new position as managing director."

"Perhaps she genuinely cared for him," suggested Gemma. "Or felt comfortable with him. They'd been friends since childhood, after all."

"If you think Annabelle did anything without an ulterior motive, you're as stupid as all the rest of the poor suckers she sank her fangs into," Martin said dismissively. "I even feel a bit sorry for Reg Mortimer—but not sorry enough."

"How can you be so bloody callous?" Gemma felt the telltale flush of anger staining her cheeks, but she didn't care. "You slept with this woman. She was your wife's sister. She loved your children. Don't you feel anything for her?"

For a moment she thought he would snarl back at her, but instead, he said with unexpected tenderness, "You've no idea what it was like to love her. . . . And then to be discarded with no more remorse than if she'd given an old pair of shoes to the jumble. To lose your home, and your children." He jabbed a finger at her. "If I were you, Sergeant, I'd look very carefully at anyone Annabelle came in contact with. Because I promise you there'll be others like me. Others whose lives she destroyed without a backwards glance. Do you think Mortimer killed her?"

"I'm more interested in where you were last Friday night, Mr. Lowell," said Gemma, keeping herself in check. "Because Annabelle had reason to search you out. She'd learned what sort of poison you'd been feeding your son. Did she come here to have it out with you?"

"I told you, I hadn't seen her in years. There was a time . . . just afterwards . . . but she wouldn't see me, wouldn't take my calls."

"There's still the little matter of the shares," said Kincaid. "Annabelle must have drawn up that will before anything happened between you. Did she tell you she'd never changed it, but that she meant to now? You could use the money, couldn't you?" He gestured round the flat. "It must be hard, paying support for two kids, and all because of her. The temptation would be tremendous."

Lowell stared at Kincaid, his face blank. "That's daft. I told you I had no idea about the will. And I didn't see Annabelle on Friday night."

"Then you won't mind telling us your movements."

"That's easy enough," said Lowell, and Gemma thought she detected a hint of relief in his voice. "I was with someone all of Friday evening. I spent the night at her flat."

"And she'll vouch for you . . . this friend?" Kincaid raised an eyebrow. "Is she married?"

"Of course she'll vouch for me. She just lives round the corner. And no, she's not married, or I wouldn't have spent the night with her, would I?" Lowell answered reasonably.

There was a soft tap at the door, then it opened a few inches and, as if on cue, a woman's voice called, "Marty?"

"Your alibi, by any chance?" guessed Kincaid.

"You might as well speak to her now," Martin said with a shrug as the woman pushed the door wider and stepped into the sitting room. "This is Brandy."

Martin's visitor couldn't have been more than nineteen. Her bleached hair was curled in a mass of long, tight ringlets, she wore a mini so skimpy Gemma felt sure her knickers would show when she sat down, and her halter top exposed a pierced navel.

"Marty?" the girl said again, looking at them curiously. "I got worried when you didn't come at six, like you said. You know you promised you'd set up my tanning lamp."

The corner of Kincaid's mouth twitched as he glanced at Gemma. He said, "Some guys have all the luck."

"JANICE IS SENDING A CONSTABLE ROUND to take a formal statement from Martin Lowell's girlfriend," Kincaid said as he returned from using the phone and sank gratefully back into his chair on Hazel's patio. "Too bloody bad we don't have enough evidence to search his flat—or Reg Mortimer's, for that matter," he added, retrieving his beer from the flagstone.

Gemma sat beside him, her legs stretched out in front of her, a bottle of cold cider cradled on her chest. She'd changed from her trousers into shorts and tank top, and had pulled her hair up off her neck with a flower-patterned scrunchy.

Hazel had invited them to stay for tabouli and a green salad, insisting that it was too hot for a cooked meal, or for Gemma to attempt preparing anything in her flat's tiny kitchen, and she'd sent them out to the patio with cool drinks while she finished putting things together.

The children were running in circles on the square of lawn, seemingly oblivious to the heat, their half-naked bodies lit in flashes by the long, low shafts of sunlight streaking through the trees.

Sipping her cider, Gemma said, "I think it's generous of you to elevate Brandy to the status of girlfriend. Martin Lowell should be ashamed of himself—and so should you for ogling her."

"I didn't ogle."

"You did so. But I suppose you should get some dispensation, as she might as well have been going about in her bra and knickers."

"You'd have thought Lowell would be more discriminating, after Jo and Annabelle," Kincaid said, hoping to redeem himself in the matter of Brandy. "But how does a thirty-something banker manage to pull half-naked teenaged birds, tasteful or not?"

"I thought surely Martin Lowell couldn't be as bad as Jo made him sound, but he's a forty-carat bastard if I've ever met one," Gemma said with feeling.

Kincaid glanced at her, amused. "I rather got the impression you didn't take to him."

"You noticed?" She smiled and settled a bit further down in her chair. "The odd thing is, I can see why they were attracted to him. Jo and Annabelle, I mean, and even Brandy."

"The Heathcliff-in-a-suit looks?"

"He made me feel like a butterfly pinned to a board. If you didn't know what a rotter he was . . ." She took a contemplative sip of cider. "Or for some women, he might be appealing even if they did."

"Including Annabelle?" Kincaid asked. The sun dropped behind the roof of the house next door, and the garden seemed instantly cooler.

"Mrs. Pargeter, Jo's neighbor, said she thought that Annabelle was so devastated by her mother's death that she grabbed the first thing that looked like love. But if that's the case, I think she must have realized fairly quickly what Martin Lowell was really like." Gemma scowled. "What I don't understand is why she told Jo. In spite of what Lowell says, Annabelle hasn't struck me as a righteous sort, or as someone who deliberately hurt people."

"Lowell seemed to want to have his cake and eat it, too, so Jo need never have known—"

"But he might have threatened Annabelle, told her he'd confess to Jo if she tried to end things. I don't think he'd have let her go easily, and maybe Annabelle saw telling Jo as the only option."

It seemed to Kincaid that Gemma was going to great lengths to whitewash Annabelle Hammond's behavior. "What about her affairs with Gordon and Lewis Finch? Surely she knew Mortimer would be hurt if he learned the truth about those."

"I think she was searching for something she hadn't found in Reg Mortimer. And she *kept* those relationships secret. Up to a point anyway. She only told Mortimer there was someone else under extreme provocation."

"*If* Mortimer is telling the truth," Kincaid agreed with some skepticism. "I still believe he's holding out on us. Did you get a look at his papers?"

Nodding, Gemma stretched out her feet and wiggled toes unencumbered by sandals. "Looked like bills and bank statements, but I didn't catch the details. Were those paintings as valuable as I thought?"

"If I remember what I read recently in the *Times*, I'd say twenty to thirty thousand pounds apiece."

Gemma whistled through her teeth. "Crikey. How could he afford that?"

"Family money?" Kincaid finished his beer, upending the bottle to get the last drops. "His father's on the Hammond's board, but from what I've seen, none of the Hammonds have that sort of lolly."

"Posh flat, expensive furniture, expensive paintings, expensive clothes . . . and a stack of bills and bank papers." Gemma wrinkled her nose. "Financial overextension? But I can't see how that would give Reg a reason to kill Annabelle. He had everything to lose and nothing to gain."

"He might have thought she'd left him her shares. Or that he'd get her position."

"A big risk, either way, but we should do a bit of digging into his affairs—as much as we can without getting up Sir Peter's nose," added Gemma.

"I'm not happy about the Finches, either—major or minor," Kincaid said, glancing at her. "I find it very hard to swallow that neither of them learned about the other."

"Reg Mortimer's story seems to bear out what Gordon told us—that he was the one who rejected her. What if it was because he found out about Annabelle and his father?"

"That would give him a bloody good motive for killing her—"

"Maybe when he found out, two or three months ago. But why kill her now? When she wanted to mend things between them?"

"We only have his word for that," Kincaid said, irritated by her defense of Finch. "For all we know, she told him it was his father she was in love with, and he snapped and killed her."

Gemma glared at him. "According to Mortimer, Annabelle said that even if the man she loved wouldn't have her, she wouldn't be satisfied with less—if you weren't being pigheaded you'd see that Mortimer's statement supports Gordon Finch's."

Stung, he retorted, "And you weren't being pigheaded when you compromised your safety by going to Gordon Finch's flat on your own yesterday?"

"Are you still on about that? Give me credit for a bit of judgement, will you? I wouldn't have gone if I hadn't felt perfectly safe, and I got results, didn't I?"

"Yes, but—"

"Since when do I need telling how to do my job?"

Kincaid realized this was escalating into a full-scale row. "Gemma, I'm sorry. I didn't mean—"

"Shhhh," she said suddenly, holding out a restraining hand. "Listen."

It took him a moment to realize that it was the silence she meant. He sat up and looked round. The children had been huddled together, giggling, the last time he'd looked, but now they were nowhere to be seen.

"Toby?" Gemma called, setting her drink on the table and starting to rise.

Kincaid stood. "I'll go see what they're up to, the little buggers." It would give him a chance to cool off.

The children were not allowed to go out the garden gate alone—even though it was only a few steps from the gate to the front door of Gemma's flat, they would be unsupervised on a busy street. Kincaid's heart quickened at the thought, and it was with difficulty that he kept his pace unhurried as he crossed the lawn, peering into the pockets of deeper shadow. They were simply hiding, he told himself, and as he neared the gate he caught a pale flash of movement behind the mock orange hedge.

Whistling faintly, he walked on by, and was rewarded by the sound of a stifled giggle. He backed up a step and stood looking round, as if confused, then whirled about and reached through a gap in the hedge. "Got you!" His hands closed on damp skin and the children squealed with delight. Gently, he extricated them from the shrubbery, then scooped Toby up under one arm and Holly under the other. Their small bodies were sticky from the drippings of the iced lollies Hazel had given them after their tea. "All right, you two. You stay where we can see you, or you'll have your baths early and up to bed."

"One more hide-and-seek, please, Duncan, pretty please," wheedled Holly, while Toby squirmed and wiggled in his grasp.

"Can't catch me, can't catch me," the boy chanted.

Kincaid tightened his grip. "I just did, you wiggle-worm. I'll tell you what. If you're both very, very, very good, I'll read you a story after your baths."

"In my room or Toby's room?" Holly demanded, always the one for details.

Kincaid stopped and made a show of thinking, the children still dangling from his arms. "If you promise to be little angels, I'll read the story in Toby's room. And I'll carry you home, Holly. How about that?"

"A fireman's carry?" Holly had recently discovered the joys of bouncing upside down over his shoulder.

"If you like." He plopped them in front of Gemma and they darted away like minnows scattering in a pond.

His arms felt weightless now, and the impressions of the children's bodies lingered like an afterimage on the retina. Suddenly, he felt a longing for Kit so intense that it took him by surprise. He sat down clumsily, as if his legs had turned to jelly.

"You should have scolded them," Gemma said crossly.

"Gemma—"

"What is it?" She turned to look at him, as if alerted by something in his voice.

"I—" he began, but he couldn't find the words to express the sense of loss he felt. Instead, he said, "I suppose it's this business with Kit that has me out of sorts. If he won't talk to me on the phone, I'm going to Cambridge to see him." He realized he'd made the decision as he was speaking.

"I thought he didn't want to see you."

"Hazel said I needed to let him know my feelings hadn't changed, no matter how he behaved. How can I do that if I can't talk to him?" he asked, his frustration rising again.

Gemma sat up in the lawn chair, frowning. "That was before Ian complicated matters by waltzing back into Kit's life. Maybe it would be less difficult for Kit now if you just let Ian get on with the job."

"Just bow out? Just trust Ian's judgement after everything we've been through? What's to stop him from moving Kit back into the Grantchester cottage, then changing his mind again in a month or two?"

Shaking her head, Gemma said, "What option do you have?"

"I can still see him," Kincaid said stubbornly, wondering why Gemma suddenly seemed to be at cross-purposes with him over everything.

"All right." Gemma sighed and sank back into the curve of her chair. "Go tomorrow, then. I'll cover for you. Just make sure you've placated the guv first, and if all hell breaks loose while you're gone"—she gave him a pinched smile—"it'll be on your wicket."

THEY ATE IN THE GARDEN, BY the light of citronella candles lit to keep the flies away. Hazel's tabouli combined the richness of feta cheese, Provençal olives, and ripe tomatoes with the freshness of lemon and mint, and Tim had opened a chilled bottle of Pinot grigio to accompany the dish. The children entertained themselves on the flag-stones with a dog-eared deck of playing cards they'd discovered in the kitchen junk drawer, allowing the adults to eat in peace.

As Kincaid glanced across the table at Gemma, she turned and laughed at something Tim had said. In the candlelight, she looked re-laxed and happy, and suddenly the thought of Annabelle Hammond intruded. Had Annabelle enjoyed her last dinner party as much as this?

She had been among friends, or at least so she thought—her sister, her fiancé, her sister's friends, and her adored nephew and niece—and then her pleasant evening had disintegrated into nightmare. First Harry Lowell, then Reg, then Gordon Finch—all male, and all, it seemed, turned against her in some way. Had Annabelle gone to some-one else for solace—a woman, perhaps?

He thought suddenly of Teresa Robbins. They'd taken her at face value, the loyal and distressed employee, a trifle plain, a bit colorless; and yet she seemed to have settled quite competently into Annabelle's job. What if Annabelle had gone to her, confiding something that Teresa was unwilling to reveal? She might be protecting Annabelle's memory—or she might be protecting Reg Mortimer.

Or perhaps such speculation was just his way of salving his guilt at the thought of taking a morning off in the midst of a murder investi-gation. But he made a mental note to ask Gemma to have another word with her in the morning.

After dinner, he offered to do the washing up while Gemma gave the children their baths. Hazel and Tim had taken the opportunity to go for a walk in the cool of the evening, so he had the kitchen to him-self. There was no dishwasher—refitting the kitchen was one of the luxuries Hazel and Tim had forgone when Hazel had quit her private practice to stay home with Holly—but Kincaid found the routine of soaping and rinsing relaxing.

As he filled the sink with lemon-scented suds and took a clean tea towel from the drawer, it abruptly occurred to him that this sort of life was what he wanted with Gemma, and that he had begun to take its eventuality for granted. But Gemma seemed to be pushing him away lately, and he didn't know how to close the distance starting to yawn between them.

The kitchen door swung open with a thump and the children burst in, dressed in their pajamas, shouting, "Story, story!" Behind them came Gemma, tendrils of damp hair that had escaped from her ponytail curling round her face.

When he'd finished his task and read to the children, Gemma poured them both a glass of wine and they took their drinks outside and sat together for a few moments on the steps that led from her flat up into the Cavendishes' garden.

He massaged her back where he knew she liked it best, between her shoulder blades, and when she leaned against him he wrapped an arm round her and brushed his lips against the nape of her neck. For a moment he felt her respond, pressing against him; then she pulled away.

"Toby's been restless the last couple of nights," she said, rising and finishing her wine. "Must be the remnants of his cold. And I didn't sleep all that well myself last night."

"I can take a hint," he said lightly, standing and kissing her chastely on the cheek. "I'll see you at Limehouse in the morning."

But once at home in his own bed he tossed and turned, unable to get comfortable, especially when Sid settled himself heavily across his feet. At last he gave the cat a gentle boot and made a concentrated attempt to clear his mind of all its circular, nagging thoughts. As he drifted off to sleep, an image came to him with the bright lucidity of a dream.

Gemma stood in a sunlit field of barley, the light sparking from her hair as she laughed. Then as he watched, he realized it wasn't Gemma he saw at all, but Annabelle Hammond.

AT A TINY TABLE WEDGED IN the pub's back corner, Teresa sat across from Reg Mortimer.

When she'd finally got home after shutting things down at the warehouse for the day, she'd found a message from him on her answer phone, asking her to meet him at The Grapes in Limehouse, on Narrow Street. It was the first she'd heard from him since he'd left the solicitor's office after lunch, and his voice held an odd note, pleading, almost. As the machine clicked off, she automatically ran a hand through her hair and straightened her blouse, then chided herself for thinking he'd asked to see her for any reason other than business.

But she'd not been able to stop herself from brushing her hair and putting on a bit of makeup before she ran out of the flat to catch the DLR at Crossharbour.

At Westferry Station she left the train and, jostled by homeward-bound commuters, made her way down the concrete steps from the platform. Squinting against the low evening sun, she turned right into Limehouse Causeway, then walked along Narrow Street until she came to the pub. The establishment was one of the historic fixtures of Lime-house, catering now to the upwardly mobile, and she knew it only by reputation, as it was not the sort of place one went on one's own for a bite of shepherd's pie or fish and chips.

She entered tentatively, squeezing her way among the suit-and-tied clientele packed sardinelike in the long, narrow space, until she spotted Reg in the far corner. He waved to her, and when she reached the table he stood and gave her an unexpected kiss on the cheek. He looked slightly flushed; his hair fell untidily on his brow and he looked even more handsome than usual.

"Thanks awfully for coming," he said as he seated her. "Have you been here before? The crowds will thin out in a bit, and the food's brilliant. I thought you could use a good meal. But first I'll get you something from the bar, shall I? There's a nice summer ale, a bit citrusy."

"Lovely," Teresa managed, and as he turned away towards the bar she leaned forwards and sniffed surreptitiously at his drink. Unadulter-ated lemonade, as far as she could tell, and not surprising, as he didn't ordinarily drink—yet she could have sworn he was tiddly. Frowning, she watched him chatting to the barman with the same feverish jollity.

He came back with her drink and a menu, and when he sat their knees touched unavoidably in the small space under the table. "I'd rec-ommend the fish cakes," he said, opening her menu for her. "I know they sound boringly pedestrian, but they're divine. And I'm sure there's some sort of historical precedent—Dickens ate them, or something. Did you know this is supposed to be the pub Dickens called the Six Jolly Fellowship Porters in *Our Mutual Friend*? He described the bar as 'not much bigger than a hackney coach,' and that's still true enough. It had the veranda overlooking the river in those days, too, though I daresay it's a bit sturdier now, and the wooden ladder that de-scended to the ships so the watermen could climb up to the bar is long gone. We'll go outside afterwards and have a drink, if you like, and in the meantime you can just imagine the bowsprit of an anchored square-rigger poking through the window and the hearty fellows drinking their pints." He nodded at the window above her head and raised his glass. "To bygone spirits."

Their eyes met as he seemed to realize what he'd said, and in the uncomfortable silence that followed neither of them spoke the name that hovered between them. Normally adept at filling silences and putting others at their ease, Reg was the least likely person she knew to make such an awkward remark. And yet tonight he seemed to be possessed by a sort of reckless desperation.

Searching for a way to rescue them both, she closed the menu without looking at it and said, "What about you, Reg? Aren't you having anything?"

"Just some soup, I think, to keep you company. Is it the fish cakes, then?"

When she nodded, he got up again and gave their order at the bar. "There's a proper restaurant upstairs," he told her as he returned. "But I'm glad they've left the pub a pub. There ought to be some immutable things in the world, don't you think?"

"Reg, I—"

"I'm sorry I buggered off this afternoon after the solicitor. I shouldn't have, leaving you on your own like that."

"Oh, no." She shook her head. "It was quite all right, really. It's just that I was a bit worried about you, when you didn't come back to the office."

"As if you hadn't enough to deal with." He looked at her, his face still for the first time, and after a moment added, "I have been a washout these last few days, haven't I? I just can't seem to stick it."

Teresa blinked, surprised by such a personal admission. He *had* been quite useless at the office, if she were to be brutal about it, seemingly unable to manage tasks that he could ordinarily do without batting an eye. But she'd no idea how she would cope if she were in his position, and she knew people reacted differently to grief. Her own response had been to buckle down to the job, because it was the concentration that kept her going.

In the end, she didn't deny his failures, but said, "Reg, if there's anything I can do to help—"

"You've been a peach as it is." He reached out and touched his fingers to her cheek. Suddenly very aware of his legs against hers, and of her response, she flushed with embarrassment, but didn't withdraw her knees. It was wicked of her to hope, even, that he found her attractive, but she'd discovered that knowing the wrongness of it didn't make the feelings go away.

The waitress arrived with their order, relieving Teresa of the necessity of responding to his comment. Rather to her surprise, she discovered that, in spite of everything, she was ravenous. The fish cakes were as good as Reg had promised and she tucked into them with enthusiasm.

He watched her, smiling, while he toyed with his soup, and when she'd finished he said, "Good girl. Couldn't have you wasting away to nothing—where would Hammond's be without you?"

The fears she'd managed to hold at bay the past few days clutched at her. "Reg, what are we going to do? Already, I'm finding things I don't know how to handle—I can't guess what Annabelle would have done—"

"Use your own judgement. Annabelle trusted you—it's time you trusted yourself."

"But I haven't the authority," she protested. "And the business was precarious enough even with Annabelle in charge."

"You know what we have to do—"

"We can't. Not now—"

"Then we had bloody well better find a way!"

Shocked at the savagery of his tone, she stared at him, until he raised his hand and touched her cheek again. "I'm sorry. I didn't mean to snap at you. Let's not talk about it tonight. I meant you to have a break from it all."

"Reg . . . There's more wrong, isn't there? It's not just Annabelle dying— Though there couldn't be anything worse . . . could there?"

"How could there possibly be anything worse?" He stood up abruptly. "Let's go outside. I'll get us another round."

She stood and followed him out onto the veranda. The sky was mottled a soft rose with the remnants of the sunset, and on the south side of the river lights twinkled in the renovated warehouses of Rotherhithe.

They stepped to the railing, and when she looked to the east she saw the revolving beacon atop Canada Tower. She turned away, her back to the river. She desperately wanted to forget the Island, even for just a short time, imagine another life altogether. On a bench at the side of the veranda a couple sat intertwined, the woman half in the man's lap, their faces inches apart, and Teresa felt a stab of envy. Why shouldn't she, for once, be the object of someone's desire? Why should she always be the one on the sidelines?

Beside her, Reg said, "I am sorry. It's just that I don't want to think tonight. Does that sound horribly callous of me, to wish I could be someone else for an hour or two?"

"No. I was thinking the same thing, but I was ashamed to admit it."

"Were you?" His arm brushed against hers as he moved closer; she could feel the warmth of his body protecting her from the small breeze that moved the river air. She thought of the way he had held her, and of the feel of his hand against the small of her back, and she shivered.

"Cold?" He put his arm round her shoulders and pulled her closer. "Who would you be, then, Teresa? For an hour or two. What would you want to do?"

Glancing up at him, she gave a mute shake of her head. She shouldn't even think it—how could she possibly say it?

"Tell me," he urged, and she felt his breath against her cheek. She closed her eyes.

"With you. I'd want to be with you." She felt as if she were falling into an abyss.

He bent his head and brushed his lips against her throat. "Like this?"

"I . . . Reg—" He had placed his hand on her back, beneath her short linen blouse, and whatever weak protest she'd been about to make died on her lips. He moved his hand, stroking the soft skin on her side, then ran his fingers under the edge of her bra beneath her breast.

She jerked away, whispering, "We can't—not here—someone will see—"

"Then we'll go. Don't move. I'll call us a taxi."

In a few moments they were away, clutching at each other in the bouncing darkness of a black cab's interior; and then they were spilling out onto the pavement in front of her building. She felt dizzy, although she'd hardly touched the second pint of ale, and arm in arm they walked to the lift and down the corridor to her flat, where she fumbled the key into the lock.

He had her blouse off by the time they'd crossed the sitting room, and she had one fleeting and dismissive thought of her balcony-usurping neighbor and her open blinds before they reached the bedroom and fell panting onto her bed.

In the end, it was disappointing, his erection dwindling away at the crucial moment. Groaning, he rolled away from her. "I'm so sorry, love. 'Sorry'—that's all I seem to be able to say to you."

"It's all right," she said softly.

"No it's not." He turned back to her, propping himself on one elbow and cupping her breast with his other hand. "It's not you, love. You have to know that. I wanted—"

"I know what you wanted. It's all right." She pulled his head down to her breast and held him, stroking his back, and she was suddenly filled with a fierce and unexpected tenderness. When he had drifted off to sleep, she slipped her numb shoulder free and lay beside him until the windows paled, wondering what she felt, and how she could begin to justify what she had done.

IN THE LONG SUMMER OF 1940, *Lewis and William learned to identify planes. Edwina had managed to procure black silhouette cards from a friend in the Royal Observer Corps, and every free afternoon they bicycled up into the hills and found a spot where they could scan the sky, cards at the ready.*

The approaching drone of an engine brought a rush of excitement, and they soon recognized some planes from the engine noise alone. Junkers 88, Heinkels, Messerschmitts, Wellingtons, Blenheims, Lancs—they wagered on their favorites. At first the German planes were only occasional raiders, and after the first few it didn't occur to the boys to be afraid.

To them the war still seemed a distant and imaginary thing. They played "English and Germans" with the other children in the village streets, and in the dark evenings they sat round the kitchen radio with John and Cook, listening to Tommy Handley's ITMA and "Appointment with Fear," which made them feel much more frightened than the news broadcasts, and Lewis learned to imitate Lord Haw-Haw so well that he kept Cook in stitches.

But as the weeks passed, more and more airplanes passed overhead and the radio broadcasts became more dire. France fell and Italy entered the war; John Pebbles joined the Home Guard, drilling on the Downs with an old shotgun borrowed from the Hall's gun room; Holland fell, then Belgium, and people began to say that on still nights you could hear a distant rumbling, the sound of the guns in France. Lewis got himself up in the small hours on several occasions and went out in the yard to listen, but all he ever heard was the hooting of the owl that lived in the barn and the shuffling noises made by the horses.

In June, when the evacuations began from Dunkirk, Winston Churchill, now prime minister, pledged over the wireless, "We shall fight on the beaches, we shall fight on the landing grounds, we shall fight in the fields and in the streets, we shall fight in the hills, we shall never surrender," and Lewis tried hard to imagine that there were people fighting, and that his brothers were somewhere among them. Inspired by Mr. Churchill's valiant words, he and William had long discussions about how they would resist if they were invaded, and in a clearing in the woods they made a makeshift shelter from an old tent of Mr. Cuddy's and some tinned goods they had begged off Cook.

Then, one night in late July, Lewis was awakened by the sound of an explosion. Struggling into his clothes in the darkness, he ran down the stairs and out into the stable yard. Sparks floated above the treetops in the direction of the village, winking out as he watched. Then there was another crack of sound, followed by a jet of flame shooting up above the trees, and Lewis heard the sound of shouting.

"What is it? Did you see?" William came banging out the kitchen door, still tucking his shirttail into his trousers, and after him came Edwina, and then Mr. Cuddy in a dressing gown over trousers and braces, his hair standing on end. John appeared last, jogging down the hill from his cottage, the shotgun in his hand glinting in the faint light.

"I heard engines before the explosion," John told them. "There's a plane down, and the sooner we get there the better. There's some in the village that might do something daft."

A meaningful glance passed between John and Edwina. "Terence Pawley?" she asked.

John nodded. "Among others."

Lewis knew that Mr. Pawley's son Neville had been reported missing in France last week and that Mr. Pawley had been ranting wildly about getting his hands on Germans.

"Right." Edwina sighed. "Come on, you two. You're old enough to make yourselves useful."

"I'll get the car—it's quicker," John said, and ran for the garage.

Mr. Cuddy tightened the belt on his dressing gown. "I'm coming with you."

Edwina turned back to him and said, "No, you'd better stay here, Warren. I need you to organize relief, if it's needed. The boys can act as runners."

Then John brought the Bentley round and the three of them piled into it and they were off down the drive. The sky above the village had begun to glow faintly red, lighting the way, and Lewis thought suddenly of how long the journey from village to house had seemed to him the first night he had come here, when the way was unfamiliar. His stomach clenched with anxiety at the thought of what they might find. He knew Edwina had been tactful as well as practical with Mr. Cuddy. The villagers had learned that the tutor spoke German: with feelings running high, there had been some talk of his being a spy.

John drove as fast as the blackout would allow, and as they rocketed round the last corner flames sprang from a crater gouged in one side of the village green, and out of the flames rose a bent, black shape: the tail of a plane—no, two planes, charred and twisted together in an obscene embrace.

As they spilled out of the car and ran towards the gathered onlookers, the smell caught Lewis in the throat—the hot oiliness of burning fuel combined with the sickly sweetness of roasting meat.

"What's happened?" he heard Edwina ask.

"A Wellington bomber," a man said, and when he turned towards them Lewis saw that his face was streaked with soot and sweat. "Must have collided with the German plane. We couldn't get anyone out."

"Roasted," said Terence Pawley beside him, with what sounded almost like glee. "The lot of them. Serves them right, bloody Huns."

"Shut up, Terence." The sooty-faced man turned towards him angrily. "There's our boys dying in there as well."

Lewis thought he heard a faint sound, an echo of a scream, and the smell threatened to rise up in his throat and choke him. He was able to make it to the edge of the green before he threw up his supper. And then he realized that he was crying, and that William was beside him, white-faced with distress.

"They must have known they were going to die, trapped like animals," William said, but Lewis only straightened up mutely and wiped a shaking hand across his mouth.

They watched from a distance until the flames died and the wreckage took shape in the slow-spreading dawn. The German plane was revealed as a Junkers 88, and there were bits of both planes scattered all over the village. "A miracle," everyone murmured, that none of the houses had been hit. As the day wore on, it became evident that the debris was not strictly mechanical—the postmistress fainted dead away upon finding a severed leg in her garden, and other grisly bits of human remains continued to turn up for days afterwards. The younger children hunted for souvenirs with great enthusiasm, but for Lewis and William the war had abruptly ceased to be a game.

As the hot days of August wore on, the raids into London became more frequent. And although life went on much as before, Lewis woke often in the night from dreams of fire that left him heartsick with fear.

On Saturday, the 7th of September, a few minutes before four o'clock in the afternoon, the boys were bicycling up Holmbury Hill when they heard the drone of engines overhead. Both stopped and glanced up—checking almost automatically now to see whether they were fighters or bombers—to find the sky filled with German planes. Hundreds of them—heavy, pregnant bombers surrounded by squads of smaller fighters—swept in majestic, inexorable order across the sky towards London.

When the last plane had disappeared into the distance, they turned and cycled back to the Hall as if the winds of Hell were behind them. They found everyone, even Edwina, gathered round the kitchen wireless, and there they waited for news. The reports were garbled, inconclusive, but as the hours passed, Lewis's dread grew into a terrible sense of certainty.

Towards evening, Cook brewed them another pot of tea, and making up some bread to go with it, she insisted that they must eat something. But that week the cat had got into the ration of butter, reducing them to putting drippings on their bread, and for Lewis what had been meant as a comfort was an unbearably sharp reminder of home. Pushing his plate aside, he ran blindly out of the kitchen.

He sought refuge in the barn. Over the months he had come to find the sounds and scents of the animals comforting, and eventually he settled down on one of the bales of hay near Zeus's stall and drifted into an exhausted sleep.

He woke in darkness, disoriented, to the sound of William's voice and a hand on his shoulder, shaking him.

"Lewis, wake up. It's the East End. They've said on the wireless. The Germans have bombed the Docks."

"What?" He sat up, his mouth dry.

"John's been up Leith Hill. You can see it from there, now it's dark."

"See what?" Lewis said again, stupidly, his brain refusing to take in the words.

"The fires. The East End is on fire, Lewis. London's burning."

CHAPTER 12

The Docks were easily identifiable from the air and were attacked more than any other civilian target. Nearly 1,000 high explosive bombs and thousands of incendiaries were dropped. . . . At the same time large areas of residential Dockland were devastated. During the whole of the blitz, 30,000 people were killed. Slightly more than half of these casualties were in London and a high proportion of these were in Dockland.

Paul Calvocoressi, from Dockland

"WHAT WAS IT YOU WANTED TO talk to me about?" Teresa Robbins asked as she moved to the table set up against the back wall of her office. The long trestle had been placed under the windows, and held cups, teapot, and electric kettle, as well as the bowls and tins Gemma had begun to associate with the paraphernalia of tea-tasting. "I'll just make us a cuppa, shall I?" she added, glancing at Gemma over her shoulder.

"Just a few routine questions," Gemma answered, nodding assent to the tea. She watched Teresa fill the kettle from a bottle of spring water; it seemed to her that the woman's fingers trembled slightly, belying the composure of her face.

Having seen Kincaid off on his way to Cambridge at Limehouse Police Station, Gemma had arrived at Hammond's shortly after opening time, intent on interviewing Teresa again.

Unlike Mortimer's, the office Teresa and Annabelle had shared was large enough to accommodate two desks facing one another yet still leave a comfortable aisle down the center of the room. Nor did it suffer from the executive pretensions that gave Reg's office such an odd air of incongruity. The desks were of workmanlike oak and looked both comfortable and well-used—except that Annabelle's had been cleared of everything except blotter and generic office accouterments.

Wooden tea chests stamped in either red or black ink were stacked about, and a simple bookcase held a collection of novelty teapots. The room smelled of tea and, beneath that, an elusive fragrance that Gemma couldn't quite identify.

Seating herself in the chair nearest Teresa's desk, Gemma studied her as she poured boiling water into a simple white pot, stirred it once, then set a small timer. "I didn't realize it was so scientific," Gemma said, nodding at the timer.

"What?" Teresa looked blank. "Oh, the timer." She turned and leaned against the table while she waited for the tea to steep. "That's one of the first things you learn, especially in tasting. If the brewing time isn't consistent, you can't compare the strengths of the teas. William insists on five minutes, but you can almost stand your spoon up in it. I'm afraid I'm a bit of a wimp, so I stick at four and a half."

"What are we having?" Gemma had not seen a label on the bag from which Teresa had spooned the tea.

"An English breakfast blend, mostly Assam—that's a strong, black, Indian tea," Teresa explained. "I usually switch to the Ceylons in the afternoon. They're a bit lighter, more flowery." The timer beeped and she poured a little milk into the two teacups she'd warmed with water from the kettle, then poured tea into the cups through a fine mesh strainer. She brought Gemma one cup, along with a spoon and sugar bowl, and sat down at her desk with her own. "It's a habit I learned from Annabelle, and Annabelle from William." The glance she gave

Annabelle's vacant desk seemed almost involuntary, and she hastily gazed back at her cup.

"Are you the one who cleared Annabelle's desk?" asked Gemma, tasting her tea. It had a malty richness to it, and she thought it better than any she had ever drunk.

"I've shoveled everything into the drawers for now," Teresa admitted. "It's just that I couldn't bear looking at her things. Silly of me, I suppose. It's not as if I don't think about her every minute anyway." She looked up and her pale, blue eyes met Gemma's. "I know you'll think I'm daft, but sometimes I can almost feel her in the room. And I keep thinking I can smell her perfume."

Gemma remembered the barely perceptible odor she had noticed a moment ago. "A sort of woodsy, citrusy scent?"

"You can smell it, too? She had it specially made. It had bergamot in it—that's what's used in Earl Grey blends. She always said it was more suited to perfumes than tea."

"I doubt we're dealing with a ghost here," Gemma assured her. "Strong scents tend to linger on things—it's just that in other circumstances you'd probably not notice."

"Yes, I suppose you're right," Teresa agreed, but she didn't sound convinced. She looked almost pretty today, in a soft blue summer dress, her fair hair pulled back with a matching blue hair slide. But she would always have paled in comparison with Annabelle, no matter the effort she made. Gemma wondered how much she had minded.

Gemma drank more of her tea, making a vow to buy some of it at the first opportunity. "Is Reg Mortimer not in this morning?" she asked.

Teresa flushed. "No, he wasn't feeling well. This has all been dreadful for him. . . . Reg was devoted to Annabelle."

"But was Annabelle devoted to him?"

"What . . . what do you mean? Of course she was—"

"Then why was she unfaithful to her fiancé on more than one occasion?"

Teresa's hand froze on the delicate handle of her teacup. "What?"

"Didn't she confide in you? I thought she might have."

"Confide what? What are you talking about?"

"Did you know that Annabelle had an affair with Martin Lowell?

That's what broke up his marriage to Jo. Reg only learned about it the night Annabelle died."

"Martin Lowell? That can't be true—there must be some mistake," Teresa breathed.

"No mistake. Harry Lowell brought it up at Jo's dinner party. Reg was livid. He's admitted it now, but not until we played ring-around-the-roses a few times."

"It can't be true," Teresa said again, her eyes enormous in her pinched face. "Why would Annabelle do such a thing?"

"I thought perhaps you could tell me."

"She did take her mother's death very hard," Teresa said slowly. "Or it seemed so to me, but I'd only worked for her a few months and didn't know her very well." Bitterly, she added, "Although it seems I didn't know her much better after five years, did I? Annabelle always made it such a point to stress honesty in business dealings—but it seems that didn't apply to her personal life." She looked up from her teacup. "You said there was someone else?"

"Plural. It seems that Annabelle had a relationship with a man called Lewis Finch, and with his son, Gordon."

"Lewis Finch? *The* Lewis Finch?" Teresa repeated. "Are you sure?"

"Do you know him?"

"No, I . . . Only by reputation," said Teresa, but she sounded uncertain.

"Were you aware that William Hammond disliked Finch?"

"But everyone admires Lewis Finch," protested Teresa. "He's done so much for the Island—I know Annabelle thought he was brilliant."

"Did Annabelle talk about him to you?"

"Not in a personal way, but I knew she'd met him."

"And his son, Gordon? Did she ever talk about him?"

"No, never. I didn't even know Lewis Finch had a son."

Gemma wondered if Annabelle had kept her own counsel out of necessity or if she'd enjoyed having secrets. She said, "Annabelle spoke to Gordon Finch the night she died—he was the busker Reg Mortimer saw in the tunnel. This was just after she'd told Reg she was in love with someone else, and after they'd had a huge row over her affair with Martin Lowell. You can see this puts things in rather a bad light for Reg."

Teresa started to rise, then closed her eyes and sat down again, looking quite white and ill. "I've been a bloody fool."

"Why? What's happened?" Gemma asked quickly.

Teresa opened her eyes and stared at Gemma as if realizing what she'd said. "It's personal. . . . Reg never said—it's nothing to do with your investigation."

"Teresa, if this has something to do with Reg, you're better off telling us now. You could make yourself an accessory if you're protecting him out of some mistaken sense of loyalty."

"No, I don't know anything, honestly. It's just . . ." She hesitated, then said in a rush, "Have you ever done something so stupid that you think you must have taken leave of your senses?"

Involuntarily, Gemma thought of dancing with Gordon Finch in the park. Had Teresa been as susceptible to Reg? "Why don't you tell me about it?" she said gently.

"No, I . . ."

Teresa jumped as the phone rang, and after a glance at Gemma fumbled it off the hook. She listened, murmuring an occasional reply, then gently returned the phone to its cradle.

"That was Mr. Hammond. He's requesting a meeting of the board tomorrow morning, at Martin Lowell's insistence."

"And this means—"

"They'll decide who's going to take over Annabelle's job as managing director."

"Is it between you and Reg, then?" asked Gemma.

"Unless William decides to take over again himself. Or they could bring someone in from outside." Teresa reached for a stack of papers, put them back, and looked about distractedly. "I've the financial reports to prepare. . . ."

Gemma leaned forward. "Teresa, you need to tell me what's happened between you and Reg. You can't judge what bearing it has on our investigation."

Teresa shook her head firmly, but Gemma saw that the fair skin on her throat had suffused with color. "No, I can't. I won't. I've just been a silly cow, because I wanted to think I could offer some comfort—" She swallowed and her hands moved over the papers again. "But it wasn't comfort he wanted. He wanted to get back at Annabelle, make it even, because he found out what she'd done. And I just happened to be convenient."

"Teresa, did you sleep with Reg? Is that what you're saying? If he confided in you—"

Teresa smiled. "Apparently, he hasn't told me half as much as he's told you. I can't help you." She rose. "I've the data to prepare for the financial reports, and it looks as though I'll be putting together the marketing reports as well, since Reg has made himself scarce."

Knowing she'd get no further at the moment, Gemma took a card from her handbag and placed it on Teresa's desk. "You ring me if you want to talk, or if you think of anything you haven't told me. Anytime, day or night, all right?"

When Teresa nodded, Gemma took her leave, but stood for a moment on the catwalk, looking down at the main floor of the warehouse. She thought about the relationships among the people who had come together in this building, bound by a web of concealments and half-truths that had just become exponentially more complicated. Because she knew something now she hadn't known half an hour ago.

If her instincts served her right, Teresa Robbins was in love with Reg Mortimer, and Reg had taken full advantage of the fact. But to what purpose?

As REG TIED HIS TIE IN his dressing table mirror, he thought of Annabelle, of how he had liked to watch her when she was getting ready to go out. She had made up her face with such concentration, like an artist putting the finishing touches on a painting, but the end result had been almost invisible—she had simply been more beautiful.

She had been as self-absorbed as a grooming cat, and at the time he had found it amusing. But that detachment had carried over into other aspects of their relationship, and he wondered now how he had found it acceptable. Even in bed she had always seemed somehow removed from him, as if there were some part of her he could never reach. Had she been that way with the others, too?

The thought made him feel physically ill, and the sweat broke out again on his forehead. This morning when he'd left Teresa's, he'd meant to go straight into work after coming home to shower and dress.

But by the time he'd reached his building, he'd felt so unwell he'd col-lapsed on the sofa until the spasms in his stomach had subsided.

Everything in his life seemed to be crumbling beneath him, and it was all he could do to keep panic at bay. He couldn't ask his parents for help—his father had bailed him out of difficulties once too often, and last year had cut him off altogether, making it clear he wouldn't soften his position.

But if he could only find some way to hold off his creditors for a while longer . . . and if he could convince William to support his nomination as managing director to the members of the board, he might have some hope of survival.

And then there was Teresa. She at least believed in him, and he won-dered how he could have failed to appreciate the virtues of such steady loyalty until now.

His phone rang, startling him. He crossed to the bedside table and picked it up.

It was Fiona, the Hammond's receptionist, telling him that Miss Robbins had asked her to inform him that Mr. Hammond had called a meeting of the board for ten o'clock tomorrow morning. When, his heart sinking, he asked why Teresa hadn't rung him herself, Fiona replied awkwardly, "I'm sure I don't know, sir," and rang off.

Reg let the phone fall back into the cradle. Whatever the bloody hell had happened now, he wasn't sure he had the bottle to face it.

IN THE AFTERNOON OF THE SECOND *day of the bombings, Edwina found Lewis in his room in the barn, packing his bits of belongings into the old, battered suitcase. He straightened and faced her defiantly, expecting to be chastised for his disobedience, because when he'd begged permission that morning to go to London, she'd refused him.*

But instead she sat down gracefully on the room's only chair, looking at him with such understanding that he was forced to turn away and stare out the window at the sparrows nesting under the eaves in the barn.

"Lewis, you must not do this," she said quietly. "I know how desper-ately worried you are, but the only thing you can do for your family is to stay where they can reach you."

"But—what if . . . I can't bear not knowing—"

"We don't know how long the bombing will go on, and this is why they sent you away, to keep you safe. How would your mother feel if you went to London and were hurt or killed, and all this year had been for nought?"

He shook his head wordlessly, but found some unexpected comfort in the thought of his mother's anger.

"The East End is in chaos," Edwina continued. "You know that— you've been listening to the reports on the wireless. And William's parents confirmed what we've heard—they managed to ring through from Greenwich to tell us that the Hammond's warehouse was not badly damaged. It's quite possible that your family has been relocated, and in that case you'd not be able to find them. The only sensible thing to do is wait. I'm sure we'll hear something soon." He heard the chair legs creak as Edwina stood, then felt the light touch of her hand on his shoulder. "Promise me you won't do anything rash."

After a moment, he managed to nod and say, "All right," but he still couldn't bring himself to look at her.

"You're a sensible boy, Lewis," Edwina said, giving his shoulder a brief squeeze. "I knew I could count on you."

Lewis heard her go down the stairs, her booted steps as quick and precise as she was in everything, but he didn't feel sensible at all. In his heart he knew he'd failed his family, left them to an unknown fate that he should have suffered with them, and that his safe and sensible retreat marked him as an outsider and a coward.

THE HOUSE ON STEBONDALE STREET WAS *was hit by an incendiary bomb on the third night of the Blitz, but this Lewis didn't learn until almost a week later, when he received a note in the post. The paper was much blotched and stained, but the neatly looped, convent-school handwriting was instantly recognizable as his mother's.*

> *Dear Lewis,*
>   *The house is gone but we are all right. The third night the bombers came a fire bomb hit right on top of the house but we had gone round to the McNeills in Chapel House Street and went down their Anderson shelter when the alarm sounded. So it was lucky for us*

wasn't it? They have given us a flat in Islington for
now with two other families, its not very clean but at
least we have a place to lay our heads. I will write more
soon remember I love you.
   Your loving mother

Lewis had gone every day to wait for the post at the bottom of the drive,
and now he stood, staring at the tattered paper, until the tears blurred his
vision and splashed onto the page. He knew that William and Edwina
and Mr. Cuddy and even Cook were watching him anxiously from the
house, as they had every day, but he couldn't seem to move.
   After a bit, William came down to him, but Lewis found he couldn't
speak, either. He was forced to hand William the letter to read for himself.
   William read, squinting at the unfamiliar script, his lips moving
silently. Then he looked up, a grin spreading across his face, and whooped
and pounded Lewis on the back, shouting, "Hooray! Bloody hooray!" and
after that it was all right.

IT WAS MID-MORNING BEFORE KINCAID STARTED for Cambridge, after
having made a stop at the Yard. He concentrated on negotiating London traffic until he reached the M11, then he popped a jazz piano tape
Gemma had given him into the Rover's tape deck and settled into the
right-hand lane, determined to make good time.

The music was improvisational, the drifting notes of the piano
sometimes as ethereal as wind in the grass, or as liquid as running water. After a bit, in the sort of free association often brought on by long-
distance driving, the music seemed to combine his thoughts of Kit
with memories of the long days of his own boyhood.

He'd spent his summer hols running wild with all the freedom of a
child growing up in the country, packing his lunch in the mornings
and setting out to roam, on foot or on his bike. Sometimes he'd gone
with friends, and sometimes alone, if he could manage to ditch his
little sister. He'd climbed trees and swum in the canals and taught
himself to fish with absorbed and infinite patience.

Of course, there must have been wet days, and boring days; in retro-
spect, however, they were all idyllic, filled with the heady tonic of

adventure. But what had made his confidence possible, he realized now, was the knowledge that when he returned home in the evenings, his mum and dad would be home from the shop, supper would be cooking, and Miranda would be wanting him to play Monopoly or catch.

His foundation had seemed unshakable; it had never occurred to him that it could collapse as easily as a house of cards.

It was almost lunchtime when he pulled into the Millers' drive and stopped the engine. Laura Miller had been Vic's secretary at the university English Faculty, and a good friend as well. Her son, Colin, had been at school with Kit, although the Millers lived in Comberton, a hamlet a few miles from Grantchester. Laura's willingness to take Kit in for the past few months had provided the boy a haven of familiarity while the school term lasted.

To Kincaid's surprise, Laura answered his ring herself. "I thought you'd be at work," he said, kissing her cheek.

"It's summer hols for me, too," she said as she let him in. She wore white shorts with a bright madras cotton blouse, and her fair skin was faintly flushed from the heat. "Come back to the kitchen. It's cooler there."

The house was a comfortable, suburban semidetached, filled with the trail of discarded shoes and sports equipment that marked habitation by boys. "Colin's gone quite football-mad this summer—I don't know what's got into him," Laura said as she cleared a kitchen chair of a ball and a pair of dirty socks. "Sit down and I'll get you something cold to drink. Ginger cordial?"

When he nodded assent, she went on, "I've been trying to ring you this morning." Handing him a glass filled with milky liquid and a few ice cubes, she sat down at the table. "What's going on, Duncan? Kit came back from London doing a perfect impersonation of the sphinx—and then yesterday Ian McClellan showed up here and said he's back in Cambridge for good. It was just this morning I finally got Kit to tell me that Ian intends to take him back to the Grantchester cottage."

"Ian's seen Kit, then?"

"He didn't stay long. That's all Kit's been willing to say about it, he won't talk about you at all, and he refuses to leave the house. I'm really quite worried about him."

"I told Kit I was his dad," Kincaid confessed reluctantly. "The night before Ian rang me up in London."

"Oh, dear." Laura looked aghast. "No wonder he came back in a royal funk."

"I knew it might take a bit of getting used to, but I rather thought he liked me. . . . I suppose I'd even hoped he might be pleased."

Laura shook her head. "You were Kit's escape from his old life, someone unconnected except for those last few weeks, a friend."

"But a father, surely—"

"I don't think you understand, Duncan. To Kit, parents are the last people you can count on. They run away and leave you. Or die. I don't think anything could have frightened him more."

Kincaid stared at her, wondering how he could not have seen it. "Oh, Christ. I didn't realize . . . How can I possibly sort things out with him after this?"

Frowning, Laura said, "I don't know. I suppose you can try to reassure him that things between you won't change." She nodded towards the patio door. "He's at the bottom of the garden."

ABANDONED GARDENING TOOLS AND A SCATTERING of empty plastic pots near the house told him that Laura had been working in the perennial beds, which got full sun before several old oaks turned the bottom of the garden into a shady retreat. He whistled for Tess, who came up to greet him, tail wagging, but he didn't see Kit until he'd rounded the first tree.

Kit sat with his back to the trunk, arms wrapped round his knees, regarding Kincaid with an expression of sullen wariness.

"Hullo, sport." Kincaid squatted and scratched Tess behind the ears. "Where's Colin?"

For a long moment Kit didn't answer, then he said grudgingly, "Next door. He went to borrow some nails."

In the grass, Kincaid saw what looked like the beginnings of a rudimentary platform at the end of a series of small trestles made with logs. "What's it for?" he asked, nodding at the platform.

"Tess." At the sound of her name, the dog left Kincaid and sat expectantly at Kit's knee.

Kincaid squinted at the pieces of plywood. "Okay. But what's it *for?*"

"It's an obstacle course," Kit said impatiently. "There's supposed to be a ramp, and a dispenser for tennis balls, but we can't figure out how to make the dispenser work."

"I could probably come up with something," Kincaid offered.

Kit shook his head. "It's our project, Colin's and mine. And besides, you haven't the time."

Kincaid ignored the dig. "I thought maybe we could get some sand-wiches in Cambridge, take out a punt."

"Punting's stupid," Kit said, looking away. "And Laura's making beefburgers. I don't want to go out."

"Okay." Kincaid sat down in the grass. "Maybe we could just talk, then."

"I don't want to talk, either." Kit pressed his lips together and wrapped his arms tighter round his knees.

"How about if I talk, and you listen?" Kincaid suggested. "You don't have to say anything."

When Kit didn't answer, he went on, picking his words carefully. "I'm sorry about what I said the other night. But it doesn't change anything between us. It's just a fact, like having blue eyes, or blond hair. It doesn't mean I'm not your friend, or that I'd have done any-thing differently if there weren't that connection between us. It's just extra, like icing on the cake." When he paused, Kit blinked, but still didn't look at him.

"I'm not going to stop being your friend, no matter what. You can still visit me in London, just like before, if it's all right with Ian—"

"I'm not going back there! Not to the cottage." Kit jumped up and turned his back on Kincaid, then kicked at the tree, but not before Kincaid had seen his eyes fill with tears. "You can't make me!"

"Kit, I didn't come here to make you do anything. But you can talk to me about it. Tell me why you don't want to go back."

Kit shook his head, but this time the gesture seemed anguished rather than stubborn.

"Is it because of your mum?" Kincaid asked very gently, praying that for once he had said the right thing.

"I can't—" Kit's voice broke and Kincaid could see the effort he was making to continue. "She's not—"

When he didn't go on, Kincaid thought furiously for a moment, then said, "Kit, do you remember when you ran away from your grandparents, and I found you at the cottage? You were asleep in your bedroom, you and Tess. And you felt safe there, didn't you?"

After what seemed a very long while, Kit nodded.

"It wasn't such a bad feeling, was it?" Slowly, knowing he was treading on very unsure ground, Kincaid added, "It might be a good thing, even, to remember some of the times with your mum—"

"I want to stay here, with Laura," Kit said, turning to face him. For the first time, this seemed a plea rather than a refusal to consider alternatives.

But it was a desire Kincaid had no power to grant. He temporized, carefully. "Well, perhaps you could just go over for a visit, have a look round, see how things feel. Have you seen Nathan lately?"

"No." Kit dug the toe of his trainer into the grass. "Not since I finished the fish project I was doing for school last month."

"You could pay Nathan a visit. I'll bet he'd like to see Tess."

Kit shrugged, frowning, but didn't reject the idea.

"I could even take you, if you like," Kincaid offered, looking away, trying to impart an impression of nonchalance.

Kit shook his head, but slowly, as if he might be thinking about what to do. "I suppose I could ride my bike." He looked up and met Kincaid's eyes for the first time. "Would he be there . . . my dad?"

Kincaid sat down on the old garden chair the boys had been using as a carpenter's bench. "I don't know. How did you leave things with him?"

"He said he had a lot of things to do this week at the college, and getting the house ready, but he'd come this weekend and move my stuff—" Kit's voice rose at the last and he clenched his hands, looking round as if the thought made him want to bolt in panic.

"Whoa. That's ages from now," Kincaid said soothingly. "You can only do things one day at a time, sport. Sometimes life is so bloody that's the only way you can get through it. But the good bit about living one day at a time is that when nice things happen, you enjoy them more than people who are always thinking about the past or the future."

Kit frowned at him, looking unconvinced, but to Kincaid's relief, his hands and shoulders had relaxed.

The odor of grilling meat reached them, and from the kitchen Kincaid heard the murmur of voices. Knowing his time was running out, he said, "What if you go over on your own this afternoon, just for a bit of a recce, then you give me ring and we'll talk about it. What do you say?"

The kitchen door opened and Colin came out to the edge of the patio and waved. "Mum says will you stay and have beefburgers?" he called out.

Kincaid cupped his hands and yelled, "Wouldn't miss it!" then turned back to Kit. "Is it a deal, then?" He held out his hand, palm up, an invitation for their customary high five.

Kit looked towards the patio, where Colin was making a face and a hurry-up gesture, then at Kincaid. He shrugged. "Okay," he said at last. "I suppose it can't hurt just to have a look." With a slap of his palm against Kincaid's, he turned and darted off towards the house, followed by a furiously barking Tess.

Kincaid watched them go, his relief at making a bit of progress marred by the awareness that he'd just done his best to give his son into the care of a man he neither liked nor trusted.

AFTER RETURNING FROM HAMMOND'S, GEMMA SPENT the remainder of the morning at Limehouse, sifting through the accumulated reports and the logs of telephone and house-to-house inquiries. When Janice returned at lunchtime, they called out for some sandwiches and coffee, clearing a space to eat on one of the desks in the incident room so that they could compare notes.

"Did we get Martin Lowell's girlfriend's statement?" Gemma asked.

"It's here somewhere." Janice dabbed at the bread crumbs that had fallen on the papers nearest at hand, then reshuffled them until she found the relevant copy. "Brandy Bannister, aged nineteen, resident of—"

Washing down a bite of her tuna on brown bread with a sip of tepid coffee, Gemma snorted dangerously, precipitating a fit of coughing.

"Brandy Bannister?" she sputtered when she had recovered sufficiently. "Suits her. You could almost feel sorry for her if she weren't such a nit."

"That bad?"

When Gemma nodded, mouth full, Janice continued, "It is a bit unfortunate. You always wonder what parents could have been thinking." She looked back at the report. "At any rate, *Brandy* says she was with Martin Lowell from eight o'clock on, when they had dinner at the Trafalgar Tavern. They left the tavern about eleven and went directly to her flat, where they gave one another full body massages"—Janice raised an eyebrow— "and she says she's sure she'd have known if he'd left at any time during the night."

"Full body massages? Not the kind that would pass a licensing board."

"Like that, was it? Do you think she's a reliable alibi, or would she lie to protect him?"

"I think she's too witless to carry off anything more complicated than saying she's sure he stayed the entire night when she actually slept like a log—and if Martin killed Annabelle he'd have needed a bigger fabrication than that."

Janice glanced at the statement again. "How so?"

"Annabelle would've had to contact him in the missing two hours, between the time both Mortimer and Gordon Finch say they saw her last: around ten, and before midnight, when the pathologist estimates she died." Frowning, Gemma took another bite of tuna sandwich. "Let's send someone round the Trafalgar—see if we can confirm they were there and stayed until eleven."

"It's a big place, lots of traffic. But suppose we can confirm it, what's to say Martin didn't go directly back to his flat and find Annabelle waiting for him?"

"I guarantee you Martin Lowell didn't take Brandy out for a nice evening of intellectual stimulation and kiss her good night at her door."

"Well, what if he stopped off at his flat for condoms or something, found Annabelle waiting for him, and killed her there? Then he went on to Brandy's flat for a good time, got up in the wee hours and went back to his flat, stuffed Annabelle's body in the boot of his car, and dumped her in the park," Janice suggested.

"I suppose it's possible. But he'd have to carry her body across the open courtyard of his building—not a very safe prospect even in the middle of the night. And he has a very nosy neighbor. We might send a PC to have a word." Gemma finished her coffee and tossed the cup in the rubbish bin.

"What about Teresa Robbins? Anything new on Mortimer from her?"

"Only what we should have guessed from the beginning—she's quite besotted with him, or at least she was until she learned Reg hadn't told her what he knew about Annabelle's affairs."

"That would give Teresa a motive," mused Janice. "What if Annabelle went to see Teresa that night—she was that upset, wanted a friend to talk to—"

"And Teresa decided to kill her so she could have Mortimer for herself? Why not let nature take its course? It doesn't sound as though Reg and Annabelle were likely to have patched things up."

"She could have helped Mortimer, though, if he killed Annabelle." Janice poked distastefully at the remains of her tomato on white. "And he's still the best fit for it, in my opinion."

"Except for the fact that if he killed her elsewhere, he'd no way of moving her. And I can't imagine how he'd have convinced her to go to the Mudchute when she was alive."

"Maybe he followed her, saw her meeting someone else?" Janice met Gemma's eyes.

"Gordon Finch?" they said at the same time.

Then Janice shook her head. "But why would she meet him in the park? It's the same problem as with Mortimer, and Finch doesn't own a car, either. His landlady didn't provide him an alibi, by the way. Says she has no idea when, or if, he came home that night, and she's not sure she'd have noticed if he'd had a visitor."

The strength of Gemma's disappointment surprised her. She hadn't realized until that moment how much she'd hoped that someone would provide him an unshakable alibi for the time of Annabelle's murder. "I wonder," she said slowly. "If we assume it was Gordon she meant when she told Reg she was in love with someone else . . . why did Annabelle call *Lewis* Finch?"

"When Gordon turned her down, she took the next available number?" Janice offered.

"I don't believe that. Not when she'd just told Reg she wouldn't settle for anything less than the real thing. Maybe she wanted a shoulder to cry on—"

"Lewis Finch? Not bloody likely! Don't make the mistake of underestimating Lewis," warned Janice. "And don't be lulled by his well-barbered looks and Savile Row suits into thinking money's made him soft. The man's a shark, and he's bloody relentless when he's after something." Janice scowled. "Which reminds me—I've been doing a bit of inquiring. With the idea of a connection between the Finches and the Hammonds, I remembered I'd heard a rumor or two that made me curious, so I stood the head of the Neighborhood Association a few pints.

"It seems that for the past several years, Finch, Ltd. has shown an extremely active interest in buying the Hammond's warehouse. The company has developed several similar riverfront properties, and Hammond's occupies a prime location, one of the last holdouts in what's now almost entirely a residential or mixed residential/commercial area."

"But nothing came of it?"

"No. Apparently, William Hammond refused to sell, and he still maintains a controlling interest in the firm, even though Annabelle had taken over as managing director. What's odd is that Finch has apparently passed up a couple of similar properties in the last year." Janice swirled the remains of the coffee in her cup, grimaced at it, then set it down and lit a cigarette. "This is just the sort of project that Gordon would actively protest."

"Why?" Gemma brushed the last crumbs from her blouse and settled into a more comfortable position in the hard plastic chair.

"You have to understand what happened here. The last of the Docks closed in the late seventies, and by the early eighties the Island was a rotting wasteland. I know because I watched it happen as I grew up, and by the time I finished school the prospects were bugger all." Janice shook her head. "But there are those who criticize any development on the Island—they hate the yuppie in-comers and the disintegration of the old neighborhoods, they're angry because there's less and less hous-

KISSED A SAD GOODBYE

ing available to the working-class people who made the Island what it is—"

"And that's how Gordon Finch feels?" Gemma asked.

"The paradox is that without the development, the Island would have become a massive slum in the last ten or fifteen years, and I think he's reasonable enough to see that. But there are problems and conflicts of interest that could be handled more sensitively." Janice sighed and tapped ash into the tin ashtray on the desk. "The irony is that both Gordon and Lewis Finch want to preserve the Island, and their aims aren't necessarily incompatible. I see both sides every day, and there are concerns that need addressing. You can't have the sort of massive re-development we've undergone on the Island without mistakes and excesses—but I'm no dinosaur: I'd not see things go back to the way they were."

Gemma doodled on the page of her open notebook as her mind sorted details. "If Lewis Finch has been aggressively pursuing Hammond's property, why didn't he mention it when we saw him? He admitted to the affair with Annabelle readily enough."

"My mate knew about that, too."

"Did he?" said Gemma, thinking that she was finding it more and more difficult to believe that Gordon hadn't. "Did he know about Gordon and Annabelle, then?"

"No, that one was a proper shocker."

Slowly, Gemma said, "What if Annabelle's interest in Gordon and his family had to do with the possible sale of the Hammond's property, rather than rebellion against her father's strictures? Remember, Gordon said she sought him out."

"Surely Gordon Finch couldn't have slept with the woman for months without finding out what she was up to—and that's assuming he wasn't already aware of his father's interest in the property. My mate in the Neighborhood Association is the world's worst gossip, and if *he* knew . . ."

Gemma was beginning to feel she'd been played for a fool all round. Snapping her notebook closed, she stood up. "I'm going to have another word with him."

"Gordon? What about Lewis?"

"I want the truth from Gordon before I tackle his father. I'll ring you in a bit." Ignoring the thought of the friction it had caused with Kincaid the last time she'd paid Gordon a visit, she gave Janice a farewell wave and took off.

LEAVING HER CAR IN THE LIMEHOUSE car park, Gemma walked the short distance down West India Dock Road and caught the DLR at Westferry Station. She'd had a sudden desire to see the Island from the elevated train, and the thought of her car's metamorphosis into a traveling oven in the afternoon heat made the prospect seem even more inviting. Clouds had begun to build as the day wore on, as they had yesterday, but a storm had yet to break the heat's grip on the city.

As the train slid into the Canary Wharf Station, Gemma looked up at the soaring glass arch of the terminal and thought about the Island. The architecture of the terminal echoed the great Victorian railway stations in boldly modern terms, as perhaps Canary Wharf itself expressed the same optimism and opportunism that had driven the Victorians who conceived the great docks.

The pneumatic doors closed with a sigh and the train moved on, crossing the middle section of the West India Docks. Office buildings and expensive flats filled the waterfront spaces once occupied by the warehouses, while sailboats and Windsurfers vied with the ghosts of the great ships that had unloaded their cargoes here.

If progress was inevitable, it seemed that Lewis Finch had done what he could to save the buildings themselves, adapting them to new uses, while Gordon strove to preserve the unique social structure of the Island, and to her it seemed a shame that father and son were unable to reach a compromise.

The train made a sharp left after the main section of the West India Docks, stopping at South Quay Station, where the damage from the IRA bomb that had exploded in the car park was still visible; then it turned right again to parallel the north-south Millwall Dock. To her right was the London Arena, followed on the left by Teresa Robbins's building and the ASDA Superstore. Beyond that were the high banks of Mudchute Park and the hoardings that hid the construction at Mudchute Station.

After Mudchute the train seemed to spring into the open, crossing the expanse of Millwall Park on the old Millwall viaduct. She caught a glimpse of East Ferry Road, and of the bowling green nestled in the walls of the Dockland Settlement, then they were crossing over Manchester Road and pulling into Island Gardens Station.

As she left the train she stood for a moment on the elevated platform, looking down at Annabelle's flat and just to the left, where she knew the entrance to the foot tunnel lay hidden by the trees of Island Gardens. She had a sense of imprinting the geography of place and players on her mind, a framework for the pattern of events that had led to Annabelle Hammond's death—then she ran down the circular stairs and set out to look for Gordon Finch.

She tried the park first, and next the tunnel, but the spot under the plane tree was empty, and the guitar player had taken up the pitch in the tunnel again, prompting Gemma to wonder how he could possibly scrape together a living from busking. Tossing a few coins of condolence into his case, she turned away and climbed back up into the sunlight.

When she emerged from the tunnel, she turned left into Ferry Street at Annabelle's flat and followed it until it made a sharp right angle at the Ferry House pub—the route Reg Mortimer said he had taken the night of Annabelle's death. At Manchester Road, Ferry Street became East Ferry Road, and a short walk brought her to Gordon Finch's flat. How easily, thought Gemma, Annabelle could have left the tunnel and gone either to the pub or the flat, and she wondered suddenly where Lewis Finch lived. Gordon had said that his father had moved back to the Island—perhaps near his office? She made a mental note to check the address when she got back to the station.

Today, no sound of the clarinet came from the flat's open windows. Gemma crossed the road and knocked at the blue door, telling herself that he might be busking at South Ken today, or even in Islington.

But after a moment, the door opened and Gordon stared at her groggily. "Gemma?"

"Did I wake you?" she asked. His hair stood even more on end than usual, and one side of his face bore faint crease marks, as if from prolonged contact with a wrinkled sheet.

He shook his head as if to clear it, said, "I suppose you did," then added, "I sat in on a recording session last night; didn't finish until dawn." He yawned. "If you've come to interrogate me, you'd better come in. Just let me put on some coffee." There was a click of toe-nails as Sam came down the stairs, and after a questioning look at his master, he went out into the small side garden and efficiently did his business.

When the dog had finished, Gemma followed them both up the stairs. The flat looked very much as she'd seen it before, except that the narrow bed was unmade. Sam stretched out beside it with a sigh and closed his eyes.

"He's getting too old for such late nights," said Gordon, giving up his attempt to straighten the covers. "Though you'd have thought he slept just as much at the studio." He squatted to rub the dog's ears. "I suppose he doesn't care for his routine being disrupted." Standing again, he gestured at the small table. "Make yourself at home, why don't you," he said, but Gemma couldn't detect any evident sarcasm. As he disappeared into the bathroom, he added, "I won't be a minute."

When he returned a few moments later, his hair had been smoothed down and his shirt buttoned the remainder of the way.

He put water on to boil and took a cafetière and a bag of ground coffee from the cupboard in the small kitchen. As he spooned out the coffee, he gave Gemma a questioning look, but she shook her head. "No thanks. I just had some at the station, unspeakable as it was. You'd think it was a deliberate attempt to poison us."

Hearing herself sound idiotic, she quelled any further impulse to babble by asking, "What were you recording?"

"Some mates of mine in a rock band wanted a clarinet solo on one of their tracks."

"Do you do much studio work?" she said, her natural curiosity pro-viding her an easy avenue.

Gordon shrugged as he poured the hot water over the coffee. "I never turn down an offer—makes a break from busking."

"I wouldn't have thought that many bands used clarinets."

"I play anything—jazz, classical, even backing for adverts; I'm not a bloody music snob. It works both ways, you know." He glanced up at her as he poured coffee into one of the two mugs he seemed to own. "The rock guys who think classical is rubbish are just as stupid as the classical blokes who think rock is rubbish."

Blowing across the top of his cup, he took an experimental sip, then sat down opposite her, his eyes now clear and focused. "So, Sergeant, what is it you want from me *today?*"

"The truth."

He raised an eyebrow. "I thought we'd done that."

Gemma plunged in. "You must have known your father was interested in buying the Hammond's warehouse and developing the property. Why didn't you tell me?"

"Hammond's? You mean Annabelle's business? Why should I have known that?" he answered reasonably. "I haven't seen my father in—"

"It was common enough knowledge that your mate in the Neighborhood Association knew about it. You expect me to believe he neglected to mention it to you? And that's assuming you hadn't heard it already from someone else."

Gordon stared at her, his face expressionless. "My father buys properties all the time—it's what he does. Why should anyone have bothered to mention one he *hadn't* managed to acquire? You're giving significance to things after the fact that hadn't any before, Sergeant."

She stared back at him, regrouping. "All right, let's try it from the other direction. All those questions you said Annabelle asked you about your family—were some of them about your father's business?"

"They might have been, I suppose, but I'd not have thought anything of it—people tend to be curious about him."

"And you never wondered, when she sought you out and seduced you, if she might have had some ulterior motive?"

"Are you saying she needed one?" His eyes met hers in a challenge.

Gemma felt the color rising in her face. "I think that once you learned who Annabelle was, you'd have made sure you heard anything that had to do with Hammond's, and especially if your father happened to be involved. What I don't understand is why you're lying about it."

When he didn't answer, she continued, "I think you knew about your father and Annabelle. I think you knew about your father's interest in her business. And I think you've lied to me from the beginning about your feelings for Annabelle. She was in love with you. That's what she told you that night, wasn't it?"

[251]

Gordon's knuckles whitened on his coffee mug. His voice dangerously calm, he said, "You know fuck-all about it. Nothing was about
love with Annabelle. It was about *power*. I'm not stupid, Gemma, and I
was only willing to be used for so long—"

"You broke things off with her because you found out she was sleeping with your father. You loved her. You never stopped loving her. But
you wouldn't forgive her."

"Forgive her?" Gordon shoved back his chair and shook a cigarette
from the packet on the counter, then lit it with an angry strike of a
match. "Why should I even have believed her? And what difference
would it have made if I had? Can you imagine what an aboveboard relationship with Annabelle Hammond would have meant? Do you
think I'd have let myself be vetted by her family to see if I passed
muster? That I'd have put on a coat and tie and gone to work as her
flunkey in the family firm?"

Gemma stood up so quickly that her chair rocked and teetered.
"You lied to me. And I put myself on the line for you!"

"Is that what this is about? You and your professional credibility?"
His face was inches from hers. "That's bollocks. I've been interviewed
by the police before, and they didn't dance with me in the park, or
come alone to my flat. You want me to be honest with you, Gemma,
then you be honest with me. You tell me this isn't about you and me."

"I . . . You . . ." Gemma couldn't look away from him, and to her
dismay she felt herself trembling.

"You can't, can you?" He was almost shouting now, and he plunged
his unfinished cigarette into his barely touched coffee. Sam opened his
eyes and looked up at them, his brow furrowed. "Don't accuse me of
holding out on you when you won't admit that."

"All right, goddamn it," Gemma said, her own voice rising. "It's
not about my credibility. It's not about the job. It's about whatever
this is between us—"

Gordon grabbed her roughly by the shoulders. He stared down at
her, and the pressure of his fingertips seemed to burn her bare skin.

In an instant of appalling clarity, Gemma saw that his fair eyelashes
were darker at the roots, that he had a small indented scar at the inner
edge of his brow from chicken pox, and that he had a crease in his

lower lip. She smelled toothpaste and coffee and cigarettes on his breath, and the strong odor of his skin that came from sleeping. Her eyes strayed to the rumpled bed and she saw Annabelle, her perfect body naked, her red hair spread out beneath him . . . and then she saw herself there, with him—

A phone rang, shrill and nearby. Gemma jumped, heart pounding. She jerked herself free from his hands. It took her a moment to realize that the phone was hers, tucked into the pocket of her handbag.

"Answer it then, why don't you?" Gordon was breathing hard.

"I—" Gemma took another step back, groping for her bag. "No . . . I—I've got to go." Her fingers closed on the strap of the handbag. She turned and ran down the stairs as if the devil himself were after her.

"TURKEY," SAID COOK. "WE'RE GOING TO *have the biggest turkey you've ever seen—just let that Mr. Hitler think he can spoil our Christmas,*" she added indignantly, wiping the tip of her red nose on her apron.

"*And mince pie?*" prompted Lewis. He sat at the kitchen table, feet tucked round the chair legs, laboring over an essay for Mr. Cuddy on the historical basis of Italy's war against Greece.

Although he was no longer awed by the Hall—he ran carelessly up and down the stairs to the first-floor schoolroom where he and William had their lessons with Mr. Cuddy, and he now knocked on the door of Edwina's drawing room without hesitation—he'd taken to doing his lessons in the kitchen. It was always warm and filled with good smells, and he'd learned he could make the occasional response to Cook's chatter without really paying attention.

"*Don't you tell a soul about my mince pies,*" cautioned Cook. "*Why, just the other day I heard that Mavis Cole trying to bribe the grocer for a few sultanas. If word got out, we'd have half the village here begging for a taste.*"

Fruit of any kind—fresh, dried, or candied—had become extremely rare, but Cook had a few jars of last Christmas's mince tucked away in the pantry and meant to make the most of it. Lewis suspected that in spite of her admonition, she'd already dropped a careful hint or two in the village, and was very much looking forward to being besieged with requests.

And if he suspected as well that Cook had a soft spot for him, he had no qualms about taking advantage. "That's because your pies are the best," he said, looking up from his paper.

"You're a flatterer, Lewis Finch; you mind yourself," said Cook, fanning herself, but her face turned just a shade ruddier and Lewis knew she was pleased. "Now what about them onions for your mum? Shall we pack them up nice with some of my marrow and ginger jam?"

"Yes, please. And some of the greengages?" Lewis gave her his best smile.

There had been no question of Lewis's going home for Christmas this year. Although the attack on Coventry on the 14th of November had marked the beginning of a decrease in raids on London, the bombs were still falling. And even had it been safe, there was not really anyplace for him to go. The damage to the Stebondale Street house had been irreparable; his parents had been finally resettled in a tiny, one-room flat in Millwall, a few blocks from the Mudchute.

The food shortages were even more evident in London than in the country, and he and Cook had conspired to send a few much-prized things, including onions from the Hall's kitchen garden. His mum had written that she'd seen a lone onion on a cushion in a greengrocer's window, priced at 6d, and that the sight of it had made her weep with longing.

His mother wrote often, full of news of fires tamed and rescues carried out in the course of her new duties as a volunteer ARP warden. After the chaos of the first few nights of bombing, she'd been determined to make herself useful and had gone about it with her usual practicality. And besides, she'd confessed to Lewis in a letter written on a late night watch, it helped take her mind off worrying about his brothers, who had been posted together to a cruiser in the North Atlantic—and about Cath, who had taken to going to the cinema and staying the night in a public shelter if the warning sounded while she was out.

"Greengages it is," Cook agreed, twinkling. "Your mum and dad will think Father Christmas came in the post."

John came in then, his arms full of faggots for the stove, and as he and Cook talked about the business of the day, Lewis went back to his essay. In the past year he had discovered, to his surprise, that he rather liked schoolwork. Mr. Cuddy even made history interesting, and he had determined that the children should understand the war in what he called an "histori-

cal context." They had put an enormous map up on the wall in the school-room, and kept track of the campaigns in Europe and the Mediterranean with pushpins and colored pencils. This made the names of places mean something to Lewis, but every once in a while a glance would remind him how close their little part of England was to Occupied France, and he would shiver. He tried not to think about what would happen if Hitler decided to send his armies across the Channel. At least for now he seemed to be busy elsewhere, though in a dream Lewis had seen Hitler's mind as a great red eye, turning this way and that, and the image had haunted him ever since.

William banged through the door from the corridor, bringing Lewis back to his unfinished essay with a start. "I've finished mine," William taunted him with a grin. "Race you to the shops. Edwina wants a newspaper before they close, and she said I could get some glue for my model."

"Right," said Lewis, letting his chewed pencil bounce onto his paper, and they jostled one another out the door and into the courtyard.

A sun the color of blood was setting against a translucent sky etched by the black skeletal silhouettes of trees, the air smelled of frost and wood smoke, and the last of the leaves swirled suddenly on the courtyard cobbles as if stirred by an invisible hand. Lewis stopped, seized by a sensation he couldn't quite put a name to, but it reminded him of the way he'd felt when he'd watched one of the great ships steam into the docks at home.

Then the moment passed as William shouted for him to hurry, and he pounded off down the drive.

A WEEK LATER, LEWIS WAS CROSSING the courtyard after finishing up his midday chores in the barn when he looked up and saw his mother standing in the kitchen doorway. He stopped and blinked, believing for a moment that his eyes were playing tricks, but it was his mum in her old bottle-green coat and the plum-colored felt hat she kept for "best," and she smiled and held out her arms to him.

He ran then, skidding across the drizzle-slick cobbles as he reached her and was enveloped in a fierce hug. To his amazement, he found that his face was on a level with hers, or perhaps a bit higher.

"Lewis Finch, I swear you've grown a foot." She held him off so that she could study him. But although she was still smiling, there was something

not quite right about her voice, a quaveriness. Up close, he saw that her pale skin had the faint blue cast of fresh milk, and there was a puffiness round about her eyes.

"You said you weren't coming to visit," he said, ignoring the tiny prickle of fear. "Did you get my present? Is that why you've come? Where's Da?" Then a sound from the kitchen drew his attention, and he looked past his mother into the room. Cook sat at the table, her apron drawn up over her face, and he suddenly knew it was a sob he'd heard, for he could see her shoulders shaking.

He looked back at his mother, stepping away. "What is it? What's happened?"

"We'll go for a walk—somewhere we can talk," she said, slipping her arm through his, but she didn't meet his eyes, and from the kitchen he heard Cook sob again.

He led her blindly, out through the gate in the back of the yard, across the blackening stubble in the pasture, to the old stone wall that marked the lip of the valley. Below them, the trees marched down the slope and up the other side, their branches as gray today as the mist that shrouded them, like wraiths standing in a sea of russet leaves.

"We had a telegram," his mother began in a careful, level voice. "A supply convoy and its naval escort were attacked in the North Atlantic—"

"Is it Tommy? Or Edward?" Lewis interrupted, the knowledge of what was coming squeezing the air from his lungs. He heard a faint buzzing in his ears, and unbidden, the names of the German battleships he'd read in the newspapers flashed before him: the Scharnhorst, *the* Gneisenau, *the* Admiral Scheer.

His mother didn't answer. When Lewis dared look at her, he saw that she was staring down into the valley, her face still except for a tiny tic at the corner of her mouth.

"No." Lewis tried to shout it, but the mist seemed to catch the word, dampening it in cotton-wool fingers.

"Your brothers were born ten months apart," his mother said slowly. "And from the very first they always wanted to be together." She turned to him at last, touching his cheek with her cold fingertips. "Oh, Lewis . . . I'm afraid that's all the comfort we have."

•　　•　　•

WHEN GEMMA HAD FIRST MOVED INTO the Cavendishes' garage flat, which had only a tiny shower, Hazel had given her carte blanche use of the bathtub in the house. She'd seldom found time to take advantage of the offer, but tonight, after the children had been bathed and got ready for bed, she'd brought over a towel, a dressing gown, and a handful of CDs and locked herself in the bathroom.

Hazel kept a small CD player on the shelf above the tub, insisting that music not only kept the children calm in the bath, but restored her own sanity, and at the moment Gemma felt in dire need of a little restorative treatment. She started the water, added lavender bath gel, lit the candles Hazel kept ready, then hesitated over the choice of music. In the end, she chose Jim Brickman over Loreena McKennitt, and as the unaccompanied notes of the piano filled the room, she slipped out of her clothes and dimmed the lights.

The bathroom was large enough to have existed as a dressing room in a previous incarnation, but Hazel had managed to make it serene and cozy at the same time. A stained-glass lamp produced multiple reflections in the mahogany dressing table's time-speckled triple mirrors; the walls had been sponged a soft, periwinkle blue with a border of seashells; and a bookcase held volumes for perusing while soaking in the clawfoot tub.

But the books didn't tempt Gemma for once, and the room did little to calm her troubled thoughts. She sank down into the foaming water, willing herself into the music as if she could absorb the clean simplicity of it.

Involuntarily, however, she looked down at her body, half submerged in the water, and touched her bare shoulders as if Gordon Finch's fingertips might have left a tactile impression on her skin. Even remembering the sensation made her shiver, then flush with shame. She'd tried telling herself that nothing had actually happened between them that afternoon, but she knew she'd teetered on the very edge of temptation—and that if she had fallen she would have compromised both her career and her relationship with Duncan irrevocably.

As much as she wanted to believe Gordon innocent, he was a suspect in a murder investigation, and her behavior had been rash and dangerous. The fact that she suspected something similar had happened to

Duncan on a case they'd worked last year didn't make her feel any better, and he'd at least not been involved with her at the time.

She closed her eyes and eased herself further down into the water, wishing she could wash away what had happened. But she knew that no amount of guilt or regret could alter the connection that existed between her and Gordon Finch—a connection she somehow had never doubted was mutual, a connection so powerful it had made her contemplate throwing away everything that made her who she was.

The thought frightened her so much she felt tears well behind her closed eyelids. She blinked them angrily away. Were her commitments to the job and to Duncan flimsy fabrications that would crumble under the slightest pressure?

Could it be that she didn't know herself at all?

CHAPTER 13

*The trade and industry which had
first brought work and workers to
the Island in the nineteenth
century, was now in terminal
decline. One by one, in the 1970s
the remaining factories closed
their gates and moved away;
rumours that the Docks too
might close, proved to be all
too true. The last ships came
and went.*

Eve Hostettler, from
Memories of Childhood
on the Isle of Dogs

TERESA ROBBINS DRESSED CARE-
fully in her best pale blue suit and
white lawn blouse, even putting on
tights, although it took the help of a
bit of talcum powder to get them
up in the morning's sticky heat. At
least the sky was solidly overcast,
she thought, and there was hope the
weather might break by the end of
the day.

She painstakingly applied her
makeup, and at the last minute
used a bit of spray to set her hair—
all the while feeling as if she were
the condemned going to face the
guillotine. Sharply, she reminded
herself that it was unlikely anything

that happened to her today could be worse than the things she had endured in the past week.

She had thought her grief for Annabelle more than she could bear, until Annabelle had been revealed to her as a liar and a cheat; she had thought she and Reg might find some comfort in one another, until she'd learned that he had used her for the most unconscionable sort of revenge.

Yesterday she'd steeled herself to face him, but he hadn't come in at all, and she'd gone home exhausted after a day spent preparing ever more dire financial predictions for this morning's meeting.

As she walked down Saunders Ness from Island Gardens Station, she wondered if she could bring herself to work for Reg if they made him managing director, or if she wanted to go on at Hammond's at all if they brought someone in from outside.

Then she'd stepped into the building and smelled the familiar combination of scents—motor oil and dust overlaid by the rich perfume of the teas—and she wondered how she could possibly bear even the thought of leaving.

William arrived first, looking stern but rather frail; then Sir Peter, dapper and cheery; then Jo; and finally, Martin Lowell, whom Teresa had never met. She stared at him curiously, but couldn't read the expression on his darkly handsome features.

Reg did not arrive until they were assembled in Teresa and Annabelle's office, and in spite of everything that had happened between them, Teresa couldn't help feeling a spasm of concern. He looked exhausted, possibly even ill. As he took his seat in one of the chairs gathered in a semicircle round the desks, he closed his eyes.

William called the meeting to order, and as Teresa read her reports she was conscious of Martin Lowell's gaze on her.

When she'd finished, there was a moment's silence. After a glance at William, who nodded, Sir Peter looked round at them and said, "There are obviously many issues that need addressing, but today our primary concern is to decide who will be in charge of the day-to-day operations of the firm. As great as is our loss, we must think of the future of Hammond's—"

"If there is any future to think of," Martin Lowell interrupted impatiently. When he knew he had their attention, he went on, "It's obvious that this firm is facing a financial crisis, and as my children now have a considerable interest, thanks to Annabelle's generosity, I intend to do whatever I can to resolve this." He smiled, and they all stared at him as if mesmerized—even Peter Mortimer, whom Teresa had seldom seen lose command of a situation.

Jo was first to recover. "Look here, Martin. You can't just start in as if you owned the bloody—"

"You have as much at stake as anyone, Jo—your own financial security as well as the children's. Surely, you're not willing to see that frittered away through mismanagement—"

"Just a minute, Martin," broke in Sir Peter. "No one's suggesting—"

"*I'm* suggesting that you cannot even begin to consider as the new managing director of this firm someone who has proved himself incompetent." Martin looked directly at Reg, who paled even further.

"Wait a minute." Reg pointed an unsteady finger in Martin's direction. "You've no right to—"

"And what's more, how can you possibly consider giving Annabelle's job to someone who is accused of murdering her?"

"You bastard! No one's accused me of anything. If anyone should be suspected of murdering Annabelle, it's you. Everything that happened that night started with you and the things you told Harry. It was you Annabelle was furious with—" Reg lunged at him.

William and Sir Peter started to their feet, but Jo was already up and shouting, "Stop it, both of you! You're like two jealous dogs fighting over a bone, and she's dead, goddamn it! Just leave it alone—"

"That's enough, all of you." The others turned to look at Sir Peter. Martin had stayed in his seat, but his color was high; Reg was white and shaking with fury; tears streaked Jo's face. "This is difficult enough for everyone without indulging in this sort of histrionics," Sir Peter continued, loudly and firmly. "And Martin, I don't believe making unfounded allegations about my son benefits anyone."

Lowell nodded but didn't apologize. Reg had opened his mouth as if he meant to defend himself, when his father cut him off. "Reg, you and Teresa are both under consideration for this position. You may vote your shares now, but you're aware your percentages are too insignificant to affect the outcome—"

"Then why bother?" Reg's face was still pinched with anger.

"As you wish," Sir Peter said smoothly. "But in that case, I think it would be best if you both left the room until we can come to a decision. Why don't you wait for us in your office."

Teresa stood up, catching sight of the grief and shock etched on William's face as she did so. A wave of weakness invaded her knees, and she suddenly realized how desperately she wanted out of the room, away from emotions so raw they seemed to rip the air.

Straightening her spine, she crossed the office with deliberate steps; at the door she turned and waited for Reg.

He took one last look round the room, as if defying anyone else to speak, then he turned and joined her.

They walked down the catwalk to his office in silence, and as he shut the door behind them, he said, "It's a bloody farce—may the best man win and all that. I'm fucked without this job, well and truly fucked—did you know that, darling Teresa?"

"I don't want—I never meant to take anything from you," she said hotly, angry tears smarting behind her eyelids. "You—"

"Then why wouldn't you talk to me? You had bloody Fiona ring me to tell me they meant to crucify me—"

"That had nothing to do with this. It was *you*—you lied to me about what happened with you and Annabelle that last night. You were furious with her because you found out what she'd done with those other men—and then with me. . . . You used me to pay her back, didn't you? Even though she was dead."

Reg stared at her blankly. "What are you talking about?"

"You . . . you made love to me because you knew Annabelle cheated on you, and I was the first thing that came along after . . ."

"That's daft, Teresa. It never even crossed my mind. I wanted you. I wanted someone who wouldn't turn away—but you did." Moving a step closer, he said, "You believe them, too, don't you? You think I killed her."

"No, I—"

Reg grabbed her, his thumbs digging painfully into the soft flesh of her arms. "Don't bloody lie, Teresa. I can see it on your face. You—"

The door swung open and Jo exclaimed, "What the—"

Slowly, Reg let Teresa go. "What's the verdict, then?" he demanded. "Banishment from the kingdom?"

"Reg, I'm sorry." Jo shook her head. "We're asking Teresa to step in as acting director."

He gave a strangled laugh that was almost a sob. "Not you, too, Jo?"

"I'm sorry," Jo repeated. "It's not because I think you murdered Annabelle—I don't believe that. But I think it's the best thing for the company. You're out of control, Reg. You need—"

"All you Hammonds can go to hell, so just shut up, Jo. Don't you dare tell me what I need." He turned away from her, back to Teresa, and his eyes were bright with tears. "They're right, you know. If anyone can salvage what Annabelle sowed, it's you—but don't say I didn't warn you about the consequences of throwing your lot in with the Hammonds. They've a bloody talent for betrayal."

JANICE LOOKED UP FROM HER DESK at Kincaid and Gemma conferring in the corridor. There was a tension between them this morning, subtle but evident if one was aware of the signs. If Gemma was trying to juggle the personal and the professional, as Janice now strongly suspected, she didn't envy her the task—although she supposed that even if Kincaid was a bit of a prat sometimes, he was not bad as far as men went.

Of course, everyone's frustration level was running high—it had been six days since they'd found Annabelle Hammond's body, and they weren't much further forward. So far, forensics had not turned up anything of significance in either Annabelle's flat or her car, and they were still processing the samples from the warehouse.

Kincaid had had another meeting with his chief superintendent that morning, and Janice knew the brass was pressuring him to come up with something. She still had her money on Mortimer—he was the obvious suspect with the clearest motive—but they'd not been able to put together enough evidence to justify searching his flat. It was too bad—

Her phone rang. She picked it up quickly, reaching for a cigarette. A distressed female voice asked for Sergeant James, and cupping her hand over the mouthpiece, Janice called out, "Gemma! Phone."

Coming into the office, Gemma took the receiver and sat on the edge of the desk, listening. "Right," she said. "We'll try the flat first. We're on our way." She passed the phone back. "That was Teresa Robbins. She says Reg Mortimer left Hammond's after the board meeting this morning, and he seemed so upset and irrational she's worried for his safety."

REG MORTIMER ANSWERED THE DOOR ON the first ring, holding it open for them without speaking. Kincaid thought his face looked blotchy, as if he'd been weeping, and as they followed him into the sitting room he wiped the back of his hand across his nose.

"Teresa rang us," said Gemma. "She was concerned about you."

"How magnanimous of her." He stood with his back to them, looking out the window at the river, gray under the scudding clouds.

In the few days since they had last seen it, the flat seemed to Kincaid to have acquired an aura of neglect. A fine coating of dust lay on the furniture, in the kitchen he could see dirty dishes piled in the sink, and the warm room held the faint smell of spoiled food.

Nor had Mortimer fared well. His clothes looked wilted, his skin was sallow, and his once-shiny chestnut hair seemed lank and lifeless.

When he didn't face them again, Gemma said to his back, "Can you tell us what happened at the meeting this morning, Mr. Mortimer?"

"They made Teresa managing director, with encouragement from Martin Lowell. You'd think he might have displayed a bit of solidarity, the two of us having been through the same war, so to speak."

"Surely she's capable—"

"Of course she's capable," Mortimer said impatiently. "And deserving. It's not that."

"Then what's the problem? You worked happily enough for Annabelle—why not Teresa?"

"No." Mortimer's voice sharpened as he turned round at last. "You don't understand. I *needed* that promotion. There's a big jump in salary. With Annabelle gone, it was the only way I could keep the vultures at bay a bit longer—that, and the hope that in that position, I could've salvaged the deal—" He broke off abruptly.

"What vultures?" Kincaid asked.

Reg stretched his lips in a smile. "I'm afraid I got in a bit over my head."

Kincaid nodded towards the canvases on the walls. "The paintings?"

"Very perceptive," Reg acknowledged. "Yes, among other things. Managing cash flow has never been my strong suit, and I was counting on a rather large sum that never . . . materialized."

"I think you had better sit down and tell us about this deal." Kincaid gestured towards the sofa.

Reg Mortimer came round and slumped onto the white cotton cushions, putting his head in his hands as if his exhaustion had finally overwhelmed him. "I suppose it doesn't matter now. Nothing does, much," he said through his splayed fingers. Then he dropped his hands to his lap and looked up at Kincaid and Gemma.

"It was a commission—a sort of finder's fee, I suppose you might call it. We came to the conclusion quite some time ago—Annabelle and Teresa and I—that the only way to keep Hammond's solvent was to sell the physical plant and use the proceeds to move the business downriver into more modern and cost-efficient premises.

"I knew a chap—a developer—who would pay any price for the property . . . if Annabelle could be persuaded to go against her father's wishes. So I brought them together."

"Hence the commission," Kincaid said, thinking aloud. "Paid only if the sale was completed?"

Mortimer nodded. "But that wasn't the only catch. The deal was only feasible if we could get a majority of the shareholders to vote against William, and the only way Annabelle would agree to move against her father was if she were convinced that the warehouse itself would be saved as an integral part of the development. She thought it might mollify William, make him feel that Hammond's still had its place in posterity."

"This developer . . . ," said Gemma. "It was Lewis Finch, wasn't it?"

As Mortimer nodded again, Kincaid frowned. "You said, 'If Annabelle were convinced.' Was that not the plan, then—to incorporate the existing building into the new structure? I thought Lewis Finch had a reputation for doing just that."

"He does. But he didn't intend it in this case. Something about 'structural flaws in the warehouse.' But Lewis and I agreed not to tell Annabelle, hoping she wouldn't insist on having a preservation clause written into the contract."

"What did you think would happen when Annabelle found out?" Gemma sounded incensed. "You were engaged to be married, and you were colluding against her."

"I was desperate. And I suppose I thought that once the deal had gone through, it wouldn't matter so much—that perhaps William would have come to see reason."

Kincaid thought he'd begun to see where this was leading. "And then you learned that Annabelle was no stranger to lies and betrayals. What happened that night, after you found out about Annabelle and Martin Lowell?"

"We were arguing when we left Jo's. One thing led to another. I said that if she would do such a thing to her own sister, and if she'd kept that from me, what else had she done?"

"Go on."

"I don't know what got into me that night. I've always hated jealousy—thought it was uncivilized. But she'd been pushing me away for months, refusing to talk about our wedding, making excuses not to stay with me . . . and suddenly it all seemed to make sense. I accused her of . . . things. Whatever came into my head. And then I thought of Lewis Finch, and of all those 'business' meetings she'd claimed they'd had. I accused her of sleeping with him. I said . . . I said Lowell was right, she was no better than a whore, sleeping with Finch to get what she wanted."

"What happened then?" Gemma asked softly.

"She laughed. She stood there and laughed at me. She said I didn't know the half of it . . . that it had cost her his son, and that she'd only learned too late what it meant to really love someone. I yelled at her, said it had cost her more than that—served her bloody right, too—and then I told her what Lewis meant to do. The instant those words left my mouth, I knew I'd gone too far—queered everything—and I said I hadn't meant it. We had an appointment with my father the next morning, to put the plan to him, and we were supposed to have talked to Jo after the party that night. I thought we could smooth it over, somehow, go on with things. . . . But she went very quiet, like she was listening to something . . . then she laughed again. 'The gods have given me a sign, Reg. So sod off,' she told me. I argued—begged her, even—until finally she said she'd meet me at the pub."

"And you walked away," said Gemma.

"Yes. And the terrible irony is that I didn't know—I never knew, until you told me—that Lewis Finch's son was the busker in the tunnel."

LEWIS FIRST SAW IRENE BURNE-JONES ON *a July evening in 1942, when Edwina sent him in the pony trap to fetch her from the station. Irene was actually her second cousin, Edwina told him, her husband's brother's granddaughter, but always one for simplifying, Edwina merely referred to the girl as her niece. Her family's house in Kilburn had taken a direct hit from a stray bomb, and Irene would be staying with them while her parents sorted things out.*

This information Lewis absorbed with some trepidation. William was away, having been allowed to visit his parents for a few weeks now that the bombing had lessened considerably, and as Lewis missed his company he thought it might be nice to have someone about for the short term—but on the other hand, he wasn't sure he could imagine a girl fitting in with their usual summer routine of walks and bathing and fruit-picking. His intimate knowledge of girls was based on his sister, and Cath had never shown the least inclination to do the sorts of things boys did.

He had hardly recognized his sister when he'd gone home to the Island for a visit in April, his first in more than two years. Cath had got a job in a shell-making factory, and she looked an alien creature when she came home in her bright-colored overall and turban; then within a few minutes she was gone again in a cloud of scent and the click of high heels. Whenever her name was mentioned, Lewis saw a look pass between his parents, and once or twice when he walked into the room, he'd had the feeling he'd interrupted a discussion.

But Lewis had been much more interested in roaming the neighborhood, trying to adjust to the sight of piles of rubble, or cleared, weed-covered lots where his house and the homes of his mates had stood. It had made him feel quite odd and hollow, and at the end of a week he'd felt a secret bit of relief at the thought of returning to Surrey.

A snort from Zeus brought his attention back to the road, and he tightened up the reins automatically, clucking to the horse soothingly. John Pebbles had taught him that, and the memory reminded him, as did so many things, of how much he missed his friend.

In the spring of 1941, John, against the pleas of both his wife and Edwina, had joined up, and was now serving as a sergeant with the 8th Army in North Africa. Lewis had taken over many of his jobs by default. The care of the horses had become solely his responsibility, as William was rather frightened of them, and as William was not mechanically inclined, Lewis maintained the seldom-used automobiles. But he and William tended the garden and chopped firewood together, and they helped Edwina with other tasks round the house and the estate to the best of their ability, as there was no one else.

To Lewis, it seemed as if the war had gone on forever. He could hardly recall the days before rationing, and even the enormous portions of meat Cook had fed him when he first arrived at the Hall were now a dim memory. They were still luckier than some, he supposed, with their garden, and in the winter of '41 Edwina had bought pigs and chickens, so that they had at least an unlimited supply of fresh eggs and the occasional rasher of bacon. Of course, the feeding and care of the animals had fallen on Lewis's head as well, but he didn't really mind except for the slaughtering of the pigs, with whom he was inclined to make friends.

Did girls like pigs? he thought, and then he wondered what on earth he would say to her on the ride back from the station. A glance at the angle of the sun told him that it was later than he'd thought, and he clucked again at Zeus to hurry him up. Edwina would have his hide if he daydreamed along until he was late.

SHE STOOD ON THE PLATFORM BESIDE an enormous suitcase. Lewis looked up and down to be sure, but there was no one else, and he breathed an inward sigh of relief. The girl looked about his own age, and seemed quite ordinary and not as frightening as he'd expected. She wore a red and white gingham dress with socks and sandals, and had hair the color of old pen-

nies pulled back in a neat plait, but the best thing was that when she saw him looking at her uncertainly, she smiled and waved.

"Are you Lewis?" she said when he reached her. "Aunt Edwina said you'd meet me. I'm Irene."

"Sorry I'm late." Lewis picked up her bulky suitcase and maneuvered it into the back of the trap. "What have you got in here? Stones?"

Irene gave him her warm smile again and jumped up into the trap unassisted. "Just about everything I own, or at least everything we could salvage from the wreckage. And I didn't mind that you were late, except I was trying to think what I'd do if you didn't come at all. I've never tried hitchhiking, and I didn't know if anyone would be brave enough to pick me up with this monster of a suitcase."

Lewis glanced at her, surprised. He and William had never quite got up the nerve to try hitchhiking. "You could have telephoned," he pointed out. "There's a call box just next to the platform. This isn't exactly the wilds of Africa, you know."

"How old are you?" Irene asked, apparently unperturbed by his sarcasm.

"Fourteen in January," he answered, sitting up a bit straighter as he backed up Zeus and got them started in the opposite direction.

"I'll be fourteen the week before Christmas. So I'm older than you." Irene's triumphant grin was so infectious he couldn't help smiling back.

It was a perfect July evening, the air still soft and smelling of newly mown hay. The road ran through leafy, light-dappled tunnels, and there was little sound expect for birdsong and the soothing clip-clop of the horse's hooves.

"How far is it to the house?" asked Irene when they'd ridden in silence for a bit.

"A couple of miles. It will take us about three-quarters of an hour." Lewis suddenly remembered how great the distances had seemed to him when he'd first come to the country, and how he hadn't been able to imagine a stretch of road without a house or shop in sight.

"It's not at all like Kilburn," Irene said, and some quality in her voice made him look more closely at her, wondering if underneath that cheerful exterior she might be just a little bit frightened.

"No, but you'll like it," he said. "I promise."

• • •

LEWIS AND IRENE BECAME FAST FRIENDS *so swiftly that the first few weeks after William's return were a bit awkward. William had come back rather full of himself, having spent his holiday immersed in his family's business. When Irene remained unimpressed with the importance of Hammond's Teas, William very politely tried to make it clear to her that she wasn't included in Lewis and his schemes. But Irene always affected not to notice: she tagged along anyway, and after a bit William gave up in exasperation. He soon seemed to forget that he'd ever tried to leave her out.*

In August, Mr. Cuddy returned from his long holiday on the Cornish coast, and they were busy with schoolwork again. If Mr. Cuddy and the boys had got into a bit of a rut with their studies, Irene soon woke them up. She was fascinated by Mr. Cuddy's geographical mapping of the war, and always had a question or an argument.

They had a special interest in the campaign in North Africa, and Irene followed the exploits of Montgomery's 8th Army against Rommel with as much partisan fervor as the boys, even though she'd never met John Pebbles. As the days shortened into autumn, they spent long afternoons before the schoolroom fire with cups of cocoa, discussing the war and their futures.

"It's going to be over before we're old enough to join," complained Lewis one day when the rain beating against the windows kept them from going outside. "North Africa's only the beginning. With the Yanks in it now, Europe's bound to be next. Old Hitler won't be able to stand up to the combined forces."

"Yes, but I remember when everyone said the war would be over in weeks." William stretched out on the rug and propped his chin on his hands, staring into the fire, and Lewis thought that he couldn't imagine William fighting anyone, even if things did stretch out that long.

"Do you ever think about losing?" asked Irene. With Edwina's cooperation, she had taken happily to wearing trousers like the boys, and sat crosslegged on the floor with her back against the old armchair. "Everyone talks as though there's no question we'll win, eventually. But what if we don't?"

"Don't be silly," retorted William. "Of course we'll win, so there's no point thinking about it."

But Lewis had thought about it. Lots of things he'd thought could never happen—his house being bombed, his two brothers dying—had happened, so he had to consider the possibility that they could lose this war.

"Of course, I hope it will end soon," said Irene, studying the flames.

"But if it doesn't, I'm going to join up when I'm old enough and I'm going to be a general."

"You're positively daft," said William. "Girls can't be generals."

"I don't see why not." Irene's chin went up the way it did when she was going to be stubborn. "I like planning maneuvers and things."

"But that's just playing at it," Lewis said, trying to be reasonable. "If it was real, you'd have to deal with wounded, and intelligence reports, and oh, all sorts of things. And you'd have to tell people what to do all the time."

"So?" Irene stuck her tongue out at him. "I could do any of those things just as well as you."

Mr. Cuddy looked up from the book he was reading. "Don't squabble. I think Irene's perfectly capable of telling people what to do. In fact," he continued, warming to his subject, "has it ever occurred to you that we might have won the war by this time if all the generals were women? Think about Artemis, the hunter goddess."

Lewis and William looked at each other and rolled their eyes. Now she'd got old Cuddy started on one of his tears, and they'd get the entire Greek mythology if they weren't careful.

"And what about Boadicea—the ancient British warrior queen who led her forces against the Romans. That's a bit closer to home." Mr. Cuddy smiled at Irene. "And she had red hair."

"I'll bet people told her she couldn't be a general, either," Irene said, tossing her head with irritating smugness.

But Lewis was willing to let the matter drop for the sake of peace, because he had a feeling that if they kept on at her, Mr. Cuddy would get really cross.

Their tutor had seemed different since he came back from his long Cornish holiday, but Lewis had not quite been able to put his finger on what it was. At first he'd thought that maybe Mr. Cuddy didn't like Irene, but that didn't seem to be it, as he was much less likely to snap at her than at William and him. But something had changed, and the small, nagging worry this caused Lewis was the only thing to mar his contentment.

As KINCAID PULLED THE CAR INTO a shady spot across from Gordon Finch's flat, Gemma saw Gordon walking down East Ferry Road from the direction of Mudchute Station, clarinet case in his hand, Sam at his side. They waited until he had almost reached his flat, then got out of the car and crossed the road to intercept him.

"We'd like a word, Mr. Finch, if you don't mind," Kincaid said, showing his warrant card as if Gordon might have forgotten who they were.

"And if I do?" Gordon said easily, but his eyes flicked towards Gemma. He wore his military gear again today, and looked disreputable beside Kincaid, who wore khakis and a blue chambray shirt, his collar unbuttoned beneath the knot of his tie.

"We can have a chat somewhere less comfortable."

Gemma felt the tension mount between the two men, then Gordon shrugged without speaking and led them up the stairs to his flat. Once inside, he looked at Gemma and threw down a challenge. "You know your way round, I think." The physical presence of the two men, so close together in the small room and radiating dislike, made her feel she'd got caught in the middle of a pissing contest.

She held her ground. "We want to know exactly what Annabelle said to you in the tunnel. Word for word."

"I've told you—"

"A very small piece—that she wanted to mend things between you. What you didn't say was that Annabelle had just found out that your father had lied to her, betrayed her, just as she meant to betray her own father."

"My father doesn't lie," Gordon said sharply.

"Then why did he tell Annabelle he would preserve the Hammond's warehouse if she sold it to him, when all along he meant to tear it down?"

"Tear it down?" he repeated, frowning.

"She didn't tell you? She must have been terribly angry with him."

"She said . . ." He looked down as if surprised at the clarinet case he continued to hold in his right hand, then he knelt and set it carefully by the music stand. "She said something about loyalties that no longer mattered. I'd heard rumors, back in the spring, about Lewis's interest in the warehouse, and that they'd been seen together a good bit. But when I asked her about it, she denied either a business interest or an affair." He looked up and met Gemma's eyes. "So I followed her. She spent the night at his flat. When I confronted her with it, she never even tried to justify herself. She said I wouldn't understand. . . . And then she let me walk away."

"But you didn't stop loving her."

Gordon rose, his hands looking awkwardly empty. "No."

"And that night, she told you she loved you. She wanted to work things out. In the video in the tunnel, she was pleading."

"She said . . . she said she'd realized that she'd thrown away what mattered to her most . . . but that my being there meant it wasn't too late—we could still work things out, if we loved each other."

Gemma sensed Kincaid move restlessly behind her, but he didn't speak. "You turned her away," she said softly, not taking her eyes from Gordon. "You didn't believe her." She heard her words fall flat as stones in a pool, and as she looked at Gordon Finch she thought the desolation on his face far worse than weeping. "There was something else, wasn't there? What else did she say, Gordon?"

When he didn't speak, she said it for him. "She said she meant to prove it, didn't she? In the video, I saw her turn back for a last word, and she was still angry, defiant even. She meant to prove she loved you."

"IT LOOKS LIKE LEWIS FINCH, DOESN'T it?" Gemma felt no sense of elation at the prospect. For Gordon to have to face the guilt of a father he obviously cared for more than he admitted was bad enough, but she herself had liked and admired Lewis Finch.

"It wasn't her engagement she said she was going to break off when she rang him that night," Kincaid said as he eased the Rover into the northbound traffic on East Ferry Road. "It was their deal. That's why he sounded angry in the message he left on her answering machine."

"And not just the deal, but her relationship with him as well—how could she keep seeing him after what she'd learned?"

"It sounds as though she was using Lewis from the beginning—"

"As he was using her." Gemma glanced up at the high banks of the

Mudchute to the right as they passed, and on the left the sun glinted off the water of Millwall Dock. "But that doesn't solve the problem of where and how they met that night, or how Lewis Finch could have got her body into the park."

"Or his motive," Kincaid mused. "It seems apparent why Annabelle was willing to defy her father's wishes in selling the warehouse. The business was more important to her than anything, and if she believed that was the only way she could keep it afloat—"

"But why was Lewis Finch willing to pay any price for the property? And why was he determined to tear it down once he had it, a contradiction of everything he believes in?"

"Did he think killing Annabelle would stop the sale from falling through?" Kincaid asked.

"He couldn't have been sure what would happen." Gemma frowned and glanced at her watch. "Do you want to try to catch him at his office? He said he's usually out on site in the afternoons."

Kincaid drummed his fingers on the steering wheel as he waited for a light to change. "No. Not until we have enough to nail him. We'll ask Janice to have a discreet word with his neighbors, see if they noticed any unusual comings and goings."

"So what do *we* do in the meantime?" asked Gemma, a little surprised, but conceding the logic of his approach.

"The reason we can't make sense of Lewis Finch's behavior is because we haven't got at the root of it," Kincaid said slowly. "And I think that root lies in the past—I can't believe it's mere coincidence that William Hammond and Lewis Finch knew each other during the war, or that Annabelle sought out Gordon Finch."

"William Hammond's made it clear he's not going to talk about it," Gemma protested.

"So we'll find someone who will." Kincaid glanced at her. "Come to Surrey with me. There's a nice B and B in Holmbury St. Mary— remember?"

Yesterday's encounter with Gordon Finch flashed unbidden into Gemma's mind— How could she face a romantic getaway with Duncan in a B&B with that on her conscience?

"I promised I'd look after the kids for Hazel tonight," she said.

Knowing that Hazel and Tim's plans to take in a movie were flexible and that she was stretching the truth, she felt guiltier still. "And you might need me this end," she added, bolstering her excuse.

"I might," Kincaid said lightly, his tone disguising the hurt she was certain she had glimpsed in his eyes.

JO LOWELL HAD TOLD GEMMA THAT she thought the house where her father had spent the war years was now a country-house hotel, and that his godmother had been named Burne-Jones. That was all the information Kincaid had to go on when he arrived in Surrey in the late afternoon and took a room at the pleasant farmhouse B&B in Holmbury St. Mary. He'd hoped he might see his friend Madeleine Wade, who lived in the village, and Holmbury was in the vicinity Jo Lowell had indicated.

Madeleine practiced massage and aromatherapy from a small flat above the village shop, which she also owned, and when Kincaid had met her on a case the previous autumn he'd found her fascinating as well as a bit disturbing. She was the most matter-of-fact of self-confessed psychics, a former investment banker with a gift for reading what she rather disparagingly referred to as "emotional auras," and he'd discovered that conversations with her could have unexpected pitfalls.

When he'd settled the few things from his emergency overnight kit in his room, he'd walked down the road into the village proper. The shop was not on the green but tucked away in a cul-de-sac on the hill above the village, and by the time he reached it he was warm and perspiring, even with his jacket slung over his shoulder.

The girl working the counter was unfamiliar, but said she thought Madeleine was at home, then watched him curiously as he thanked her and let himself out with a jingle of the bells on the door. He climbed the white-painted steps that ran up the side of the building and knocked at the glossy white door at the top. After a moment, it swung open. Madeleine regarded him with a faint smile. "You've not lost your knack for good timing, I see."

She looked just as he remembered—her bobbed, platinum hair and sharp nose receding into insignificance the moment you met her deep, moss-green eyes.

"You're not surprised to see me?" he asked, looking round as he stepped into the small flat. He had last been here in November, but on this warm summer evening the two windows overlooking the shop-front were open to the breeze that moved the cheerful red-polka-dot curtains.

Her smile broadened. "No conjuring tricks this time," she said, referring to the fact that the last time he'd called in unannounced, he'd found the table set for two. "But I did put a bottle of wine in the fridge to chill, just in case some old friend happened to drop by unexpectedly."

"Madeleine, you're astounding."

"And you're easily impressed," she retorted, but she looked pleased as she retrieved a bottle of Australian sauvignon blanc from the fridge and uncorked it.

When she'd filled their glasses with the wine and they had sat down in the sitting area, she studied him for a moment before speaking. "So what brings you here, Duncan? It's not strictly pleasure, I'm sure."

"No, unfortunately." He swirled the wine in his glass. "Do you happen to know of a country-house hotel nearby, used to be owned by a woman named Burne-Jones?"

Madeleine frowned as she thought. "The name sounds vaguely familiar. . . ." Her face cleared. "Wait, I've got it. There is a place, up near Friday Green."

"Any of the family still about, by any chance?"

"It does seem as though I'd heard something about one of the family still living on the grounds, in the old tied cottage. A distant cousin, female, I believe. . . . Sorry, I can't seem to dredge up any more."

"It's a place to start."

"I can give you directions, at least," said Madeleine. "It's quite near here, actually."

Kincaid jotted them down, then slipped the notebook back into the pocket of his jacket and returned his attention to her. "How are things, then?" he asked.

Madeleine laughed. "Blessedly dull since you went away, Superintendent, thank you very much. The ripples have subsided, and we've all gone back to pretending we never suspected one another of murder. And what about you?"

As he told her a bit about the Hammond case, she listened intently, and when he mentioned Lewis Finch's name, she made a small movement of surprise. "Do you know him?" Kincaid asked.

"I did, in my previous incarnation, you might say. He had quite a reputation in the City."

"A good one?"

"Yes, surprisingly; after all, success and honesty don't often go hand in hand. Then again, Finch didn't get where he is without a good deal of ruthlessness. Your Annabelle was a strong character indeed if she stood up to that one."

"To her cost."

"Do you think Lewis Finch killed her?"

"He seems the most likely possibility. Her former brother-in-law is the only one who professes to hate her, but he has a tidy alibi. Her fiancé seems to have had everything to lose and nothing to gain by killing her, and while he might have lost control enough to have a bloody great row with her, there's a great gap between that and murder." He studied his wine. "And Lewis Finch's son has no motive that I can see—he'd known about her relationship with his father for months, and Annabelle pleaded with him to make up with her."

Madeleine refilled their glasses, her expression pensive. "That's a volatile situation—a father and son in love with the same woman . . . and if she threw the father over for the son . . ."

"What did you think of him?"

"You want me to tell you if I think Lewis Finch is capable of murder?" She frowned. "I suppose a man as driven as I remember Lewis Finch being might go over the edge. But I also sensed in him a great deal of grief—the sort of sadness that's carried so long it becomes an integral part of the personality." She gave Kincaid a swift glance over the rim of her glass, and he keenly remembered how exposed she could make him feel. "So tell me about you," Madeleine demanded.

With anyone else, Kincaid would have found it easy to dissemble. He took a sip of his wine. "My ex-wife died—was murdered."

"Oh, Duncan, I'm so sorry. Were you close?"

"Not for years. I wish we had been . . . friends." He met Madeleine's eyes, looked away. She seemed to be waiting. "And I learned I have a son. Kit. He's eleven."

"Your ex-wife's child? But how wonderful for you."

"And complicated," Kincaid said a bit ruefully.

"How's your sergeant coping with all of this?"

"Gemma? I think she can take anything in her stride."

"Do you?" Madeleine's voice held its characteristic trace of wry amusement.

Without warning, he was assailed by a longing for Gemma. He finished his wine, wishing she had agreed to come with him—wishing they could have had this one night alone together, uninterrupted.

"Another glass?" asked Madeleine, but he shook his head, recalling the unusually incapacitating effect of drinking with Madeleine, especially on an empty stomach.

"Thank you, but I'd better not," he said, standing, and Madeleine gracefully uncoiled herself from the sofa and walked him to her door. "It was good to see you, Madeleine. I like to think of you here, sometimes. A calm center."

"If you start quoting Yeats at me, I won't have you back," she said lightly, her marvelous eyes level with his.

"Never fear, then. I'm forewarned. And I will come again." He kissed her cheek and turned away.

"Duncan."

All the amusement had vanished from her voice and he stopped, compelled to look back.

"Whatever it is that's happened to you, it won't go away on its own," said Madeleine. "Please take care."

THE SKY HAD PALED FROM BLUE to violet to cobalt, but Gordon Finch had not stirred to turn on a light. In his lap the dressing gown he had bought for Annabelle, his only tangible connection with her, lay crumpled beneath his fingers.

Until today, he had not allowed himself to think it out. Until today, he had not had all the pieces—had not been forced to follow events through to their logical conclusion. Had Gemma and her watchful-eyed superintendent taken the same path? If not, how long would it take for them to realize where Annabelle had gone and what she had done?

All that remained was for him to decide how much loyalty he owed his father . . . and what vengeance Annabelle demanded.

CHAPTER 14

For the majority of families whose livelihood depended on river trade activity, the abandonment of the upstream docks was as unexpected and destructive as a natural catastrophe. It was their Great Fire. They could only watch and accept the consequences of a process which they had no part in initiating and little chance of controlling.

George Nicholson, from Dockland

"YOU WILL NOT TALK WHEN I AM *speaking to you," said Mr. Haliburton, his shaking hand raised to the chalkboard, his back still turned to the children, in the too-quiet voice Lewis had learned to recognize as a danger signal.*

It had been Irene, leaning over to whisper something to Lewis, whom Mr. Haliburton had heard while he was lecturing to them on the structure of the Houses of Parliament. Now Lewis gave her a warning look and held his breath, hoping the moment would pass.

The shaking hand began to move

[280]

again, and Lewis relaxed as much as was possible while in the same room with their new tutor. Chafing his freezing fingers together under the table, he tried not to think of Mr. Cuddy, tried not to remember the days when the four of them had sat round the schoolroom table arguing excitedly over a book they were reading or a point of history—because all that had changed on that June morning when Mr. Cuddy had gathered them together in the schoolroom as his annual holiday was to begin. As he'd asked them to sit down, Lewis had seen, to his surprise, that his tutor had tears in his eyes.

"I cannot put this off any longer," Mr. Cuddy had said then. "You all know that I'm going away, but I'm not going on holiday as I've told you, and I'm afraid that I won't be coming back."

Irene recovered first. "Don't be silly, Mr. Cuddy. Why ever wouldn't you come back?"

Mr. Cuddy had turned away from them, a slight, balding, familiar figure in spectacles and moth-eaten jacket, and Lewis had felt the first stirring of fear.

"I have been torn this last year between what I saw as my duty to you, and what I felt was my duty to my country, and I'm afraid I have let myself be swayed by my desire to stay with you three children. But I have realized that you are not children any longer." Mr. Cuddy turned back to them, his hands in his pockets, and Lewis knew he would be fingering the old watch he always kept there. "I have told you that I believe the Allies will shortly be invading Italy and the Mediterranean. Translators will be needed—"

"Are you saying you've joined up?" asked William, with an expression of astonishment that was almost comical.

"They refused me at the beginning of the war, but I speak Greek as well as rudimentary Italian and German, and it seems the army has come to see the advantages of that." The light glinted from Mr. Cuddy's spectacles as he nodded. "Yes, I have enlisted. And if this war goes on as it has, you boys will be doing the same before long."

"But you're too old," blurted Lewis, without thinking.

Mr. Cuddy smiled. "I tried telling myself that. But for this it doesn't matter. I won't be fighting at the front, just trying to keep things running smoothly behind the scenes."

"But what about us?" Irene was frowning so hard that Lewis guessed she was holding back tears.

"You will all be perfectly fine without me," Mr. Cuddy had replied. *"William will rebuild his father's business when the war is over. Lewis, I think you can do anything you set your mind to, once you decide what that is. And Irene—our Irene is going to be prime minister, of course."* He lifted Irene's chin gently with his forefinger, the first time Lewis remembered him touching any of them, then he had bid them a determined goodbye.

They'd watched him from the window, tramping down the drive with his rucksack as if he were going on holiday after all, and Lewis had felt as if he'd awakened from a silly sort of bad dream and found it not to be a dream.

In the autumn, Edwina had enrolled them in the village school, and while they were bored with their schoolwork, life at the Hall had gone on very much as before.

At first, Lewis wouldn't talk about Mr. Cuddy when William or Irene brought his name up, and when letters came from Italy, he pretended disinterest and refused to read them. But sometimes in the evenings, when everyone had gone to bed, he would creep into Edwina's drawing room. There he could pore over the letters alone, by the light of a guttering candle, as many times as he wanted.

Mr. Cuddy had been posted to General Clark's 5th Army, which had landed at Salerno, on the shin of Italy, a few days after Montgomery's 8th Army entered Italy at its toe on the 3rd of September. As the weeks passed and William and Irene speculated about whether Mr. Cuddy would eventually meet up with John Pebbles, Lewis occasionally let slip that he knew more than he admitted. Irene looked at him but said nothing, and somehow this made their friendship closer.

Raids had been light and infrequent over the past eighteen months, since the Blitz had ended in May of '41. They were all allowed home for a long holiday at Christmas—William to his family's home in Greenwich; Irene to Kilburn, where her house had been repaired enough to be at least habitable; and Lewis to his parents' tiny flat in Millwall.

As they sat down to tea the first evening in the room that served his family as bedroom, parlor, and kitchen, Lewis had glanced at the three places set on the makeshift table and asked, "Where's Cath, then?" thinking she must be working an evening shift at her factory.

The look he'd come to recognize passed between his parents again, then his father stared down at the pile of mashed turnips on his plate and muttered, "Bloody Yanks."

Lewis turned to his mother for enlightenment. He'd seen the American soldiers in the street, and the American military police everyone called "snow-drops," in their white belts and hats, but he didn't make the immediate connection.

His mother gave another glance at his da before she said softly, "Your sister's gone, Lewis. I hadn't the heart to tell you in a letter. She's married an American flier who's been invalided home—" Faltering, she touched his father's arm, but he shook his head, refusing her comfort. "And she's going to have a baby," his mother finished quickly.

Lewis had heard enough village gossip to guess the order of events, but that didn't quell his rising anger. "You mean she's gone off to the States without even saying goodbye?"

"It was all that quick, in the Registry Office . . . and your da didn't want any fuss." His mum's eyes filled with tears and she pushed a covered dish towards Lewis. "The greengrocer saved me a special treat for your tea—fresh Brussels sprouts."

Feeling suddenly nauseated, Lewis pushed back his chair. "I'm sorry," he muttered. "I'm not hungry."

The air outside was dense with a freezing fog that seemed to creep inside his clothes and cling to his skin, but Lewis found himself trudging along West Ferry Road in the dark, the thin fabric of his coat pulled up round his chin. There was nothing he could do about the cold nipping at his wrists and ankles. His sleeves were too short, as were his trousers: he'd already outgrown the few items allotted by his ration coupons.

It seemed there was nothing he could do about people leaving, either, he thought, kicking savagely at an empty tin in the street. A man hurrying in the opposite direction gave him an angry look as he stopped and picked it up. "Don't you know there's a salvage drive on, sonny?" the man said roughly, pushing past him.

Fury washed through Lewis and he turned, fists up, but the man had disappeared into the blackness.

How could his sister leave them, knowing they would probably never see one another again, and not even send him a letter?

He walked on, as far as Island Gardens, but the river was invisible in the heavy overcast and he felt it only as an icy void sucking more of the warmth from his body. At last, he turned and trudged back to the flat, but that evening seemed to set the tone for the rest of his holiday.

His parents had changed. It seemed to Lewis that his sister's desertion, following so soon on his brothers' deaths, had made his gentle father bitter, while his mother was simply worn down with repeated grief and loss. And he found he had changed, as well. When he met his old mates they jeered at his accent, and their lives were filled with talk of going down the pub and concerns that seemed foreign to him. Most had left school at fourteen, in favor of factory work until they were old enough to enlist, and although he felt an outcast, to his surprise he didn't envy them.

The days dragged by. He thought several times of William, just across the river, but Greenwich seemed a world away and William had not invited him to visit. On Boxing Day, with guilty relief, he kissed his parents goodbye and caught the train back to Surrey, but his pleasure at returning there had been short-lived.

As he watched Mr. Haliburton at the chalkboard, he thought of the first time he had seen him in Edwina's drawing room, on New Year's Day. William and Irene had returned and they'd all gathered in the kitchen, poking spoons and fingers into Cook's pots while she scolded and flapped at them with her apron. After a few weeks of subsisting mostly on turnips and potatoes, Lewis's stomach was growling at the thought of the ham Cook had promised for their New Year's feast, and there was to be a tart as well, made from the preserved gooseberries they'd picked in the autumn. He'd been inching towards the larder with the idea of just having a peek at the sweet when Edwina had come into the kitchen and asked them to join her.

"Maybe we'll get a glass of sherry for a New Year's toast," William whispered, elbowing him as they followed Edwina down the corridor, but Lewis had been more interested in watching Irene. She wore a wool skirt and jumper rather than trousers, her glossy copper hair bounced on her shoulders, and it seemed to him that there was something different about the way she walked. Irene had looked back then and smiled at him, and it had made him feel quite odd.

As they entered the drawing room, Lewis first saw through the window the strange car in the drive, its bonnet glistening with rain. Then he noticed the tall, thin man standing before the fire, smoking, his back to them.

He *didn't turn round to greet them and Lewis noticed that the hand holding the cigarette shook.*

Edwina *glanced at the man and lit a cigarette of her own before she spoke. "This is my cousin, Freddie Haliburton. He's been invalided out of the RAF and will be staying with us for a while." She paused, sipping at a glass of the sherry she hadn't offered them. Lewis had been smirking at William's disappointment and not paying much attention when she'd continued, "Freddie is going to be your new tutor, so I wanted you to get acquainted right away."*

This brought Lewis up with a snap, and as the stranger turned round slowly, he heard Irene give a small gasp beside him.

It took all of Lewis's effort not to react, though a sidelong glance told him that Irene had raised a hand to her mouth and William had lost his color. The left side of Freddie Haliburton's face was a shining mass of red scar tissue, closing his eye, dragging the corner of his brow down and the corner of his mouth up in a way that might have looked comical, but did not.

"It's Group Captain *Haliburton," the man said, and Lewis knew he'd seen the horror in their eyes. "But since we're going to be such good friends, you may call me Mister Haliburton." His light, mocking drawl had a slight rasp to it, as if he had difficulty breathing. Then he smiled. Or at least the right side of his mouth rose in a grotesque parody of a smile that was even more unpleasant than his face in repose, and Lewis had suddenly had a very bad feeling about it all.*

Now, Freddie Haliburton turned from the chalkboard to face them, and while the shock of seeing his face had lessened, Lewis's dislike of him had not.

"Mr. Finch," said Freddie, with the smile Lewis had come to loathe, "shall we see if your ability to think logically about the House of Commons has improved since yesterday? Or could it be that common is as common does?"

KINCAID SLEPT FITFULLY ON THE NARROW bed, waking with the duvet kicked onto the floor, a dull headache, and an image of Annabelle Hammond that had somehow become entwined with a vivid dream of Vic.

But the day that greeted him when he stepped from his room in the farmhouse's converted stable block was fresh and clear enough to revive his spirits. When he'd breakfasted and thanked his hosts, he set out in the Rover with Madeleine's directions on the seat beside him.

His route wound up into the hills, and the occasional gap in the thick woodlands gave a superb view of the Surrey Weald. He thought of walking in these woods with Gemma the previous autumn, when they'd climbed Leith Hill together, and the moment's reminiscing caused him to bypass the turning for the hotel.

After carefully backing up in the narrow road, he entered the drive and bumped slowly along it. As he rounded a curve, the building came into view—massive, redbrick, late Victorian Gothic, and although it was most impressive, he could see why the structure was no longer used as a private house.

Behind the hotel and to the right, the land dropped away down the hillside; to the left the elevation rose slightly, and among the trees he caught a glimpse of a chimney and a red-tiled roof that he assumed must belong to the cottage Madeleine had mentioned.

He left the Rover in the car park in front of the house and walked up the small, graveled lane that led into the woods. As he neared the cottage, he heard voices—no, it was only one voice, he decided as he came closer, rising and falling, then pausing before beginning again.

Another few yards brought him to a clearing in which stood a redbrick cottage surrounded by a low-walled garden. On a sunny patch of lawn he saw a woman, her back to him, pacing and speaking to herself. She wore trousers and a pale blue cotton shirt, and her slender figure was almost boyish, an impression furthered by the short cropping of her auburn hair. She reached the end of her circuit and turned, then came to a surprised halt as she looked up and saw him standing at the bottom of her garden. As her face came into the sunlight, he saw that she was considerably older than he'd first thought, well past middle age, perhaps.

"Hullo," he called. "I didn't mean to startle you. I'm looking for someone called Burne-Jones."

Coming forward, she rested her hands on the rusting, wrought-iron gate and examined him. "My name is Burne-Jones. What can I do for you?" Her face was pleasant and open, and her eyes, although on close inspection surrounded by a network of fine lines, were a bright and inquisitive blue.

Kincaid slipped his warrant card from his jacket and presented it. "My name's Kincaid, with Scotland Yard. I've some questions about the house"—he gestured back towards the way he had come—"and the people who stayed here during the war."

"The war?" She frowned and took the card from his hand, scanning it carefully before handing it back. "What could you possibly—" Pausing, she looked back at the cottage, then seemed to come to a decision. "Right. Come in, Superintendent. I was about to make coffee.

"It's just that I've a deadline," she explained, looking back over her shoulder as he followed her into the house. "When I'm a bit stuck on something, I work it out in the garden."

As they entered the front room of the cottage, he saw that the worktable set against the front window held a computer monitor and keyboard, and that a good portion of the pleasant room was filled with well-stuffed bookcases. "Are you a writer, Miss Burne-Jones?" he asked, taking in the comfort of the room, with its squashy, chintz furniture, worn Aubusson carpet, and robin's-egg-blue walls. A large, new television and VCR were positioned to one side of the fireplace.

"A freelance political journalist. And you can dispense with the awkwardness—I'm Irene. Just have a seat and I'll be back in a moment," she added as she disappeared through a door he thought must lead to the kitchen. But instead of sitting, he had a look at the bookcases.

Irene Burne-Jones's taste in reading matter was wide-ranging, with a concentration in British history and political biography, and he gathered from the number of volumes on him that she had a particular fondness for Winston Churchill.

He had removed William Manchester's *The Last Lion* and was thumbing through it when Irene reentered with a tray. "Sorry," she said as she pushed a stack of obviously unread newspapers aside to make room for the tray on the coffee table. "Things tend to accumulate when I'm finishing up an article. Do you like books, Mr. Kincaid?" She glanced at him as she poured coffee into mugs.

"Second nature. My parents own a bookshop," he answered, returning the volume to its spot and taking a seat in the armchair.

"I'm not sure I'd have liked that," Irene replied. "Taking books for granted, that is. My parents weren't great readers, so I found books a revelation." She added a dash of cream to her coffee and sat back, regarding him curiously. "Now, tell me how I can help you."

"Did your family own the Hall during the war, Miss Burne—Irene?" he corrected himself.

Irene shook a cigarette from the packet of Dunhills on the table and lit it thoughtfully. "It belonged to my aunt Edwina. There were no surviving Haliburtons, so when she died she left the estate to my father, and upon his death it passed to me. I'm afraid our family has suffered the attrition of spinsters and childless marriages until I'm all that's left of it." The glance she gave him was wry and not the least self-pitying.

"And you sold it?"

"What else was I to do?" she said. "The very idea of living there was preposterous. This was in the mid-seventies; I had my life and my career in London, and the upkeep on the place had become prohibitive. You know what happens with these old houses. I kept the cottage as a weekend retreat—my lover at the time was married, so it came in quite handy. . . ." She gave him an amused glance, as if checking to see if she'd shocked him.

Suddenly wishing he'd known her a quarter of a century ago, he smiled at her, and she went on, "Then a few years ago I decided I'd had enough of the city and moved down here full-time. With a fax and a modem it's not really necessary to be in the middle of things these days."

"I believe your aunt Edwina had a boy staying here during the war, her godson. His name was William Hammond."

"William?" Irene stared at him. "Why do you want to know about William? Has something happened to him?"

"You knew him?" Kincaid asked, his interest quickening.

"Well, of course." Irene took an impatient drag on her cigarette. "I spent two and a half years of the war here myself, evacuated from London when our house was bombed. We were inseparable . . . William, Lewis, and I," she said more softly. Then, raking Kincaid again with her bright blue glance, she ground her cigarette out in the ashtray. "Tell me what's happened to William."

"You won't have seen it, then," Kincaid said, with a gesture at the stack of unread papers. "It's his youngest daughter, Annabelle, who had taken over as managing director of the firm. She's been murdered."

"Murdered?" Irene exclaimed. "How awful for him. But I don't understand what that has to do with the Hall."

Kincaid reached for his coffee before asking, "Did you mean Lewis Finch, a moment ago?"

"Yes, of course. But how would you know that?" Irene frowned. "And what has Lewis to do with William's daughter?"

"He was having an affair with her, for a start."

"Lewis? And William's daughter?" She sounded astonished. And perhaps a bit amused? "Well, I'll be damned."

"Annabelle Hammond not only had a relationship with Lewis, she sought out his son and seduced him—although I don't imagine he gave her much argument."

"She was beautiful?"

"Yes. But it wasn't only that. She was a very strong personality, used to having her way."

"Have you any idea why she took such an interest—if you want to call it that—in the Finches?"

"She was extremely curious about Lewis Finch, and that seems to have extended to members of his family. Did you know that Finch has been actively trying to buy William Hammond's property the last few years?" Kincaid asked.

"No, but it doesn't surprise me. The Hammond's warehouse is just the sort of thing Lewis would snap up in a minute."

"Apparently, Annabelle was as eager to sell as Lewis was to buy— she felt the warehouse was a liability to the future of the firm, and that the profit from such a sale should be used to set up the business in more modern and cost-efficient premises downriver. The thorn in all this was William Hammond. He refused to consider a sale under any circumstances, and he still owned enough shares to block it unless all the other major shareholders voted against him."

Irene leaned forward and tapped another Dunhill from the packet, then made a slow business of lighting it and extinguishing the match. "You'd think William would have seen that change was inevitable, but he was always a bit obsessive about Hammond's. I suppose he was fortunate that one of his children inherited his passion for tea, if not for preserving the family heritage. His daughter's death must have been a dreadful shock for him. And for poor Lewis, if he cared for her. Who'd have thought things would come to such a pass for any of us?" She sighed. "There were a few magic years when I thought we three could overcome anything."

"During the war?"

"You have to understand our circumstances, Mr. Kincaid. Our friendship was so uncomplicated at first—we were so young, and we had all been removed from our homes, our security. We became family to one another. But we were growing up that last year, and things changed between us."

"You fell in love with William," guessed Kincaid.

"Oh, no. It wasn't like that at all," Irene said quietly, gazing out the casement of the sitting room window, where fat bees sampled the roses and lavender in the perennial bed. She looked up and met his eyes with her direct gaze. "You see, Superintendent, I fell in love with Lewis."

"Doodlebugs," said Irene. "That's what Edwina's friends at the War Office are calling them." She kicked her heels against a hay bale outside Zeus's stall, and the white cotton shirt she was wearing above an old pair of Edwina's jodhpurs looked luminous in the light of the barn. They had turned the horses out to graze on the lush June grass, then Irene had followed Lewis back into the barn with the determined expression that meant she had something to say.

He looked up from forking the dirty straw out of the stall but didn't answer. He supposed it had been too much to hope that the raids of the winter and spring would be the last Hitler could throw at them. But with the Allied invasion of Europe earlier in the month, they had begun to hear rumors of a German retaliation weapon, and three days ago had come the first serious assault on Greater London.

"Everyone's saying they're really pilotless planes, and that you hear the engine stop just before they explode," Irene continued, hugging herself as if the thought made her cold in spite of the summer warmth.

"I'm still going home, bombs or no bombs. Anything's better than that bastard digging at me all the time." There was no need to say who he

KISSED A SAD GOODBYE

meant: the presence of Freddie Haliburton seemed to have worked its way into every nook and cranny of their lives.

At first they'd thought Edwina would get over feeling sorry for him because of his injuries and begin to see him for what he was. But they learned soon enough that Freddie presented a different side to Edwina, and it seemed that she was too honest herself to suspect deception in others.

Freddie was always watching the three of them, always eavesdropping, always ferreting out a weakness or the smallest misdeed as a target for his ruthless tongue. That morning he'd picked apart Lewis's translation of Virgil with such vicious sarcasm that Lewis's face had flamed from the humiliation of it, and when he'd protested, Freddie had pinched his earlobe so hard he'd nearly cried aloud. It was only Irene's quick hand on his arm and a quelling glance from William that had kept him in his seat, and he'd been simmering ever since.

"Well, I think you're bloody selfish, Lewis Finch." Irene glared at him, her chin up. "We swore a blood pact, the three of us, that we'd stick together no matter what—"

Lewis jammed the fork into the straw. "It's all right for you. He doesn't call you a guttersnipe, and a . . . a barrow boy—"

"Why is that worse than him making fun of me because I'm a girl? We're all in this, and it's not been easy for William, either. You know how Freddie loves to tell him horrid stories about the war just because he knows how much they upset him." She slid down the bale until her booted feet touched the ground and her face was almost on a level with his. "Sometimes I think you're the only thing that keeps William from doing something really silly. You can't just leave us—"

"You'd be all right; you and William will stick up for each other—"

"How can you be so bloody stupid, Lewis? I'm trying to tell you that I don't want you to go. Can't you see that?"

Baffled, he stared at her. Under the thin white shirt her chest was rising and falling quickly, and her blue eyes snapped with anger.

"But . . ." His tongue refused to cooperate. "I don't—"

Irene stretched up on tiptoe, placed her hands on his shoulders, and kissed him hard on the mouth. Then she stepped back and put her hands on her hips. "Now tell me you want to go."

"I—" Lewis's head spun with confusion and a rush of desire. For months he'd tried to ignore the way Irene had made him feel; he'd never

dreamed it might be the same for her. "I—" he began again, then gave up trying to sort things out in words and reached for her. This time her lips were soft against his and he felt the pressure of her breasts against his chest.

"Irene." He pulled away with a groan. "What about William? If he sees us—"

"He won't. He's working on some project in the attic and he told me to sod off, it was none of my business." She added, "This can be our secret," as she kissed him again.

Lewis felt he might drown in the pleasure of it, but he didn't care. With his hands, he felt the curve of her back and the definition of her ribs, then the beginning of the swell of her breasts. So lost was he that it took a moment for the faint cough to register, and before he could react he heard Freddie say, "How sweet. Love amidst the hay."

Lewis and Irene jumped apart as if shot and whirled towards the door. Freddie stood just inside, his shoulder propped against the jamb, his thumbs hooked through his braces. He stepped forward, smiling and shaking his head. "My, my. It's a good thing I'm the one volunteered to look for you two, isn't it? It might have been Edwina, and then where would we be?"

Beside Lewis, Irene drew a swift breath and opened her mouth, then shut it again with a sharp shake of her head.

"Look," said Lewis, anger overcoming his fear. "You won't say anything to Edwina."

Freddie's smile grew wider, distorting the grotesque mask of his face. "Not unless it suits me," he said, very softly, and the menace in his words made the hair rise on Lewis's arms. "But just now she wants you inside, Lewis, and if I were you I'd pop along like a good lad."

"I'm coming with you to the house," said Irene as Lewis took a step towards Freddie, and taking Lewis by the elbow, she tugged him from the barn.

"Don't be stupid," she hissed as they crossed the yard. "That's just what he wants."

"What do you suppose he means to do?" whispered Lewis worriedly.

"Hold us hostage." Irene gave him a quick glance, then released his arm. "But I don't care. It's worth it."

"Irene—"

"It'll be all right; we'll talk later. You'd best go see what Edwina wants." Then she slipped ahead of him through the kitchen door and went to help Cook with the scones for tea.

In the corridor, Lewis straightened his collar and smoothed his hair before tapping on Edwina's door. Edwina seldom asked to see him on his own and his pulse gave a moment's anxious jump, but there was no way she could know about what had just happened in the barn. He took a breath and went in.

Edwina stood before the open window, staring out and smoking, and the first thing Lewis noticed was that the cigarette in her right hand had an inch of ash on its end. As he watched, the ash fell to the carpet and shattered, but she didn't seem to notice.

It was then that he saw the yellowed slip of paper she held in her left hand, half crumpled in her fist. His first thought was that it was John Pebbles, or Mr. Cuddy, killed in action—but for that she'd certainly have called the others in as well.

Then she raised her head and met his eyes, and he knew.

"I SUPPOSE IT WAS A TERRIBLE irony," Irene said. "His parents survived so much, then to be killed in the first wave of the V1s. If I remember correctly, they were just coming out of the corner shop, such an ordinary thing, on a June day much like this one. . . ." She shook her head and lit another Dunhill.

"Lewis refused to let William come to the funeral, or me, but Edwina insisted on going with him. He would never speak about it afterwards, or about his parents. Except once."

Kincaid waited in silence as she smoked for a bit, and in the clear light he could see the deep creases running from her nose to the corners of her mouth—laugh lines, his mother had always called them, but he thought Irene's face expressed a multitude of joys *and* griefs.

"He said if he'd been there, it might not have happened," she went on at last. "He might have heard the rocket in time."

"And you blamed yourself for his guilt, because you wanted him to stay," Kincaid said. He knew about guilt, about the relentless game of *what if* the mind could play.

"Yes. And I tried to comfort him." For a moment, Irene seemed lost in the memory, then her blue eyes met his. "But nothing could have prepared us for what happened afterwards. You see, Edwina and Freddie Haliburton, our tutor, were killed in an accident very shortly after Lewis's parents died." She ground out her half smoked cigarette in the ashtray. "Edwina's death . . . it was just too much grief—for all of us, but particularly for Lewis, who had lost both his brothers early in the war, as well as his parents. He left after Edwina's funeral. There was nothing I could do to persuade him to stay."

"It must have been hard for you."

"I went back to my family in Kilburn, bombs and all, but we made it through the last of the war without incident."

"And William Hammond?"

"William went home to Greenwich. I had the occasional letter, then they dwindled to Christmas cards."

"And you never heard from Lewis?"

Irene's smile was self-mocking. "I had fantasies for years that he would find me again someday. Then in the sixties his name began appearing in the papers, and I did some research. He must have lied about his age, because he did a brief stint in the army at the end of the war. Then when he was demobbed at the end of 1945, he joined a rebuilding crew and worked his way up in the construction business. There were great opportunities after the war for those with the brains and the talent to take advantage, and Lewis Finch had both."

"But you never contacted him?"

"No. I toyed with the idea, of course, but I'd learned he was married. I've never been much of a masochist," she added with a smile.

Kincaid thought for a moment. "William Hammond's older daughter told us that he had warned her and Annabelle against Lewis Finch. Have you any idea why?"

"I can't imagine," said Irene, but Kincaid thought he detected a note of doubt in her voice. She rose, and going to her desk, she idly straightened the papers on its surface. "Although I suppose there was some tension between them that summer."

"Was William jealous of you and Lewis?"

Irene frowned. "I'm not sure William even noticed what was happening between Lewis and me. He had concerns of his own." Kincaid waited for her to continue. Softly, she said, "I promised myself I'd never become one of those old biddies who drone on about their youth. But we led an idyllic life in the year and a half we had together, William and Lewis and I, in spite of the hardships of the war. Then Freddie Haliburton came, and everything changed." Turning, she met Kincaid's eyes again. "He had a talent for digging out weaknesses and making lives miserable that I've seldom seen since."

"You said he died?" Kincaid asked.

"Yes. It's a wonder he wasn't killed when his fighter crashed in the war, if he flew with the same disregard for the laws of nature he demonstrated when he got behind the wheel of a car. He went up to London every few weeks to drink himself senseless in the officers' club, and I suspect to do other things that I didn't understand at the time." She shook her head. "I can't say I've met many truly wicked people in my life, but Freddie . . . Freddie was the serpent in the garden of Eden."

Lewis stared out the schoolroom window at the rain-washed July morning and tried not to think of other July mornings. . . . The July he and William had learned to spot planes . . . summer hikes with Mr. Cuddy on the Downs, imagining themselves to be Roman soldiers . . . teaching Irene to ride Edwina's hunter. There were so many closed roads in his mind now . . . places he could no longer bear to go . . . and always the one that teased at the edge of thought. Home. His mum, and his dad . . .

He turned back to the five pages of Latin translation Freddie had assigned him before their regular class time began, as punishment for some transgression, but really because he knew how much Lewis hated it. And hated him.

The door opened and Lewis tensed. He never knew now when the ruler might smack down across his knuckles, or the cruel fingers pinch his earlobe until the blood came.

"What a good boy you are," said Freddie behind him, and Lewis heard the rasping of his breath. The same fire that had destroyed half of Freddie Haliburton's face had seared the delicate tissues of his lungs, and Lewis found himself wishing more and more often that the burning plane had left nothing behind but scraps of charred flesh. The thought made him shudder.

Freddie said, "Cold?" and moved a step closer. Then Lewis felt Freddie's hand settle on his shoulder, and he steeled himself for the pain.

But the pain didn't come, only a gentle stroking of his shoulder—and somehow this was far worse. "Don't." He wrenched himself free, his feet tangling in the chair legs as he tried to scramble away; then he turned and, stumbling, faced his tormentor. "Don't touch me," he said huskily, panting against the nausea that threatened to overwhelm him.

"You wound me, Lewis. I might even think you find me distasteful," Freddie said in his most dangerous drawl. "I'll wager you don't say that to Irene when she touches you. It's quite unfair, don't you think, that her fair face should render her your favor?"

"You leave Irene out of this," said Lewis, not understanding everything Freddie had said, but hearing the threat.

"Oh, but you're the one who won't leave Irene alone, Lewis. I've seen the way you look at her. I've even seen the way you touch her when you think no one's looking. And sometimes I do wonder what Edwina would think if she knew . . ." He smiled and Lewis backed up another step.

"You don't seriously think she would approve, do you, boy? You can't seriously think Edwina would consider a trumped-up barrow boy good enough for her own niece? Because you'll never be good enough. You'll never be anything but slum rubbish, no matter how much education you have, no matter how hard you try to speak like a gentleman—" He leaned forward and hissed, "You will never be one. You do understand that, Lewis?"

Lewis stared at the drop of spittle that had collected at the corner of Freddie's ruined mouth, hoping desperately that if he kept his mind on some small and disgusting detail, the words would bounce away harmlessly, like hail against the slates.

"Answer me, boy." The ruler appeared in Freddie's hand as if by magic.

Then came the sound of voices in the hall, and a moment later William and Irene burst in, laughter dying on their lips as they took in the faces before them.

"Aren't we eager this morning," drawled Freddie, making a quick recovery, while Lewis slipped back into his chair and bent over his copybook.

Freddie started them on drills, but the atmosphere in the schoolroom was more uneasy than usual, and Lewis found it impossible to meet Irene's eyes.

By mid-morning they were sweating from the heat, and Freddie had begun the restless pacing that Lewis had learned meant trouble was brewing. After a bit, Freddie stopped behind William and looked over his shoul-

der until William began to fidget. Then he said, conversationally, "Have you seen the papers this morning, William? They're reporting a successful bombing run last night over Germany, a score of direct hits. Of course"—he paused—"it's too bad some of those targets happened to be in heavily populated areas."

William went white, then pressed his lips together, refusing to be baited. They all knew his views on civilian bombings. It was a subject he and Lewis had avoided by mutual consent after a few charged discussions.

William had argued that any civilian deaths were unconscionable, whatever the victim's nationality, and that Lewis should feel the same because of what had happened to his parents—while to Lewis it seemed just the opposite, and he couldn't understand how William could condone restraint against the Germans after what they had done to London.

"Women, children . . . ," Freddie clucked sympathetically, and turned on his heel, pacing again. "Of course, there were pilots shot down, too, and that is rather a shame, wouldn't you agree?" He stopped near his desk and studied William. "Or perhaps you wouldn't agree with that, dear Will? Perhaps your sympathies lie elsewhere?" Reaching into his desk, he pulled out a twine-wrapped bundle and brought it over, dropping it on the table before them. "I do think you could spend your time in the attic a bit more profitably."

William reached out a hand as if to snatch the bundle, but Freddie tapped him on the knuckles with the ruler and drawled, "I imagine Lewis and Irene would like to see what you've been doing." He jerked at the twine, and leaflets spilled out across the tabletop.

Lewis stared curiously, then with growing horror as he realized what they were—pacifist tracts, with a crudely drawn cartoon showing a leering RAF pilot deliberately strafing a fleeing German child.

"I . . . they sent them to me, this group in London," protested William. "I hadn't given them out to anyone." He reached for them again, but once more Freddie interceded, gathering them back into a bundle.

"I'll keep these for you," Freddie said kindly. "Just in case Edwina or any of her friends at the War Office should want to see them."

Eyes on William, Lewis said, "How could you do such a thing?" He stood up, past caring if it made Freddie angry. "I think they're . . . they're disgusting."

"I didn't mean—" William began, but Lewis had pushed back his chair and started for the door. "Lewis, wait!" William shouted after him.

Lewis glanced back, once, before slamming the schoolroom door shut behind him, and the expressions on their faces stayed burned into his memory—Irene, her brow furrowed with concern, her lips shaping his name; William, his eyes dark with fright; and Freddie, the good half of his face stretched into a grimace of satisfaction.

HE KNEW HIS FATHER'S HABITS. LEWIS would leave his office mid-afternoon to check round the building sites—he never trusted anyone else to get things right; that was one of the things that had made working with him impossible. And so Gordon waited near the gunmetal-gray Mercedes in the Heron Quays car park, smoking, watching the sky darken as heavy banks of clouds moved in from the west. The stifling air smelled faintly sulphurous.

Gordon had given up trying to prepare what he would say. His mind was blank, suspended between fragmented thoughts of Annabelle and a recurring memory of his father lifting him from the waves when he was a child. When he saw Lewis come round the end of the building, he ground out his cigarette with the heel of his boot and moved to intercept him.

"Dad."

Lewis looked up, hand on the Mercedes's door. "Gordon! What are you doing here?"

"I need to speak to you."

"We can go back in the office—"

"No, here. I want to know what happened the night Annabelle died. She came to see you, didn't she?"

"I never knew until that night that there was something between you. I'd not have kept on seeing her—"

"You couldn't let me have one thing you hadn't stamped as yours, could you? You always had—"

"No, it wasn't like that," Lewis said tiredly, and Gordon saw lines in his father's face he hadn't noticed before. "I never meant to hurt you— never meant to hurt Annabelle—"

"Then why did you plan to cheat her?"

"How did you know about that?" Lewis said quietly.

"You're a fucking hypocrite, Lewis Finch. After you spent years drumming the importance of integrity into me, it turns out you're no better than all the rest. Annabelle told me that night what you'd done—"

"You wouldn't understand. It wasn't about Annabelle. It wasn't even about the business, except as a means to an end."

"And what end was that?"

"I wanted to take something from him, something he loved as much as I loved Irene, and Edwina, and he always cared more for the business and his bloody family name than he did people. But it's nothing to do with you—"

"Do you mean William Hammond? Did you kill Annabelle to get back at William Hammond?" Gordon was shouting, past caring if anyone heard.

"What?" Lewis sounded utterly baffled. "What are you talking about?"

"When she came to see you, she told you the deal was off, didn't she? And she told you she loved me—she said she meant to prove she loved me—and you killed her!"

"You think *I* killed Annabelle?" Lewis spoke slowly, as if trying to get it clear in his own head, and for the first time Gordon felt doubt. "But I thought you . . . When she left that night I thought it was you she was going to see. . . . I was afraid . . ."

Gordon stared at his father. "Are you saying that all this time you thought it was *me*?" His throat tightened with a wave of relief he wasn't sure he could allow himself to feel. "And I thought . . . they said it was someone who loved her, someone who laid her body out so carefully, and I couldn't believe that you'd killed her and just left her. . . ."

"Laid her body out?"

"They said she looked serene. . . ." Gordon saw that his father was no longer listening.

"I should have seen it from the beginning," Lewis said softly, his gaze still far away. A gust swirled dust and rubbish round their ankles, and in the west lightning arced from cloud to cloud.

"Seen what?"

Lewis yanked open the door of the Mercedes. "This time I'm not going to let him get away with it."

"What are you talking about? Let who get away with it?" As Gordon reached for his father, the slamming car door brushed the tips of his fingers. "Dad!"

But Lewis was already reversing out of the parking space, and the spinning tires threw grit into Gordon's eyes as the car accelerated away.

CHAPTER 15

*Trade-union and community
campaigns to prevent this decline
were transmuted in the 1980s
into campaigns to redevelop the
area in the best interests of local
people, to encourage investment
which would bring more jobs, to
improve transport, schooling and
health care. Alongside these
concerns was a concern that the
community should not lose touch
with its roots.*

Eve Hostettler, from
Memories of Childhood

"WE COULD USE A BIT OF RAIN,
old girl," said George Brent. He was
on his knees in the vegetable patch
in his back garden, with Sheba
sitting beside him, watching him
as if he might turn up something
tasty. "Marrows are getting to be
as scrawny as I am, in this blasted
heat."

Sheba lifted her sleek black muzzle, sniffing the air, and George
straightened his back a bit as he
sniffed, too. His nose wasn't what it
used to be, but he could smell rain,
and the sky to the west looked
thunderous. "Rheumatism's playing
up—that's a good sign," he added as

he stood and worked the stiffness from his joints. "Maybe we'd best pick them ripe tomatoes, just in case." He was proud of his tomatoes— he started them early in the spring, on the kitchen windowsill, and bragged on them to the neighbors whenever the opportunity arose. Reaching for the basket he'd left on the grass, he bent to the task and had it half filled when he heard a whistle and a shout from the house.

"Dad. What are you doing out here in the garden with a storm coming on, you stubborn old goat?"

"Eh, lad, come and give me a hand," called George, beaming at the sight of his only son, who had been out on his merchant ship these past two weeks.

A large, good-natured man with dark, curling hair just beginning to recede, George Brent, Jr., was never called anything other than "Georgie." He strode across the small square of lawn and thumped his dad on the shoulder, then took the basket. "These will make a proper feast with the sausages I've brought for tea, and I've put the kettle on."

"Good lad."

When they had settled at the small, oilclothed table with their sausages, fried bread, tomatoes, and steaming cups of tea, George proceeded to tell his son about the events that had taken place in his absence. He could talk now about finding the body without getting a lump in his throat, and in every telling the red-haired young woman grew more and more beautiful. "Like an angel, she was," he said now, wiping up the last of his tomato with a bit of bread, and thinking of Lewis Finch with a twinge of guilt. He couldn't quite bring himself to tell Georgie what he had confessed to Janice Coppin.

A crack of thunder rattled the crockery on the shelves and Sheba yipped. "This one's going to be a corker," George said, but as he poured them another cuppa, he wished he could bring the image that had been nagging at him into focus. A face seen at the wrong time and in the wrong place, it hovered at the very edge of his consciousness. He gave up, shaking his head in disgust, and proceeded to inform his son that perhaps that Janice wasn't so bad after all.

As DROPS OF RAIN SPATTERED AGAINST the windscreen, Lewis put the wipers on *delay* and switched on the headlamps. He drove blindly, instinctively south, besieged by the memories he had kept buried for so long. He had thought he owned them, that he could use the knowledge of the past to fuel his hatred and yet remain unscathed. But he'd been wrong; he saw that now. And he saw, too late, that Annabelle had reminded him of Irene—

IRENE HAD COME TO HIM THAT *night, in his room over the stable.*

"Lewis," she'd whispered, sitting on the edge of his bed and shaking his shoulder. "I want to talk to you."

He'd awakened instantly. "What are you doing here? You shouldn't—"

"It'll be all right—they're all asleep." She settled herself more comfortably against his hip as he struggled to prop himself up on his elbows. "Listen, you mustn't mind about William. You know he doesn't mean any harm—"

"That's no excuse," said Lewis, his anger rushing back. "Where does he think that sort of rubbish comes from? Straight from the Germans, that's where. And when our men are dying—it could be John next, or Mr. Cuddy—"

"He's only thinking about innocent people being killed, and he doesn't understand how you feel about your parents, not really. He thinks you can be logical about something like that—"

"Logical? What does he bloody know about anything?" And to his shame, Lewis began to cry—the hiccuping, wrenching sobs he'd never let out, even at his parents' funeral. Irene sat quite still, her hand on his shoulder, silent and concerned, and when he could manage, he said, "I know it's stupid, but I keep thinking if I'd only been with them, I might have saved them somehow—"

"Lewis, you'd have been killed, too, you know that. That's the last thing your mum and dad would have wanted." She pulled back his blanket and slid into bed beside him, wrapping her arms round him.

"Irene—"

"I want to be with you, Lewis. We could be bombed, too—the rockets fall short of their targets all the time—and I don't want to die not knowing what it's like."

She kissed him, pressing her body against his, and for a long moment he let go—then he pulled away, panting. "We can't; what would Edwina—

"It doesn't matter," she whispered, her mouth against his ear. "Nothing matters but us. Now, I want to be everything to you—mother, sister, lover—and I want you to need me more than you've ever needed anyone."

He felt her trembling against him, and when he kissed her she tasted of tears. She was right—no one had ever loved him like this. Nothing mattered but this. And then sensation washed his mind clean of any thought at all.

LEWIS WOKE, AS HE USUALLY DID, when the first hint of dawn lightened the oblong of his window. Irene still lay beside him, her chest rising and falling gently as she slept. When he woke her, she sat up groggily and smiled at him.

"I suppose I'd better get back before anyone stirs," she said, yawning and snuggling back down under the covers.

"You'd better hurry," he urged. "You know how early Cook gets up sometimes." As tempted as he was by her warm body against his, he felt suddenly uneasy, and he pushed her out of his bed with a hasty kiss.

From his window, he watched her cross the yard in the faint gray light, and for an instant he could have sworn he saw a curtain twitch at one of the upstairs windows.

ALTHOUGH LEWIS HAD KEPT HIS ROOM above the stable, he had for several years shared a bathroom on the second floor with William.

That evening, after tea, he'd finished his bath and had just stepped from the tub when he heard the door open behind him. William, come to patch things up at last, he thought as he reached for his towel, but when he glanced up at the mirror he saw nothing but the fog from his bath. "It's taken you long enough," he said, determined to make light of it, for they had been avoiding one another all day.

Then he heard hoarse breathing close by, and arms went round him, pinning him hard with his knees against the cast-iron tub.

"Hasn't it?" said Freddie, and Lewis felt him fumbling against him, and then came a searing pain.

For an instant, he didn't understand what was happening. Then, as Freddie thrust against him, he began to struggle with all the strength of *his rage and humiliation. Freddie tightened his grasp, hissing, "You'll do what I want, boy. I saw her leave this morning—I know what you've been—"*

The door opened and Lewis wrenched himself round, but he couldn't free himself from Freddie's grip.

William stood in the doorway.

And Freddie smiled. "You know all about it, don't you, William? You learned it at school. And if you know what's good for you . . . and your little cause . . . you'll bugger off . . . now."

William stood frozen, white-faced with shock, his hand raised, his lips parted in protest.

Then he met Lewis's eyes—and turned away. The door clicked shut behind him.

GORDON STOOD OUTSIDE THE CALL BOX at Mudchute Station, staring at the smudged card he'd found in his trouser pocket. Gemma had given it to him the first time she'd come to his flat—it seemed ages ago, not a mere five days—and she'd scribbled her mobile number on the back.

He'd already provided the police with enough information to damn his father—would he make things even worse by ringing her now? But as he turned away, he saw again Lewis's face as he had sped off in the car, and an urgency that made his stomach feel hollow drove him back to the phone.

When Gemma answered, he said without preamble, "Lewis didn't kill Annabelle."

"Gordon?"

"All the time I thought he'd killed her, he was thinking the same about me. And when he realized it wasn't me, he said—it didn't make sense. . . ."

"Go on," said Gemma, her voice tense.

"He said . . ." Gordon paused, struggling to remember the exact words. "He said he should have known . . . and then something about not letting him get away with it again. Then he drove off. . . . He looked . . . I'm afraid he'll do something crazy. . . ."

"Gordon?"

He didn't answer. Without warning, the pieces had come together in a way he hadn't thought possible, and he felt a surge of anger so intense it left him shaking.

"Gordon?"

Realizing he was still holding the receiver to his ear, he said, "I have to go," and aimed the phone at the cradle as he turned away.

He reached his flat in minutes and took the stairs three at a time, startling Sam into a volley of barking when he burst through the door. "It's all right, boy," he said automatically. But he knew nothing was all right unless he could make it so.

Dropping to his knees, he dug under the bed until his fingers touched the smooth wood of the box stored there, a gift from his father on his twenty-first birthday, one of the few possessions he had carted from place to place over the years. He slid it free and clicked up the latches.

"It's a goddamned antique," he muttered to Sam. A sentimental memento—he'd never dreamed of shooting anyone with it. But his father's Webley Mark IV lay snug in its red felt cradle, clean and oiled, and beside it was an unopened box of .38 cartridges.

KINCAID HAD DRIVEN BACK FROM SURREY slowly, thinking about Irene Burne-Jones and the things she had told him. He doubted Irene had ever loved anyone the way she'd loved Lewis Finch, and he'd found he hadn't the heart to suggest to her that Lewis might have murdered Annabelle Hammond.

Knowing something now of Lewis Finch's history, he tried to imagine that Annabelle's rejection of Lewis that night had been the loss that had tipped him into despair, driving him to murder. But for the first time he had doubts, and he still didn't understand what had made Lewis so determined to take William Hammond's property from him.

He was still mulling it over when he pulled into the car park at Limehouse Station and saw Gemma coming out the door. She wore a black, sleeveless dress that just brushed the tops of her knees, but his pleasure at the sight of her faded when he saw her distracted frown. When he called out to her, she looked his way and came to intercept him. "What's going on?" he asked.

"Gordon Finch just rang me. He said he was sure his father didn't kill Annabelle—and then he hung up."

"Was he ringing from his flat?"

"Probably a call box. He doesn't have a phone."

"We'll try the flat first. Get in."

She came round the car, and as she buckled herself in, he asked, "Is that all he said?"

"No. Duncan, they were protecting each other—Gordon and Lewis—but neither of them knew it. When Lewis realized Gordon hadn't killed her, he said he should have known, and that he wasn't going to 'let him get away with it again.' "

"Let who?"

"I don't know. I don't think Gordon knew."

Kincaid's phone rang as he pulled out into West India Dock Road. He answered, then said to Gemma as he rang off, "That was Janice. Forensics just called. They've found a trace amount of hair and blood in a sample taken from one of the tea chests in Annabelle Hammond's office."

"So it looks like she was killed at Hammond's," Gemma said. "Who would she have met there in the middle of the night?"

"If we assume it was neither of the Finches?" He switched on his wipers as rain spattered the windscreen. "Martin Lowell? If he wouldn't let her come to his flat, and she wanted to have it out with him?"

"We've had Brandy Bannister in again this morning. She hasn't budged an inch on her statement. It looks as though Lowell's alibi is good." Gemma sounded unhappy about it.

Kincaid frowned. "Maybe we should look at this from another angle. Who, besides Annabelle, had access to the warehouse?"

"Reg Mortimer and Teresa, of course, but Mortimer's the most obvious. He knew Annabelle liked to go there when she was troubled, and he desperately wanted to talk to her."

"But if he killed her in the warehouse, how did he get her body to the park?" Kincaid asked. "We're back to square one." Then, as he shook his head in frustration, he remembered something. "Teresa Robbins said that since his wife died, William Hammond turned up at the warehouse at odd hours, that he couldn't bear to let go of the business. . . . What if it wasn't a case of Annabelle arranging to meet someone, but an accidental encounter. . . ."

"And you think William might have seen someone?"

"It's possible," Kincaid said slowly. "But it's also possible that it was William who killed her."

"William Hammond?" Gemma's voice rose on a note of disbelief. "Her own father? The poor man was devastated—you saw him."

"I don't doubt that. But . . . everything seems to come back to William Hammond and Lewis Finch." He told her about his interview with Irene Burne-Jones. As he negotiated Westferry Circus and headed south on Westferry Road, thunder boomed and rain began to beat against the roof of the car. "What did Hammond have against Finch? And why was Finch so determined to buy the warehouse when he knew its importance to William Hammond? Something happened in the last few months the three of them were together—William, Lewis, and Irene—that Irene isn't willing to talk about, even after all these years."

"It doesn't make sense," protested Gemma. "Why would William Hammond kill Annabelle when she'd just made up her mind to call off the deal with Lewis?"

"I don't know. But if Lewis Finch said he wasn't going to 'let him get away with it again,' what could he have meant but murder? Someone *was* killed in those last few months those three children were together—the children's tutor. Irene said it was an accident. . . ."

"But what if it wasn't?" said Gemma. She shook her head. "We're missing too many pieces. Gordon must know something we don't—"

"And I don't think it's very likely we're going to find him sitting at his flat, waiting for us." He peered through the windscreen, but the curtain of rain obscured virtually everything. "Ring William Hammond's house—do you have his number?"

"In my notebook." Gemma found the number and dialed her mobile. "No answer."

"Try Lewis Finch."

"At home?"

Glancing at his watch, Kincaid nodded. "It's already after five."

But Lewis Finch didn't answer, either, and after a moment Gemma disconnected. Slowly, she said, "If it *was* William Hammond Lewis meant, and he thought he might find him at the warehouse . . ."

"It's worth a try," Kincaid said as a flash of lightning illuminated the long line of cars crawling down Westferry Road ahead of them. "But we're not getting anywhere in a hurry."

As LEWIS PULLED UP THE MERCEDES on Saunders Ness, the square bulk of the Hammond's warehouse was scarcely visible in the blinding rain. His hands shook as he lifted them from the wheel. He was sweating and nauseated, as powerless to stop the flow of memories now as he had once been to stop Freddie Haliburton. . . .

He had passed the night in a black fury unabated by exhaustion. Unable to bear the thought of seeing anyone, or speaking to anyone, he had started on his chores in the barn without going up to the Hall for breakfast. He didn't know what he would do if he saw William—he didn't even want to think about William—but Irene was not so easy to avoid.

She came looking for him, as he knew she would, gliding silently through the barn door and stopping in the shaft of sunlight that fell from the high window. "Lewis? What happened to you last night? Why didn't you come to breakfast this morning?"

"Just go away, Irene. I don't want to talk to you," he said roughly, turning back to the hay he was forking into Zeus's manger. He felt her watching him, but she didn't speak, and after a moment she went out again. Knowing how much he'd hurt her only stoked his rage. How could he touch her after what Freddie had done to him? And how could he stop it from happening again? Freddie had made clear that his refusal would mean compromising Irene, and that was the one thing Lewis could not allow to happen.

It seemed to him that he had only one option . . . and that would mean never seeing her again.

IT WAS MID-MORNING WHEN FREDDIE FOUND him, sitting hunched against the stone wall that ran behind the kitchen garden.

"*There you are,*" *Freddie said sweetly as he came round the corner.* "*It's not like you to miss lessons, Lewis. Whatever is the matter?*"

Lewis rose, fists clenched, but Freddie stopped just out of reach.

"*Cook's quite worried about you, you know. If you miss another meal she'll feel it's her duty to tell Edwina, and I don't think we want that, do we?*" *Freddie stretched his face into the grimace that mimicked a smile.* "*Oh, and when you've had your breakfast, you can get my car ready for me, there's a good boy. I'm going up to town for the night and I want everything shipshape.*"

He turned away, as if that settled everything between them, but when he reached the end of the wall he looked over his shoulder and said, "*But I'll be back—and there's always tomorrow, isn't there, Lewis?*"

IT CAME TO HIM AS HE *lay beneath Freddie's car. It was so simple—a nick in a hydraulic line and the whole system would lose pressure—that he wondered why he hadn't seen it before. Everyone knew Freddie Haliburton drove like a maniac—even Cook was always clucking and predicting he'd come to a bad end. No one would think anything of it. He would be safe, and Irene would be safe, and William . . . he didn't care about William.*

He felt as if he were divided into two people—one who concentrated on the task, and one who observed. That Lewis heard his mother's voice, but the Lewis who acted ignored them both, and his hands were steady and precise with the knowledge John Pebbles had given him. It was not until he had finished and slid from beneath the car that he realized he was being watched.

William stood just inside the stable door, and Lewis had no idea how long he had been there or what he'd seen. "*You have to understand,*" *William said, stepping forward, and Lewis saw that his face was white and strained.* "*My grandfather was killed in the Somme. My father was decorated, even though he was only nineteen, and he's suffered from the gas ever since. If they found out—*"

"*I don't care about your bloody pamphlets! You could have stopped him—*"

"*There was nothing I could do! And now he says maybe he'll tell my parents anyway, just because he hates cowards. They'll disown me—*"

"Then it serves you bloody right, William Hammond!" Lewis shoved William hard in the chest and bolted out the door.

He ran through the yard and down the hill to the meadow, then along the stream, legs and heart pumping, until at last he collapsed facedown in the soft moss along the bank, sobbing as if his heart would break.

It was an hour before he returned to the house, calm from his weeping, determined to undo what he had done. Then he would tell Irene goodbye and leave. . . . It was the only way. He'd lie about his age and join up, or get work somewhere, it didn't matter.

But when he reached the stable yard he heard a wail of anguish from the kitchen, and he knew he had come too late.

IT WAS IRENE WHO TOLD HIM that Edwina had been killed with Freddie. There had been a farm cart in the lane, just over the crest of the hill, and the car had been unable to stop in time. It was Irene who had grown up from one minute to the next and taken charge, helping Cook to her bed and going to ring her father with the news; Irene who had left Lewis alone in the kitchen with William. . . .

"She wasn't supposed to go," Lewis said numbly. His brain and his tongue felt as if they were frozen, and the words seemed to hang in the air, brittle as ice.

"She . . . she changed her mind at the last minute." William sat slumped at the kitchen table, his face blotchy with weeping. "He was taking her to see my parents. He said . . . he said he was going to tell them. I didn't think. I didn't think she'd be . . ."

The import of William's words dawned slowly on Lewis. He shook his head from side to side to stop the ringing in his ears. "You mean you knew? You knew about the car . . . and you let Edwina go?"

"I'm not as stupid as you think. You jumped when you saw me standing in the barn, so when you ran away I looked. . . . I only thought it would delay them—"

"Delay them? You know how Freddie drives and you let Edwina go?" He lunged for William, yanking him from his chair by his collar. "You— you bastard!" Lewis shouted, shaking him. "I'll kill you for this." When his fist struck William's face, the sight of the bright blood flowing from William's nose only made him angrier.

William hit him back and they grappled, straining for a better hold, another blow.

Then Irene was between them, shouting, pulling them apart.

"Stop it! What's the matter with you? Stop it! Lewis, how could you?"

Panting, he stared at her. "I . . . He . . ." In that moment Lewis realized he couldn't tell Irene what he'd done that day—he could never tell her. And when he met William's eyes, he saw that William knew it, too.

He had no memory of the days before Edwina's funeral, only of Irene, afterwards, coming to him in the barn. His case was packed; he had meant to leave without telling her goodbye.

"You can't tell me you don't love me," she said. "I won't believe you."

"No," he had answered her. "I won't tell you that. But it doesn't matter now. Nothing does. I'm sorry."

He had left Irene then, left the Hall, left them all behind. And he'd never told anyone the truth . . . until the night Annabelle had told him she loved his son and called him a cheat and a liar. She'd said she'd never hurt her father for him, that she couldn't believe she had ever considered doing something that would cause William Hammond so much pain.

He hadn't known until that moment how much Annabelle had come to mean to him—that she should turn against him was beyond bearing. His words poured out—he'd wanted to hurt her—and he told her that her precious father was a coward and a murderer, and he told her exactly what William had done.

Lewis opened the door of the car and stumbled out into the rain. He was soaked by the time he reached the warehouse, but he hardly felt it. The door was unlocked, and he stepped for the first time into the building he had tried for years to destroy.

As his eyes adjusted to the shadows, he saw that the large main floor was empty, but a light shone from a door on the catwalk that ran along the left-hand side of the building. Feeling his way carefully to the stairs, he began to climb. He heard a faint sound, and as he neared the top of the staircase, the sound sorted itself into a singsong voice, rising and falling beyond the open doorway.

William Hammond sat behind one of the scarred oak desks in the nter of the room. He was talking to himself, his hands busy with the colorful tea tins on the desktop, but when he looked up and saw Lewis he didn't seem at all surprised.

"She was beautiful, wasn't she?" said William, his eyes drifting back to the tins. "She made these for me. My favorite colors, cobalt and russet. Russet like her hair. She looked like her mother, so beautiful."

"William." Lewis stepped further into the room. "Why did you do it? What did Annabelle say to you?"

"Do you remember, Lewis?" William's gaze skated across his again. "Do you remember the watercress? And the deer? I've been thinking. . . . It all seems so vivid, like it was just yesterday."

"Did Annabelle find you here, William? She was angry with you, wasn't she?"

For an instant William's eyes were clear. "Annabelle loved me. She was a perfect daughter."

"I know she was. But she found out, didn't she . . . about Edwina."

William froze, the tea tins suspended in mid-shuffle like a shell game gone awry. "She said things . . . terrible things. She said she'd tell people . . . Sir Peter, even. That she would sell . . . this." His hand looked almost translucent as he gestured round the room. "And she said . . . she said she'd spent her whole life trying to live up to me— and that I was a hollow man. A hollow man," he repeated. "I didn't mean—"

"You didn't mean to kill her?" said a voice behind Lewis, and without turning he knew it was his son.

Lifting a hand to halt him, Lewis warned, "Gordon, no." But Gordon came on, and as Lewis felt the force of his son's fury, he realized his own had drained away at last.

William rose. "I only wanted to stop her from saying those things. I never meant . . ." He looked impossibly frail.

"But I do." A gun appeared in Gordon's hand—and Lewis saw that it was his own.

IT WAS STILL POURING WHEN THEY reached the warehouse. Kinca killed the engine as the Rover coasted to a stop behind a gray Merced

"Lewis's car?" asked Gemma, thinking she remembered seeing the car park at Heron Quays.

Kincaid nodded, meeting her eyes. "Careful."

They dashed through the pelting rain to the warehouse. The door stood open a few inches. Kincaid eased inside and Gemma followed, coming to a halt beside him in the shadowy interior.

They heard the voices immediately, coming from the open door of Annabelle and Teresa's office high above them. Gemma felt Kincaid touch her arm, lightly, then move away towards the staircase. She followed as quietly as she could, cursing the fact that she'd worn slick-soled shoes.

Halfway up, she found she could distinguish the voices—Lewis's; Gordon's; and, though less familiar to her, William's—if not quite make out the words. Then, as they neared the top, she heard Lewis shout, "Gordon, don't be a bloody fool! Give it to me."

There was the sound of a scuffle, then the smack of something hard hitting the floorboards.

Gemma skidded to a halt inches from Kincaid and peered through the doorway. Gordon and Lewis Finch were locked together as if frozen in the midst of a dance, Lewis's hand clamped round Gordon's wrist, Gordon's fingers splayed, empty. Their eyes were fixed on the opposite side of the room, where William Hammond stooped and straightened again, a gun in his hand.

He held it awkwardly, staring at it as if not quite certain what it was. Then he looked up at them, and Gemma saw in his faded blue eyes not surprise, but a grief so bleak it made her bones feel cold.

He lifted the gun. Before Gemma or Kincaid could react, Lewis shouted, "William, no!" and lunged towards him.

But William Hammond touched the barrel of the revolver to his temple and pulled the trigger.

CHAPTER 16

*There is a growing movement
determined to bring the river
back to life.*

George Nicholson, from Dockland

"HE LOVED HER," GEMMA SAID
slowly. She sat in Janice's office at
Limehouse Station, drinking revolting coffee from the machine. "Annabelle was the child of his dreams, the
one who would carry on for him, ful-
fill his ambitions. How hard it must
have been for her, living up to that."

Janice said, "And he couldn't bear
for her to destroy his image of her—"

"Or his own image. William
Hammond spent fifty years living a
lie so thoroughly that he even convinced himself."

A week had passed, and they were
still sorting out the details of the
case. Lewis Finch had made a detailed

statement, as had Gordon, and it seemed to Gemma that their shared loss might go a long way towards healing the rift between them.

"And Lewis?" said Janice. "He was responsible for Edwina Burne-Jones's and the tutor's deaths as well. Will he be prosecuted?"

"Unlikely, I should think. There's no evidence, except for Lewis's own statement, and I doubt the Crown Prosecution Service would waste their time." Softly, Gemma added, "I have a feeling Lewis Finch has paid enough."

Janice nodded. "I was wrong about Reg Mortimer," she said wryly, making a face as she sipped at her coffee. "And it seems I was wrong about George Brent, too. He did know something. When I told him what happened, he remembered that the night Annabelle was killed, he'd stepped outside sometime after midnight to see his lady friend home. He saw a car come slowly up Seyssel Street and turn right into Manchester Road, and he knew the driver's face—although he'd never actually met him, he'd seen him many times over the years."

"William Hammond?"

"He must have had his car at the warehouse when Annabelle arrived unexpectedly, and that's the way he would have gone, taking Annabelle's body to the park. What I don't understand is why he didn't turn himself in when he realized he'd killed her."

"I suppose even then he couldn't face the truth of what he'd done to Annabelle—or to Edwina. But it destroyed him." Gemma thought of the way he had left his daughter's body, so lovingly arranged . . . and she thought of Jo Lowell, bereft now of mother, sister, and father, burdened with the terrible knowledge of what her father had done. But she thought Jo, like Annabelle, had taken her strength from their mother, and that she would be all right.

"There's one good thing to come out of this, maybe," Janice said a bit hesitantly. When Gemma looked at her, she went on with a little smile, "George Brent's son's been round to see me. He was an old beau, efore I met Bill."

"And?" asked Gemma, grinning.

We have a proper dinner date. Tonight. He's a nice enough bloke," e added, defensively.

sure he is," said Gemma, and surprised Janice by giving her a ıg before collecting her things and saying goodbye.

DURING LAST FRIDAY'S STORM, LIGHTNING HAD struck the DLR tracks, but the damage had been repaired and Gemma had taken the tube and then the train out to Limehouse.

The storm had brought a week of clear skies and mild weather as well, and as Gemma boarded the DLR at Westferry, she looked forward to her walk home alone from the Angel tube stop. All week she had been plagued by a sort of melancholy that not even the thought of tomorrow's piano lesson had relieved, and although she knew she was indulging it, she couldn't seem to shake it off.

She had tried to put Gordon Finch from her mind—it had been an impossible relationship from the beginning, she knew that. But still she had this nagging sense of opportunities missed, of doors not opened, and when she emerged from the Angel and saw that the music shop across Pentonville Road was still open, she went in.

She browsed for a bit, looking over simple arrangements that she thought she might be able to learn to play, but in the end she bought what she knew she had come in for—the sheet music for Rodgers and Hart's "Where or When." Tomorrow, she'd ask Wendy if she could work towards learning it.

Tucking the music a bit guiltily into her bag as she left the shop, she walked back to the Liverpool Road, past the Sainsbury's where she'd first seen Gordon, turning into Richmond Avenue for the last few blocks before she reached Thornhill Gardens.

Suddenly, she stopped, listening, thinking at first she was imagining the notes of the clarinet, faint on the clear air. Then she saw him, sitting on a swing in the empty school yard, clarinet in hand. He stood and came towards her.

"I took a chance," he said.

"But how—"

"I used to watch the way you walked home. I wanted to know ab‹ you."

"But you—" She shook her head. He had never seemed to noti‹ at all.

"I've seen your son, too. How old is he?"

"He's three," said Gemma, bemused. "His name's Toby. Gordon, about your dad—how is he?"

"He's gone to Surrey—something about laying ghosts. But that's not why I wanted to see you," he added quickly. "I think we have some unfinished business, you and I . . . and . . ." He looked away, rubbing his fingers absently over the keys of the clarinet. "And it seems to me that the past has done enough damage, that we shouldn't let what's happened chart our course."

Gemma met his eyes then, and what she saw there made her throat tighten with emotion. Gordon Finch would never say he was lonely, would never admit to needing anyone, and she knew the effort it must have taken him to come here.

But she also saw something else. He had put before her the choice she'd never expected to have the option of making. Reaching up, she kissed him on the lips, then stepped back and looked at him. "I can't," she said. "I'm sorry." And before she could change her mind, she turned and walked away.

THERE WAS NO ANSWER WHEN TERESA rang Reg Mortimer's bell, but when she tried the door it swung open.

"Reg?" she called softly as she stepped inside and looked round. The sitting room was a maze of cardboard boxes, some sealed, some still standing open, and the bare walls made the flat feel even more abandoned.

She had called out again when she saw him, sitting in a chair on the little round balcony, huddled into a shapeless old cardigan even though it was quite warm.

When she went out to him, he said, "I will miss the view," as if continuing a conversation.

"Where are you going?"

"To my parents' for a bit. Until I can find a job, get back on my feet. e removal men come tomorrow."

I want to talk to you." She moved between him and the river, so ae had to look at her. "About Hammond's."

esa, I—"

listen to me. I thought about leaving, too. I didn't know if I could go on, with everything that's happened. . . . But there's Jo to consider now. She needs me. And I . . . I don't think I can do it without you," she finished hurriedly. How could she say things any more clearly and still retain a shred of pride?

Reg looked past her, frowning. "I've told you, you don't give yourself enough credit, Teresa. You'll be fine."

"All right, I'll give myself credit," she said on a rush of anger. "I may be fine, but you're not. You're—you're a mess, Reg. Look at you."

He seemed to take her command seriously, picking at his shabby cardigan, but when he looked up and met her eyes for the first time, she saw a trace of amusement in his. "I was cold."

"You know what I meant."

"The funny thing is, I was so afraid of failure, afraid of losing Annabelle. And now that there's nothing to fear, it's rather peaceful. I'm not sure I want to put myself in jeopardy again."

"I'm not Annabelle," Teresa said softly, and for the first time, she was glad.

"No." He said it with a sort of wonder that made Teresa's pulse spring with hope. "You're not."

BRAVING THE FRIDAY AFTERNOON TRAFFIC ON his way back from Cambridge, Kincaid fought to hold the Midget on course as a lorry roared past him on the motorway and the little car shook and rattled in its tailwind. He really must do something about the damned old thing, he thought, swearing. But he had promised Kit he'd keep it, and he was learning not to take such promises lightly.

Ian had rung him earlier in the week, asking him to come to Cambridge at the earliest opportunity. Since Ian had brought Kit back to the Grantchester cottage, the boy had been silent and unresponsive, spending all his time down by the river with the dog.

That was where Kincaid had found him, stretched out on his stomach on the damp bank under the chestnut trees, making holes in mud with a stick.

"I used to do that," Kincaid said, sitting down beside him, scratching Tess behind the ears. "The water will bubble up in after a bit."

Kit gave him a sideways glance and went back to his digging. "I didn't think you'd come."

"I said I would." Kincaid took a stick and poked a hole himself. "Do you want to come to London next weekend? I've a few days off."

"Are they really off?"

"Yes. I promise." He would make sure of it, even if it meant tossing his phone and pager in the nearest bin.

"I might," said Kit, but he dug a little harder.

"What's up with you and Ian?" Kincaid asked casually, reaching for a flat stone and skimming it across the water. "He's worried about you."

Kit pushed himself up to his knees and sat back, staring at the river. After a moment, he said, "I asked him if you were really my dad, and he said he thought you might be—but that it didn't matter. He says he and I are family, and he wants us to be together."

Kincaid waited as Kit snapped his stick into pieces and fed them to the current.

When the last piece of wood had lodged in the roots of a chestnut tree, Kit said, "But he left last time."

"I think," Kincaid said slowly, "that Ian needs to be with you just now. He's done some things he knows were wrong, and this is his way of trying to make it up. You could help him."

Kit gave him a surprised glance. "Me?"

"I think so. And I know he misses your mum, and he needs someone to share that with."

Sitting back, Kit wrapped one arm round his knees and absently petted the dog with his free hand, but it seemed to Kincaid that there was a receptive quality to the boy's silence.

After a bit, Kincaid said, "Hungry?" and Kit looked up and smiled. "Starving."

Kincaid took him to tea at The Orchard, and they spent an easy ᴐur under the apple trees with the wasps while Kit worked his way ᴐugh the menu.

ʰen it was time to go, Kincaid walked him back to the cottage ᵻid, "I'll ring you about next weekend." Then he offered his hand ᵻ customary high five, and it seemed to him that his son left his ᵻis just an instant longer than usual.

HE FOUND THAT GEMMA HAD LEFT him a note on her door, and another on the Cavendishes', directing him to the sitting room. Bemused, he followed the trail and found her sitting at Hazel's upright piano. She wore a crinkly, white cotton dress that ended just above her bare ankles, and she'd pulled her hair back loosely at the nape of her neck with a seashell slide.

"Where are Hazel and Tim and the kids?" he asked, pulling a chair up beside her.

"They went to the pictures. A Friday night treat."

"You didn't want to go?"

"I thought I'd be here when you got back. How was it with Kit?"

"All right," he said, suddenly realizing that perhaps, at least for the time being, it was. "What's this?" he added, noticing the piano primer standing open on the music rack.

Gemma poised her hands over the keys, then tentatively touched middle C. "I've started lessons."

"Why didn't you tell me?" he asked, surprised. "I'd no idea you wanted to play."

"I thought you might laugh. And . . . I know it's silly, but I wanted something in my life that was just mine."

"I don't understand," he said, baffled.

"I know." Gemma turned to him. "I've been thinking about Annabelle Hammond."

"What has Annabelle to do with this?"

"She lived by other people's expectations—because she was so beautiful, everyone in her life had their idea of who she was, what they wanted her to be. And what seems tragic to me is that she finally made different choices, her *own* choices, about what mattered to her—but she never got to see where they might have led. Or who she migh* have become."

Kincaid still didn't understand, but he saw the fear that had b hovering at the back of his mind for what it was. "Gemma, if t' about Gordon Finch—if you want—"

"No. This isn't about Gordon . . . or only a little bit. I* don't know what I want. . . . I only know that I'm in the becoming,.and I want to see where it takes me, who I might be. I love you, Duncan. I do know that."

"Well, that's something, anyway," he said, trying to make light of the chasm yawning before him.

But Gemma regarded him with perfect gravity. "It's all we ever have, really. Isn't it?" she said.

LEWIS SAT FACING IRENE IN THE rusting iron chairs of the cottage's rose garden. Their knees touched, and she held his hand in both of hers lightly.

It had been John Pebbles's cottage once, and John had tended these fragrant roses with as much care as Irene evidently did now. It was fitting, Lewis thought, that Irene should be here, and that he had come back at last.

He had told her everything, and she had listened without comment. Now she looked up at him, and in the clear afternoon light he could see the tracing of fine lines in her fair skin. Her eyes were as blue as he remembered, and she looked the way he'd imagined she would, as if she'd grown into herself.

"Why didn't you tell me, Lewis?"

"I couldn't. I suppose I was just as guilty as William in that sense. I couldn't bear you knowing I wasn't what you thought."

"How were you to know what I thought?" she said sharply. "Or what we might have made of our lives if you had told me? Who were you to decide that it was better for me to spend my life alone than to share the burden of your guilt?"

"I—"

"Never mind," Irene said with a sigh. "We are who we are now, and that path's not worth following. But it seems to me that Freddie Haliburton has ruined enough lives. And that you underestimated my ɔacity for forgiveness. Let it go now, Lewis. It's time."

Ie met her eyes, and he knew he had found the only absolution that ɔred.

ABOUT THE AUTHOR

Winner of the Macavity for Best Novel of 1997 for *Dreaming of the Bones*, Deborah Crombie received international acclaim for her first four mysteries, as well as nominations for the Edgar and the Agatha Awards. She grew up in Dallas, Texas, and later lived in Edinburgh and in Chester, England. She travels to Great Britain yearly to research her books. She now lives in a small north Texas town with her husband, daughter, cocker spaniel, and four cats, and is at work on the seventh book in the Duncan Kincaid/Gemma James series, which includes *All Shall Be Well*, *A Share in Death*, *Leave the Grave Green*, *Mourn Not Your Dead*, and the award-winning *Dreaming of the Bones*.